# CLOUDS WITHOUT
# WATER

## GARRY HARPER

ISBN 978-0-578-28206-0

Cover design by Ana Grigoriu
www.books-design.com

Printed in the United States of America
First printing edition 2022

For inquires, contact press@cloudswithoutwater.net

## October 22, 1844

THE WIND HOWLED across Ascension Rock as William looked westward toward the setting sun. He inhaled the cool air deeply and took in the enormity of the moment. Gazing up at the overcast sky, he was overcome by a strange sensation: everything was about to change. He could feel the presence of Christ drawing near, the Son of Man returning as foretold. The world was coming to an end.

Behind him stood the people of Calvary, New York. They had spent their latter months preparing for this day with passion and dedication, weathering the adversities that followed the opening of each seal—held together through it all by an unbreakable bond of hope and fear. They, too, peered out along the horizon at the bloodred sun. Families young and old huddled together, clasping each other's trembling hands as the sky continued to dim, while the most zealous of the worshippers remained steady, eyes raised upward and hands stretched out from the sleeves of their white robes and into the air, yearning to be as close to Heaven as they could.

As he stood a distance apart from the crowd at the edge

of the overlook, William felt the warmth of his community at his back. The people had first met him with reservation and even jeers when he'd returned six months earlier, but they were now a thousand strong on the hill that commanded a view of the eastern banks of the Hudson—and a million strong across the global valley below. The gospel had traveled far and wide, and William was honored to be its messenger, delivering unto the uneducated masses the wisdom of the divine and the knowledge of man, two parallel paths that converged upon one road of truth: that the King of Kings was coming to redeem all mankind.

Though all were united in anticipation of what was said to arrive at dusk, there were those among them who were unsure if it was truly going to happen—some even skeptical of whether William actually believed it himself. But they dared not speak their concerns aloud in the presence of the faithful who had given up their livelihoods to prepare for this moment. There was too much at stake to voice any kind of disbelief; and still, even in the most doubtful there remained a latent, unsettling feeling that their reckoning just might be upon them.

The wind was lightly blowing. The clouds further enveloped the sky. William could only see the dull outline of the sun behind the silver shawl. But this was all proceeding just as it was written. Scripture had a way of being theatric, he thought to himself. Like a curtain draped across the heavens, the clouds would conceal the Bridegroom until dusk—when the tableau would be pulled apart to reveal their savior and bring about the final act of history.

"It's really happening, Brother William," said Josiah, standing beside him with tears in his eyes. "The time has finally come."

"Yes," William replied. "And our faith shall be duly rewarded."

The sun kissed the horizon. The congregation began to sing, their voices carrying canorously through the heavy air. Out from their quivering lips came songs of praise, mercy, and redemption—preludes to the impending blare of the angels' seven trumpets.

William listened, satisfied and proud. He had led his people to the well, and now it was time to drink their share of salvation. In just a few moments, they would ascend. Those who atoned and believed in the imminence of Christ would soon sit beside the Heavenly throne, draped in garments of righteousness for all eternity. Christ would reign for one thousand years until New Jerusalem would descend from the sky and Heaven and earth become one. But those who did not believe—*the fearful, and the abominable, and murderers, and whoremongers, and sorcerers, and idolaters, and all liars*—would face boundless scorn for thirty generations, left behind to walk the earth as it is swallowed by God's wrath, until the dead are raised for the final judgment and the coming of their second, everlasting death.

The families gathered closer together as the sun sunk lower. The westward view of the Hudson River Valley seemed to stretch into infinity, an eternal horizon upon which William had once gazed in contemplation many years ago, before deciding that he must leave behind his hometown for the seminary and learn the truth behind the secrets of Scripture. And now it was before this horizon that he found himself again over twenty years later, no longer on that journey alone. It was God's guidance that had brought him here, and he knew there was nothing to fear. In a few more moments, the world would be silent, and Christ would come to deliver the faithful chosen.

William felt a joy in his heart unlike any that he had felt before. In that moment, he understood that this sensation was the spiritual satisfaction for which he had longed his entire life. His calculation was correct. It had taken decades of research and scholarship, years of reading countless tomes of history and commentary, numerology, and mathematics, and a lifetime of devotion to Scripture. But the culmination of his work was finally here, and it was this very work that had compelled those behind him to prepare their imperfect souls for salvation. He had saved them all—he had fulfilled his holy purpose on earth.

The sun began to melt into the horizon.

"He is appearing," William announced with exhilaration as his eyes widened. "I feel Christ near!"

Many in the crowd were overcome with emotion, some falling to the ground and wailing in fits of hysteria. But the shrieking and crying quickly faded around him as William was deafened by the purity of the scene. Blood rushed into his ears and silenced everything else on the hilltop. He no longer noticed anything behind him—his vision focused only on the sky as the sun fell further, moment by moment, until it was but a sliver of light above the horizon. All of the concerns and doubt he'd had since his return were dissolving along with the remaining rays of light. He waited for the final beams to cross the plane as dusk fell at last.

"Behold! It is accomplished!" William shouted passionately. "The Bridegroom cometh!"

The sun disappeared, and the world held its breath. It

was time—the moment that he had foretold and spread throughout Calvary and beyond had arrived.

William closed his eyes gently and waited for the darkness to give way to light.

# Part One

---

"Return, ye backsliding children,
and I will heal your backslidings.
Behold, we come unto thee:
for thou art the Lord our God."

# Chapter 1

A CLOUD OF STEAM erupted with a loud hiss as Dr. Clarke lowered the hot iron into a crucible. Benji's sternum fluttered as he inhaled the vapors through his nose and mouth. Feeling the effects instantly, he leaned his head farther toward the cauldron, which Dr. Clarke had positioned firmly atop the oak plank that stretched across his supine body, and devoured the remaining bolus of steam before slouching back meekly against his straw pillow.

"Is he going to be all right?" Rosemary asked anxiously, her eyes glimmering in the light across the foot of the bed.

Dr. Clarke removed the iron, taking care not to spill any of the boiled water onto the young boy's exposed chest, and placed it in a wooden bucket beside the nightstand.

"Is Benji going to be all right?" Rosemary asked again, with more desperate urgency.

Still seated on a stool beside the children's shared bed, Dr. Clarke dabbed the condensation from his forehead. He raised his eyes and answered Rosemary's question through her father.

"His lungs are continuing to constrict, Henry," he said.

Henry stared ahead silently, his face unmoved, as if his mind were on another plane of existence. His two daughters huddled closely together and continued to look his way, waiting for a response that never came.

"What does that mean?" Abigail turned to Dr. Clarke and asked at last, breaking the silence in the room.

"It means you'll have to repeat this treatment whenever he has an episode," said Dr. Clarke, slowly pushing himself from the stool. "I'll have the herbs shipped from the apothecary in Albany to Harriman's general store the first of every month, for use as needed."

Rosemary looked up at her father with pleading eyes. "Benji's not going to die, is he?"

Henry gazed at his son, whose eyelids slowly grew narrower with each breath as he drifted off to sleep. He knew this was not a peaceful rest, but one that overtakes the body after a mortal struggle—a deer after a chase, a soldier at the conclusion of a bloody battle. There was nothing more he could do.

"That's only for God to answer," he said.

Tears began to well up in the eyes of both of his daughters as they stared back at him in despondence. Dr. Clarke, surprised by Henry's lack of paternal reassurance, quickly acted before the two girls would begin sobbing in earnest.

"Come, let's not discuss these sorts of dreadful things in front of the boy," he began, turning toward the younger and more lachrymose of the two. "Rosemary, how is school? Are you liking your classes?"

"Yes, Dr. Clarke." She sniffled as she began to restore her composure.

"Things must be changing quite a bit now that Reverend Miller is back in town," he continued. "I hear he has resumed his duties as headmaster."

"Yes, Dr. Clarke," Rosemary answered again with quiet reservation.

Dr. Clarke began to put away his medical supplies while Benji's strained breathing continued to normalize, putting Abigail and Rosemary more at ease.

"William was just a young man when he left for the seminary. I figured I'd never see his face here again," said Dr. Clarke.

"Hardly anyone has seen him since he came back, apparently. His return even took Pastor Thomas by surprise," said Abigail.

Rosemary looked at her sister suspiciously.

"How would you know that?" she asked. "We haven't been to church since last Sabbath."

Abigail hesitated before gathering her response. "There's lots of talk about it in town," she replied. "Some of the older residents are worried that he might be here to sell off the church property that he inherited from his father."

"He's indeed always been a very savvy person in that way, even as a boy," said Dr. Clarke. "I remember one time when he was just thirteen or fourteen, he took bets that he could recite any passage in the King James Bible by heart—a penny per verse. He must have cleared ten dollars that day, never losing once. But the lashing he took from his father when he found out I'm sure was not worth twice the sum."

Rosemary raised her eyes with incredulity. "Ten dollars at a penny per verse?" she repeated. "That's a thousand verses. There's no way that's true."

"Believe it, young lady," said Dr. Clarke. "And that's just the English version. He supposedly had the whole thing memorized in Greek and vulgate as well."

"Well I don't imagine he's come back to perform parlor tricks for us," said Abigail. "I just hope Pastor Thomas gets a fair hand in all of this, no matter what William's purpose for returning may be."

"With all of those years the reverend spent at the university, he can at the very least impart some of his knowledge to the classroom," said Dr. Clarke. "I'm sure you two will have a lot to learn from him."

Abigail laughed to herself at the implication. "Doctor, I'm not in school anymore. I'm seventeen now."

"Seventeen!" Dr. Clarke exclaimed, raising the white wires of his brow with surprise. "Time goes by so fast. It seems like yesterday that I was calling on your mother when she was first starting to carry you. Now you're almost that age where you're ready for that yourself. You know, my son is—"

"It's no matter," she assured him. "My father needs me here. It's nearly time to plant the summer crops."

"Bah, there's more to life than toiling around the house for your father," he said, waving his hand. "You'll understand that when you have a family of your own . . ."

Their conversation faded into the recesses of Henry's mind as he stood at the threshold of the bedroom, watching his only son fall into a deep slumber. The small talk purveyed by Dr. Clarke to distract the children for a time withdrew like the tide—each word like a wave receding further back until the room was devoid of sight and sound. His universe was now entirely black, lit only by a soft, yellow glow where Benji lay. Henry watched as his son's thin, bare chest filled and unfilled, slowly ebbed and flowed.

The room flooded with light again as Henry pulled himself from his daze, and Dr. Clarke's gravelly voice returned in full volume.

"If you don't get out and live your life, you'll find yourself standing alone one day, old and gray like me, asking yourself how it all went by so fast. I've seen it happen to so many young women over the years."

Henry walked out of the children's room without a word and into the main living area. He paused to look around the house that he had built long ago when his wife was newly pregnant with their first child. It was a humble home—two snug bedrooms and simple living quarters—that he had hoped would be all that was needed for their small family. But he wondered if perhaps he could have done more: if more space could give way to more comfort, if more comfort would alleviate the physical stress on the body, if an alleviation of bodily stress could help the boy heal more easily.

He needed to breathe. Henry walked across the sturdy puncheon floors, past the family dining table, through the kitchen, and out the back door. Closing the door behind him, he stood on the wooden planks of his back porch for a moment and inhaled the April air. The weather was starting to get warm.

Henry peered out across the rows of his unsown farmland and into the pale sky above, hoping to remove himself from the mire to which he risked succumbing. He knew that the cyclical thoughts of doom—ruminations on illness, suffering, death—were like quicksand: the more he struggled against it, the deeper he would sink. He had been there before. All he could do was lie still, keep up his routine, keep living, and hope that he would eventually be delivered.

Dr. Clarke quietly opened the door behind him and hobbled onto the back porch. Although he intended to leave Henry be, the sound of his gait was unmistakable, a crooked limp from shrapnel in his knee he'd received during his time as a field medic in the war some thirty years before.

"You know I can sense you coming from a mile away," Henry said without turning around.

"Just wait until your hearing starts to go, young man," Dr. Clarke said dryly.

"Are you all finished in there?" asked Henry.

"I think it's your daughters who are finished with me," he said. "Can't say I blame them. When I was fourteen or seventeen, the last person I wanted to pay any mind would be an old coot trying to advise me on how to live."

Henry feigned a smile as thoughts of his son's mortality reentered his consciousness. Dr. Clarke noticed his consternation and stepped forward to stand beside him.

"Things will work themselves out, Henry. Benji's only twelve years old; his lungs still have time to grow. In the meantime, you'll have his medication. This blend of lobelia and sage can do wonders for the bronchial passages—an old Thomsonian colleague of mine in Albany swears by it. You just let me know if the boy's condition worsens, and I can write for more at any time."

Henry continued staring ahead quietly. He had known Dr. Clarke long enough to discern the incertitude in his voice.

"How are you doing with everything that's going on now that William is back? I know you two have a bit of a history together," Dr. Clarke asked.

"That's all long in the past," said Henry. "He probably wouldn't even remember me if he saw me."

"Still, his return has a lot of people spooked, as if a ghost has appeared. The man didn't even come home for his father's funeral a few years ago, but now here he is."

Henry swept his eyes across the land before him, ignoring the temptation to speculate. "Summer wheat season will be here soon. That's all I can focus on for now—putting food on the table."

"I see," said Dr. Clarke, sensing his friend's desire to be left alone. "Well, I don't want to keep you. I know it's been a long morning."

Dr. Clarke placed his hat atop his head and reached out to the handle of the door, pausing to hold it open as he spoke to Henry once more.

"Just remember to take care of yourself, too. Your daughters need you, Henry."

Henry nodded to Dr. Clarke, who tipped his hat before going inside. Henry returned his eyes to the acres of unsown ground before him, an endless continuum beneath the gray firmament. He still had the power to do something with this: to cultivate the land, to sow his fields, to grow life out of dust. If nothing else, he could still make a miracle with his own hands.

With the voices of his daughters echoing through the wooden frame behind him, Henry stepped down from his porch, grabbed the hoe that leaned against the rail, and began to till the soil.

# Chapter 2

THE VIBRATION OF the church bells juddered beneath Henry's boots as he stopped before the doorway with his children in tow. A fresh coat of white paint had recently been layered on the exterior walls, accentuating the black letters of the UNITED CALVARY sign above the door. Henry had been coming to the church every week since he was a child, and yet he still felt a sense of admiration for it each time he stood before the building upon the hill that bore the town's name. It was a frame built by and for the common man, holding just as much gravitas to the people of Calvary as a French cathedral; humble in its construction, but colossal in what it represented to the town. Atop the snow-white walls, the narrow wooden steeple could be seen slouching toward the homes below from as far away as the farms—reaching out like the figurehead of a vessel bound for the promised land, puffing its chest over the houses in the town, whose arched roofs converged like hands folded in prayer, knees bent in supplication.

"Go on with them to our seats, Abigail," he said. "Your brother needs to get off his feet."

Benji looked up at his father obstinately. "But I don't need to sit down," he insisted. "I'm feeling much better today."

The color had indeed returned to his face since the dyspneic episode earlier that week, his eyes now fuller and his cheeks more sanguine than they had been in months. Dr. Clarke's remedy appeared to be working, but nevertheless, Henry ignored his appeal and motioned again for Abigail to take him to their seats. She followed accordingly and led her brother and sister to their traditional Sabbath pew midway down the aisle.

Henry waited inside the entrance of the church to greet his neighbors as the townspeople continued to file in. Although he would never admit it outwardly, this Sunday ritual had become the bright spot of his week. The winter was isolating for him, and with Abigail grown and Rosemary on her way, there was little practical need for him to make the journey into town during the weekdays and see his old companions in the business district. And so, the prelude to Sunday worship was the most opportune occasion for him to connect with his peers through idle chatter and to finally engage in much-needed discourse with men of his own age.

Henry stood guard by the door as the morning draught crept in with each group that passed through. Two more gusts of wind soon brought in two more families, and, mouthing the same instructions to their wives and children that Henry had given to his, two men broke off to stand beside him as their families made their way into the nave.

"Nathaniel, Jacob," Henry said as the men approached, shaking their hands firmly in succession.

"Henry," Nathaniel said in return.

"Henry," Jacob repeated in kind.

The two appeared unnaturally lopsided standing beside one another, as if they had been transplanted from two different epochs of two distant civilizations and into this new locale in the upper Hudson River Valley. Nathaniel Harriman, tall and fair-haired, had the shoulders of a carpenter and the chest of an ox, despite choosing a profession—proprietor of the town's first general store—that made no appropriate use of his burly frame. Jacob White, on the other hand, had an atypical look and build for his life as a dairy farmer—barrel-shaped and squat, bearing a single tuft of brown hair that bridged together the perimeter of neck-length curls draped around the sides of his skull. Both were seemingly unbothered by the physical imbalance and carried on without notice.

"I haven't seen you around the store lately," Nathaniel said to Henry.

"Summer wheat planting is keeping me busy."

"How's your tillage coming along this year?" Jacob asked.

"It's been a dry spring so far," said Henry, shaking his head. "I'm hoping these clouds will bring us some rain."

Jacob nodded in agreement. "It's high time that we have a good storm. My livestock are near grazing dirt at this point. The well's bound to dry up sooner or later if we don't get some relief."

"You know what they say," Nathaniel began in an attempt to allay his friends' concerns. "'Labor, and let the care and worry with God.'"

Henry looked between the duo's shoulders toward his family's pew. Amongst the other churchgoers, he spotted the vibrant purple and yellow ribbons tied around the backs of his daughters' bonnets as Abigail and Rosemary chatted with one another, facing the altar. Beside them, Benji was kneeling on the pew in the opposite direction with his arms folded across the back of the bench, talking to the children seated behind him with a juvenescent exuberance that Henry hadn't seen in him all season.

Henry kept his eyes fixed on his son as he continued the conversation.

"Everything will be fine," he said. "It's all going to be all right."

As more parishioners continued to enter through the heavy wooden doors, Henry noticed several faces that he had seldom seen outside of the Easter or Christmas worship. The church had typically been filling to about half capacity as of late, and he wondered if Reverend Miller's return might be piquing the town's curiosity and inspiring greater attendance for the first Sabbath services since he'd come back. It had been more than two decades since his departure, and rumors and hearsay had a way of animating the dehydrated gossips of their quiet town into action, he thought to himself. Henry scanned the room, looking at both the new and the familiar congregants to see if his hypothesis could be confirmed.

In the back, the latest arrival, Josiah Young, searched for a place to sit. As the owner and sole editor of the local paper, the *Calvary Crier*, Josiah was eager to listen to the services and perhaps draft a story for his next edition, chronicling the return of the fabled reverend doctor to his humble roots after his long tenure at the elite universities to the east. Crane-like and clumsy, Josiah approached several solitary empty spots with hesitation, raising a finger to indicate a request to have the seat, only to become a victim of his own forbearance as the crowd of newfound churchgoers turned their heads or assured him that they were saving a space for a tardy neighbor, a mingling relative, or simply as a place to stretch their legs. After several vain attempts, he eventually thought it better to spare what was left of his pride, and he took a seat with an obstructed view in the corner pew of the rearmost row.

A larger group of congregants began gathering toward the front of the nave, where George Wainscott was holding court with some of the community's elders and business owners. Though Calvary had no formal governing body, George was, in a sense, the de facto mayoral figure of the town. The Wainscott family owned the riverside port that controlled all of the commerce to and from the vicinity, and they had over the years dedicated much of their profit to public expenditures, including the first paved road that stretched from the ports through the commercial center of town and to the base of the hill where the church resided. As things were, there was seldom any need for a governing force to intervene in the town affairs, but when the rare occasion would arise, George was the man with the resources and respect to call a quorum and help execute whatever democratic proposal the townspeople would collectively design.

Dressed in a princely navy-blue bang-up, George perched himself on a thin walking stick and held a captive audience with his well-practiced politicking and urbane charm, greeting the locals through his big wooden teeth that jutted outside the double smile of his lips and side-whiskers.

"Gentlemen, it appears we have a full house today," he

said to the circle that had gathered around him. "I suppose the reverend has a lot of questions to answer."

"There are quite the rumors floating about," said one of the merchants. "I've been hearing that he arrived by coach after midnight and has been holed up in his rectory since. Strange that he would spend nearly a full week in solitude after half a lifetime away from town."

"The sexton who saw him pull in told me that he carried with him little more than a satchel of books and some kind of object shrouded in a muslin sheet," said another in the group. "But who knows if that is the truth or just conjecture carried by the wind."

"If you ask me, he can stay hidden away with his books," said one of the elders. "We were doing just fine without him."

"Fine is only so fine until you see something better," countered another. "I for one think this could be a great development for our church. William has twenty years of experience studying and teaching at institutions of great prestige since leaving Calvary. It's about time we had an intellectual in town."

The men continued debating amongst themselves as George stood and listened quietly, taking in their hopes and concerns.

"Has Reverend Miller come to see you yet, Mr. Wain-scott?" one man asked eagerly at last.

All eyes turned to George.

"I haven't had a chance to speak with him," he said, adjusting the lapel of his coat. "But I do not think that he would make such a journey by carriage in this weather at this time of year without having something important to say. So I suspect that whatever his reason for coming back is going to be of the utmost interest to us one way or another. I say let us hear him out—but always with a cautious ear."

As George continued to shape the conversation, the only resident afforded more respect than him entered the church behind them. Making her way down the aisle was Helen Chandler, the oldest woman in Calvary and one of two remaining descendants of the town's founding families. At her side was the other scion, her daughter, Marigold, who clutched her mother's arm to help steady her balance.

Guided by the gentle hand of Marigold and the aid of a cane, Helen passed the trio of Henry, Nathaniel, and Jacob and proceeded to the front of the church. The parishioners knew to leave two seats in the first pew empty for their town matriarch, who had sat in the same seat every Sabbath day since the elder Reverend Miller built the church a generation before.

Helen never failed to impress with her Sunday finest every week. Despite the hours of preparation time, she made sure to adorn herself in a flowing lavender redingote and an ostentatious Marie Antoinette hat, which still evinced a quality of contemporary high fashion for the rural farm town. Likewise, she would not travel anywhere without her signature accoutrement, a feather parasol adorned at the top by a silver ferrule in the shape of a dove, which on sunny days could be seen shimmering from nearly halfway across town. The other congregants looked over and admired her ensemble while Marigold navigated her to her seat. But as Helen attempted to lower herself in the ornate outfit, her cane began to shake, and her daughter struggled to help her maintain her footing.

Henry caught sight of the scene and took two steps toward her to intervene, but promptly and proudly found that Benji had already darted out of his pew and taken the liberty of helping Marigold stabilize her mother and safely seat her on the wooden bench.

"What a kind boy you are," said Marigold.

"It's not a bother, Miss Marigold," Benji replied.

Finally situated, Helen lifted her cloudy, cataractous eyes and looked straight ahead as Benji remained at her side, only able to see a shadow of the boy who'd assisted her.

"Who is that being such a gentleman?" she asked.

"That's Benjamin Smith, mother," said Marigold.

"Henry and Mary's son? Why thank you, dear," said Helen in Benji's direction. "You tell your father that Helen Chandler said you're earning your place next to St. Peter."

"Yes, ma'am," Benji said with a flush of red across his cheeks before running back to his seat.

Henry took the occasion to say his farewells to Nathaniel and Jacob, and with a taciturn nod broke away from the men and rejoined his family at their pew. Henry sat beside his son and tousled his hair playfully as the rest of the parishioners quickly took to their seats. The pastor of the church, Thomas Aleman, was entering from the side corridor.

Though the pastor was young, he had over time earned the trust and respect of the parish in the years since he had assumed the responsibilities of the church leadership. Reverend Samuel Miller, William's father, had taken Thomas under his wing when he was only seventeen and trained the boy in the fundamentals of Scripture over the course of several years as if he were his own son. Thomas eventually found himself leading sermons and planning the worship calendar as the elder Reverend Miller's health continued to deteriorate, eventually taking over in full upon his passing four years prior.

Thomas looked out at the parishioners with a moue of disappointment, bit his tongue, and silently walked past the altar. The congregation began to rustle as their pastor declined to take his typical position at the pulpit and instead sat himself at the side deacon's bench that he had once occupied while still under Samuel Miller's tutelage.

"Is Pastor Thomas not leading the services?" Abigail asked her father.

"It's Reverend Miller's church," Henry replied. "Always has been, even when he was away."

"But Thomas has been here every Sunday for ten years now," said Abigail, becoming more defensive.

"That's just the way it sometimes has to be." Henry shrugged.

Abigail looked out at the deacon's bench and locked eyes with Thomas, wordlessly exchanging a look of mutual dissatisfaction. Thomas lowered his eyes to the ground and then upward to the side of the altar.

The door to the stairwell suddenly burst open as if it were concealing a tempest, and the congregation went silent. Reverend Miller stood at the archway in his old ministerial garb with a Bible tucked against his chest, quietly surveying the attendance of his congregation for several moments. Henry focused his eyes on the preacher whom he had not seen since adolescence. William had never been imposing in stature, Henry recalled, and he remained unimpressive in appearance to him as an older man: short, almost delicate in frame, a stark contrast to the well-tempered bodies of the farmers and dockworkers before him. Henry could see the same bookishness of William's youth was still within him as his small, rounded glasses reflected in the light while he studied the church attendees. But behind his eyes was now a certain self-assurance, as if he had discovered a secret that he knew was his alone to reveal.

He stepped forward. Each purposeful stride reverberated throughout the pews and into the bones of the congregants. The older parishioners had not seen him for twenty years; the younger generation had no memory of him at all. But whatever doubts they had, whatever whispers ran across their lips, whatever reservations they held about their former neighbor returning to reassert his claim to the church he'd left behind all vanished in that single moment he stood before them. He looked all the forty years of his age but held a fierce, virile energy in his eyes—two ocean-blue orbs that pierced the souls of the parishioners, just as those of Samuel Miller had done before him.

A powerful voice resounded through the room as he commenced his sermon.

## Chapter 3

WHAT SHALL BEFALL *us in our latter days?*

"This eternal question has perhaps aroused more passion and confounded more men than any other since the dawn of time. One can certainly relate to the desire to uncover this mystery in one's own life—for the instant we are of the age to recognize our existence, we find ourselves likewise pondering death. This is a natural consequence of our sin: since our banishment from Eden, God has made it so that all things must one day come to an end. Finitude, thenceforth, has become an intrinsic property of life. And though we may never know how we will each meet our individual ends, Scripture has made it clear precisely how the world at large will one day cease to be.

"I speak of the prophecy of Daniel, the first divine vision of the end times given to man. This vision, delivered unto him by the angel Gabriel, foretells a series of events throughout history, beginning in ancient times, spanning the rise and fall of empires, our Messiah's birth, death, and resurrection. And just as it has foretold the past, so, too, does it tell us what is to come.

"See now, my brethren, through the eyes of the prophet! See a time of great tribulation, such as there has never been in any time of any nation. Look yonder at the terrible discord—of the violence and bloodshed, of disarray and death—for a great war looms between good and evil, and you and I and the children of God are those soldiers inside the ranks. Hear the battle cry as civilizations fall! Find the righteous believers stalwart, refusing to surrender while the armies of Satan attempt to beat us into submission. Look again, and see those too cowardly to choose a side trembling fearfully as they wait in vain for the bedlam to subside. For it is only at the time appointed by God that the end shall be—when those who remain standing are judged according to their deeds in the Book of Life, and the chosen are delivered by Christ as he comes to redeem mankind.

"We call this vision an 'apocalypse,' from the Greek *apokaluptein*: to 'uncover' or to 'unseal.' For the scroll onto which the fuller breadth of the end times had been written was sealed away following Daniel's epiphany, taken to the Heavenly throne room, where it would remain for centuries until the Lord deemed mankind worthy of the truth.

"It was only after Jesus Christ had taken away the sin of the world that the remainder of the prophecy would at last be unsealed on the island of Patmos. This is where our next apocalypse begins, the vision granted to the prophet John and captured for us in the Book of Revelation. It is here that John was presented with the images behind each of the seven seals that bound the holy scroll and held the secrets of the rapture. And lo, he heard a voice of thunder say, 'Come and see.' And he saw what is to come when the end is near.

"See it with us now: the four horsemen who wait behind the first four seals. The first shall come a mighty warrior named Conquest who rides upon a white horse, armed with a bow to bring the civilized world to its knees; and behind him on a horse the color of blood, the wielder of a great sword whose name follows conquest in natural form: War, the bringer of civil disorder, division, and destruction. Next, upon a black horse, one who carries with him even more agony than the others who preceded him. For who is the only killer in our world's history deadlier than the sword? Famine—he who controls the balance of food and trade, deliverer of starvation and immeasurable suffering to the land. And lastly, the consummate butcher of all: Death himself arriving upon his pale horse, who shall bring sickness and disease many magnitudes greater than the sum of our torment since man had been expelled from Eden. But these are no comparison to the tribulations that will yet come.

"Now cup thine ears to Heaven and ye shall hear the cries of the martyrs resounding from above! This is the opening of the fifth seal, which marks the beginning of the time of final atonement—our last opportunity to repent and accept Jesus as our savior whilst our faith is tested in ways we dare not imagine. For what lies behind that sixth seal is unlike anything we have ever witnessed in history. As it is opened, the world will shake violently under our feet; but look not just down at thy stead, cast thy view overhead to see the sun become black as night and the moon red as blood and the stars in the heavens now crashing down and falling upon the earth in a fiery blaze; and stop for just one moment to feel the air around you as a mighty wind sweeps across the land and makes all our trees fruitless and bare.

"And thus, when the Lord decrees that time shall be no longer, the four angels in the four corners of the earth who each hold the four winds shall halt their operations on the sea and land as we await our final judgment. This will be the calm before our day of reckoning, as the seventh and final seal brings us a brief silence. This is the moment when those who have remained faithful and have washed themselves in the blood of the Lamb will be spared from the wrath of the Almighty, and Christ shall come and wipe away their tears.

"But soon the sounding of seven trumpets will follow for all to hear, if ye be unfortunate enough to not ascend. And, my friends, how I pray that you and I—such unworthy and humble servants—never hear those trumpets ring! For each note shall unleash devastation unto mankind: a great conflagration of fire, hail, and blood, if you can imagine it so, will burn the grass and trees of the earth; the waters of the rivers and seas will become as blood, and the rest bitter and foul to drink; the celestial light dimmed as hope fades away. Then, at last, the woes: menaces out from the pits of Abaddon that will plague mankind with such brutality that those who do not die will wish for death; an army of demons waging war on the living; the kingdoms of earth dashed to pieces as Hell reigns supreme.

"But can you believe if I say that this is not the end to the suffering? What more must be said to convince the sons of Adam to repent for their sins and accept Christ as the one true savior? If this has not been enough to move a man to action, then surely he will fall to his knees after hearing of the seven bowls of wrath. Picture these terrible images, my friends: boils on the flesh of all who remain; all waters turned to blood until every living creature of the sea is dead; the sun swelling until the earth is baked in unbearable, inescapable heat; then darkness, O most terrible, mystifying darkness, to follow. Those left behind will curse His name and seek respite with false prophets, until a great battle is waged and the cities of the world are left in ruin.

"It is after one thousand years of torment that mankind will fully surrender to all the corrupt passions of the human heart. All nonbelievers and blasphemers will stumble drunk on the blood of the martyrs; laws will cease to be regarded; all authority will be trampled underfoot; anarchy will be the new world order; chaos will abound and will fill the earth with horror and despair. And when that day comes, God will wait no longer for repentance, no longer to be gracious and merciful as He has been for all our history—His eternal wrath will await all ye unspared.

"This time of strife is yet in the future, but it hangs—O it hangs, my friends—over our heads, ready to break upon us in tenfold vengeance. It is possible we live in the proximity of these times, blissfully unaware of the imminence of the advent. It is possible that we carry on about our days, assuming that these terrors are merely adornments of the modern world to which we have long become accustomed. But we cannot allow ourselves to be ignorant and unprepared, for when the time of holy tribunal comes, we will be judged by how we spent our remaining hours. Those who are righteous shall be purified white; but even as the wicked bear witness to this, they will not understand what God hath wrought. Only the wise shall know that this is the final judgment; and to that I say: let us not be the damned, who shut their eyes to the signs around them. Let us be the wise who believe in the coming of God's everlasting kingdom! And let us remember the words of undying hope from Daniel to give us comfort and instill us with the resolve we need as we are drawn ever closer to the advent: 'Blessed is he that waiteth.'"

Amen.

## Chapter 4

"THIS WEEK'S *CRIER* out today! Get them while they last!" Josiah Young shouted to the morning swell of residents in the main square of town. His body curved out from behind his newspaper cart like a parenthesis, stretching above the stacks of freshly pressed prints and into the cobblestone walkway.

"Calvary's centennial celebration, local news, New York politics, and more," he continued, waving a copy in the air as the townspeople carried on about their day.

Few paid any attention to Josiah's impassioned overtures, as the only news on their collective mind was the apocalyptic pronouncement of the previous day's sermon. Speculation and debate were relayed between the passersby as they walked throughout the town, turning away their ears and waving off any less noteworthy stories coming from the wooden cart. With every person who passed him without acknowledgment, Josiah's voice increased in pitch, growing more desperate after each wordless rejection. By the time the

Smith children turned the corner on the way to school, he had reached an embarrassingly high octave.

"Come now, get the *Calvary Crier* here, folks!" he screeched just as he espied Abigail out of the corner of his eye, forcing him to collect his wits.

"Good morning, Abigail—er, Miss Smith," said Josiah, adjusting the cadence of his voice and tipping his hat sheepishly as she approached the cart.

"How do you do, Josiah?" she responded without slowing.

"Care to purchase a copy of this week's *Crier*?" he asked. "This edition has this season's farmer's almanac."

Abigail shook her head. "My father says those predictions never lead to an accurate yield."

"I assure you, these are based on the calculations of the leading experts in agriculture and meteorology. Their methods are proven true year after year."

Abigail continued walking with a slight turn of her head. "I'm sorry, Josiah. It's neither worth the penny nor the time."

Josiah stopped himself from pleading further as Abigail corralled Rosemary and Benji to cross the street and continue toward the schoolyard. A layer of fog hung over the pavement as they made their way deeper into the heart of the town, where figures began to appear and disappear like apparitions through the mist, bringing with them whispered embellishments of the various scenes of the eschaton described in William's services the day before. A general foreboding carried in the air as Abigail overheard the ominous words of their preacher through the brume— the coming hellfire, the promises of woe and doom. But still, there was a curious sense of enticement in each hidden voice, a yearning to understand what else was to come, what more William could tell them, even if the answers were too dreadful to hear.

Abigail tried to ignore it all the best she could. The sun was starting to peek out from behind the morning fog, lighting a path for the children to the hillside and drowning out the gloom of the passing conversations. It was a mystical feeling for Abigail, the first sensation of warmth for the season. After a long winter, she finally began to feel hopeful about what was ahead of her. The last several years had been hard on the family; adulthood had been foisted upon her as the only solution to care for her younger siblings while her father ploughed the fields, tended to the livestock, and maintained the small farm by himself. Though she knew it weighed most heavily on her father's shoulders, the burden was fluid, dispersing across each member of the family in its own way. But with the warmth finding an avenue to the earth despite its struggle through the clouds, it felt as if this was the season in which some balance could be restored, and things could at last move forward. Abigail breathed in the spring slowly, and time stood still for a brief moment.

The church bells began to chime in the distance and stirred her to attention. Abigail increased the stride she set for her siblings, who would be late to class if they didn't hurry. Benji had missed too many days in bed the week prior, and she was determined not to let him fall further behind.

"What's the rush?" Rosemary asked as she danced over the uneven cobblestones. "We still have plenty of time."

"You heard what father said. He doesn't want you two missing any more schooling if we can help it," said Abigail.

"It's not like the lessons are that difficult," said Rosemary. "Anyone can repeat a bunch of math tables. Mrs. Edwards plans the coursework like we're all children."

"You *are* all children," said Abigail. "Now come, pick up the pace."

Rosemary huffed and clenched her jaw as the three continued to walk farther into town, past Harriman's general store and the rows of houses and merchants that lined the main road. Unlike the timber farmhouses along the outer plains of Calvary, the buildings in town were constructed in the sturdier Dutch Colonial style of the region—walls made of stone that supported the broad gambrel roofs and flaring eaves that gave the Washington County villages their distinctive look. Anyone who did not own a farm or a ranch in Calvary lived along this street or one of its tributaries, where the community naturally nestled between the docks and the hill where the church was built. Abigail never liked to tarry about this part of town for too long—like her father, it felt more natural for her to be away from the busier realms of society and instead under the open skies of the home in which she had been raised, five miles or so inland from the river.

"I think he likes you, you know," Rosemary teased.

"Who?" asked Abigail, furrowing her brow at her sister.

"The newspaperman," said Rosemary. "I saw how he was looking at you when you walked away from him."

"And what would you know about how men look at women?" Abigail asked incredulously.

"I know more than you think—" Rosemary began before being interrupted by her brother.

"How come we never get to buy one?" Benji asked. "What if I wanted to read the newspaper, Abigail?"

"When you're old enough to walk to school yourself, you can spend your earnings on whatever diversions you'd like."

Abigail's response appeared to have further darkened Rosemary's disposition that morning.

"The dead will walk the earth before that happens, if I'm any measure," she muttered to herself.

"I don't remember you complaining about this to mother when you were Benji's age."

"That's just what I mean. That was almost two years ago. And father still has you accompany me to school as if I'll get lost without you."

Abigail was disheartened by the budding hostility between her and her sister. She remembered when Rosemary used to look forward to going to school together in the morning—matching her big sister's gown and bonnet, stopping to pick wild berries together, copying her every movement as they traipsed through the woods on their way into town. But after their mother became too ill to take them anymore, Abigail was given the responsibility of being the chaperone, and things began to change. It seemed that they could not go one day without some kind of argument—the hardheadedness, the needless confrontation, the passive-aggressiveness and insubordination. Abigail wouldn't escalate it though. This was something that Rosemary would need to grow out of on her own.

"Fine," said Abigail. "You want to go on by yourself— then go. I have errands to run anyway."

Rosemary glared at her sister, deliberating whether or not to call her bluff.

"Come on, Rosemary," Benji interceded. "I bet I can race you to the top in under five minutes."

Before Rosemary could respond, Benji was already off ahead of her, his white stockings flapping below his flannel shirt in the distance. Rosemary quickly resolved her impasse with Abigail, who turned with a conciliatory motion toward their brother. Forgetting the world for a moment, Rosemary sprinted ahead, and she and Benji gleefully chased one another up the hill as Abigail observed from afar.

Abigail shielded her eyes from the morning sun as she watched her siblings pass the fingerboard along the north-bound path to the school. A smile eked across her face, and memories came racing back to her. She recalled the summers of years past, chasing the two of them through the amber rows of wheat on their family farm while their mother watched from the porch. As the eldest, Abigail was always able to keep up no matter how quickly and dexter-ously they dashed through the fields and darted about the stooks of harvested grain. But now it was she who stood still and watched, just as her mother had before, as Rose-mary and Benji ran up the hill until they were no longer in her sight, fading away into the distance like two ships into the horizon.

Abigail took in a deep breath as she waited for the patch of sunlight upon her to expand its glow. But behind her she heard a steady clamor echoing in the air and turned to see a small gathering across the street. In the center was a man who'd attracted a semicircle of listeners as he recited the final chapters of the New Testament from a ragged Bible in his hands. Abigail watched as the townspeople listened curi-ously to the man speaking of the horrors that would befall the earth and the infinite desolation that awaited those who are not chosen.

"'Babylon the great is fallen, is fallen, and is become the habitation of devils, and the hold of every foul spirit, and a cage of every unclean and hateful bird,'" he read aloud. "'For all nations have drunk of the wine of the wrath of her fornication, and the kings of the earth have committed fornication with her, and the merchants of the earth are waxed rich through the abundance of her delicacies. And I heard another voice from heaven, saying, *Come out of her, my people*, that ye be not partakers of her sins, and that ye receive not of her plagues.'"

Abigail felt a sudden chill and shivered as the sun faded behind the clouds above her. As the light receded, she watched the fog once again begin to snake across the street, winding down the road and soon enveloping the speaker and his audience until they could no longer be seen, an inescapable captor among the cold pavement of the town.

# Chapter 5

ROSEMARY AND BENJI entered the small classroom in the single-room schoolhouse as the bells continued to ring. Their teacher, Mrs. Edwards, was not yet present, and so the children were left to their own wild devices for a time. Some sat in a circle and traded candies that they'd procured from the merchants on the way to school; some perched themselves atop the wooden desks like Gothic statues, a fad that was in vogue with the older children that semester; others jabbered about with their friends and siblings, momentarily free from the watchful eye of a parent, instructor, or preacher. In the back of the room, a group of children led by a twin brother and sister played a clapping game set to a mischievous rhyme that they had made up over the course of the school year:

*"Old Lady Edwards's life begun*
*Never learned to have fun;*
*So she looked to the steeple*
*Said 'I'm gon' teach these people'*
*And now our lives are done."*

Rosemary sifted through the horseplay and took her seat next to her brother in the middle row. She always preferred the desk near the window, as she had a habit of daydreaming of another life when she became disenchanted by Mrs. Edwards's basic and banal curricula or when she could discern no practical relevance they would have to daily living. She was in this kind of dreamy mind-state that morning, and she settled in to gaze out the window rather than participate in the rudderless skylarking with her classmates.

The church bells desisted as their large, block-shaped teacher entered the room and silenced the air immediately. The older children sitting on the desks spun their bodies around and into their seats; the loud chatter faded quickly into a distant murmur; and the forbidden rhymes halted as if they had never been uttered at all. Mrs. Edwards surveyed the class to ensure all were on their best behavior, then proceeded with an invocation.

"Please bow your heads as we pray," she instructed.

The children each lowered their heads and clasped their hands accordingly. Mrs. Edwards closed her eyes tightly with the earnestness of a nun.

"Our Father in Heaven, who has blessed the pupils and the teacher of this school with another day, come grant us a continuance of thy protection and blessing during the next. Come then, and be in this classroom and likewise grant us the help we need to be faithful and successful in our duty. Amen."

"Amen," the class repeated.

"Very good, children," said Mrs. Edwards. "Now let us return to our tables from last week."

The class judiciously awaited her direction as Rosemary sighed to herself. The remedial arithmetic they had been studying year after year as new students entered and older students left neither interested her nor challenged her on any intellectual or spiritual level. Nothing could be less gainful than rote recitation, which to her was as easy as memorizing a song or a psalm.

Mrs. Edwards opened a textbook and commenced her instructions.

"Zero times zero," she began.

"Zero," the children answered in perfunctory unison.

"One times one."

"One."

"Two times one."

"Two."

"Two times two."

"Four."

Rosemary slouched into her open hand and stared longingly out the window. Some remaining clouds were still stubbornly wrapped around the sun like ivy about a tree as it rose higher in an attempt to shuffle off their grasp. While the repetition of numbers continued around her, Rosemary focused more intently on the rising sun, drowning out the string of integers that grew in automatic multiples.

Hypnotized by the monotony of the math tables and the slow shift in the sky, Rosemary's mind began to wander. She thought back to a lesson from earlier in the year, when the students were taught the concept of infinity—a boundless number that had no observable quantity or natural limit. It was impervious to any kind of manipulation, a value that could not be increased, decreased, or subdivided. It was a divine number, they were told, that measured the properties of God and time—the Lord's infinite wisdom, eternity stretching infinitely backward and infinitely into the future.

But then, if this concept were as true as she was assured it was, why would they begin all other lessons at zero? Surely, zero did exist—she could see it before her: she had zero pencils on her desk, she was holding up zero fingers, she had been to the Egyptian pyramids zero times. But she could not see the infinite in the world: the river was not infinitely long, her father did not have infinite seeds of wheat, no one was infinitely old. Zero existed, beginnings were observable; and, likewise, if there was a singular beginning, then there must also be a finite end.

Rosemary could feel her teacher's eyes upon her, and so she lifted herself out of her existential deliberation before she could be chastised. She quickly sprung up her hand as Mrs. Edwards was getting to the fours.

"The privy, please?" Rosemary pantomimed silently.

Mrs. Edwards looked at her between recitations and crinkled her lips, reluctantly bowing her head to grant her permission to leave the classroom. Rosemary swiftly untucked herself from her seat.

"Where are you going?" Benji asked in a whisper.

"Sshh. None of your business," she said as she attempted to get up without drawing too much attention.

Rosemary hastily crossed between the students and her

teacher and exited the classroom to the hallway. She was free for a moment, despite being in an enclosed corridor. The mechanical recitations were a dampened patter behind the classroom door, and there was not another soul in sight. Rosemary was not concerned with the time—any delay in her return could be excused away. Perhaps the privy was locked and she had to go around to the church; a family from out of town was asking for directions to the riverfront; a rabid skunk was loose in the hallway. It was no matter to her now. Spending her time in worry would negate the purpose of her small diversion, and it was better to allow her head to clear and her mind to wander elsewhere.

Rosemary began to hum to herself as she walked aimlessly down the hallway, skipping ahead at each high note as she slowly progressed forward. The narrow corridor connected the school directly to the church transept and had been built to shelter the children from the snow when they would need to travel between buildings in the winter. She looked around at the old wooden walls that the elder Reverend Miller had constructed by hand long before she was born, finding a waist-high divot between the boards. She followed the crack with her finger, sliding it along as she continued to skip down the hall.

As Rosemary glided down the covered walkway, thoughts of the infinite reentered her mind. She began to ponder the story of Creation. The Bible seemed paradoxical on this matter—Scripture specifies that there was a beginning, but also a time before the beginning. She recalled that there was first a period when the earth was without form, the time before the light of the sun, when all the universe was a void of darkness. She imagined this time—an abyss of reality inhabited only by the Ancient of Days, readying for the moment of Creation—a time that stretched into a retrograde eternity. Is this what is meant by infinity? Perhaps it is only earth and man that are bound to finite principles, and God and space and time play by a set of their own rules, where limitlessness instead is their intrinsic property. Perhaps, then, one can only discover the infinite after reaching the finite limit of the earth, where existence returns to what it was before Creation—everlasting, only now moving eternally forward.

The space between the boards terminated at the end of the hall where the school met the church. Rosemary stopped humming and pressed her ear against the door to see if there was any kind of service happening that morning. Hearing nothing but the faint sounds of the classroom to her rear, Rosemary turned the doorknob to peek her head inside and felt it clear to enter when she saw that it was vacant.

She had never been in the church when it was empty before and was surprised by how calming and peaceful it felt to her. She quietly walked through the transept, her shoes clattering on the floor and echoing against the tall ceilings with each step, as she inspected the unfilled pews where her family would sit every Sunday. The solitude soon imbued her with a sense of daring as she gamboled to the pulpit, impish and eager in her approach, but ultimately hesitant to set foot onto it.

As she mulled exploring further, Rosemary's heart jumped at the sudden sound of a voice in the distance. She stopped to listen—and then heard another muffled sentence resounding from afar. It didn't appear to be directed at her, she concluded, as she further attempted to locate the source of the sound. Finally, she heard a second voice, louder than the first, and realized that it was echoing from the stairwell across the room. The door to it was open. Rosemary's trepidation gave way to curiosity as she drew closer, quietly, to eavesdrop on the nameless men.

"This is utterly profane!" she heard one voice shout clearly as she reached the opening of the stairwell. "Do you honestly think the ministers at the Convention would approve of one of their partner parishes teaching this?"

"That is where you're confused, pastor," the other responded. "I do not seek their approval."

Rosemary placed her foot softly on the spiral stairs and leaned against the railing, careful to not make a noise. She slowly inched her way toward the voices to get a better listen as the wooden steps creaked under her weight. The argument was coming from the church rectory, and she recognized the first, younger voice as that of Thomas Aleman.

"Consider this from my perspective, reverend," said Thomas. "While you were away for all of these years, I was a student here under your own father's tutelage. We had a mutual agreement: he would show me how to care for the church and provide for the spiritual needs of the people of Calvary just as he had done for fifty years; and in turn, he trusted that I would help shepherd the congregation when he became too frail to continue any longer. But I was to always leave this rectory uninhabited, for one day, he assured me, his prodigal son—the Reverend Doctor William Miller—would return to his hometown and lead the church toward the path of righteousness just as he promised to him before he left for the seminary.

"For the man who saved me from drowning in iniquity,

who instead gave me new life out of the waters of my baptism, I of course obliged and kept this door open. And as the years went on, your father never rescinded that accord. Week after week, I began to fill out the sermon calendars myself, took over responsibilities as headmaster and held the school to a high standard, and soon led the Sabbath services in good faith and began to foster a burgeoning relationship with those in this parish. All the while, nary a letter from you or any indication that you would keep your vow. Even as he lay on his deathbed, you still did not return."

"I was in the midst of a breakthrough," William inserted calmly. "My father ought have understood."

"Yet he continued to insist that you would come back," said Thomas. "What a great man William Miller must be, I thought, for his father to have such faith and hold him in such high regard that he continued to contend that he must be the one to lead this church. So I kept my word, though no one imagined that day would ever come. And now, ten years after I started my training and over twenty since you left yours, you suddenly return bearing this . . . prophecy."

William remained poised as Thomas caught his breath.

"You must calm yourself, Pastor Aleman," he began. "I assure you this is no whim or flight of fancy. This is the sum of decades of scholarship—evidence in Scripture and history, converging on this date."

Rosemary tiptoed farther up the stairs until she could see a ray of light coming through the window, penetrating the swirls of old dust. The door to the rectory was open wide, and she surmised that she might be able to get a look at the argument without being seen herself. Lifting her eyes to the room, she was able to see the two men—Thomas pacing the floor in growing agitation while William remained unflustered in the seat behind his desk.

"It would be immoral to keep the truth from our congregation any longer," William continued. "Matters this consequential demand urgent action."

"So what are you going to do?" said Thomas. "This is not a town of scholars and academics. Do you expect to first teach them advanced mathematics or ancient Greek to understand what these numbers mean?"

"What I've told you may seem like an enigma, but the calculus is clear as day. Every numeral in Scripture is a detail from God: every 'day,' a year; every 'year,' a corresponding date in the Jewish calendar. Each vision of Daniel, the revelations of John, they all have meaning beyond the abstract or the allegorical. And that is precisely our calling as preachers, Thomas: to mill the grains of the divine and turn these words into bread for the people."

Thomas turned and stepped toward the window to look out into the waning clouds.

"What is this really about, William? I know it must be difficult returning after all of these years, seeing your neighbors and friends growing without you, moving on with the junior pastor at your own father's church."

"You dare imply some kind of ulterior motive?"

"Sunday's sermon you described the end of days, the Millennium. A vivid and animated description, I must admit, but hardly the kind of topic upon which one would expect Christ himself to preach. And now you reveal to me the subject of your next sermon, supported by these vast and complex interpretations of the apocalypses in Daniel and Revelation. If this is some kind of spectacle to regain the interest of your parishioners, then I will at least understand your perspective."

"This is no pageantry or performance," said William, leaning forward in his seat. "God has given me a looking glass. One that reveals His final, immutable truth."

"Enough with this blather!" Thomas snapped, turning back toward William. "You cannot truly believe what you're saying—that you can see the future with certainty."

"It is not a matter of believing. I have studied the greatest scholars on the subject, and I have spoken to those held in esteem at the most prestigious institutions of learning, who all helped me come to this conclusion. This is not speculation—this is science."

Rosemary listened intently as William at last stood up from his desk.

"I would like to show you something," he said to Thomas as he opened a storage chest against the wall.

With a delicate hand, William removed an object covered by a muslin sheet, placing it upon the desk and untying the string around it as Thomas—and Rosemary—observed with great curiosity.

Beneath the protective layer was a thick parchment scroll. William inspected the paper meticulously to ensure that it had not been damaged in his travels along the cold and craggy road to Calvary; once satisfied with its condition, he removed the mandorla seal of his former university that bound it together. William placed the top corners against the flat surface of the wall behind his desk and clamped them beneath the brackets of two parallel candle sockets. Firmly pressing it against the wall, he slowly began to unfurl the scroll—and on it, the history of the world.

## A CHRONOLOGICAL CHART OF THE
## VISIONS OF DANIEL AND JOHN

The title was spelled across the top of the page in an authoritative arch. Beneath it, a growing prophecy was revealed across four columns. In the first, passages from Scripture with exegetic commentary; in the second, apocalyptic visions from the Books of Daniel and Revelation brought to life, every element of each prophetic scene illustrated with precise detail; in the third, a corresponding event or epoch in history, dated and accompanied by a thorough annotation and description; and lastly, in the excited pencraft of William's own hand, a final column with a series of calculations devised to prognosticate each event throughout the history.

The visual timeline began with the prophecies outlined in the Book of Daniel, commencing with the Jewish exile in Babylon, spanning their persecution and subordination by each subsequent power that followed. Babylon, Persia, Media, Greece—each sovereign of Israel, which Daniel beheld as four allegorical beasts in his holy vision. History marched on as William continued to unfurl the scroll, as Daniel's visions proceeded to the Abomination of Desolation, the Maccabean Revolt, the rise of Pagan Rome, and, at last, the establishment of the Catholic Church.

Rosemary took one more soft step up the stairs and into the pale light that shined through the rectory window. She stood at the edge of the top stair and raised her head to gaze at the chart William had placed against the rear wall. On it, she spied the hellish beasts of Babylon, Persia and Media, Greece, and Rome with horrible hanging eyes and bloodthirsty fangs. She saw the chimeric, forsaken abominations that followed: a red dragon with seven crowned heads, a monster with the face of a man resting upon its horn like a pike, a mutated lion that sprouted other creatures from its skull and a dead-eyed pope sitting upon its back. Something stirred inside Rosemary as she saw these images, affecting her unlike any words had before. The sum of all her fears was displayed before her, ready to jump off the canvas and devour the world.

"The calculations beside the date of each moment in history have allowed me to decode the mysteries of Scripture," William explained. "Here they reveal the precise unit of time that passed between each event, which had previously been obfuscated by the intricacies of biblical translation across the centuries. These calculations now serve as the mathematical proof of the equation, the foundational system of measurement that can be extrapolated to the future prophecies of Daniel and John."

Together on the chart, the two sets of apocalyptic chronicles became interwoven like a tapestry, crossing through moments in history that were yet in the future when first recorded: the division of Rome, the creation of the Papal States, battles over the Holy Land throughout the Mahometan era, the rise of the Holy Roman Empire, and the conquests of Napoleon. With every event unfolding on the page and every illustration growing more violent and disturbing as the timeline expanded, Rosemary's eyes grew wider and her heart began to throb faster. Blood rushed to her ears like a choir of angels singing louder and louder as the years advanced closer to the current era.

And then history stopped. William focused his eyes

onto the end of the chart. Each year was accounted for precisely in Scripture, each interval assigned a value. The calculations that resided in the rightmost column now converged with the other columns as one in the center, into the present. Scrawled atop the final date was a passage from Daniel, which William read aloud.

"'And he said unto me, Unto two thousand and three hundred days; then shall the sanctuary be cleansed.' This is it. The indisputable truth of the imminent end."

Thomas deliberated in silence, looking over the scroll that hung unfurled before him. His eyes drew across each date, each image, and each equation, then lowered to the floor with resignation.

"I made a vow to your father that I would keep this door open for your return," Thomas began. "But I also made a vow that I would maintain the integrity of the church he built after he died. And I cannot keep the former without breaking the latter."

William remained composed as he stood across from Thomas and looked into his eyes.

"Then your service is no longer needed," he declared. "It is the right of the people of this church to know what imminently awaits them, and I intend on sharing these tidings with them on the next Sabbath. We are living on the threshold of eternity, pastor—and I see souls perishing by the thousands."

Rosemary stared up at the images of seven angels blowing their trumpets, recalling William's prior sermon, and remembered the suffering that would follow their call— the war, the pestilence, the calamity and death that would come. At that moment, the sun shook off the grip of the clouds outside and filled the rectory with light, revealing the bottom of the scroll.

GOD'S EVERLASTING KINGDOM was printed triumphantly beside an image of the angel of mercy. What followed below it was history's final date, the revelation for which William had journeyed far from the east, crossing the narrow bridges over the icy rivers and through the windswept mountains to deliver. The Parousia, the rapture, the ascension—the day the world would come to an end.

Rosemary knew it immediately. It was clear and unerring, supported by the irrefutable proof from God's word itself. It was Truth. Her eyes focused in on the sum of the calculations beside the image of the trumpets, and she felt as if the air had been taken from her lungs as she read the date. OCTOBER 22, 1844—not more than six months from the present day.

Unable to catch her breath, Rosemary turned and rushed down the stairs, attempting in vain to not draw attention with her movements. Her vision began to tunnel before her; the spiral stairs seemed to stretch on forever as she rotated down step by step. Reaching the ground and passing the stairwell door at last, she ran back to the nave, found her family's pew, and knelt down to pray.

# Chapter 6

THOMAS INCHED HIMSELF closer as the two reclined against the hay bale outside of his barn. His hand gently brushed against the back of hers and left a trail of goose bumps up the smooth skin of her arm. The sun was beaming brightly overhead, and this closeness warmed him further still.

His troubles were only a distant memory when he was with her. The passions of his argument with William that morning were still a dull ache in the depths of his mind, but they were temporarily numbed by the serenity of the scene that surrounded them that afternoon. He could smell the fragrance of the grass rising through the soil; the birds were calling from the trees that fortified the perimeter of his farm. There was not a cloud in the sky.

"Stay here with me all day," Thomas said softly.

"That sounds like Heaven," said Abigail, smiling as she adjusted her bonnet against the pillow of hay and nestled under his arm.

His promise to not take up residence in William's rectory had been an easy one to keep these past several years. Thomas preferred life on his small homestead at the outskirts of the community, as living farther away from the church afforded him a privacy that was seldom granted to a town's sole preacher. With a one-room cottage and a modest barn of his own, he could, at least for a time, escape the needful nature of his congregation, the fishy smell of the port, and the noise of the wagons bustling through the town atop the cobblestone pavement. Situated less than a mile from the center of Calvary, he was far enough removed from the main road without being at the reclusive distance of the larger farms and ranches in the outer reaches of the town. This gave him the opportunity for a twice-daily walk to the church, for the goodness of exercising the muscles of his body and exorcising the perils of the day from his spirit, and allowed him to gather his thoughts and plan his sermons as he believed God intended—not in the dark cloisters of the church, but under the light of the temple that was all around them, whose doors were never shut.

The couple lay and watched the springtime bloom around them as Thomas continued to calm his weary mind. The serviceberry flowers were beginning to open and bobbed buoyantly in the breeze. Bees by the dozen descended upon the flowering trees beside the barn, floating benignly past them to indulge in the first deposits of pollen for the year. Thomas had once heard that the name of the serviceberry tree came from the original settlers of the region, who observed that the annual bloom of the white flowers coincided with a thawing of the snow, signaling that the treacherous Appalachian roads were now again in service and safe to pass through. But as he thought about the perilous paths that connected the town to the rest of civilization, the concerns of the day began to resurface, and his demeanor quickly changed.

Thomas drew down his straw hat to shade his face, and he clenched his eyes tightly as the sun continued to reign over them. Abigail sat further upright beside him and leaned against the heavy bale, her dress puffing out around her lap like a mushroom.

"You seem like you have something on your mind," she said.

"I suppose I'm not doing a good job of concealing it then," he admitted.

"It's Reverend Miller, isn't it? I can't say his return hasn't also made me feel unwell."

Thomas looked at her curiously from under the brim of his hat.

"I saw a man in town today reading aloud from Scripture," she said. "He had a decent-sized crowd before him as well."

"Well of course that made you feel unwell. I could never imagine you taking a shine to someone who reads to an audience from the Bible."

Abigail grinned and coyly nudged Thomas's exposed side.

"You know what I mean. There was something different in his eyes. They were wide and unblinking, like he was so desperately trying to fulfill some kind of spiritual duty. And the words that came from him were the same kind of frightful premonitions that we heard at the services yesterday. It was like he was possessed."

"If only you knew what William was planning for the

next," Thomas said, shaking his head. "The hubris of it all. He spends years away and now returns saying that he knows exactly when and how God's plan will be enacted—as if he has discovered the key to omniscience itself. It borders on sacrilege."

Abigail nodded in agreement. "The world has enough evil in it without the constant reminder."

Thomas sat up and turned toward Abigail, blocking the sun so that his face was all that she could see. At twenty-seven years old, he had not a wrinkle under his eyes and managed to maintain the same adolescent quality that he'd had when Samuel Miller first brought him under his tutelage. Fair-skinned and always clean-shaven, he was considered by many women in town to be quite handsome, and several had attempted, unsuccessfully, to set their cap at him numerous times since he took his role at United Calvary.

But it was Abigail alone who caught his eye some months prior. Her beauty was unmistakable, but it transcended physical appearance; to him, it was the outward reflection of her spirit and values that he adored most. He had watched the way she carried herself at church—graceful and mature beyond her years, a maternal figure for her younger siblings, yet holding a quiet dignity that effaced all bitterness from the undertaking. The admiration was reciprocated by Abigail when the two had an opportunity to speak while setting up the Christmastime festivities, and their courtship quickly began in earnest thereafter. But in order to prevent a potential scandal, they both agreed to rendezvous in private, away from the gossips and restless birds who might bruit their relationship about town, until the time was right.

Thomas had never before felt the love that he had when he was with her these past months. And this made it hurt all the more to know that he had to tell her.

"I need to do something about this, Abigail," he said. "I never had a problem with the idea of ceding control of the church to the man. It is indeed his birthright, and I have no doubt that there is much that he can teach us. But if William does what he claims he will do and delivers those grotesque prognostications, I fear for what his words will bring—shame to the church, his father's legacy, or worse."

"But you said it's his birthright—that there's nothing you can do to stop him from preaching here."

"United Calvary is a partner parish in the Baptist Convention of Upper New York. That was the only way William's father could fund the church when it was first built and legitimize it in the eyes of the original families in town. And as long as it operates as a member, it's subject to the scrutiny of the Convention delegates. So I may not be able to stop him from this doomsaying now, but if I speak with the other ministers about what is being sanctioned under the auspices of the Convention, then I can perhaps stop it from devolving any further. Once the church loses its backing, William's sovereignty will be over."

Abigail looked at the open sky above her and folded her arms around her knees.

"These other ministers . . . how far away are they?" she asked with a sense of futility.

Thomas sighed and answered reluctantly.

"They are spread across the state. It may take several months to get to them all, but I must speak to them in person to make my case. I can't risk any letters I send being misconstrued, leading them to conclude that this is merely some feeble attempt at usurpation or the falsehood of a bitter pastor who has been removed from his position at the church. They need to understand that this is about more than my reappointment in the clergy. They need to recognize the gravity of what might transpire if William's teachings go unchecked."

"Several months," Abigail repeated quietly. "But . . . what will come of us?"

Thomas reached across her lap and covered her hands with his, looking into her eyes as they shimmered like glass in the sun.

"Come with me," he said, surprising himself with the extemporaneous proposal. "Join me, Abigail."

Abigail attempted to find her words as she shook her head sorrowfully.

"That can't happen, Thomas. What would people say?"

"I am not as young as I once was. William never took a bride, and look what he has turned into. A man married to the church, joys and crosses of it all. That is not what I want."

Abigail hesitated and then slid her hand from Thomas's.

"You know I can't leave my father alone like that."

"I'm sure he will understand, once we explain."

"And my brother . . ."

"He has your sister."

"She's too young to care for him herself!"

Not allowing any further tears to form in her eyes, Abigail raised herself from the ground and brushed the needles off of her dress. She looked down at Thomas with a disappointed glare.

"Why do you offer me something that you know I cannot accept?" she asked with exasperation. "Is it because if I say no, then it becomes my fault that we are not together—and not yours for leaving?"

Thomas lifted himself to his knees as he looked up at her silhouette painted against the sky.

"That's not it at all. I don't want to leave you, but I need you to understand . . . I have to do this."

"But why you, Thomas? You know how dangerous the mountain roads are—what if something happens to you out there? Why do you feel this need to take the burden upon yourself?"

Abigail waited as Thomas continued to look ahead, searching to find an answer to her question. Part of him knew she was right—that William would eventually be exposed by nature of time passing and his predictions failing, that the congregation would inevitably have to reject his teachings and move on. But he could not help feeling a sense of urgency and determination to expedite the process, as if he was being compelled by a higher power to prevent a deeper, more sinister weed from taking root.

"It's getting late," Abigail said, breaking through his silent deliberation. "I have to get back to the school before it lets out."

"Stay with me awhile longer," said Thomas, his knees still in the grass.

"I'm sorry," she said, holding back her tears. "I have to go."

"Abigail . . ." Thomas began faintly.

Before he could say another word, Abigail turned and walked toward the woods to the trails leading back into the town. Thomas looked on as the afternoon sun irradiated her white dress like an angel, and for a moment, he considered standing up and chasing after her—taking her in his arms, saying that he would stay and wait with her for everything to pass, choosing her over this invisible force that he could not put into words.

But he could not bring himself to his feet. The sooner his journey would begin, the sooner it could all be over. Thomas remained in the grass, anguished but resolute, as he watched the thatches on her gown glint in the sun until she at last receded into the shadows.

# Chapter 7

ROSEMARY COULD NOT shake the sinking sensation in her stomach. From the moment she overheard the discussion in the rectory, she'd felt as if there was a heavy pendulum within her swinging in perpetual motion, a constant reminder of the revelation she had witnessed. She found herself lost in the abyss throughout her lessons in school, unable to focus on anything else as she stared out the window and into the boundless sky. Her walks with Abigail and Benji were quiet and gray, clouded by the invasive thoughts of Armageddon that made all other conversation seem meaningless and insignificant, any other subject trivial. At home, she avoided her father and siblings when possible, for they would only make matters worse with their well-intentioned but futile attempts to assuage her underlying angst. She went to sleep praying to herself silently, hoping that she would wake up in the morning and the feeling would subside. But as dawn broke each day throughout the week, the pendulum swung again, reminding her of the secret that she dared not speak aloud.

It was only in the small pasture on their farm where she could find momentary comfort amongst the flock of sheep that her father kept for wool—the four docile, peaceful creatures that she had come to see as pets since she was a young girl. She spent what time she could with them in their pen, caressing the soft skin and fine fleece of the freshly sheared ewes, feeding them forbs and flowers she had collected near the house and talking to them by name to help distract herself from the millenarian dread that constantly threatened to surface.

Rosemary attempted to hold on to the placidity she felt in the pasture until it was time to go to bed, where she would continue to pray herself to sleep, continue to wake at sunrise, and continue to feel the pendulum swing again as the haunting words from that day returned to her.

*I see souls perishing by the thousands.*

Each cyclical, sobering realization that these words were not just a dream further cast her unto an island by herself. Her family, classmates, and friends continued to go about their days in ignorance as the countdown to the advent began, unaware of the torments that awaited them behind the seven seals, the imminence of the rapture, and their inevitable judgment on that day in October. But what weighed on Rosemary most was not the carnage and chaos that hung in their future, but that she was alone in her understanding of it. She wanted to confide in her family, shake her classmates and warn them to tell theirs—but she knew it would be in vain. No one would believe her if she tried.

Rosemary looked up at the agglomeration of white

clouds that swelled over United Calvary as she arrived at church with her family on Sunday. But below them appeared a darker, tumid mass that began to bubble and expand, rising up from the depths of the lower stratosphere to meet the tufted pillows that hovered before the sun. The two systems clashed atop the steeple, swirling, crashing, and coagulating in turbulent conflict—until a single gray crown emerged victorious at the top.

"Looks like a storm is brewing," Henry observed as they stood before the entrance. "Let's get inside before the weather turns."

Rosemary lingered outside as the rest of her family walked through the door. Finding it nearly impossible to move, she watched their shadows cross the threshold into the black, as if they were passing a stygian gate, never to return. She remained stuck in place, weighed down by the heavy pendulum as the sky continued to darken, until Benji returned from the void to call for her.

"Come on, Rosemary," he urged cheerfully. "There's nothing to worry about."

The pendulum held in place for a brief moment as she swallowed her consternation and linked arms with her young brother, then set foot inside.

The church was more alive with discussion than Rosemary had ever heard it, even during the post-baptismal celebrations that brought together the whole of the congregation two or three times a year when they welcomed a new convert or a child passing into adulthood through the waters of Christ. The town had been awash with a week of gossip after hearing the news that Thomas had left on sabbatical, though no one knew why or for how long. Questions and fanciful suppositions fluttered throughout the small nave about their missing pastor—that he had been banished by William upon returning to find his father's church in disrepute; that, unable to compete with the older preacher's erudition and verbosity, he had left on a voluntary measure to establish his own parish elsewhere; that he had ensconced in a monastery deep in the Green Mountains in a fit of jealousy. But there was only conjecture for now, birds chirping throughout the chamber with competing calls.

Rosemary took her seat at the pew beside Abigail and Benji, afraid of what was to come. She looked over her shoulder to find her father talking to Nathaniel and Jacob as he always did every Sunday morning. But she wanted him there with her—to sit down and heed the sermon, to at last begin to share in her understanding and perhaps diffuse the anxiety she felt every morning keeping this news to herself. She looked in his direction, waiting for him to at last glance over. Henry soon noticed her wide eyes looking his way, and he finished his conversation to return to his seat beside her.

Just as Henry sat down, William entered from the stairwell, Bible in hand. Rosemary grasped the wooden bench, curling her fingers until her knuckles turned white, as he made his way to the pulpit. Her knee began to bounce uncontrollably beneath her wool dress, rustling against her sister's thighs.

"What's wrong?" Abigail asked, placing her hand on Rosemary's leg to stop the shaking.

Rosemary remained silent as the pendulum began to swing again and a cold feeling came over her. William's voice thundered throughout the church.

"Before I left for the seminary, my father gave me these

words that I have long carried with me since," he began. "'Truth,' he said, 'is an undeviating path that grows brighter and brighter the more it is trodden.'

"I have walked down that path, long and rugged it be. It has taken me far from this town, away from my church, my home, and my kin. I've spent the better half of my life traversing it, at first in such darkness that I knew not where I stepped. But as I made my way through the bogs and morass of theology, the natural sciences, and secular history, the light began to erase the shadows before me and soon burned brighter than a thousand suns as I drew ever closer to my destination. It was there at the end that I finally saw what was waiting."

William held up the Holy Bible.

"It is this Bible that holds all of the answers to the fundamental questions of the universe—to thousands of years of debate and deliberation, to the deepest philosophical quandaries—for those who wish to seek them. But what I have found is that the only way to reveal the full meaning behind its words is with the light from that long journey toward the truth—the travels through the bogs, the morass, and the shadows that so brighten its pages. And so as I return to where my path began, I come to share with you the summation of my journey, and the illuminated words of God that have for so long been hidden from man.

"Last week we spoke of the apocalypses of Daniel and John, transcribed for us in Scripture with precise and exhaustive detail. Every moment leading up to the end of days is captured in that text with such vividness and terrifying specificity that it could melt the hearts of even the most indurate of men. Now, some of you may be tempted to deny what you heard last week, closing off your ears to the sounds of the rapture and burying your heads in the sand to avoid witnessing the horrors and havoc that will befall mankind. But before we hide like recreants who are too afraid to accept what is plainly given to us by the Lord, we must first understand the purpose of these prophecies. Why has God granted us a vision of the future, knowing that we can do nothing to prevent these events from transpiring? The answer, my friends, lies in the supreme benevolence of our creator, for these apocalypses serve as a gift to fortify us, the believers, during these times. They are here to help prepare us for the ultimate tribulation—and to give us hope that there is salvation at the end of it all.

"This is not the only time a prophecy was written to solidify the resolve of the faithful. We can see it in the first visions of Daniel, who outlined the future of Israel as delivered to him by God centuries before these events occurred. Daniel's people had become captive to Babylon, their temple in Jerusalem destroyed at the hands of King Nebuchadnezzar, and it was to be a long and arduous path of suffering ahead of them before their Messiah would come to restore their kingdom. That is why God instructed Daniel to chronicle every step in their journey, each attributed with a precise unit of time, so that all those who read the Scripture would know that everything was a part of God's plan—that their people would eventually be delivered, as long as they could maintain their faith and persevere through these trying times. And this holy vision, we will see, has been shown to be clear and verifiable, the flowers of the divinations blooming throughout the ages—the evidence in the history of our world itself."

William stepped down from the pulpit and began to walk down the aisle as he looked into the eyes of the congregants in each row.

"For it was foretold! It would be one hundred and thirty-nine years from when the first beast of Babylon took the king of Judah in its maw until Cyrus the Great decreed that the Temple of Jerusalem shall be restored. And so it came to pass in the seventh year of the reign of Artaxerxes after him that this decree went into effect, in 457 B.C., and Daniel's twenty-three-hundred-year prophecy commenced.

"For it was foretold! It would be exactly one hundred and twenty-five years more that Alexander the Great would conquer the Levant and commence the Hellenization of the people of Israel. And it would be one hundred and sixty-eight years hence until the great persecution by his successor, Antiochus, would end—he who forced upon the people the Abomination of Desolation that was the rite of pagan sacrifice. And so it came to pass that Antiochus fell from his chariot and was devoured by worms precisely on the date that God had given to Daniel.

"For it was foretold! Six years later, the Israelites would enter into a compact with the Romans, ushering in an era of illusory peace—illusory, for we know that these new boundaries would provide the grounds for the trial, conviction, passion, and death of our Lord and savior, Jesus Christ. And so, too, it came to pass."

William paused as he turned back toward the pulpit. All eyes were upon him, waiting eagerly for his tapestry to be completed. Rosemary trembled in her seat as she remembered the scroll and the remainder of the years that were to come.

"I have studied these dates in Scripture and have seen how each prophecy has been fulfilled," William continued. "And I know with confidence that the final visions of Daniel and John are fated to come with that same inevitability, which I have returned to share with you here today. Some will have you believe that these events cannot be known with certainty, that God's will is never to be fully understood by man. Some may even go so far as to leave our community to seek outside counsel as they wrestle with the tidings that I will soon deliver. But let me assure you, my friends, that these facts are as true now as they have always been. And the truth can be seen throughout the course of civilization.

"These moments are all empirical—anyone with access to a small library can verify their occurrence, which I encourage you to do if you are filled even with one iota of doubt—and these dates thus give us what we need to decipher the times of the remaining prophecies of Daniel and John. I've validated my calculus with the nation's leading theologians, numerologists, historians—who all can confirm its authenticity. But I did not share with them the final results of the calculation, the last piece of this divine puzzle—no. For it is too consequential to impart first to strangers, too momentous of a discovery to risk falling into the hands of an untrustworthy rogue. Only now will I share this news with my own congregation, as we look ahead to what Daniel and John saw would follow the first coming of the Messiah—and what will come in the future.

"Extrapolating from the prophecies using these methods I just outlined, we arrive in the years of our Lord and come to an important date in the history of the world and in Christendom. This year is 538 A.D., when papal authority over Rome was granted by Emperor Justinian; and thus, the papal-cesarean church was formed while the true church of God was cast away in exile. Both Daniel and John reveal that this civil reign of the papacy, led by those who would falsely claim to be the vicars of Christ, would last times, times, and a half—one thousand two hundred and sixty years—until the generation of our grandfathers. And lo, in February of 1798, even the youngest schoolchildren here know what transpired—the armies of Bonaparte marched into Rome and dethroned Pope Pius the Sixth on their way to conquering the Papal States. The civil power of the papacy was no more; the true church was restored.

"This is a most consequential time in the grand scale of prophecy, for it is foretold that following the restoration, the final day of reckoning will fall upon us with precipitous speed. And that glorious day shall be the culmination of Daniel's twenty-three-hundred-year vision, the time when Jesus Christ will return to take his church as his bride. Call it what you may: the Second Coming, the Millennium, the advent and the eschaton.

"I hope for all my speaking today and in days to come that I will have laid out the case quite clearly, and that you will likewise come to accept the unerring nature of Scripture before it is too late for us to act. For there will soon be a moment at sundown when the clouds will burst asunder and the Bridegroom will descend to deliver the righteous from this earth. And I am here to tell you that this day will arrive imminently: the Day of Atonement; that is, the twenty-second of October in this year of our Lord eighteen hundred and forty-four."

A long silence overtook the congregation as the parishioners began to absorb the true meaning of the words delivered to them—that within six months, every person in that church and beyond would perish; their homes, farms, and businesses would disappear; their families would be no more; the world as they knew it would end.

The quiet rumination was finally broken as Mrs. Edwards belted out a cacophonous wail that nearly shook the room. A feverish chatter amongst the parishioners followed. Rosemary looked around the pews at those nearby. Ahead of her Marigold Chandler raised a kerchief to her mouth in fright, while her mother remained upright and unflappable, a hint of a smirk upon her face. Nearby to them, George Wainscott attempted to calm his shrieking neighbors as they buried their heads into their hands, as if to hide themselves from the news. To her rear, Nathaniel and Jacob spoke to one another intensely as their wives and children sat dumbstruck beside them. Josiah Young, sitting alone, began frantically writing in his pocket notebook with a pencil. Rosemary lastly looked beside her, as Benji attempted to don a veneer of bravery while he covertly grasped Abigail's hand, who held back tightly in return. Henry remained unmoved, staring straight ahead at William, an intimation of doubt in his eyes.

William outstretched his hands to calm the voices.

"My friends, my friends," he urged. "Now is not the time to fret and agonize over this news. This is a time to thank God in all His wisdom for granting us this knowledge of the eternal glory that is to come! And so I say: to all the sinners, repent; to all the righteous, praise His name! We have but six months to come out of Babylon, to ask for forgiveness, to change our wicked ways, and to believe and believe and believe! The Bridegroom awaits us, and all who are worthy will soon take their vow."

Among the screaming and clamor of the parishioners, Rosemary found herself in an unexpected calm. Everybody now knew the secret that she had been holding with her for a week; they now had the information they needed to responsibly prepare for their coming judgment. The knowledge was no longer hers to bear alone. With a comforting sense of relief, Rosemary closed her eyes and exhaled, as the pendulum ceased its sway.

# Chapter 8

I T TOOK ONE day for George Wainscott to organize a town hall. Word of the Millennium had spread to every corner of Calvary overnight—those who didn't attend the Sabbath services heard about it from neighbors who had, and those who had no neighbor were visited by a cousin, an uncle, or a postal carrier who brought them the news with dire concern or curious delight. One could not patronize a shop, see a barber, enter a carriage, or walk portside without being prompted to discuss October the twenty-second and the doom-laden promises of Reverend Miller—and one could not have a discussion without likewise being petitioned to choose to take a side between caution or dismissal. It was the most interesting thing that had happened in the town in a generation. And so by the time the forum was scheduled to begin after sunset, a crowd of eager attendees was overflowing into the street outside the meetinghouse, waiting to hear from the collective of the community and decide what they must do next.

When the doors were finally opened, nearly every able-bodied adult in Calvary flooded into the hall, ready to engage in the deliberation. It appeared that William's prognostication had gotten to them all. Even Henry, typically removed from such caprices of the town, had made the trek from his distant farm, his clothes and beard covered in dirt and dust as he stood in the back of the enormous crowd to hear what, if any, practical impact the outcome of the meeting might have on his life.

Situated in the front of the meetinghouse was George, who leaned over a wooden table to wait patiently for the scheduled hour to arrive and for the utterances to cease. On the walls surrounding him were oil paintings celebrating the legacy of the town, state, and nation: the largest to his left was a reprint of Thomas Sully's *The Passage of the Delaware*, depicting George Washington and his men at the Battle of Trenton, which had been installed in Calvary in commemoration of the centennial of their county namesake's birth; adjacent to the painting was a portrait of Martin Van Buren, native son of the region, commissioned during his short term as the state's governor some years prior; opposing the two on the other wall was a portrait of Cecil Goodman, grandfather of Helen Chandler and great-grandfather of Marigold Chandler, the first to settle Calvary when the land was still considered the untamed frontier; and lastly displayed was a framed replica of the Declaration of Independence, the founding document situated beside the founding family. Behind George hung a large outstretched American flag, suspended from banister to banister, which served as the backdrop for all matters of civic discourse during the town halls.

George studied the room and, determining that they had more than sufficient attendance for quorum, let down a gavel to quiet the impassioned crowd.

"Hear ye," he projected. "Please remain orderly. This is still a civil society for the time being."

The crowd hushed as the residents turned their attention to the center of the room, where George stood up to open the forum.

"Now I know you are all understandably troubled by yesterday's sermon and may have some strong opinions as to what was said," he began. "But we have persevered through times of strife before by remembering our common purpose here and maintaining our composure."

George's opening remarks were immediately interrupted by a shout from the crowd.

"Mr. Wainscott, what are we to do? We cannot just remain idle!"

George sighed as he saw that the source of the question came from Mr. Edwards, a mercurial but obedient dock foreman who'd worked at his family's pier for years, husband to the long-tenured schoolteacher who stood at his side.

"Mr. Edwards, the town of Calvary has always been a democratic institution," George said calmly. "Since its founding, our forebears gathered at this very hall to share in the responsibility of communal discourse to make decisions together without malice or prejudice. In that tradition, I propose we hear the thoughts of the men here, one at a time, before coming to any rash conclusions as to what must be done."

Goaded by his wife, Mr. Edwards stepped to the front of the crowd to initiate the debate as George formally granted him the floor. Beginning to sweat from the attention, he turned around and nervously addressed the audience.

"I am a God-fearing man," he began. "If the events leading up to the advent—the war, the famine, the pestilence—are even halfway as devastating as Reverend Miller describes, then we are set to face suffering unlike any this world has ever seen. These are serious times, friends! So I say henceforth, starting from the moment we leave this hall tonight, my wife and I shall be on our knees every day pleading for the Lord's mercy and forgiveness—as we all should—until kingdom come."

Voices of support began to grow amongst the crowd as Mr. Edwards remained in position, soaking up the affirmations, while the other half of the crowd dismissed his worries as a foolish, neurotic overreaction.

"And how do you know what William says is true?" a deep voice echoed from the side of the hall.

The crowd turned to see a man with a bushy red beard leaning against the wall in the shadows, his arms folded against his chest. Over the heads of the others in the back, Henry recognized the man as the church sexton, who had long worked at the United Calvary cemetery under Thomas Aleman and the elder Reverend Miller before him. Usually reserved and aloof, it was a surprise for those in attendance to be hearing from him directly.

"Were you not listening, man?" asked Mr. Edwards. "His source is the Bible itself! Are you denying the word of God?"

"Mr. Edwards, you are not a mathematician nor are you a historian. We are all humble members of the laity here.

There is not one of us in this room who can confirm his calculations one way or to the contrary."

"Reverend Miller said he consulted the leading experts in the world about this," said Mr. Edwards. "Who are we to question their authority?"

"I heed not the authority of any man when it comes to matters of faith," said the sexton. "But I will consider the opinions of those more learned than I on Scripture—and those whom I have come to trust due to their loyalty to their church and their town. I will therefore be waiting for the one pastor who has not spent twenty years away from us chasing a theory to return from sabbatical and confirm or discredit the reverend's prediction, so that I may make an informed decision for myself."

"You can wait for Pastor Aleman all you want. But I know our time is getting shorter with each hour we delay, and I will begin to ready myself for that moment of deliverance. If there is ever a time to reconsider how we choose to live our lives, it is now."

As the townspeople took sides in the debate, the middle ground quickly began to vanish—one either became a vocal proponent for the prophecy or a believer that prudence would ultimately prevail. George's calls for order were disregarded as nameless voices began to shout counterpoints across the room.

"And what exactly are we to do with this knowledge?" one voice demanded.

"We reflect and repent, just as the reverend says," answered another.

"We spend every waking moment of our remaining days making sure that our souls are worthy of salvation," added Mr. Edwards.

"Think of the children!" Mrs. Edwards screeched. "We must protect them too!"

"I have a farm to plough," one bystander argued. "I cannot spend all of my hours on my knees begging God for forgiveness."

"Spoken like a man who cares more about his reap than his redemption," said Mr. Edwards.

"Spoken like a man who would be fooled by the snake and snake oil salesman alike," the farmer countered.

The crowd continued to squabble as the voices grew louder and more unruly. Breaking through the noise, Mr. Edwards stomped his foot and shouted for all to hear.

"You are free to condemn yourselves to eternal damnation. But now that we have the knowledge of the end's imminence, I am going to respect what God will bring—and prepare for this very ground we walk on to turn to flames."

Sensing that some compromise was needed, George banged his gavel to silence further argument and attempted to restore good faith to their discourse.

"I'll allow that there perhaps is a point to be had here," George mused out loud. "That is, when we think about how we spend the next few months, which is the bigger risk: to behave as though our judgment will come and find it to be disproven in October—or to behave as if it will not and find ourselves unready to face God's eternal wrath? After all, it is better we step on a cold ember with a boot than to be caught with a hot coal barefooted . . ."

"Oh, humbug to your boot talk, George," a voice called out from the crowd.

As the townspeople turned to see who this speaker was, the small figure of Helen Chandler emerged from within the group, cane in hand, and slowly walked to the center of the floor. The spirited arguments ceased as the residents waited intently to hear what more she had to say. Finding the open space in the front of the room, Helen turned back to the crowd and leaned on her cane to project her voice.

"I may be going blind, but that doesn't mean I can't see what is happening here," she began. "My family founded this town nearly one hundred years ago, and we've had our fair share of drummers come through since. Charlatans, Shakers, Indian medicine men—all claiming God told them this or that, holding on to one divination or another. And now we have our dear Reverend Miller returning after how many years, peddling his moonshine."

A few in the crowd snickered under their breaths as Marigold shook her head, mortified by the temerity of her mother's words.

"Mother . . ." she said lightly from the front of the audience, her admonition promptly ignored.

"Frankly," Helen continued, "I am shocked that some of the men here are lending themselves to such fear and hysterics. Remember who you descended from, my neighbors: frontiersmen who braved squall and tempest, those who blazed their own path and tamed the wilds of this land because they refused to bow to the threats and decrees of tyrants. This is not the spirit of the Calvary I know."

"Respectfully, Mrs. Chandler," George began, "are you not afraid that what the reverend prognosticated might be true? Surely you'd want to exercise some caution."

"If we believed every prophecy of doom, we'd still be dwelling in caves, hiding from the thunder," said Helen, stepping out farther into the center space.

"Most of you will be too young to remember this, but I am reminded of a story of another alleged prophetess in the old country, hailing from a town called Leeds. She, too, foretold that the Second Coming of Christ would happen imminently, just like Reverend Miller claimed yesterday. The people of Leeds believed she had nothing to gain from misleading them, and so all were soon convinced that they needed to start preparing for the end of days. Over time, she was visited by an untold number of pilgrims, faithful begging for forgiveness and fanatics who tossed pennies upon her feet in hopes that they would be blessed with the mark of the chosen when the time should come. The town was in a frenzy waiting for the fulfillment of the revelation.

"The prophetess drew so much attention that a young reporter from London visited the area to see the source of all this commotion and chronicle it for his newspaper. And there he found that she took quite an extraordinary form." Helen paused for effect. "For upon arriving, he discovered that this prophetess was neither a preacher nor a mystic nor a soothsayer—but rather . . . a common barn hen. Yes, this prophetess was a chicken who laid eggs inscribed with the words 'Christ is coming.'

"Many, you ought believe, accepted this as a true sign from God because they had witnessed the eggs being lain before their very eyes. But, perhaps unsurprising to us now, it was later discovered that these inscriptions were not divine messages at all—but etchings made by the owner of the hen herself, who would write the words on each shell and reinsert them back into the poor fowl and wait for it to complete the ruse.

"Now I heard the sincerity and the conviction with

which William Miller told us of the advent yesterday, and I can understand how it could at first strike fear into the weakhearted like our good Mr. Edwards here. After all, it is not every day that we learn the world is going to end. But in that moment of silence in the church, the seconds that passed after the reverend said we have but six months left, I could not help but to ponder to myself this old story of the Prophetess of Leeds. And standing here this evening, having fully digested the words of doom and damnation, I can come to but one conclusion: the reverend has simply laid another egg."

The crowd immediately burst into uproarious laughter as Helen concluded her anecdote, and the friction that pervaded the room appeared to be lifted in an instant. Even Mr. Edwards managed to exchange a smile with the sexton across the floor, silently settling any bad blood that may have manifested between the two men.

"Reverend Miller may well believe what he says," Helen resumed in a more solemn tone as the laughter began to abate. "But I've been in this world for seventy-four years and I'll be damned if I haven't learned a thing or two about it. So he can try to convince me all he wants that he has evidence from the Bible or history or what have you, but I tell you now that none of it is going to change how I go about what remains of my life. And those still with your ruddy cheeks of youth, those who inherit the spirit of our ancestors who came to this country without any fear in their hearts, shouldn't dare change yours either."

The room erupted with applause as Helen returned to her daughter's side in the front of the crowd. All but a few lingering voices of dissent were untethered from the feelings of dread that had enveloped them for the past day and became united in the newfound ethos of the meetinghouse. The debate, it seemed, had been settled. George banged his gavel once more and the meeting was adjourned.

Henry stepped aside to allow the crowd to disperse out of the small egress, led in the front by Helen as the rest followed behind. Josiah Young stood across from him, silently letting the people pass through as he studiously sifted through his notebook, reviewing the dates and events that he had written down from William's sermon the day before.

The exit, not having been designed to accommodate such a large capacity, forced the attendees to merge at the door and consolidate into a dense mass. The group, now connected limb to limb and still eager to leave, slowly writhed its way through the doorway to the outside, one pulsation at a time; the body bound to a tail, swayed and directed by the sum of its parts—an ophidian beast beating with a hundred hearts.

## Chapter 9

WITH THE INITIAL panic pacified by Helen Chandler's stand at the town hall, Calvary returned to its usual way of life throughout the course of May. The sap rose and fell as the days became warmer. Farmers planted their new share of crops in the morning and mowed the brush that was beginning to spring up across the valley in the afternoon. Sheep were sheared and wives and daughters spent the daytime hours carding the wool for use at home or for sale in town, where storefronts were beginning to bustle with the season's new merchandise. The children, mostly oblivious to the controversy of the weeks prior, returned to their lessons at school as if nothing had changed.

Church attendance slowly began to dwindle as the advent continued to be the focus of William's sermons and many parishioners gradually grew tired of the gloom and the incessant diatribes on the importance of faith, charity, and contrition. Even Helen Chandler, who had not missed a

Sunday sermon in years, abstained from attendance in order to protest the new leadership of Reverend Miller, leaving her seat in the front pew next to her daughter noticeably open for all to see. William nevertheless remained consistent with his millennial rhetoric, warning of the consequences of apostasy and the impending wrath that would strike the unbelievers. But the parish collectively paid little heed to these exhortations, and many secretly longed for the eventual return of Thomas, whom they hoped would come and offer an end to the doomsaying that had a stranglehold on their town.

The only person in Calvary who seemed to truly appreciate William's ongoing series of sermons was Josiah Young. He was captivated not only by the magnitude of the information, but by the care and specificity that William had put into his exegeses and historiography. Week after week, Josiah continued to write down every detail that William used to support his thesis and compiled his notes by candlelight in the evenings, organizing the timelines for himself and searching for any kind of error in the calculations. But finding no discernible flaws nor gaps in the reasoning, he could only conclude that the prophecies were true; and, in turn, he could not understand why there was no greater urgency amongst the people of the town to act accordingly.

"This week's edition here!" Josiah announced throughout the town square while wheeling his newspaper cart across the cobblestones. "Silas Wright visits Albany on the campaign trail."

His words generated little interest as the residents continued to walk past him without a hint of consideration. Josiah was angry with himself for leading with that story for this week. Half the people of Calvary didn't know the name of the president, let alone the governor, and yet he had foolishly convinced himself that the regional brush with politics would be a worthy headline for his publication. At least the seasonal almanac was of some value to the farmers, he thought to himself in hindsight—this, meanwhile, had no bearing on anyone.

"Read all about it in the *Calvary Crier*," Josiah continued more languidly.

Although enervated by the failings of the week, Josiah fought back against his cynicism as he reflected on his initial motivations for taking up this enterprise in the first place. Was this not exactly the purpose of a local paper, he reasoned—to educate the masses and *make* them care about the events that do not square directly with their everyday lives? Indeed, that was his foundational mission for the *Crier*, the publication he had mortgaged his life to start at the age of twenty-two, not five years earlier.

Josiah had considered himself something of a revolutionary in its early days, and he believed that in a revolution, the pen is even more important than the sword. Inspired by the journalistic and moral crusades of William Lloyd Garrison and Isaac Knapp, who appealed to the decency and devoutness of their readers in order to advance their righteous causes, and bolstered by the vocal parishes that had set the whole of Upstate New York ablaze in the decade prior, the *Crier* was started as the county's first abolitionist publication, featuring weekly editorial treatises on the immorality of human bondage, just as *The Liberator* had done some time before. Seizing on the sensational ecstasy he derived from being at the forefront of an enlightened movement, Josiah in turn expanded his venture to other radical notions of the day—pacifism, women's suffrage, temperance—imploring his readers to liberalize their mores and at last cast aside the complacency of the times and begin to take a principled stand in their lives. The paper failed to catch on.

Out of financial necessity, the *Calvary Crier* evolved greatly after its inception to cover more relevant quotidian topics for its readership, but Josiah still would not give up on his dream of seeing it one day blossom into his original grand vision. He had ambitions of becoming his generation's Shepard Kollock—amplifying the voice of the small-town periodical to reverberate throughout the region, the country, even the world—but it was indeed a slow start to the lofty trail he wished to blaze. The people of Calvary simply did not like him. He attributed it mostly to the perverse air of anti-intellectualism that pervaded the community, but nonetheless, no one said it would be an easy road to make. After all, the *Massachusetts Spy* was a constant target of suppression during the Revolution, and that publication lived on well across several decades. His, too, could therefore just be a newly germinating seed that needed only to withstand the frost of apathy to soon grow into a solid oak, standing tall and firmly rooting itself in the bedrock of his town.

"Come get them while they last," he said with an ironic sense of finality, looking at the stack of papers that remained before him in his cart. He still had twenty-one to go to turn a profit for the week.

Josiah shook his head and turned the corner toward Harriman's general store in hopes of finding more passersby on their way to or from the nearby port. But before he could raise his latest edition in the air, he noticed William exiting the store with an armful of building supplies, loading them into the small carryall behind his white horse.

It was unusual to see a preacher take on the role of a carpenter, save the rabbi Himself, and as such, William turned the heads of a number of others on the street corner as well. As he loaded his wagon to return to the churchyard, several of the townspeople—still sharing in the spirit of raillery born out of the town hall meeting—nudged their companions with their elbows, drew their attention to the preacher, and snickered puckishly behind his back. Trying to outwit one another, some of the younger men proceeded to place their fingers on their heads to imitate devil horns, as they teased the reverend for his weekly sermons on the hellfire that imminently awaited them.

Josiah observed the craven mockery with disgust. He not only admired the rationality of William's sermons, but he had always respected the man himself, or at least what he had heard about him growing up. Here was someone who'd made a laudable career at numerous acclaimed universities and still chose to return to their humble town and deliver this great news to his neighbors before anyone else. What's more, William was supporting his claims with verifiable facts—mathematical calculations, evidence from history, citations from Scripture— encouraging his congregation to validate the findings for themselves if they had any doubt. That few were taking him seriously was shameful enough in Josiah's eyes, but the public derision that morning was beyond reproach.

Josiah could not quell his feelings of indignation. Knowing that this week would not be profitable for him regardless, he hastily covered his wares and left his cart behind to trail the reverend on foot as he made his way to the church grounds.

He continued following him up the hill and around the building to the open field behind the church, where William had tied his horse's reins to a hitching post and left his wagon unattended. Josiah lagged behind just long enough to find the reverend had already unloaded the hardware that he had just purchased and distributed it across the grassy terrain. By the time he arrived, William was stripped of his customary frock, now wearing a white cotton shirt and galluses, and on his knee, driving a pike into the dirt. Josiah approached him gingerly, uncertain as to what he wanted to say or what he even wanted to accomplish in doing so.

Still on one knee, William shielded his eyes from the sun as Josiah's straw-like shadow extended before him.

"Who goes there?" he asked.

"Josiah Young, reverend. I'm one of your congregation members."

"Yes, I see. You're the fellow who always sits in the back with a notebook in hand."

"That's right," said Josiah. "It's a lot for one to take in by heart alone."

"Well I am sorry to tell you that there's no service today," said William as he resumed his work on the grounds.

Josiah looked out to the plot of land. A series of ropes formed a large square more than twice the perimeter of the church itself. At each corner lay several sandbags, brass rods, and an array of antiquated tools left over from the time William's father had constructed the church and schoolhouse. Josiah couldn't fathom what could possibly be erected in that large of an arena.

"What is it that you are working on?" he finally asked after standing in silence for several moments.

"I'm laying out the groundwork for an expansion. The church is too small for a sermon this large."

"That is, in a way, what I wanted to speak with you about, reverend," said Josiah, gathering his thoughts at last. "There's been some talk about the town ever since your announcement about the Millennium."

"I should hope there has been," said William, lifting himself to his feet. He began to move to the next corner while Josiah followed closely behind.

"I mean they're talking about you," Josiah clarified. "Helen Chandler implied that your preachings are nothing but a grift and likened you to some kind of foul charlatan. Some are even questioning your fitness to run the parish once Pastor Aleman returns from his leave."

William knelt down to drive another pike into the ground.

"Let the jackasses bray."

"But reverend, I just can't stand to see it. I've personally checked your calculations. It took a bit of time to locate the histories and commentary to support each point, but I have found that it is unerring—it's perfect. And as the only other man of high education in this town, it pains me to see the bile with which you are treated personally and the contempt with which they repudiate your work. They are dismissing you without a thought. They are abandoning all reason. They are . . . laughing at you."

William finished hammering and stood up, brushing the dirt off his hands.

"When Noah said a great rain would bring the end of all flesh, was he not cast aside as an old fool, a doomsayer?"

"I believe he was," said Josiah.

"And when he built his ark as God commanded, was he not mocked and ridiculed while the others continued their lives of sin?"

Josiah nodded, beginning to understand William's implication.

"You are a smart man, so I believe you will see my point in all of this, Josiah," William concluded. "I spent years away on a mission by myself to uncover these mysteries that are hidden in Scripture. And when I was finished, God spoke to me, and He told me to come back to the place where it all began. There is a reason for that."

"And what is it?" asked Josiah.

"Look around you." William gestured to the open grounds atop the hill. "This is my ark. This is what will protect us on the Day of Judgment."

Josiah realized, at that moment, that William's was perhaps the same mission as his—to bring truth to the unenlightened, to spur action in those who languish in the mud, to help educate the ones who need it most.

"But how can we convince them, reverend?" Josiah asked. "I know the people here well, and they are not ones to take up a cause larger than themselves. I have been trying for so many years—and still it is as if they see knowledge as their enemy."

William stepped forth and stared into Josiah's eyes, his glowing a deep blue as the sky reflected upon them.

"The rains will soon come, Josiah. The people of Calvary have a choice before them: join me here . . . or perish in the flood."

# Chapter 10

HENRY'S DRAW HOE snapped with a lethal crack as he plunged it into the hard, dry terrain. As he lifted it from the dirt, the metal head hung from the splintered shaft like the neck of a dead rabbit, rendering it all but useless. Henry looked out at the expanse of undrilled land before him. The sky was beginning to darken overhead, and it seemed like a storm was swiftly rolling into the valley. There was too much that needed to be done before the rain would come, and he knew he couldn't afford to spend the entire morning half mending the tool. Without wasting any more time, Henry packed up his supplies and began to hurriedly make his way into town in hopes of salvaging the day.

The street outside of Harriman's general store was teeming with patrons, both farmers and business operators, who likewise saw the dark clouds looming and sought to purchase supplies while they still could. Nathaniel had just placed his May stock on display on the porch outside the shop—dry goods for lighter spring and summer clothing, summer hats from the haberdasher in the next village over, flower bulbs for the gardens, and hardware that would serve to mend the roofs and windows before the wind would carry in the inevitable spring showers from the western lakes. Henry passed the display and entered quickly, not wanting to leave his farm unattended for another minute before the storm would arrive. He could hear thunder rumbling in the distance as he stepped inside.

The all-purpose shop had grown over the past several years as commerce expanded at the riverside ports. It was the town's only general store, so all of the miscellany unloaded from the docks from various industries upriver would eventually find their way there for sale, along with the wares of the local artisans and traveling merchants passing through on their way to Albany. Combing through the various sections of the small store, Henry found a suitable replacement for his draw hoe in the back of the shop and slung the new tool over his shoulder. He approached the sales counter, where he saw Jacob White waiting ahead of him to pick up his weekly order of chewing tobacco that Nathaniel had shipped in from Virginia.

"I heard our reverend came in here and bought up half the supplies," Jacob said with a wry grin.

"He did indeed," said Nathaniel. "He tried putting them on credit . . . said he'd pay it off on October twenty-third."

Nathaniel burst into laughter at his own joke, as Jacob slammed his fist against the counter and let out a wheezy howl, his eyes bulging like a goat.

"Well, that money'll be of no use where you're headed anyway, friend."

Nathaniel loaded the box of tobacco and sighed to himself. "I almost feel bad for the old fool. Did you hear the latest?"

Jacob shook his head and leaned in, eager to learn more.

"You'd never believe it," Nathaniel continued. "I heard from Elias Cooper that he knows someone who saw Reverend Miller before he came back here to Calvary. Apparently, his cousin works at the lunatic asylum downstate and says that William Miller was living there—as a patient—for the past four years. Imagine that! All of that talk of his research at the university was nothing more than a cover for his time in bedlam."

"Just as well explains it," said Jacob. "His sermons sound like the ravings of a madman. It wouldn't surprise me to find the minister wearing a black veil at the next Sabbath."

The two laughed derisively as Henry approached the counter and paid for the hoe.

"What do you say, Henry?" asked Nathaniel. "Are you getting your boots ready for hellfire come October?"

Not one to partake in the ridicule, Henry shook his head as Nathaniel and Jacob continued sniggering together.

"I tell you, Henry," Jacob said as he leaned against the door, stuffing his lip for the walk back to his ranch. "Sometimes you have to find humor in life's crazy turns."

As Henry prepared to leave, the floorboards beneath the men suddenly rattled as a deafening crackle ripped through the confines of the store from outside. The hearing returned to their ears just in time to catch the sound of a woman's shrill, horrified scream that followed. Nathaniel, Jacob, and Henry exchanged a look of concern and at once exited the store and hastened down the road to the origin of the commotion, holding on to their hats as the wind began whipping across the town.

A large crowd had already gathered outside the gates of the Chandler estate, the oldest and largest property directly in the center of the residential section of Calvary. As the three continued toward the gathering, the wind began to carry a pervasive stench toward them—a rich, nauseatingly sweet bouquet of burnt hair and fat that grew more acrid the nearer they came to the source, until a heavy metallic tang could be felt upon their tongues. The men covered their mouths, nearly retching from the odor as they approached.

As they arrived at the property gates, they found the onlookers frozen like statues, each fixed in place, stationary and silent. A pair of men stood with their hats over their hearts, eyes lowered, solemnly staring at the cobblestone road before them. Another three women stood amongst them, each holding a gloved hand over their mouth and nose—too aghast to turn away, too calcified for tears.

Marigold sat on the pavement before the crowd with her arms wrapped around her legs in a state of shock. White steam rose from a charred pile beside her as she averted her eyes and looked out into the distance. Between the boots of the men in the crowd, Henry could see the burnt fringes of a blue dress waving in the wind like the feathers of a bird crushed beneath a wagon wheel. He pushed between the bystanders and stepped forward to find the remains of a small body. A shawl had been placed over her face. He knelt down to confirm the worst of his suspicions.

"Don't move it," warned one onlooker. "You don't want to see what's under there."

Henry turned toward Marigold. He had known her

nearly all his life, through all of her family's misfortune, but had never seen such an emptiness in her as he did at that moment.

"Marigold, what happened?" Henry asked.

Marigold continued staring into the distance with her eyes wide open, taking time to gather her words. "We were just walking home, and suddenly there was a flash of light," she said. "Everything went dark for a moment. Then I woke up . . . and she was gone."

Henry looked at the ash on the cobblestone pavement and saw the silver-tipped dove of her mother's parasol glowing beside her. Marigold planted her face between her knees as she began to sob irreconcilably.

As Marigold wept, a larger crowd began to accumulate around the area. The nearby residents had left their houses after hearing the thunderous noise, and all who walked down the road stopped to see what had happened to the Didonian matriarch of Calvary. Within several minutes, dozens of onlookers had arrived to the scene.

Henry could not stand by while such a sight was on public display, and he motioned to Nathaniel and Jacob to help him.

"Marigold, you wait here," Henry said tenderly as he left her in the company of the neighbors who had gathered beside her. "We'll bring her to her bed inside."

Marigold raised herself to her feet and stood in quiet disbelief as the three men encircled Helen's body, careful to preserve her modesty as they knelt down to lift her off the ground. But as they began to carry her toward the gates, a sudden draught of wind traced the side of the street and swept off the shawl that had been carefully placed over her head. As Helen's face was exposed, the gathering collectively gasped aloud, and the women in the crowd screamed in fright. Marigold, beholding the image before her, lost her constitution and fainted to the ground.

## Chapter 11

"THERE WAS NOTHING more that you could have done," Dr. Clarke said to the men. "At least take comfort in knowing you were able to bring her into her own room to be at peace."

His postmortem examination complete, Dr. Clarke returned his medical supplies to his satchel and covered Helen's face with a white sheet. He stood up from her bedside, sleeves rolled up and face puckered with exhaustion, and ambled toward Henry, Jacob, and Nathaniel across the room.

The storm had already passed without a drop of rain, and the light had begun to shine in through the window, thickening the air as the aroma of burnt flesh remained.

"At peace?" Nathaniel whispered, careful as not to disturb Marigold, who was recovering in her bedroom down the hall. "But her face . . . that was a look of sheer terror."

"Sometimes a lightning strike can cause that kind of

rigor mortis," said Dr. Clarke. "But I assure you, she did not feel anything for very long before she passed."

"I think I'm going to be sick, doc," Jacob said, holding his stomach.

Dr. Clarke looked at him disconcertedly. "Why don't you go home, Jacob. Be with your family. Reverend Miller is already on his way here to deliver a prayer."

Henry felt a sudden pang of sentimentality as he looked over at Helen in repose. She had always been like a mother to everyone in town—the one who nursed the fledgling community into existence, and always seemingly the one who kept it together. One of the last of the hardened colonial women in New York, Helen was a daughter of the Revolution—Calvary's final surviving member of the generation who weathered the strife and uncertainty of the war and the years that followed. She understood the capriciousness of history, how quickly society around her could transform, and always made a point to impart the wisdom of her years to the younger residents of the town, lest they be unknowingly swept up into these raging currents of change.

The people of Calvary knew Helen as the successor of the founding Goodman family, though she had relinquished her historical name upon marriage. But that did not matter. What they saw in her was a torchbearer to the lineage of the original settlers, those who believed that the land could be more than a consortium of farms—but a community of friends and neighbors who could collectively build a better society of shared mores and values. Helen was instrumental in seeing that vision through, organizing town holidays, festivals, and banquets throughout the years. And as Calvary matured, changed, and expanded, the original spirit of her forefathers always lived on through her.

"Is anyone else coming to see her before the burial?" Nathaniel asked, interrupting Henry's nostalgic meandering.

"Just Marigold. That's all the family she has within a month's worth of travel," said Dr. Clarke.

Helen had nine children in total, eight of whom survived past childbirth. Marigold was the youngest of the lot and remained in their large house through adulthood. She was just a small child when her father was killed by a drunk wagon driver not far from where Helen was struck by the lightning, and the trail of her family's misfortune continued on thereafter. The town was overrun by an epidemic of typhus the following winter, which spread throughout the long halls of the Chandler estate like wildfire. Marigold's four brothers and three sisters were among those who perished in the outbreak, and only she and her mother were spared. The remaining members of the Goodman family, Helen's brothers and their wives and children—frontiersmen by blood—took the incident as a sign from God to move on from their ancestral hometown and left for the Michigan Territory shortly after. Within two years, Helen and Marigold were all who remained of the family.

As Helen's health began to decline, Marigold took it upon herself to care for her in her old age and stayed with her as the sole occupants of the large private manor. This sense of filial duty was like a bulwark against suitors, and aside from the occasional flirtation or attempted courtship of her youth, Marigold seldom displayed any interest in moving out or starting a family of her own. And thus she remained unmarried into her forties, her life dedicated solely to the care of her mother.

"How is she doing?" Nathaniel asked.

"A little bruised from her spell," Dr. Clarke replied. "But you know how close those two were. I'm sure the trauma of seeing her this way was a lot to bear."

The men all reflected on the horror that lay under the sheet and could hardly imagine what it must have felt like for Marigold to see it with her own eyes.

Henry shook his head. There had been enough idle staring for the day. "I don't believe we can be much more help for her at this point. Only the passage of time will be her remedy."

Feeling the weight of the day upon them, Nathaniel and Jacob agreed with Henry, and the men prepared to leave the room. But as they turned to the door, they found Marigold standing at the threshold, staring quietly at the white sheets before her. Dr. Clarke approached her with calming assurance.

"Marigold, you should be resting. Save your energy."

Marigold did not take her eyes off the bed. "We didn't listen," she whispered.

The men looked at one another, unsure of what she could possibly mean.

"We didn't listen," she repeated more loudly. "We didn't heed his warning. We ignored the signs. Every Sunday since she lost her children, my mother made sure that she went to Sabbath services and sat in the very front pew, no matter how frail or incapacitated she became. It was important to her that she form a close relationship with God. And now as soon as she betrayed that relationship, this is what happens."

"Now Marigold, this was an act of nature, not of God. Nothing your mother said or did could have caused this," said Nathaniel.

Marigold turned her eyes from the bed and glared at him.

"It wasn't just what *she* said or did. It was everyone's collective insolence. I was there with her during the town hall. I heard the jeering and the dismissal. And I saw what happened in this town the weeks after. Her words poisoned the community, turned us against the reverend's teachings. And for that, the Lord sent us a message."

Tears began to fall down Marigold's cheeks in parallel streams like rain on a glass window.

"I saw a flash of God when that lightning struck. In that moment, I saw Him grant me mercy and spare my soul for another day. But now I realize that my mother saw something else—it was imprinted on her face when the wind took off that veil. I saw it in her: she knew that she would not be spared. I saw the dread in her eyes. She was blind, but yet what she saw was the Hell that waited for her."

Marigold approached Henry and grabbed him by the hands as she began to tremble through her tears. "It was all of us who brought this on her. It was her fault for speaking out against God. It was mine for not stopping her. And it was everyone else's for listening. We should have known! We should have known!"

Nathaniel and Jacob lowered their eyes as Marigold began to sob. Her hands still gripping Henry's, she slumped to her knees, and he leaned down to catch her before she could fall flatly to the floor. Dr. Clarke hurried over and grabbed her by the arms, lifting her off the ground alongside

Henry and supporting her weight on his shoulder. Jacob and Nathaniel remained in place, their eyes unblinking, stirred to the soul.

"All right, Marigold, come with me. We'll calm your nerves," said Dr. Clarke.

"It was all of us!" Marigold repeated again. "We should have known! We should have known!"

Her words echoed through the hallway as they passed William, who stood at the door as witness to the scene. William paused to wait for the sounds of Marigold's grief to dissipate as Dr. Clarke administered his medication in her bedroom.

"Thank you for your help," William said to the men. "But it's time for me to issue a final prayer."

Jacob and Nathaniel kept their heads low and exited quietly, still shaken by Marigold's rebuke. Henry looked at the white sheet covering Helen one final time as the room cleared and William stepped inside.

"Henry. It's been a long time," said William.

Henry kept his eyes averted. "It has indeed," he said, shaking his head. "The last of the founding families. So much has changed since you've been gone."

William took another step forward. "And I'm afraid to say the changes have only just begun."

Henry lifted his eyes from the bed as the two men stood across from one another in opposite corners of the room— Henry in the light from the window and William in the shadows of the entrance.

"I must be on my way now, William. My children will be home from school soon."

William bowed his head as Henry walked past him into the hallway.

"Henry," William said, stopping him at the threshold. "I was very sorry to hear about your wife. She was a good woman."

Henry stood with his back to William and paused as he attempted to gather a response, choosing instead to straighten his wind-battered shirt and leave without a further word.

Now alone, William sat down in the seat beside Helen and placed his Bible on her nightstand. Leaning over the bed, he gently lowered the sheet, revealing her face. Underneath the covering lay Helen in her final rigidified countenance of terror—her face contorted, mangled, and twisted, her jaw agape. Silver coins had been placed over her eyes, but they could not block the visions that she had witnessed. Helen had seen what was behind the seals and beyond. The woe and the wrath. The false prophet and the beast. The rusted gates of Babylon ajar.

William raised his eyes to the heavens and delivered his prayer.

# Chapter 12

THE SMELL OF death lingered in the air for days. Each morning, a street cleaner attempted to remove the ashen spot that stained the thoroughfare in front of the Chandler estate—working with a push broom and a bucket of warm water to scrub the face of the cobblestone as the townspeople made their way to the ports, the shops, or the school, covering their mouths and noses to spare themselves the fetid remembrance of that day until the odor was sufficiently diffused across the town. But nothing would lift the shadow from the ground. It became a memory indelibly etched into the stone, a grisly reminder for all who passed—a sign that could no longer be ignored.

Nearly every pew in United Calvary was filled during the Sabbath services for the first time since the town hall. The rumors and embellished details of Helen's death had spurred the prompt reawakening of scores of parishioners who had eschewed services in the weeks prior—those who had begun to feel a tacit sense of remorse and dread for disregarding the warnings and treating their reverend with skepticism or ridicule, and who now held with them an unspoken fear that they might be struck down next.

"I tell you, it's not the way I'd like to go out," Nathaniel said, shaking his head. "Dying with the devil's words upon my lips."

"It really makes you appreciate the mysterious ways in which the Lord works," Jacob replied. "One day Mrs. Chandler's speaking out against the teachings of the church, the next she's cold as a wagon tire. It's like God was sending us all a message."

The men, standing beside the church entrance, looked to the front pew at the unoccupied seat that Helen once filled. Marigold sat beside the empty space, staring blankly ahead, her eyes like polished marble from the effects of Dr. Clarke's narcotics.

"I do still feel terribly for Marigold. The Hell she must be in just thinking about her mother being turned away from the gates of St. Peter."

"Yes, but I reckon she'll start taking these times more seriously now. No longer being so passive when there's blasphemy within earshot."

The door opened behind them as Henry entered with his family. He had not spoken to Nathaniel or Jacob since Helen's death, nor had he ventured into town, where the news had proliferated in the days that followed. The turnout in the congregation took him by surprise—it appeared that the entire population of Calvary was there to pay their respects.

"Let's sit down before someone takes our pew," he said to his children, declining to partake in his weekly tradition at the door.

The four walked down the aisle slowly as a requiem began to play on the portable organ next to the deacon's bench.

"Poor Mrs. Chandler," said Abigail, looking at the chasm where she once sat. "To think about how ghastly of an end she faced."

"How did she die, Abigail?" Benji looked up and asked his eldest sister.

Abigail struggled to find the words to respond to him delicately as their father led them to the seats in their pew.

"I'll tell you," Rosemary said as they sat down. "God burnt her to a crisp for speaking out against the Second Coming."

"He did?" Benji gasped.

"That's enough, Rosemary," Henry chided.

"What did I say that's untrue? It's what all of the children at school are hearing from their own parents."

"All you need to know is that she's in a better place now," said Henry. "There is no sense in being obscene."

Rosemary sunk into the bench and crossed her arms, sulking at her father's chastisement as the rest of the congregation continued to fill in the remaining seats and waited nervously for their preacher to arrive. Appearing in the shadow of the stairwell, William paused to study the throngs of parishioners, and a look of self-satisfaction grew across his face as he saw the full-capacity attendance before him. With renewed purpose, he took to the pulpit and raised his voice over the final chords of the organ.

"As we gather here on this solemn occasion, let us remember our dear friend Helen Chandler, who was taken from us this past week with such suddenness and such force that we are all rightfully left humbled and in awe of God's unimaginable power. Let us pray for her soul: that the Lord shows her mercy, that He grants her eternal passage. Let us pray to thee, O God, that thou judgest her from the whole of her book of life—not merely from the final page that she hath wrote for herself.

"But let us also give prayers of gratitude that God has granted those of us sitting here today more time to prepare for that final demonstration of might that is to come on October the twenty-second. For how providential it is for Mrs. Chandler to be taken in such a way as to remind us of what John the Revelator witnessed as he gazed upon the throne of Heaven: 'lightnings and thunderings and voices.' Could it likewise be that the thunder we heard this week was God's call, the lightning his message?"

William stepped forward from the pulpit and closer to the parishioners in the pews.

"Now I must speak to you with candor. I am not deaf to the rumors that have been eddying about this town; these walls do not fortify me from the gossip and hearsay hovering in the air outside. I have heard allegations related to my whereabouts for the past several years—accusations that I have not been forthcoming in my previous residence."

The parishioners averted their eyes with shame-faced guilt as they waited for their admonishment.

"But I must tell you now . . ." William said with a pause. "These rumors are true. I have indeed lived in a madhouse—though not for four, but for all forty years of my life!"

The congregation began to buzz as the parishioners attempted to decipher the meaning behind the sudden revelation. William remained poised and purposeful as he raised his voice and lifted his finger, leaning in toward his audience with a spirited fervency as he continued his sermon.

"Yes, that's right! I have been living in a madhouse occupied by so-called Christians who refuse to heed the words of inevitable doom that are so clearly spelled out before us. A madhouse in which the most consequential tidings in the history of man are dismissed forthwith and we continue to carry on about our days as if everything is unchanged. A madhouse in which God smites the most vocal unbeliever as a warning to us all, and yet we still remain on our feet rather than falling to our knees to beg for forgiveness. Yes, all the world must be a madhouse, for one must be a madman to ignore the signs of our great reckoning.

"It's time now to drink the dregs of thy coming reality. Continue to scoff and mock, and ye shall be left without a vessel when the rain cometh. Continue to ignore what is in front of thine eyes, and ye shall see what shall happen to thy soul. Ask now, ye impenitent, ye callous and unbelieving: where wilt thou reign when the Millennium is here? In Hell! Yes, a dreadful word! But important to understand what truly awaits. Hell. To lift one's eyes and find oneself surrounded by those eternal flames, to find oneself in perpetual torment. Stop, sinner, and think! Consider thy latter end hence."

Benji struggled to find his breath as he listened to the warnings of damnation that awaited the denier and saw the fire burning in William's eyes. With each word came a more strained inhalation, and he soon found himself unconsciously opening his mouth in a feeble attempt to swallow more air than his lungs could take in, until his teeth began to chatter from the tension.

"Benji, are you all right?" Rosemary asked.

Benji closed his mouth and nodded, trying not to exhibit panic or cause any commotion in front of his family.

"What are the signs of the times?" William continued as he paced in front of the parishioners. "We are inclined to think about the prophecies of Daniel and John as sequential events; that is, distinct acts that are carried out one after another. But God's plan does not flow in a single path; rather, these signs in Scripture are woven together like tributary streams that fill up the grand river of prophecy, until the sum of it ends in the ocean of eternity.

"My friends, you may not realize it, but we are already sailing downstream. By my assessment, the first and second seals have long been opened. Perhaps you have already seen the white horse, great conqueror of nations, in the paintings of Bonaparte of France, who vanquished the Holy Roman Empire and deposed the last of the civil popes, just as it was foretold in Revelation. And likewise, you may have read in the newspapers of the red horse that rode behind him: the bloodshed that continues to flow mightily in the wars and revolutions that followed. But this is just the beginning; do not think ye shall be spared from the rest. We now await what is behind the third seal, which by my calculation is to be opened in the coming weeks: the black horse, the destroyer of wheat and barley, oil and wine. And it pains me to say, but it is verily so, that a great famine will follow."

Overwhelmed by the imminence of the coming destruction, several parishioners rushed to the aisle and fell to their knees, throwing up their hands in submission to God. Palms in the air, they closed their eyes and cried aloud.

"God save us!"

"Forgive us!"

"Grant us thy mercy!"

The church became awash in a series of beseechments and acts of spiritual mania. Many of the previously skeptical begged for forgiveness as they came to realize the grave error of their ways. Others watched with shock and apprehension as their neighbors plunged into hysteria. With the pandemonium overtaking half the congregation and the sounds of their cries reverberating between the walls, Henry could not hear Benji beginning to wheeze.

William outstretched his hands to mollify the outbursts of his congregants.

"O my friends! What can we do to save our souls before it is too late?" he asked through the increasing commotion. "How can we, meek and humble servants, prepare for that final holy day as we bear witness to these signs?"

"Help us, reverend!" pleaded one parishioner. "Tell us what we can do!"

William answered stridently. "We must strive to save those who are not yet ready for the coming of our Lord. It is our foremost duty to bring these tidings to all our brothers and sisters in this town and beyond. Look to your left and then to your right. One man or woman next to you is not prepared for salvation. It is now your mission from God to convince them of their error, to change their ways. This is how the righteous will earn their place in the Heavenly keep; for salvation is not just ours—but it is a gift to be shared with all the world."

Several parishioners stood up and delivered rapturous praises to William's pronouncement.

"Tell your spouse, tell your children, tell your neighbor—shout it in the streets, shout it from the mountaintop," William said over the applause. "The Bridegroom cometh, ye shall say! New Jerusalem shall rise!"

The congregants in the center pews surrounding the Smith family rose to their feet, enclosing the space over Benji like an impermeable dome, as the darkness overtook him and he began to desperately hang open his mouth to gasp for air.

## Chapter 13

WITH EACH BREATH of the herbal aroma, Benji began to draw closer to an equilibrium. The color of his cheeks grew brighter, the cavity of his chest filled with air, and the rhythm of his lungs was restored to a steady iambic pattern. His vitality had returned; and now Henry, too, could at last breathe easy.

Although each episode brought with it renewed angst to the household, the Smith family had gotten used to the systematic routine they'd developed to care for its youngest member. As Benji lay in bed to minimize the impact of each attack, Abigail would begin to prepare his medication, grinding the dried herbs with a mortar and pestle to release the oils needed to create the soothing vapor. Rosemary was charged with drawing water from the well and heating the iron over the stove until it was hot enough to produce steam at the touch. Henry, meanwhile, spared the girls of the most unpleasant and intimate of responsibilities—cleaning out the basin that was left at Benji's bedside to capture the persistent expectoration of phlegm and mucus; cooling his head with a cold, damp rag whenever a fever accompanied an episode; and, lastly, administering the medication when it was ready and combined with water in the cauldron. Henry took it upon himself to fulfill these duties, but for him, it was worth a thousandfold the labor for the joy of watching his son come alive again and seeing his spirit swiftly return to his eyes.

As soon as he finished the remainder of the remedy, Benji immediately attempted to climb out of bed to join his sisters in the other room, refusing to let his affliction slow him down.

"Not so fast," Henry said as he pulled the sheets back over his chest. "I'll have Abigail bring you your lunch in here. You get your rest until then."

Benji relented obediently and curled the blanket over his shoulders, lying in silence for several moments as Henry remained beside him.

"Father," Benji began hesitantly. "Is it all right if I skip lunch today?"

"Absolutely not. You need to regain your strength after this morning," said Henry.

"But what if we run out of food? I don't want you and Abigail and Rosemary to starve."

"What makes you think that would happen?" Henry asked, taken aback by the question.

"Reverend Miller said there's going to be a great famine next . . . What if we don't store up enough food to get through it?"

Henry attempted to remain even-tempered as his frustration with the effects of the reverend's sermons on his family mounted within him.

"I don't want you worrying about those sorts of things," Henry said with his hand on his shoulder. "I promise that nothing like that will happen."

"But they said Mrs. Chandler was struck down because she didn't believe," Benji argued. "And now Reverend Miller says that we're going to see the next seal open any day now. I don't want to be a nonbeliever and have something worse happen here!"

Henry exhaled deeply as he continued to repress the resentment that he felt bubbling inside. He thought about the commotion that these same messages had caused in the church, watching some of his formerly rational neighbors turn into crazed madmen before his eyes as they shrieked and genuflected on the floor beside him. He thought about poor Marigold, always so sweet and demure, now in a state of catatonia, beside herself with guilt for allowing her mother to sow doubts about the revelation. He thought about his son, who once spoke of little more than his dreams of sailing the ocean and discovering uncharted lands, now ruminating over war and famine and fearing for what the future might bring. He was too young to be thinking so negatively—he had plenty of years ahead of him before his hands would be calloused, his heart would harden. For now, life should be an open sea before him.

"I'll let you in on a secret, just between you and me, Benji," Henry began. "Those things the reverend says are just stories. They're tall tales with good intentions, a way to ensure that everyone believes in the power of God. But you already believe in God, don't you?"

Benji nodded his head. "Yes, father."

"These stories are also told in order to convince people that they must behave as good Christians, to avoid sinning and ask for forgiveness when they do. And we already live a goodly life in this house, don't we?"

Benji thought to himself and nodded his head again.

"Well then, Reverend Miller's sermons aren't really meant for us," Henry concluded. "So I think we're going to take a little break from church for a time, perhaps until the subject of the sermons starts to change. Besides, you saw how crowded it was in there. We'll be doing someone a favor by freeing up four new seats."

"All right, father. I trust you," Benji said, yawning and smiling confidently at his plan. "That would be nice of us to make room for new members of the parish."

Reassured by the secret his father had given him, Benji closed his eyes and peacefully drifted off to sleep.

Henry left the bedroom and stepped into the living quarters. All was finally quiet in the house, save for the sounds of the fire hissing in the hearth and his daughters preparing the meal across the room. A hiatus from the church would be good for them, too, he thought to himself. While his neighbors may have been shaken into newfound religiosity over the vengeful warning from God, the last thing that Henry wanted was for his own children to come to the wrong conclusion about what had transpired with Helen Chandler—that they would believe the vicissitudes of fortune were not driven by chance, but were directed by God as retribution for a wrongdoing or a punishment for a sin. With an ailing family member in their home, he needed to put to rest any supposition that their actions could be to blame for their brother's affliction or whatever might follow next.

Abigail and Rosemary stood side by side, their backs turned to the bedroom entrance, neither noticing that

Henry had left the room. Henry leaned against the door and watched as the ribbons of their bonnets, one purple and one yellow, fluttered from the draught of heat from the fireplace. Although they were sisters, the two were very much dissimilar in disposition, temperament, even appearance. But just like the colors of their ribbons, he felt that they had grown to form a sense of harmony in their opposition—two complementary personalities who balanced out one another and made their home feel more complete. He wouldn't want it any other way.

Henry found himself losing track of time as he stared wistfully at his growing children. With all of the turmoil of the past week, he had nearly forgotten what day it was.

Pushing himself off of the door and walking past his daughters, Henry stepped outside and ambled past the outer perimeter of his budding wheat field. He continued beyond the edge of the crops, past the small chicken coops and grazing pen for the sheep, until he came to his cellar. Henry opened the wooden door of the small storage area and descended the stairs, returning with a crate of bulbs that he'd purchased from the general store earlier in the month. They were white lilies, her favorite flower.

Carefully carrying the shallow crate, Henry walked around the side of the house toward the trails that led to the town. The grassy terrain alongside his home was too uneven to cultivate any crops, so he instead had preserved the small verdant meadow from any grazing or activity that would otherwise spoil the serene setting. At the center of the open space stood his favorite part of the property: a hearty sycamore, rooted atop a small knoll, its limbs stretching out across the empty sky. This was where Henry had always wanted to build a homestead. The ground had been no more than a swamp when he first came across it, a remnant of when the Hudson surged deeper into the valley; yet out from it grew this ancient and mighty tree—and he knew that this was a sign of what the land could yield, the potential it would bring, as long as enough care was given to it.

The deep green leaves whispered from the boughs as Henry placed the wooden crate beside the trunk of the tree. Kneeling down into the grass, he brushed the pollen off of a wooden cross firmly planted in the ground underneath the shadows of the sycamore. An etching was revealed in the center: MARY SMITH. She would have been thirty-eight today.

Henry once read that it was the ancient Greeks who first began the tradition of flower-setting. They would plant them on the graves of fallen soldiers in battle, believing that if they took root, it was a sign the deceased had found peace in the Elysian Fields below. And so, Henry took on this tradition as his own—every year planting his wife's favorite flowers on her birthday, and watching the lilies grow out of her place of eternal rest, a perennial reminder that she had found peace with God in a far better place than here.

Henry dug into the soil before the cross with his hands, pressing his calloused fingers into the dirt until the holes were deep enough to fully cover the bulbs. He carefully placed in each seedling and pushed the soil back over until only the newly sprouting bud was aboveground, ready to absorb the sunlight and flourish in the springtime air. Remaining on his knees, he leaned back and looked at the freshly turned soil before him as the sun shined upon the grave. It had not rained there all season. But he was hopeful that they would still find a way to bloom.

# Chapter 14

JOSIAH HAD NEVER witnessed anything like it before. Sitting in the back of the church, he could see the full impact of William's words upon the people— the exuberance, the inspiration, the epiphany with which the congregation at last began to appreciate that the advent was coming. He watched in awe as many were overtaken by the spiritual fervor, falling to their knees in the aisle, hands outstretched to the heavens; others shouting praises to God as they filled the donation trays with jewels, coins, and other pecuniary tokens from their pockets that would only weigh them down during the ascension; and more still who were weeping in their seats, pleading relentlessly for mercy and forgiveness. The people at last began to think rationally.

He observed the scene quietly from his pew as he began to process the profound changes that were happening right before his eyes. All his life he'd felt like an outsider in his own town. He was never interested in following in the footsteps of his father or his brothers, becoming a swineherd or a yeoman cultivating a few acres of corn for the livestock, nor did he care to join an apprenticeship in the growing commercial sector and work his fingers until they were ossified and arthritic, retiring just in time to die. No, what interested him most was the pursuit of knowledge, putting his mind to work rather than his body, and helping others understand, too, that they need not be satisfied with the sheltered life that Calvary offered them.

It was this very thirst that had been quenched by Reverend Miller's new sermons. He drank in every word of it—admiring the careful translations behind every prophecy in the King James Bible, appreciating the algorithmic nature of every calculation, marveling at the fated alignment with each date and its reference point in history, empathizing with the effort and attention that this undertaking took to create. And now, the people whom he'd always hoped would join him on this pursuit were beginning to understand as well.

Josiah hadn't felt this energized to go home and work in years. As soon as he returned to his small domicile in the center of town, he sat down at the escritoire beside his printing press, opened a fresh well of ink, and began to write. He felt a sense of divine inspiration, as if his hand was being controlled by an angel or some other spiritual puppeteer. Although he had a detailed reference guide in his notebook beside him, there was a greater wealth of information captured behind the levees of his mind, and the words thus flowed onto the pages with the fluency of a poet reciting an epic from heart, pouring like a fountain from the top of his memory.

Josiah worked ceaselessly through the day, taking no

break to eat or drink or relieve himself, stopping only to light a candle as night began to fall and it became too dark to see the pages in front of him without its aid. By the time he finished, the tallow had melted into a globular pile before him, and his hand felt nearly broken. But, determined to get the article typeset in time for a late edition for the week, Josiah pressed forward, carefully rereading and proofing his work until he fell asleep at his escritoire with his pince-nez still upon his nose.

Josiah awoke in the middle of the night and managed to climb into his bed that hung above the printing press. Without the funds to build or rent a separate space for his business, the *Calvary Crier* was an operation running solely out of his own living quarters. The machine took up most of the space in his single-room residence, and Josiah had lofted his bed above it as the only way to fit the metal apparatus inside. Every night, the scent of the ink and oil wafted into his nostrils, and every morning, he awoke to the sight of the reams of flammable paper that he had shipped in from Albany weekly, which were stacked in the nooks of remaining floor space. It was a lifestyle that was becoming a debilitating burden for the young man. But this night was different. His heart was back into his business—he at last felt the same feeling he had when he first had enough money to afford the printing press machinery. And, for the first time since those initial days, he now looked forward to being lulled to sleep by the cacophonous sounds of it running all evening.

As soon as the sun rose in the morning, Josiah climbed down from his bed and tiptoed over the stacks of paper to gather the handwritten pages of his next front-page story.

He threw on his overcoat and headed immediately for United Calvary, his heart throbbing in his chest with each stride he took back up the hill, into the church, and up the stairs to William's rectory.

"Josiah?" William asked, looking up from an open book on his desk to find the disheveled man before him. "What are you doing here?"

Josiah peered around the room and marveled at the volumes of sources and references on the shelves behind him: editions of the Bible written in Hebrew, Greek, and English; the histories of the Levant and Asia Minor, the Greco-Roman empires, the Catholic Church, and the Holy Roman Empire; the philosophical treatises of the great Christian theologians from Augustine to Aquinas; and books on the natural sciences, numerology, and mathematics throughout the millennia—the ultimate unassailable corroboration to support his calculations.

Josiah removed his hat and caught his breath.

"I am but a humble servant," he began. "I may not be able to fill your donation plate, but I come to you with an offer that is more valuable than the alms of the richest man in New York."

William returned a skeptical look, closed the book before him, and leaned back in his chair. Josiah remained resolute.

"Reverend Miller, let me grant you my newspaper, the *Calvary Crier*, this town's first and only institution of the press, as a conduit for these tidings you've brought here. I spent all of yesterday going through my notes and my memory, envigored by the charge you have lain before us, and I've summarized the full breadth of your teachings here on these pages."

Josiah sprawled his folio across the desk. William stared at the staggering amount of work produced in a single day, slowly thumbing through each sheet of paper and scanning the density of the composition.

"What makes you think that the word of God needs any vessel beyond the members of this parish?" he asked, as he continued reading. "Our congregation is now on a mission, as you know."

"You told me yourself: this church is too small to hold a sermon this large. If we are to shout this message from the mountaintops, what higher summit, what greater reach, than the printed word? Together, I know we can touch every soul in this town, and maybe even beyond."

The chair behind the desk scraped loudly against the floor as William stood to his feet. Despite their difference in height, Josiah unwittingly swayed backward, as if he were preparing to be tackled.

"What sort of motive truly begets such generosity?" William asked. "Is it fame? Fortune? Forgive me for my caution."

Josiah placed his hand against his heart.

"All my life, I wanted to effect change through my reporting. And now I realize what sinful vanity this was. It's not my word that the people need to hear—rather, it's the word of God, directed through your teachings and channeled through my pen. There are countless believers who have in them the will to change their ways before it's too late. All they need is to know that the Messiah is coming. And if they don't see that now, they will after reading our paper. We can save them, reverend. Thousands of souls, maybe more."

William held his tongue as he walked across the room to the storage chest beside his bookshelf. Josiah stood by as his palms began to sweat with anxiety at the thought of another rejected plan, another dream dashed.

"If we are going to do this," William began as he returned with an object wrapped in a muslin sheet, "there are some additional details that must be filled in. Can you print illustrations, Josiah?"

Josiah nodded eagerly. "Yes, it just takes some time."

William removed the covering, unveiling the scroll in his hands. Pinning it against the window behind his desk, he slowly unfurled the chronology of the world as the morning sun illuminated it before Josiah, who stared in awe, as if being presented with the tablets of the covenant.

"We must hurry then," said William. "For we have little time to wait."

# Chapter 15

ABIGAIL'S EYES WERE fixated on the latest *Calvary Crier* as she drank her morning tea at the family table. Having just returned from walking Rosemary and Benji to school, she had some time to herself before beginning the daily housework while her father tended to the newly burgeoning wheat fields. It was a rare and much-needed respite after the intensive rehabilitation of her brother, who had recuperated from his ailment two days prior just enough to return to class. But her solitude was only temporary, as Henry opened the porch door before her tea could cool. He noticed the paper in her hands and shook his head.

"Not worth the penny nor the time," he said.

Abigail raised her eyes from the paper and turned to him.

"All creation is reading it today," she insisted. "I got the very last copy from Josiah on the way back from the school."

"And what is going on in the world that has everyone

so interested now?" Henry asked as he hung a copper kettle over the fire for himself.

"It's a full summation of all of Reverend Miller's lectures. Everything that he's said in his sermons—the history of the prophecies of the past and future—illustrated with the maths to prove it."

"It seems like the more I try to escape this kind of talk, the more it keeps following me," Henry grumbled. "Don't let your brother catch sight of it—I don't want him infected with any more gloom, let alone gloom that was bought with my hard-earned money."

"You're right," said Abigail as she lowered her eyes and folded up the paper, placing it on the table. "I suppose it's just hard not to take notice when it's all anyone in town can talk about. You couldn't go one foot into the market without hearing about it."

"News is as fleeting as the weather," said Henry. "I'm sure they'll all tire of talking about it in two weeks' time. And hopefully then the doomsaying will stop and we can go back to attending service like normal again."

Abigail cleared her teacup and stood up. "I'm going to start the wash now. And for Heaven's sakes, father, don't get so bent about a penny."

Henry dismissed her with an amicable wave as he waited by the fire for his water to boil. Abigail moved past him in the kitchen to begin the laundry, lifting the basket of linens to her chest and nudging the back door open with her elbow as she carried it outside.

Henry waited for the door to close behind her before walking over to the table. This was the first time he could ever remember the *Crier* being discussed in town as more than a novelty or a joke, and his interest was reluctantly piqued. Henry looked over his shoulder to ensure that Abigail could not see him, then unfolded the paper and flipped it over to the cover page.

COMING OUT OF BABYLON: THE SIGNS OF
THE TIMES BY REV. WILLIAM MILLER

Wrapped around the edges of the text of the article was an illustration of a large statue—a bearded man with a head of gold, chest of silver, torso of brass, legs of iron, feet of clay. Each section of the statue was labeled with the names of ancient kingdoms and inscribed with passages from Scripture and associated dates below. Henry stared at this image quizzically and began to skim through the article to discern any kind of possible meaning from it. He found that the contents were just as William had recited in his past several sermons, but distilled, processed, and refined in simpler language made understandable for a layman like him. All of the divinations were expanded and explained, the calculations and evidence to support William's hypothesis laid out in a clear and concise manner, with images to accompany each set of exegeses.

As he studied the text, Henry began to hear a quiet rumble in the distance. He paused and looked around the room to locate the genesis of the noise and saw that the kettle was juddering above the fire as the water was beginning to boil. Unconcerned, he returned to the newspaper and opened the next page, darting his eyes across the mountains of copy before him. William's dire warnings of what was to come were all listed in elaborate detail—the seals, the trumpets, the bowls of wrath; the predictions of plague, poison, conflagration, falling stars, moving mountains, and evaporating oceans; the cruel fate that awaited the world for the thousand years that would follow after Christ redeemed those who were worthy; the beast from the land and beast from the sea, a seven-headed dragon, the Whore of Babylon, and a lake of fire. Henry shook his head to himself and wondered how anyone could believe such fantastical tales.

Henry placed the paper back on the table as steam began to erupt from the kettle. But as he removed it from the heat, he noticed that the sound of rumbling remained in the air. Henry held the kettle in his hand and listened closely. What was once a gentle hum had progressed into an increasingly loud rattle as if the source of the noise was drawing nearer by the second. Within a moment, the rattle evolved into an earthshaking blare, and Henry felt as if his entire house was going to collapse into rubble.

Before he could move, Abigail let out a chilling cry from outside. Henry dropped the kettle of boiling water on the floor and sprinted toward the porch. He pushed through the back door to find his daughter standing in a shivering state of shock—her body and face covered in thick, sticky filth that looked like splotches of tar, black as pitch—too aghast to even scream.

✺

The nearest to the window, Rosemary was the first in her class to hear the distant buzzing. The room was entirely quiet as the children completed an assignment in their notebooks while Mrs. Edwards sat at her desk in the front, reading the *Calvary Crier* with her full attention. Noticing that the sound was slowly transforming into a steady roar, Rosemary stopped writing and raised her eyes from her book. The rest of the class followed as the noise grew in intensity.

"Class, continue your assignment," Mrs. Edwards instructed as she put down the newspaper and stood up from the desk.

Mrs. Edwards slowly walked toward the window, curious about the sound herself, while the students ignored her directive. Pencil after pencil fell to each desk as they watched Mrs. Edwards abruptly freeze in place before the window. Rosemary could see the whites of her teacher's eyes being overtaken by a darkness as she recoiled in terror of what she beheld.

Outside, the sun was blotted by black patches as a swarm of locusts descended upon the school like a cloud of sable smoke. The cloud grew quickly as countless thousands of creatures proliferated before them, darkening the sky as if the day had suddenly turned to night. Their sound became so thunderous that the younger students were forced to press their hands over their ears, feeling as if the creatures had crawled inside their heads and were desperately screaming to escape. Rosemary dropped to the floor and hid under her desk.

"Benji, get down," she yelled to her brother beside her, stretching out her arm to pull him to the ground with her.

Undeterred, Benji stood up and began walking toward the window for a better view of the bedlam, fascinated by what was transpiring.

"Benji, stop!" Rosemary exclaimed as her brother was drawn toward the plague like a moth to a flame.

Mrs. Edwards stepped back and pressed herself against the chalkboard in the front of the room, white dust rising around her. "The third seal!" she cried in a bout of hysteria. "The third seal has been opened! Save us, O Lord!"

The entirety of the classroom cowered under their desks as they waited for the chaos to pass. Only Benji stood tall and intrepid, watching as the storm of insects continued to speed past him in a mesmerizing vortex. But as he stepped closer to the window, the pane began to shake violently, and the force of the swarm shattered the glass before him, knocking him to the floor. The students screamed in horror as some of the winged creatures flailed into the classroom, thrashing and convulsing on their backs, battered and cut by the broken shards.

Josiah leaned against the printing press, exhausted from the long morning spent peddling all of the copies of the *Crier* he could manage to print the night before. He had been awake going on thirty hours but needed to ensure that another run of the paper would be available the next day, as he had promised Mr. Edwards that he'd be able to deliver additional copies to be distributed down the river to nearby villages by morning. This was the first time he had actually engendered enough interest to expand his reach beyond Calvary, and he knew that if he were able to keep up with demand, he would be back upon the precipice of solvency within a month.

But as he stood up in a state of near-delirium, seeds of self-doubt began to form within him about the sustainability of the series. William's teachings were brilliant, but he knew how fickle the world could be. One day's news could just as easily be superseded by another story of a storm, a war, a foreign royal's passing. He feared that people would tire of the same lede and would eventually become disinterested—or worse, unbelieving.

He thought back to last year's farmer's almanac. The reports that he'd compiled predicted a dry season, but the rains were heavier than they had been in years, even swelling the Hudson to its highest levels recorded since accurate measurements began. The farmers did not forget the error—and this year's edition sold about half of what he had hoped. What if this happened again with the new series? What if this time, the rains never came?

Josiah worked through his concerns and began cranking the noisy machine to churn out copy after copy until a new batch of paper needed to be loaded. But the room did not fall silent when he stopped the press. A loud droning persisted, the noise coming from outside. Wondering if his lack of sleep had given way to a waking, auditory madness, Josiah cautiously walked toward the front of his house and opened the door.

The torrent of locusts flew by him like a sonic wave, frenetically twirling and crashing, leaving plumes of dust in their wake. Josiah's eyes grew wide as he stood dumbstruck by the sight before him. He shut the door and quickly reopened it to make sure he was not hallucinating. But then he knew.

Josiah's hand fell off of the doorknob as he dropped to his knees. He watched as the flood of pests continued rushing past him, causing carnage and havoc, and tears swelled in his eyes. The words from William's mouth to his pen had come true. The end times were here, and they filled Josiah with true meaning and purpose for the first time in his life, as he wept with unfathomable joy.

⌘

Henry trepidatiously stepped outside onto the porch when the swarm had finally passed. Abigail, still feeling the trauma of what had happened, sunk to the ground and leaned her back against the siding of their house, unable to speak.

Henry continued walking slowly across the porch. He passed the overturned wash bucket, water and wet linens spilled out like entrails on a battlefield, and stepped over the tar-like remains of the eviscerated creatures that had met their end against the exterior of his house. Their blood dotted the wooden posts like they had been splashed with mud, the viscera on the boards sticking to his boots with each step. He was afraid to look any further.

Henry finally stepped down from his porch and onto the grounds of his farm and gazed across what remained of his newly planted wheat field. The once knee-high stalks had been ripped up and devoured, the remnants scattered about the barren rows of dry soil. All but a few patches were spared—the rest looked like ash. The summer yield was ruined.

Henry knelt down at the outskirts of the former field, picking up one of the locusts left behind. It had lost a wing and writhed and squirmed on its back in a futile attempt to preserve what remained of its short life. Henry put the inch-long beast between his fingers and inspected it for a brief moment, raising it to his eyes with the expanse of destroyed farmland behind it. Henry dropped the creature back onto the dirt and lowered his head.

After taking a moment to collect himself, Henry looked into the horizon, bloodred from the rising clouds of dust, and he thought about what lay ahead for him and his family. It was going to be a long summer.

# Chapter 16

A WARM BREEZE WAFTED through Abigail's hair as she stared peacefully at the river before her. She seldom had the opportunity to free her bun from her bonnet and savored the feeling of her hair upon her shoulders, blowing in the summer air as the sun warmed her face. The sensation drifted her into momentary serenity as she briefly closed her eyelids and absorbed the phantasmagoria that lived behind them. All was silent except for the sounds of the river, and she was able to forget about the cares of the world for a time.

Benji lay flat on his stomach across from his sister, soles of his shoes lifted to the sky as he watched the water roll downstream from the grassy bank beside the river. Next to him was a white paper boat that Abigail had made for him earlier as he bided his time for its maiden voyage. Rosemary sat not much farther away, lost in her own thoughts, picking wildflowers from the grass.

Abigail opened her eyes to find Benji looking over his shoulder, turned her way.

"The water's too rough today," he said.

Abigail shuffled herself upright from the lush embankment and made sure the rest of the paper stock was still at her side. She had picked it up from the suppliers at the port earlier that week, and with Josiah's publication business thriving, the demand was too high to risk losing it to the wind.

"It's the July current," Abigail said. "All of the ice is melted and now the rapids are coming in from the north. You just need to give it a careful push and it will carry on."

Benji stood up hesitantly with the paper boat in hand and walked toward the water's edge. Carefully wedging his feet between the slippery rocks of the riverbank, he made his way to the sand, where he knelt down and gently released the vessel into the water. He waited patiently as it was carried partway across the river, hopeful that he'd get a good turn into the smoother streams. But as it reached the first real resistance from the current, the boat suddenly tipped, spun around in a quick pirouette, and was swiftly swallowed by a rapid. Benji lowered his head in frustration and stomped his foot into the sand.

"Dang it," he said to himself as he helplessly watched his boat disappear.

Benji plodded back to his starting position on the riverbank and sat down. Abigail began to fold the card stock on her lap to make another paper boat for her brother, as Rosemary continued to create her multicolored bouquet. Benji watched the water flow before him once again, while thoughts and daydreams likewise silently flowed through them all as the sun continued to arc across the sky.

"Abigail," Benji said softly after several minutes. "Do you think this will be our last summer?"

"What do you mean?" Abigail asked.

"It's like they said in church. If Judgment Day is in October, then that means there won't be any more summers after that."

It saddened Abigail to hear such thoughts come from her young brother, especially on such a placid Sunday like this. It had been almost two months since they had been to church services, but Reverend Miller's teachings had clearly left their mark on Benji's malleable, nascent mind. She was beginning to understand why her father had come to his decision to stay home and why he was so adamant about distancing the family from such apocalyptic notions.

"Don't worry about that, Benji. One way or another, there's not much we can do, so there's no point in dwelling on it. You just focus on the present, all right?"

Rosemary, overhearing the conversation, paused her flower collection and turned to Abigail.

"Reverend Miller says that nearsightedness begets blindness."

"Since when have you been speaking to Reverend Miller?"

"They taught us that at school. Mrs. Edwards reads from the reverend's lectures during class. All of our studies are focused on the Millennium nowadays."

Abigail turned to Benji for confirmation. "Is that true?"

"Oh yes, for some time now," he answered, nodding his

head nonchalantly. "Teacher says there's no use in us learning anything else."

Abigail shook her head to herself as she continued making the next paper boat. It seemed that there was no escaping the talk, as much as their father tried to hide them from it. All she could do for now was try to find other ways to occupy their time.

The seabirds began squawking as she heard a foghorn upriver. She looked into the distance and thought about Thomas. She hadn't heard from him since she walked away from his homestead that day he told her he had to leave Calvary. The town felt incomplete without him—bereft of their voice of reason as the millennial fever spread like an epidemic. Her neighbors, she believed, had short memories. Thomas had been their pastor for four years, and it only took two months for them to move on as if he was never there to begin with. But she wouldn't forget. As much as she sometimes wanted to, she could still hear his soothing words and she could still feel his touch upon her skin.

Abigail finished making the boat and held it out to Benji. Immediately forgetting his existential deliberations, Benji took the completed vessel and galloped toward the water with his new sturdy ship. Now wading in the water up to his calves, he was determined to make this voyage a success. He lowered his arm and patiently waited for the right moment, then cast the boat into the river with greater momentum than before to successfully propel it past the outer rapids. Benji watched with glee as the boat made its way downstream, picking up speed as it glided farther across the river. It sailed steadily about twenty feet more until a mild gale blew it off course, turning the boat back toward the bank and into a protruding outlet of slimy, algal rocks.

Benji stomped back ashore again, vexed by his losing battle with the elements, and sat down at the riverside. From his seat on the sediment, he began to skip small stones into the water to take out his frustration as Abigail casually removed another piece of paper. Rosemary remained in the grass, detached from her siblings as she stared down at her flower bouquet and began to pluck the petals one by one.

Abigail couldn't stop herself from reliving that day. She, too, had not felt complete since Thomas left. She wondered if she'd made a mistake in rejecting his proposal to join him on his sojourn and bring word of William's heretical sermons to the regional ministers. She had never been outside of Calvary before, and New York was a big place. Maybe it would have allowed her to circumvent the fear and perturbation that the news of the advent had brought to her town, or perhaps it would have offered her some respite from the labors and travails that dominated her daily life at home. But her bigger regret was what the decision meant for her and Thomas. She had not received any word from him in the month that he had been gone. Perhaps he felt jilted by her refusal, that she was too harsh and unsympathetic to him when he'd asked her, or perhaps he believed that it would only be a distraction to focus on her from afar. But her worst fear was not that he held on to any kind of malice or anger—it was that he had forgotten about her altogether.

"Abigail." Rosemary broke the silence. "I do worry for us sometimes. For our family, I mean."

Abigail continued folding the paper as she glanced over at her sister.

"What is there to worry about?"

"The rest of the town is at church every day to hear Reverend Miller's sermons. But father won't even bring us on the Sabbath. We just might be the only ones not there today. Doesn't that make you feel nervous?"

"Father still has much work to do on the farm. He hasn't taken a single day of rest since the locusts came through and wrecked the summer yield. And we can't just leave the house unattended all day while he's out there."

"But Reverend Miller says that we all have work to do before Christ returns again."

Abigail sat up and turned to face Rosemary, becoming annoyed by her persistent criticism.

"Is that work at the church filling our granaries or putting food on your plate? Is it making sure that there are clean sheets and warm water for your brother when he has his spells?"

Rosemary glowered at her sister, then shook her head.

"Well then, there's no better work to be done than what we are doing now. This family is living a pious life. Father just doesn't believe that we need to hear about the impending doom of the rapture every day to remind us why."

As Rosemary prepared to argue further, a loud whooping emanated from Benji. He struggled to catch his breath as if he were choking, his face turning bright pink. Abigail dropped the paper boat and Rosemary cast aside her flowers as the two both readied themselves to come to his aid. But before they could stand, Benji leaned forward, hands on his knees, and coughed up a penny-sized dollop of phlegm that had been caught in his air passage, then returned to regular breathing.

Abigail carefully monitored her brother's every breath. All of her cares in the world were distilled and consolidated into his sickly, shimmering eyes. Thoughts of famine, death, destruction, and the rapture were but mild distractions; any feelings of past regrets dissipated in that moment. Thomas may not need her, but her family certainly did; and as much as she still felt that lingering pain in her heart, she knew deeper still that she had made the right decision. Her only concern now was for Benji's future—keeping him afloat was all that mattered. He would be her salvation.

"Come now," she said as she pulled herself to her feet. "We should make our way home; it's nearing lunchtime."

Benji spun around, reanimated as he petitioned to his sister.

"Can we stay awhile longer? Please—just one more?"

Abigail deliberated to herself as she tucked her hair back into her bonnet for the walk home. After a moment, she picked up the final boat and walked toward the edge of the river. The sun reflected upon the water and basked her in its powerful glow as her feet became awash in the cold northern current. With a deft hand, she lowered the paper craft and released it into the river. Benji and Rosemary stood to watch from behind, their minds now firmly fixated on nothing else but the boat as it successfully sailed into the downstream horizon.

## Chapter 17

THE LANTERN THAT hung in the back of Thomas's shared four-person stagecoach swung in the cool midnight air as he watched the shadows of his strange companions roll across the inside of the canvas. He was somewhere between Utica and Albany in the foothills of the Adirondacks, and the mountain chill was keeping him wide awake.

He looked at the strangers with whom he was sharing the overnight carriage. He did not know from whence they came or where they were ultimately headed, but their faces told the stories of their journey. Across from him were two men, weathered and woebegone, short on years but not experience—runaways and ruffians who clutched their carpetbags against their chests out of fear of being robbed along their destinationless passage. Sitting beside him was a third man who leaned his head insouciantly against Thomas's shoulder, free from any care or concern about whether the pastor would welcome the physical intimacy. Thomas sur-

mised that he was at least half-Indian, based on the beaded
luggage with which he traveled and the tattooed skin that
showed behind the holes in his shirt. Although he didn't
know their names, Thomas knew the order to which they,
and now he, belonged—those who hadn't the funds for private cars to traverse the wide stretches of the northern half
of the state, but who had to persist nevertheless, for whatever they had left behind must be in worse condition than
the perilous roads before them.

All except he and the driver were asleep, the others
perhaps long accustomed to resting under such rugged conditions. But Thomas's months on the road were not enough
to harden him fully yet, and his mind was traveling at far too
fast a speed for him to close his eyes. Shuffling through his
belongings, he removed a paper and pencil from his luggage.
The coach was unsteady and shook aggressively with every
bump and fissure its tires rolled over on the treacherous
mountain dugway. Thomas pressed the paper tightly against
the cover of his Bible to help stabilize his hand through the
vibrations, and began to draft a letter. It was the only thing
he could do to make some sense of his thoughts.

> *I write to you amidst the natural ridges and furrows
> along the winding road to Albany, where a drunken
> Indian lies upon my shoulder and has taken the tails of
> my frock as his blanket for the evening. A potent scent
> of stale alcohol pervades the inside of the carriage, and
> I cannot determine if it is emanating from my fellow
> travelers or the reinsman in front of us—or possibly both.
> We are approaching the devil's hour indeed.*
> *I've taken it upon myself to share an overnight coach*

with a triad of vagabonds rather than venture another disagreeable stay in another small village along the route. I've commonly found myself in these towns with little recourse, sleeping atop the hard oak frame of a church pew, wrapped in my own coat as I await a tardy minister to shake me awake in the morning; or, finding a stable sufficient on a warmer night, making acquaintance with new bedmates of sheep or bleating goats for the evening. Other nights have been even less pleasant, if you dare imagine it.

That is not to say that all my days have been filled with complete discomfort. Some folks along the way have been quite welcoming—oftentimes I'll meet a congenial taverner or an innkeeper's wife who is able to convince her husband to let a traveling man of cloth stay with free room and board should there be a vacancy for the night, or a local librarian who is nice enough to let a visitor use a reading room for an evening's shelter as long as he supplies his own lantern oil. And never underestimate the kindness of a devout farmer—had it not been for their generosity, I'd have had little to eat and little energy to keep going after the first week. The rations have been meager, but a diet of bread and eggs provided by these benevolent strangers is plenty for me, since I need to reserve what little I have in my purse for wagon fare as I have tonight. Thank Baucis and Philemon for showing them the way, lest I have been destitute or dead from exposure by the last month's end.

I am finding this process to be taking longer than expected, and sometimes I question why I am doing this to myself at all. Many of the senior members of the Upper

*New York Baptist Convention refuse to make the time for
me. Others, when I do manage to get their ear, react to
the news of William's sermons with apathy or perfunctory,
half-hearted admonition. Many will say to me "Well, let
them believe what they want—it's no harm to you" or
"No one is forcing you to believe, young pastor; let them
alone in their wicked ways." And in truth, I find that
I often have no strong argument against it, and I must
carry on with my head down in dejection.*

*Worse yet is that the news of William's advent
sermons appears to be outpacing the speed of my own
movements. I will never forget the horror I felt on the
first leg of my journey up to Plattsburgh, in which I sat
for services in a small congregation some miles outside of
the town limits, only to hear the preacher brandish the
same threats as our reverend: repent, or be sentenced to
an eternity of damnation on October the twenty-second.
I could not believe my ears. I feigned ignorance when
speaking with the minister after the services concluded,
telling him that I was just an itinerant salesman passing
through, and asked him where he heard this proclamation
of the end times. And when he showed me a copy of that
rag of Josiah Young's as the progenitor of his sermon, I
began to question the rest of my faculties as well.*

*But I soon realized that I was not losing my senses.
Throughout the course of my travels, I discovered that
the* Crier *has somehow infiltrated even the smallest
of farm towns as far west as Rochester. From the port
villages to the cities, it seems that everyone is reading
the transcriptions of William's sermons and studying the
ridiculous chart that he first showed me in his rectory. It*

*is one thing to hear the words from a wayward priest, but I've found that once the people read something in print, then it becomes legitimized as fact. And now the news has spread like the plague.*

*Despite this, my spirit remains strong. I've found that the larger parishes have thus far withstood the madness and fearmongering that is seemingly omnipresent in the smaller locales. It was in Rochester that I came across my first ray of hope. The city is alive with the spirit of Christ; the people have truly awakened to His word. One cannot turn a corner there without encountering a newly built church or hearing a preacher profess on the side of the street, hoping to inspire a small consortium of Christians to join him for worship to learn more. But the most successful of these holy men, by far, is Reverend Storrs, who is also an influential minister in the regional Baptist Convention that will be so critical in putting an end to William's abominable lectures.*

*The reverend runs a parish of nearly five hundred, and his energy and enthusiasm know no bounds. I was fortunate enough to speak to him after Sunday services, and he was already aware of the October prophecy that had been circulating throughout the city. When I told him that I hail from the same church as William Miller, a spark in his eyes immediately kindled as he asked me question after question of how this all began. After conversing with him throughout the morning, the reverend did not hesitate in agreeing to meet me in Albany at the beginning of July, where we would charter a ship to Calvary so he could witness the heresy for himself.*

Reinvigorated by the success in Rochester, I made
haste to Syracuse, where I knew the great Reverend
Marsh resided—the man who has long operated the
most prestigious Baptist parish in the region and perhaps
the state at large. Reverend Marsh may be a stubborn
old man of seventy, but he is of high importance to the
Convention, so it was of great significance that I show
him the light—or shall I say, the darkness—no matter
how long it might take. I spent a good week speaking
with him after his daily services, returning each day with
more details and copies of the Calvary Crier that had
made their way into the hands of his own congregants.
It was only after these incessant audiences with him
that he finally began to wear down and speak to me
candidly about his underlying concerns. He told me of
his unease with other growing denominations around
him, which sprung up like uncontrollable weeds—the
Methodists, the Presbyterians, the Congregationalists, and
Christian Connexion sects. He confided in me that he
was beginning to fear being left behind by his congregants
due to a lack of vitality in his older age, preaching the
same doctrines every day—and he worried that novelty of
these modern faiths would inspire others to abandon the
church for the newer, more theatric sermons. After much
deliberation, I thank the Lord that he, too, finally agreed
to join me in Albany to help root out this evil.

And that is where my next destination lies—in
Albany, at the church of Reverend Fitch. I've gotten
word that he is held in high regard in his parish and
beyond—a man of great virtue and venerable status in
the Baptist community—and securing his alignment will

*give me what I need in order to finally return home. I have full faith that Reverend Fitch will agree to join us, swayed by the promises of his colleagues to assemble there at the banks of the Hudson. (They like to travel in packs, apparently, like old hunting mates.) With his support and the arrival of Reverends Storrs and Marsh, I am hopeful that this stop will be my last, and the three would suffice for a formal deputation to United Calvary, straight into the mouth of Babylon.*

*Lord knows that these ministers will have no true bearing on the goings-on of our parish without seeing it for themselves. I've been reading with a heavy heart about what our town has become. The meetings that hold these sermons seem more like a circus than a church; and I suspect the ringleader is less William Miller and more Josiah Young, who seems to fancy himself an organizer, even placing advertisements in his paper enticing his readers to come join the show. There is a madness to it all that sometimes makes it hard to believe it's even real— and hard to find pity for those who fall for such artifices.*

*In my darkest times on the road, I've begun to wonder if the people who attend these services are bringing this mania upon themselves, and if it is better to simply wait until October and let them find out it was all a lie—and to let them suffer the consequences of their own spiritual weakness. But even though my body is weary, it's important that my mind stay focused and that I remember my purpose in this mission. And thus, on those lonely evenings, I've done what I can to help sharpen my wits and read through the works of others who likewise faced down the cynicism that is born out of* popular demagoguery—in hopes, God willing, that these words will help restore some meaning to these struggles.

When I was fortunate to stay in a public library of one of the towns along the road to Syracuse, I came across a volume of letters by Voltaire, which struck me so that I felt it important to note down on a piece of paper that I now carry with me in my pocket:

"Truly, whoever can make you believe absurdities can make you commit atrocities. If the God-given understanding of your mind does not resist a demand to believe what is impossible, then you will not resist a demand to do wrong to that God-given sense of justice in your heart. As soon as one faculty of your soul has been dominated, other faculties will follow as well."

Perhaps this is the response that I could not articulate when first challenged by the other preachers to simply leave William be. The "liberty of the soul" is the core tenet of our movement, they would say; that is, the people in his congregation are free to choose what they believe will bring them salvation. But I fear that their beliefs will not stop at the depths of the soul. I fear that these beliefs will rise through the soul, into the heart, and up through the throat and tongue and fist. It has happened before, and we are not so enlightened that it could not happen again.

Let us pray that it does not come to pass in such a way. By the grace of God, I hope that there will be an end to this madness. And it is with that hope that I must persist for our sake, Abigail. For when that day comes, we will be able to at last turn the focus of our passions unto one another. I imagine the time when this ends: entering my house, finding you there waiting with your loving

*embrace, when we can take each other in our arms, close*
*our eyes, and be warmed by the eternal glow of our spirits*
*coming as one. This is what keeps me standing. This is*
*what keeps me moving forward. And I will wait for the*
*day as long as you, too, wait for me.*

*Yours eternally,*
*Thomas*

The stagecoach rocked violently as the wheel dipped into another deep crevice, tossing the travelers awake from their slumber.

"Hey, Jehu, swerve them holes!" one of the young transients shouted. "Are you trying to get us killed?"

"I'll leave you in that ditch back there if you don't shut yer mouth," the driver snarled back.

The half-Indian lifted his head from Thomas's shoulder, roused by the commotion. "What's this?" he muttered in a daze. "Have we arrived? Is it over?"

Thomas folded up the paper on which he was writing and creased it halfway through. He shook his head.

"Not yet," he said. "We still have some miles to go."

The half-Indian shrugged and curled into the back corner of the carriage as it continued to shake and sway down the road, and the others continued to exchange gibes and threats that never amounted to anything more than words. Thomas remained wide awake. Holding the folded paper in his hand, he opened his bag and deposited it neatly alongside the dozens of other letters that he had written to Abigail along his journey, but never sent.

# Chapter 18

THOMAS ALIGHTED FROM the carriage as they reached the front of the church at the top of the hill. It was his first time breathing the Calvary air in months. But even that appeared to have changed. There was a certain miasma around him, an invisible cloud that hovered above the empty church building and fanned out across the town below. Thomas could not see it, but he could feel the weight upon him. He turned to look out to the farms in the distance and sighed to himself.

"What's the matter, son?" Reverend Fitch asked him, stepping down from the carriage behind him. "Homesick, are you?"

"I suppose you could call it that," he replied, shedding himself of his momentary burden. "But never mind it—there is no room to delay. What we do must be done quickly."

As much as it disgusted him, Thomas had read all of the editions of the *Calvary Crier* he could obtain on the road in order to stay up to date on the affairs of the town.

He had only one chance to prove to the ministers that William's congregation justified a formal censure by the Baptist Convention, and he did not want anything to catch him off guard. He had learned about the daily services from the pen of Josiah Young, who described the effervescent spectacles and the glorious moments of religious catharsis that were regular occurrences during William's sermons. But the church appeared entirely devoid of congregants—and Thomas wondered if it all might have just been a fabrication to entice naïve outsiders into joining the radical movement.

As they waited for any sign of the congregation, Thomas noticed a swath of worshippers walking around the schoolyard to the back of the church grounds. He gestured to his companions to join him behind the line of parishioners and quickly followed them to the rear of United Calvary. As they turned around the side of the building, they gazed upward at the structure before them. The church grounds that he'd tended for years had morphed into something he did not recognize. A goliath tent rose like a promontory from the sea, towering higher than the church bells themselves. The heavy beige canvas loomed over them, buttressed by a sturdy interconnection of wood and brass poles, metal fasteners, rope, and anchors. William could not have built this himself, Thomas concluded, and determined that it must have been a collective effort utilizing the most skillful of the town's craftsmen to arrange a construction of this magnitude in less than two months' time. Shielding his eyes from the sun, he looked upward still and read the words on the streamer that fluttered from the masthead atop the tent: THY KINGDOM COME.

Reverend Storrs stood beside him and marveled at the grandeur of the sight.

"This must hold at least a thousand people," he estimated. "Pastor Aleman, was your parish always this full?"

"It appears the congregation has overgrown the church proper since I left," said Thomas, shaking his head. "We only had a few dozen parishioners on a given Sabbath day."

The ministers remained in awe of their surroundings as they continued toward the structure. The camp outside was like a small village of its own. They passed scores of newcomers to the town who lined the path near the entrance—wide-eyed pilgrims from distant locales who had just arrived to finally hear Reverend Miller in person, families standing beside their carpetbags that held the entirety of their worldly belongings, weary travelers who gave up their lives elsewhere to join the worship in Calvary. Many were entering and exiting the tent at their leisure, as there seemed to be no formal structure or schedule to the services.

As the preachers approached the entrance, a group of several devotees passed by them in silence, walking solemnly in long robes of white linen with hoods shrouding their faces, as if monks in a mountain cloister.

"What the devil are those people wearing?" asked Reverend Marsh.

"I've read that they call them 'ascension robes,'" said Thomas. "Some of the more ardent fanatics have shed their secular garments in favor of these new costumes. They see it as a symbol of purity for when the Bridegroom returns."

Reverend Marsh furrowed his brow as they passed another pair of ascension-robed worshippers and proceeded toward the tent, ducking under the canvas opening to enter.

As he shepherded the group inside, Thomas was taken aback by the liveliness of the scene before them. The new church was full of parishioners—some seated on the long wooden benches that served as makeshift pews, others standing on their toes in the back to get any glimpse of William they could—who were all responding in praise, lifting their hands and reaching to the heavens with each word that was read from the gospel. The tent captured the summer heat like a greenhouse; most of the congregants glistened with sweat, but yet they were unperturbed and immovable, waving handheld fans and folded hymn booklets to cool themselves without distracting from the worship.

Other parishioners quickly pushed the priests aside as they hurried in to get an unobstructed view of the front altar. Careful not to attract attention to their syndicate, Thomas guided his guests to a corner in the back of the tent, allowing them to surreptitiously observe the sermon from the shadows. From their vantage point, they had a clear sight of William, who paced amongst the crowd in the open space near the center, his glasses removed and his sleeves rolled up to his elbows. The ministers had arrived midway through his homily, though it soon appeared that there was no beginning nor end to the services; rather, they were one continuous loop that rose and fell and regained momentum like a waterwheel churning ceaselessly throughout the day.

"Is that him—the reverend doctor?" Reverend Fitch asked Thomas.

"He refers to himself as 'Brother William' now, apparently," Thomas corrected him. "It's one of those verbal flourishes he's adopted to insinuate that they are all one collective family in Christ—that they are all in this together."

Reverend Fitch exchanged an intrigued look with his

other companions as they settled into their positions and listened to William continue his sermon.

"It is incumbent on us in these times of holy judgment that we humble ourselves before God," William declared whilst surveying the faithful that surrounded him. "We stand here together, from all walks of life, all origins, all backgrounds. Some rich, some poor; some freedmen, some debtors. Lifetime purveyors of righteousness and merchants of iniquity. Now is the time to cast aside who thou once wert! Now is the time to be born again! All past virtue is annulled; all past sin absolved. For just as we are equal in the Lord's creation, so, too, are we equal in His destruction."

William seemed more alive with the Holy Spirit than Thomas had seen in the service before he left. His arms moved and pulsed with every word, harnessing the collective energy of the room as he continued his sermon with unwavering conviction to the enraptured audience.

"Humble thyself, and believe! Humble thyself, and repent! Humble thyself, and preach His word! There is not one of us who is above worship, no work more essential than that of achieving absolution. This is our season to begin anew, but we can only be reborn by practicing our sacraments, our holy duties. For it is when we dedicate our remaining time to salvation, we shall rise from our knees; to stand, to be saved."

The three ministers looked at one another as they measured the intensity of his charge.

"He truly has them by the ear," whispered Reverend Fitch.

"Look at all of these people coming from afar just to get a glimpse of him," said Reverend Storrs.

"Yes," said Reverend Marsh. "It appears that his faith is highly contagious."

William lowered his voice and paced his speech, controlling the flow of the sermon like a conductor of a symphony.

"Think now what that imminence means. Think of how consequential our remaining days shall be. Will we spend them carrying on with meaningless diversions? Are we to fritter away the day in the fields, in the workshops of our villages or factories of our cities? Are we to waste our precious time on leisure, concern ourselves with trivial matters, both large and small? No, I say. If the governor himself passes through our blessed camp and proclaims, 'But Brother William, I cannot spend my time here. I have a campaign to run; I must make this speech or that, curry favor with voters here or there'; to him I would reply, 'Brother Governor, art thou campaigning to govern the lake of fire and sea of sulfur? Because that is what shall become of this land beginning the evening of October the twenty-second!'"

The tent erupted in an uproar of whistling and applause as the congregants jumped to their feet, roused by the image of their pastor speaking to the governor just as he would speak to the poorest among them. The visiting reverends were mystified by the excitement around them. It was not something any had ever seen at a political rally, let alone in a house of worship.

"Before we move on to a very special ceremony today, I'd like to leave you with a passage from the Book of Revelation, to serve as a warning of what we shall expect when the day of reckoning comes and as a reminder of the graveness of our call," William continued, as he recited from memory. "Just before that final seal is opened, 'Heaven departed as a scroll when it is rolled together; and every mountain and island were moved out of their places. And the kings of the earth, and the great men, and the rich men, and the chief captains, and the mighty men, and every bondman, and every free man, hid themselves in the dens and in the rocks of the mountains; And said to the mountains and rocks, Fall on us, and hide us from the face of him that sitteth on the throne, and from the wrath of the Lamb: For the great day of his wrath is come; *and who shall be able to stand?*'"

He paused and closed his eyes in prayer. "May God grant us mercy and strength in these times before us. May He grant us forgiveness, and allow us to *rise up* on that day to *stand* beside the throne of His begotten Son. Amen."

"Praise Him! Amen!" shouted the parishioners in fevered jubilation, as music from the portable organ rang throughout the tent to provide a short interlude between sermons.

William walked away from the center space, dabbing the sweat on his forehead with a white cloth. One of his volunteers handed him a cup of water to drink quickly as the organ continued to play, and two others drew the curtain behind the open pulpit to reveal a hidden part of the meeting space. Many in the crowd began to clap as they saw what lay behind the curtain—a series of wooden steps leading to a large baptismal font in the shape of a crucifix, its water shimmering before the congregation as a ray of sunlight snuck in between the canvas lining and struck its surface.

William finished his drink and reached out to beckon a pair of worshippers from the crowd to join him in the center space. From the audience emerged a young family—a mother carrying an infant baby in her arms and her lanky husband straggling farther behind. The family stood beside

William as the music came to an end and the congregation quieted down, and all attention was placed upon them.

"Today's service is a particularly blessed one, as we welcome three new children of God into our temple." William motioned to his guests. "This family has traveled all the way from Raleigh, North Carolina, to be here with us today. Please tell us, now, what made you decide to come so far and join our worship."

"Brother William," the young mother began, "I heard of the coming advent not days after our son was born, and it filled me with great worry that he might not be accepted into the kingdom of Heaven when that day comes. He's only an infant child, and he knows nothing of sin, repentance, and salvation. I knew I needed to bring him to you—you are the only one who can save him."

"My sister, you are right to be concerned for the soul of your child, for he bears with him the sin of Adam and he has not yet the volition to have that sin washed away," said William.

The young mother held her baby tightly as William's words confirmed the worst of her fears.

"But the Lord is merciful and just," he continued, "and your son shall have the opportunity to clutch his mother's breast when you are lifted to Heaven—as long as you believe, and commit yourself to this baptism in His name."

"I believe!" the mother cried. "I am ready, Brother William."

The young mother gave the child to her husband as William extended his hand to walk her up the wooden stairs to the font. Supported by the two volunteers who had drawn the curtain, William led the young mother down into the pool of water, as the congregation shouted words of love and encouragement. Heeding the instructions whispered by William, she crossed her hands over her chest and waited breathlessly for his prayer.

"As our body is immersed in this holy water, we are buried with Jesus into death. And just as He was raised up from the dead by the glory of the Father, so, too, shall we walk in the newness of life as we are lifted from these waters and become born again."

William placed his palm on the young mother's upper back and the other hand gently clasped hers. He looked deeply into her eyes.

"Do you accept Jesus Christ as your Lord and savior?"

"Yes, I do."

"Do you repent for your sins and ask for absolution?"

"Yes, I do."

"And do you accept the imminence of Christ's return and swear to remain pure until the day He comes?"

"Yes, praise God, I do!"

"In the name of the Father, the Son, and the Holy Spirit, I baptize thee."

Without delay, William plunged the young mother into the pool until she was fully immersed in the water, and in the same continuous motion, the two volunteers helped him quickly raise her to the surface. After rising back into the air, a toothy smile broke through the wet curtain of hair that stuck to her face as the congregation applauded and shouted calls of praise. William shook her hand and congratulated her as he helped her out of the water and back to the altar, where she took her child into her soaking arms and held him to her chest.

As the parishioners continued to cheer, William turned to the young father, who remained conspicuously quiet throughout the acclamation.

"And what say you to this, young man?" he asked, silencing the crowd. "It seems that you are shadowed in doubt where you stand."

The young father shuffled his feet anxiously as his wife looked at him with a critical glare.

"Well, you see," he began bashfully, "my wife in her bed rest took to reading some of the circulars that had been going around town, and she told me that we have some one hundred days before the Day of Judgment. I didn't give it much mind at first, but she told me she was comin' up with our child to see you whether I joined her or not. And I ain't about to let her undertake that journey alone, even though I ain't much of a believer myself."

"Please forgive him, Brother William," the young mother interjected. "He doesn't understand the danger his soul is in. If we had known earlier . . ."

"Do not lament, my sister. What providence that you have come in time to save not only two, but three souls together!"

William turned to the young father and stared intensely into his eyes.

"Tell me, brother, what would it take for you to believe if I said there was a great hurricane coming to Raleigh tomorrow?"

"Well . . . I don't reckon I understand the question, pastor," the young father said, rubbing the back of his neck.

"Would you trust that it would come if I showed you

all of the scientific calculations, the maps of the Gulf Stream created by Benjamin Franklin himself that say it is to be?"

"Why . . . I don't much understand that sort of thing," the young father replied.

William paused and allowed his audience a moment to consider the trajectory of his argument themselves.

"What if I showed you the history of the weather for that region, dating back to the settlers of Jamestown, and showed you an incontrovertible pattern that proves that hurricanes always make landfall on this date?"

The man pondered to himself and then replied. "Sir, I believe the only way I'd trust that you were right is if I saw the storm coming with my own eyes."

Without a moment's hesitation, William whipped around to address his congregation directly.

"My brothers and sisters, regale this soul with visions witnessed by thine own eyes! Visions of the very signs that are foretold by Daniel and John!"

"We've seen the signs, brother!" one man shouted immediately. "It was foretold there would be a great famine, and not a week passed and our summer yield was destroyed by a plague of locusts."

Echoes of other testaments resounded through the tent. All who bore witness poured their truth to the young man, who absorbed them like a series of forceful blows.

"The sun fell dark during the summer solstice," one woman cried.

"It was black as funeral garb, just as the Bible has said!" another added.

"Seven black ravens sat atop my roof the very next day!" shouted a man. "Seven ravens for the seven seals!"

"I've heard the cry of the martyrs!"

"Death is ravaging the nations of the world!"

"A mighty wind has blown!"

The voices of the crowd began to blend together, a garbled but ardent recitation of the signs of the apocalypse, witnessed by the very people in the tent. The newborn child started to cry as the voices grew louder, and a cascade of sweat formed across the young father's brow. He dropped to his knees.

"I hear you! I hear it all!" he exclaimed in wild distress. "I believe! O I believe and I believe!"

William placed his hand on the young man's shoulder as his wife spouted tears of relief.

"Will you join your wife in baptism, so that you may thus join your family in eternal glory?"

"I will, Brother William," he said. "I will."

William quickly led the young father up the baptismal font and into the water, where he in turn crossed his hands over his chest and awaited the instructions. William placed his palm on the young father's back and closed his eyes.

"Father in Heaven, we thank you for the grace you have given to open the eyes of this family before it is too late. We pray that you continue to grant your beneficence to the millions of souls across the world who have it in their hearts to wish for forgiveness. But for now, this young man has seen the light, repents for his sins, and accepts the imminence of your return."

William opened his eyes and placed his other hand on the man's chest. "In the name of the Father, the Son, and the Holy Spirit, I baptize thee."

William pushed the young father into the water and

signaled to the volunteers to remain steady as he continued pressing on his chest to keep him submerged. The young father, not expecting to be immersed for more than a brief moment, began to kick and struggle against the force of his hand as the water splashed and tossed about in the pool. But William maintained his advantageous position above, holding him underwater and counting to himself for seven seconds, until he nodded to the volunteers and they helped raise the man from the water.

The young father gasped for air as he at last surfaced, dripping water from his nose and mouth. After collecting his wits, he at last opened his eyes and reached out to shake William's hand.

"Thank you, Brother William," he sobbed. "Thank you, thank you, thank you."

The congregation broke out into cheers and unfettered exaltation. The young father remained on his knees, too overwhelmed to stand, wobbling in a state of delirium, as William held him steady in the water and his wife and child were embraced by the surrounding parishioners.

Thomas turned to speak to the ministers, but they were too transfixed by the sight before them to hear anything else.

# Chapter 19

IT WAS NEARLY dusk before the council called Thomas to their room. He had been waiting in the lobby of the inn all afternoon, pacing the floor in front of the taciturn innkeeper and his wife, hoping that their decision would be reached imminently. Separated from his home that he had not seen in months by only a mile, Thomas longed for the day to be over, when he could finally return and attempt to restore a semblance of normalcy to his life. Stubble had begun to show on his cheeks and chin, his eyes dry and heavy from the long day, and he desperately wanted to splash warm water on his face and at last take a rest. He thought about his homestead, his bed, the warming hearth in his humble quarters. He thought about Abigail, the words he would say to her when it was all over, and dreamed again of her eventual embrace. But the visions of his long-awaited reunion would merely be a mirage until the delegation was complete.

"Pastor Aleman," Reverend Fitch called to him from the top of the staircase. "Come. We've made our decision."

Sleep-deprived and powered only by his hope that a call for censure awaited, Thomas followed the reverend up the stairs and into their room. As Thomas stepped inside, he found Reverends Storrs and Marsh waiting austerely at a round wooden table that had been moved in for their meeting.

"Reverend Storrs, Reverend Marsh, Reverend Fitch," he greeted them venerably. "Can I trust that you've concluded that today's display necessitates a formal denunciation of Reverend Miller and his teachings?"

Reverend Fitch took a seat across from Thomas and gazed at him coldly.

"There's something we must admit, pastor," he began as Thomas sat down at the table. "Our motive in joining you here in person was not simply because you brought these teachings to our attention. We each had been curious about the sermons for some time before this."

"You are not the first one to come to us and speak about this October advent," Reverend Storrs added. "Many of our parishioners have been clamoring for us to address these predictions for several months now. They share the publications, the pamphlets, and transcripts of the sermons amongst themselves. And they look to us for guidance on whether or not to interpret what they've read as true, you see."

"Today has surely proven one thing," said Reverend Marsh. "The predictions of this Reverend Miller can no longer be ignored."

Thomas relaxed his shoulders, pleased that he was finally hearing some concord on the nature of William's teachings.

"That's exactly why I wanted you to see for yourselves. To witness in person the kind of sacrilege that is taking hold of my town. Once the Convention issues its decree, I have no doubt in my mind that it will bring a swift end to this madness."

Reverend Fitch shuffled in his seat and turned his eyes as if silently conferring with his colleagues.

"I don't think you quite understand, Thomas. You saw what kind of fever the people here had today, and you saw how quickly it can spread. Can you imagine if we were to refuse to acknowledge this kind of movement in our own churches?"

"The people would begin to wonder why we are the leaders of their parishes," said Reverend Storrs. "They'd castigate us for not taking these warnings seriously—for putting their souls in jeopardy."

Reverend Marsh slammed his fist on the table. "They'd tear us apart!"

Thomas was dumbstruck by the pronouncement and shook his head rapidly as he stared down at the table and attempted to gather his thoughts.

"I cannot believe what I am hearing," he said at last. "This kind of biblical prognostication was labeled heterodox long ago. What about the countless ecumenical precedents you'd be ignoring? What about the Fifth Lateran Council— has not this kind of apocalyptic speculation been rejected for centuries?"

"Are we following Catholic doctrine now?" Reverend Marsh asked pointedly. "My congregation is getting smaller by the week. If I started speaking about ancient, esoteric decrees, they'd oust me by the end of the month. But this—

this adventism—is exactly what I need to restore the energy to my church, to be the first to embrace the October date at large and stop them from bleeding into these other factions."

"He's right," said Reverend Fitch. "We have no choice in this matter. If we don't preach what our congregants want to hear, then they will surely take their spirits elsewhere."

"But surely it's just a minority of your parishioners who actually want to hear this topic addressed," Thomas argued. "And you are not only refusing to denounce these fictitious claims, but now you say that you are going to preach them yourselves? You're going along with this absurdity just to appease the calls of a small group of fanatics?"

"They may be small, but their voices are not," said Reverend Storrs. "And if it is truly our parishioners' eternal salvation that is at stake, then we must err on the side of caution."

"But what if he is wrong?" Thomas exclaimed in exasperation. "What if none of this comes to pass?"

"Don't be naïve, pastor," Reverend Fitch chided. "October twenty-second is drawing nigh. When the dust settles, would you rather be one of many fools standing together— or the only fool left behind?"

Struck down by the perfidious blows of the reverends, Thomas could do no more than slump back into his seat in disbelief. Their words soon came as an incoherent din as they continued to tell him of their plans to speak to Reverend Miller in the morning, to return to their parishes the next day, and their assurances that their decision was not only prudent, but moral and righteous.

Thomas could not bear to hear any more. Unable to say anything further to convince them of the contrary, he stood up and walked out of the room without a word, slamming their door behind him.

❧

Night had fallen by the time he returned to his house, and Thomas was hardly able to stand any longer. His plan had been a remarkable failure. The ministers would be returning to their congregations with an answer for those who believed that the rapture was coming, and it was an answer that left Thomas devoid of any hope that an end to the mania that infected his town would be coming soon. Worse, he felt like he himself was responsible for spreading this plague—carrying the rats upon his ship to new locales where the people had no immunity nor treatments to combat it.

But at least he was home. The cicadas were buzzing in the night. The air was warm; the breeze was mild. He looked at the barn and the dark windows of his small house and felt a sense of contentment. He would perhaps find some peace here at last.

Thomas took the oil lamp from the socket on the porch and entered the doorway. He stepped inside his house and closed the door behind him. The sound of the cicadas ceased behind the walls, and all was silent. He stood and looked into the dark corridor before him as if, in his state of hallucinatory lassitude, he was waiting—yearning—for someone to appear and greet him. But all that he found was his own single shadow, cast upon the wall by the dim glow of the lantern.

## Chapter 20

JACOB WHITE KICKED the heels of his obstreper-
ous sheep as Henry reluctantly trailed behind him with
a board and pencil in hand.

"Git in there, ye devils," he bellowed.

The sheep bleated and snorted in protest but nevertheless dutifully fell in line to their pen. Jacob flipped the hatch
of their gate and secured them inside.

"I don't know what else to say, Henry," he said, shaking
his head.

"You're now the fourth rancher in town to tell me you
don't need grain for the feed," Henry lamented. "What do
you expect will happen to your cattle in the winter?"

Jacob turned from the gate and continued stomping
through piles of manure toward his cattle stanchions. Henry
followed him through the muck, refusing to let his questions go unanswered. He knew Jacob was hiding something.

"I told you," Jacob said as he picked up a pitchfork.
"No one need worry about the winter, least of all the heif-

ers. Once the twenty-second of October arrives, all of these concerns will be left behind along with everyone who has refused to reckon with their sins."

Jacob dug the pitchfork into the hayloft and scooped several helpings of fodder into the troughs for his dairy cows, then boorishly grabbed a nearby bucket of grain to mix in supplementary servings of wheat. Henry stood by in perplexment, astounded that anyone would make such a rash and myopic decision as this.

"But what are you going to do until then? Your grounds will be grazed to dust!"

"If that's the worst of it, then I should thank God for showing us such mercy."

Losing his patience, Henry reached out his hand, wrapped it across the top of his friend's corpulent shoulder, and spun him around so they were face-to-face. Henry looked at him squarely in the eyes.

"You have a family, Jacob. I don't care what you believe will happen in the fall, but if you let your livestock wither away, you'll likewise do so yourselves long before you see that day come. I know you know this, so why don't you tell me the truth already?"

Jacob speared his pitchfork into the ground and spit a brown stream of tobacco into the dirt beside him.

"I'm selling my land, Henry," he admitted at last.

Henry couldn't believe what he was hearing. Jacob had been operating the dairy farm for even longer than Henry had had his homestead; his father had been a dairy farmer before him, his grandfather before that, and a long lineage of Whites had been tending livestock in the old country for untold generations prior. The man knew nothing else but sheep, pigs, and cattle.

"You've been maintaining this ranch for some twenty years," Henry said in astonishment. "What will you do for a livelihood? How will you eat?"

"I didn't want to say anything until the deal is done. But I've been in talks with a developer from out of town, an industrialist. They've been buying up properties all over the county the past few years for machine work and what have you. What he wants to do with the land is his business, but all I know is that there is no sense in spending my remaining time here when my family and I can be worshipping with the rest of the community at the church. And this offer should allow us enough capital to order our daily provisions from the fishermen or the other farmers and keep our bellies full 'til kingdom come."

"Jacob, we've known each other since we were boys. So I tell you this with nothing but respect: I think you're making a dreadful mistake."

"And I could say the same to you, my friend. Brother William has assured me that this is the way."

"But what if he's wrong? What happens if the sun rises on October twenty-third and we're all still here?"

Jacob looked up at him with a solemnity that Henry had rarely seen in his friend's eyes. "God's word has never been wrong. That I am sure of."

Jacob turned away and grabbed his pitchfork to continue feeding his cattle while Henry remained in place, sinking further into the muck. With such a scant harvest in the summer, Henry needed the ranchers' annual orders of livestock feed to recoup any semblance of earnings for the season. The locusts had devoured the heartier yield fit for a granary and human consumption, and all he was left with now were the immature grains that could only be fed to cattle or swine.

But Jacob was neither the first nor the last of his regular customers to decline a purchase for the year. The fever had struck the lot of his neighbors, from dairy farmers to swineherds to shipping merchants, who, like Jacob, found no reason to put in their orders and prepare for their lives beyond the Day of Atonement. To some of the most devout, continuing their business was even considered something of an affront to God—a sign that they did not have full faith that the Son of Man would imminently return—and relinquishing their earthly claims was therefore one of the most righteous and holy acts of faith that they could demonstrate. Unable to convince Jacob of anything to the contrary, Henry at last relented and began his long march home.

The road back to his farm took him through the center of the town. Henry had seldom found himself there since the locusts came, as most of his time was spent in the fields attempting to salvage what remained of his crops or taking orders at the ranches surrounding Calvary proper. But as he walked farther into the commercial district, he noticed that his hometown was changing before his eyes. Outsiders had begun to surge into Calvary with every week that passed as news of William's sermons spread throughout the country. Foreign pilgrims and local worshippers now walked the road from the ports to the church grounds at any given time of the day; behind them, fully stocked carryalls brought in a continuous influx of food and other supplies to the round-the-clock sermons at the camp. Some residents took in the travelers in hopes that their pious acts of charity would be recognized in October; but most of the new arrivals were content staying along the open outskirts of the town, pitching their lodgings in the form of small tarpaulin tents or covered wagons that they had converted into shelters. The humble dwellings were of no mind to the worshippers, as they would spend the majority of their waking hours at the camp to hear William speak or discussing the sermons with the rest of the congregation after services had concluded. Everything else, it seemed, was an exercise in patience.

Henry passed the tents along the perimeter of Calvary and made his way down the cobblestone roads of the town square. He found the same zeal that had pierced the souls of the ranchers had also seemed to penetrate the daily lives of those in the commercial and residential centers. Countless devotees in white ascension robes dotted the path leading up the hill to the church, as if they were already making their final ascent into the clouds. Many of the other residents began to publicly display their belief in the advent in their homes or storefronts—to both serve as a reminder for the hesitant to prepare for the coming rapture and to flaunt the ardency of their own faith for all to see. The main thoroughfare was peppered with crucifixes, banners, flags, and verses from Scripture that hung in windows, doors, and hitching posts—displays that proliferated like spores of mold, as no one wanted to be the only neighbor in a cluster of houses without a sign in their home or yard to prove their devotion.

Businesses likewise began to focus their wares on items that were essential to the end-of-days preparation and the festivities at the camp—catering mostly to the out-of-town worshippers who had few supplies with them but still needed select items and materials to survive for the next several months. Even Harriman's general store, which typically only stocked its shelves with the products of local artisans or whatever commodities the port merchants had at a discount, began to replace the dry goods and imported hats with ascension robes and pamphlets that detailed William's lectures, which sold out weekly as the population of Calvary continued to grow.

But the most ubiquitous exhibitions of faith that Henry encountered were the countdown markers to the Millennium—posts hammered into the ground that held replaceable wooden squares to change out the numerals as each day passed—which could be found beside nearly every door of the houses of the believers. The markers were traditionally turned over in the late afternoon before the evening worship began, to coincide with the coming of dusk that would mark the number of days to the exact moment of their ascension on the twenty-second of October.

Henry continued his trek away from the boisterous crowds of worshippers and vendors and neared the dirt road toward his farm, where the properties became wider and the houses more intermittent the farther they were from the main thoroughfare. Unnerved by the zealotry on display behind him, Henry increased his pace as he passed the remaining row of homes before the wooded path. As he came closer to the forest, he caught sight of the resident of the final house painting a large mural across his picket fence.

FOR AT THE TIME APPOINTED, THE END SHALL BE

The egg-white paint of the final "E" dripped down the side of the wooden fence like sap down the bark of a tree, punctuating the end of the statement. Henry heard the voices of two children singing in the front yard beside it and saw the young twins who went to school with Rosemary and Benji sitting across from one another in the grass, as they clapped their hands together in a new rhyme.

> *"Fire, fire, brimstone and blood*
> *Christ is coming to bring His love;*
> *Ashes, ashes, fury and woe*
> *O my Lord, we thank you so!"*

Henry felt a sense of foreboding in the air as he continued past them, down the road to the forest. The rest of their song echoed in the distance.

> *"Mercy, mercy, mercy, please spare my soul*
> *The righteous will make the kingdom whole . . ."*

The reverberations of their voices were soon swallowed by the trunks of the trees that sprung up around him as he proceeded down the trails. Henry marched deeper into the ancient woods, away from the town, away from the images of praise and preparation and the sounds of worship, until he could no longer hear the clamor of the day. But amongst the quietude of nature, he still could not find peace. Accompanied by the chorus of birds that whistled above him in the trees, the voices of the children continued to linger in his ear, the verses of their song repeating ceaselessly in the depths of his mind as he made his way home before the coming of dusk.

## Chapter 21

"'IN THE BEGINNING was the Word, and the Word was with God, and the Word was God.'"

Mrs. Edwards read to the class from an open pamphlet, which had been developed by William, printed by Josiah, and distributed to the school as part of the summer's evolving curriculum. She herself was learning with them.

"Now what does that mean, children?" she asked, lowering the paper from her eyes.

The students stared at the front of the room in silence. Mrs. Edwards adjusted her bifocals as she searched for the answer to her own question on the next page.

"It means," she began as she scanned the brochure, "that before Creation, the only being that existed in all of the universe was the Holy Trinity."

Mrs. Edwards turned to the chalkboard and began to copy definitions from the pamphlet as she recited each section out loud.

"The WORD itself is the Holy Spirit—the divine message of God. The LIVING WORD that stands with God is Jesus Christ—the divine messenger. And finally, GOD is the Father—the author of the message."

Mrs. Edwards fumbled with the paper as the class remained nonplussed by her lesson.

"Why is this important for us to understand?" she asked rhetorically, eventually finding the information that she needed. "Because Brother William teaches us that once the seventh seal is lifted, we will bear witness to the powers of each part of the Holy Trinity. God the Father, sitting upon His eternal throne in Heaven, will send His Son—the messenger—to call us to our judgment. The Son will then deliver the Word—the Holy Spirit—to guide us toward salvation as the believers ascend to the Heavenly throne."

The room remained quiet as Mrs. Edwards laid down the chalk upon her desk. Several of the children began to stir in their seats, restlessly swinging their feet, as they waited for the bells to chime. Only Rosemary continued to study the definitions before her in deep contemplation, attempting to unravel the paradoxes of Scripture.

"Mrs. Edwards, I have a question," Rosemary began, raising her hand. "How is it that God can be both the Word and the author of the Word at the same time?"

Mrs. Edwards swayed her heavy frame as she pondered to herself, feigning an air of expertise.

"Because God is made up of the Holy Trinity. He is the Father, the Son, and the Holy Spirit all at once."

Rosemary shook her head as she tried to understand. "But if the Word of God is the Holy Spirit, and God is the author of the Word—then wouldn't God have existed before the Holy Spirit?" she asked. "Wouldn't that mean that there was a time before the Word, when there was no Trinity?"

"Well . . . you see . . ." Mrs. Edwards began as she searched through the pamphlet for some kind of explanation.

" . . . And likewise," Rosemary continued, "if God is the Father and Jesus is the Son of God, then wouldn't there be a time before the Father begat the Son? How can they all exist in the beginning of time when one is born from the other?"

As Mrs. Edwards struggled to find a response, the church bells interceded and called an end to the lesson of the day. The students all eagerly stood up at once and began to gather their items and head toward the door.

"This is truly one of the sublime mysteries of the universe," Mrs. Edwards concluded as the students began to shuffle out of the classroom. "In the meantime, listen to the message within us all, children. Beware the signs of the times!"

Rosemary lingered in her seat as the rest of the class filed out around her. She continued to be captivated by the writing on the chalkboard, her mind racing as she wrestled with the concepts of the Trinity, nature, and time. It was only when Benji nudged her shoulder that she broke out of her trance, raised herself from her desk, and accompanied him outside.

It was the first time that Abigail had entrusted her to walk her brother home from school. Their limited food supply necessitated that she spend additional hours on dinner preparation—slow-cooking leftover chicken bones and table scraps to make a broth, softening the livestock feed into an edible porridge for breakfast, locating adequate substitutes for any missing ingredients in town—so Abigail found no alternative but to cede the responsibility of chaperoning Benji to her sister until things would go back to normal. She instructed Rosemary to bring her brother home straight from school, lest she have the weight of another worry on her mind on top of all else, and she trusted that her sister would appreciate the situation and comply with her request.

Rosemary took the long way back that afternoon. Eager to explore their own meandering paths free from the supervision of their sister, Rosemary and Benji journeyed into the town center, which they had heard was changing into something of a cosmopolitan oasis in otherwise rural Washington County. As they made their way to the town square, the two quickly became overwhelmed by the volume of people on the road, most of whom were traveling against them toward the hilltop. Merchants and peddlers roamed the streets, hawking food, novelties, and foreign merchandise for the worshippers. Wagon tires grated along the cobblestone paths as the supplies made their way to the camp, while calls from Josiah's new newspaper stands resounded from the legion of boys who had been hired to sell the week's publication to the townspeople and the pilgrims who continued flocking to the town.

As they maundered down the main road and took in the sights and sounds of the advent preparation, Rosemary stopped before the ashen spot that still remained burned into the ground in front of the Chandler estate. The dark oval where Helen Chandler took her final breath brought her back to the grim reality of her surroundings. Behind her she could hear the distant melody of "When Thou My Righteous Judge Shalt Come" echoing from the tent at the top of the hill. The song brought a sense of disappointment and longing to Rosemary as it dawned on her why the crowds all seemed to move in the opposite direction as them. Most parents had their children join them across the lawn at the church camp after school for the daily worship, using their class dismissal as the time to close up business and attend services as a family for the rest of the day. But Henry had consistently refused to consider the notion, despite her subtle attempts to sway his decision. As she stood amongst the speeding carriages and robed masses hurrying toward the church grounds, she felt orphaned—as if she and Benji were the only children in town who were not worthy to be taken up to the exaltation and the glory that was the adventist ministration. She felt the pendulum inside her stomach slowly begin to swing again as the anxiety crept into her, and so she grabbed her brother by the hand and led him toward the river.

She knew that it would make Benji's day to watch the ships come and go from the Wainscott family port. The docks had rapidly been transformed in the decade prior and entrenched Calvary as part of the continuum of commercial channels that expanded by the year. The old wooden boards that local fishermen and leisurists once used to cast off their small rowboats into the shallow banks of the river now grew into tall posts and sturdy platforms that stretched into the harbor, where the trading vessels would come downriver to unload their shipments before their terminus in Albany or the New York Harbor some two hundred miles south.

The children stepped onto the creaking boards of the docks and sauntered toward the water's edge. Benji was able to espy a steamboat in the distance amongst the smaller wooden ships and immediately focused all his attention on the sight, leaning against a post to hold himself up as he stared upstream in wonder. His cheeks were becoming gaunter, and the color had been disappearing from his face over the past month, but breathing in the fluvial air seemed to be the only thing that could inspire new energy within him, as he watched with exuberance while the vessels traveled in a row down the water.

Rosemary walked to the opposite edge of the dock and sat down on the warm wooden boards as she watched the current gently brush beside the pilings. Mesmerized by the calm, viridian water, she soon became lost in its stillness. The wisping clouds above were mirrored in the water below, and she watched as they swirled, rearranged, and materialized into the writing that had been on the classroom chalkboard earlier in the day.

Rosemary could not escape the enigma of the triune God. There was an incongruity in the logic of it all, just as there was in her understanding of the infinite that had confounded her once before. She wondered if perhaps the two concepts were intertwined like some kind of divine knot, solvable only by untangling the threads of both ideas at once. She thought about how the world would begin its era of infinity after this life ended—how she once had imagined eternity as a return to that timeless existence before Creation, when it was only the Father, Son, and Holy Spirit that occupied the abyss. This was a time when the laws of nature were not yet established—and so maybe then, the paradox of the Trinity was not a paradox at all. He who is, was, and is to come may exist simultaneously if God exists outside of time itself; for within the retrograde infinite, there is no order. Nothing is first and nothing is last—the past, present, and future occur at once. Perhaps, she thought, this is likewise what awaits when the world becomes eternal: their spirits becoming as one with the Trinity, all moments converged into one singularity, unbound by time.

Rosemary stared at her reflection in the water while the notions continued to swell in her like the rising tide. But as the ships neared the port, the ripples in the water transformed her reflection to that of another figure, appearing behind her like a second soul merging into hers. She recognized the face right away as the wavelets cleared.

"Miss Marigold?" she asked, turning around.

"Hello, Rosemary. I'm sorry to startle you."

Marigold stepped to the end of the dock and looked out into the downstream clearing. Rosemary could see that her eyes were bloodshot, her face still etched with sorrow.

"This is a good place to think, isn't it?" said Marigold. "Sometimes the worship gets too rambunctious at this hour for my taste. But I can stay here all afternoon and speak with God alone when no one else is around."

"I wish I had the time to do that more often myself."

"I find myself with so much time these days. Ironic, isn't it? Having all the time in the world now that our time is running out."

Rosemary raised herself to her feet and stood beside Marigold in silence. The two continued to observe the river.

"We haven't seen you in church lately. You must know that now is not the time to let your faith lapse," said Marigold.

Rosemary's face grew red. "Our father doesn't want us going. He says he doesn't want us thinking about the end of the world."

"The end will come for us all; there's no avoiding it."

Rosemary turned her eyes toward her brother, who leaned forward in eager anticipation as the ships drew closer.

"I hear Benjamin has taken ill," Marigold said, noticing her look of concern. "I pray for him every day during the services."

"I pray for him, too. After what happened to my mother . . ."

"Do you take care of him?"

Rosemary nodded her head. "Yes, we all do."

"If there is anything I can impart to you from my experience, it is this: it's one thing to care for his sickness; it's another to care for his soul. I wish someone could have told me that before it was too late. This body is only temporary, but the soul is eternal. If you love your brother, you mustn't take that for granted."

"We're trying to live as pious a life as we can," Rosemary insisted. "I pray that God will see that."

"Time flows like this river," Marigold continued. "If you wade in it idly, you'll soon find yourselves swept out to the blackness of the sea."

The foghorn from the steamboat blared through the air like the sound of a great trumpet. Rosemary looked back over to Benji, who excitedly jumped up and waved at the passing merchant vessel.

"I think we ought to be going home now," Rosemary said as she backed away from Marigold.

"Look after him, Rosemary," Marigold called out. "Do not let him fall under!"

Rosemary hurried to Benji and signaled to him that it was time to leave. Hand in hand, the two walked along the swaying docks and back toward the road that led to the farmhouses, as Marigold's shadow faded in the distance.

Rosemary stared outside the classroom window the next day as the clouds trekked across the sky. The air was thick, and she could still hear the hymns carrying from the camp services, which continued throughout the morning. The bell had not yet rung, and the rest of the students took the time to play amongst themselves before Mrs. Edwards arrived. But Rosemary remained immersed in thought, ruminating over the warning that she had received the day before.

Rosemary broke from her meditation as Benji sat down at the desk next to hers with his head held low. He sniffled lightly as he attempted to conceal his tears from his sister, who knew something was amiss.

"Benji, what's wrong?" she asked.

Benji wiped a teardrop from his cheek and averted his eyes. "Nothing," he said.

"Benji . . . tell me what happened."

Benji at last lifted his face from his desk. "It's the twins. They say I'm not allowed to play with them anymore."

Rosemary looked to the back of the classroom to see the young boy and girl, both wearing child-sized ascension robes, leading another clapping rhyme amongst a group of students.

"And why is that?" asked Rosemary.

Benji remained silent as he turned his eyes back to his desk and kept to himself. There was a soft wheeze to his breaths as he attempted to suppress his tears lest they further labor his breathing.

Rosemary felt a sudden rage boiling within her. Screeching the wooden legs of her desk against the floor, she pushed herself to her feet and walked to the back of the class, parting the circle of children around the twins, who ceased their laughter and gaiety as she cast her shadow over them. Rosemary was about five years their senior and made sure to it that they understood their place in the classroom hierarchy.

"Just who do you think you are, telling my brother he isn't welcome to play with you?" she asked, her fists folded against her hip.

"He's not allowed here," said the boy, unafraid of her menacing stance.

"It's a free country," the girl added. "We don't have to play with anyone we don't want to."

The children returned to their game as Rosemary clenched her fists tighter. Benji called to her from the front of the room.

"Rosemary, it's all right," he pleaded. "Just forget it."

Rosemary ignored him and pointed her finger toward the twins.

"You two: you've always let my brother in on your stupid little games before. Tell me what's changed now."

The twins looked at one another in a silent, fraternal communication. The girl at last turned back to Rosemary.

"Our parents say we aren't allowed to be around your family."

Rosemary was taken aback as the other children in the room stopped talking to listen.

"Excuse me?" She moved in closer.

"We aren't supposed to talk to nonbelievers," the boy

added. "Our mother and father said you'd be a bad influence on us as the Millennium gets closer. We're not allowed to play with children who are going to Hell."

The church bells began to ring, and Rosemary saw nothing but red. By the time she regained her constitution, she was on top of the boy on the floor with her knees pressed into his shoulders, whaling her fists across his face.

Mrs. Edwards hurriedly entered the classroom to find the students cheering on the fight.

"Cease this now!" she exclaimed as she waddled toward the fracas.

Rosemary continued to hit the boy until his white robe was speckled with a crimson trail leading up to his bloody nose. Mrs. Edwards finally pulled her off him as he moaned in agony.

"Rosemary Smith—you sit outside with your back against the wall!" she commanded as she tended to the dazed child. "As soon as Brother William breaks for his rectory, you will march yourself up there and confess your sin at once."

Rosemary pursed her lips and unclenched her bruised fists, then stomped outside into the hallway as Mrs. Edwards continued to examine the boy's injuries. She waited on the floor, her arms wrapped around her knees, as her anger slowly began to subside. She was embarrassed—not for losing her temper or for causing a scene, but embarrassed by the thought of other adults speaking about her family's fated damnation, by her father's views that kept them from the worship that was necessary to save their souls. She stirred in her position against the wall until the organ from the tent began to play in the distance, indicating that the services were in recess and William would soon return to plan his next sermon.

Rosemary's heart began to beat rapidly as she stood up and walked down the hallway that connected to the church transept. She had never been in trouble in school before, and whatever apoplexy had consumed her initially had now been replaced by fear of her coming punishment. Rosemary attempted to repress her consternation as she climbed each step of the spiral staircase up to William's rectory. But as she advanced farther, she felt a sudden pang in her stomach when she thought back to the last time she had been in the stairwell. It was the moment that she'd learned of the fate of humanity, a burden that was, for a time, hers to bear alone. She remembered how she fell to her knees to pray for her soul and the souls of her family to be saved, and how she feared that they would be eternally separated from one another if they failed their final judgment—a fear that persisted each day they came nearer to the end. The pendulum returned as she proceeded upward.

Rosemary hesitated at the top of the stairs. The door to the rectory was open, and a beam of light was shining through just as it had the last time she was here. But something about the light was different this time—she felt as if it was drawing her closer to its radiance and warmth, that it was now showing her the way to her destiny. She breathed in and entered the room.

William raised his eyes from his desk. Despite the long morning sermon, he was already sitting in front of a paper with pen in hand, writing notes for his next homily. The light reflected in his pupils as he looked at the entrance.

"Yes, can I help you?"

"Mrs. Edwards said I needed to come see you," Rosemary said with a nervous stammer. "I'm supposed to confess to you that I got into a fight today."

William returned to his notes and continued speaking with her as she stood at the doorway.

"This fight, is it something for which you seek forgiveness?"

Rosemary could not understand the sensation, but as she stood before William, she felt that she could not hide the truth from him—as if he already knew every thought in her mind.

"No, Brother William," she replied. "I was defending my brother. The greater sin would have been to stand by as he continued to be bullied."

William placed down his pen and raised his eyes to her again, surprised by her unabashed honesty.

"Even still, Christ tells us to turn the other cheek."

"But does that apply when we are witnessing the harm of others? What if the only way to protect the innocent is to harm the wicked?"

William leaned back in his chair and furrowed his brow, intrigued by the profundity of such a question from a fourteen-year-old student.

"Why don't you have a seat," William offered warmly, opening his hand to the wooden chair before him.

Rosemary sat down with a sudden urge to sob as the thoughts that she had been internalizing for so long began to surface. Everything she was too afraid to admit, even to herself, was now rising to the tip of her tongue, and she trusted that she would be guided toward righteousness, away from the strife that was tearing her apart from the inside out.

"It's just . . . I think my brother is very sick. My father won't say it, but I remember what it was like for my mother before she passed. And it feels like it's happening all over again."

"And you fear for your brother," William inferred. "Is that why you felt it within you to strike another? The fear for his health?"

"I fear for his soul, Brother William. Everyone in my family acts as if the revelation of His coming has no impact on how we live our lives. My brother and I . . . we wake up in the morning, go to school, and come straight home while others go to worship; we eat our food at the dinner table while others consume the gospel at the church; we speak about idle nonsense while others speak of salvation. Then we go to sleep and begin the next day like nothing has changed. My father . . . he doesn't want us even thinking about the end, let alone preparing for it."

"Perhaps your anger then was misplaced."

"What do you mean?"

"Perhaps you are not angry at the student who was bullying your brother. Rather, you are angry that your brother is being denied his spiritual right to seek salvation."

Rosemary lowered her eyes and mulled over the reverend's words.

"You are Henry Smith's daughter, aren't you?"

"Yes, Brother William. Rosemary Smith."

"I've known your father for a long time," he said. "I knew your mother, too, when we were young. We all went to this very school together when my father was the headmaster."

"Then you must be aware of how stubborn my father can be."

William held back a smirk and leaned in closer. "I'll tell you what we shall do. I break before the midafternoon worship to plan my next sermons in here every day. Why don't you join me during that time, and we can discuss these items together."

"But what about class?"

"I'll speak with Mrs. Edwards. We can call it detention. Besides, there are books here that can teach you more about the world than anything you can learn in a classroom with young children."

Rosemary raised her eyes, now beaming in the light, and accepted the offer without speaking a word.

"You know, I got into some trouble like this in school when I was your age as well," said William. "Looking back, it was not because there was some kind of evil or wickedness in me—but it was because I was not challenged by the curriculum. And the boredom led to idleness, and idleness to mischief."

"It's not that I am bored," said Rosemary. "All through-out the day, I find myself thinking about the new lessons you've provided to Mrs. Edwards. But all she has are ques-tions and no answers."

"I see. It seems you may have outgrown the class—and maybe even your teacher."

Rosemary smiled as she felt the warming light upon her melt away the reservations she'd had walking down the dark hall.

"Brother William, may I ask you something?" she began. "Yesterday, we learned about the nature of the Trinity at the beginning of time, before Creation, and something just isn't making sense to me. How is it that God can be both the Word and the author of the Word at the same time? How can He be both the Father and the Son without one entity existing before the other?"

"Augustine would have us consider the nature of love," William replied without hesitation. "It, too, is a kind of trinity, for love itself requires three coequal elements: the lover, the beloved, and the feeling of love that is between them. Love cannot exist without the lover, the lover cannot exist without love; likewise, the beloved ceases to be the beloved without a lover to imbue the nature of love unto them. Just as with God, these elements are separate, yet the same part of the whole—it is merely the relationship between each that distinguishes them. To put it in simpler terms: God is love, Christ is the lover, and the Holy Spirit which exists in us all is the beloved."

"And, like God, these pieces can never fully be divorced from one another," Rosemary thought out loud. "There is no God without Christ, there is no Christ without God, and the Holy Spirit cannot exist without God the author and Christ the messenger. None can therefore come before or after another. It's like a never-ending cycle . . . an infinity."

"Very good," William said as he swayed back in his chair. "I believe we will have much more to discuss on this moving forward. For there are many other questions to consider, and little time to tarry."

Rosemary looked up and scanned her eyes across the volumes of texts that lined the shelves of the room, wondering to herself what answers they might bring, as they continued to talk about life, God, and time everlasting.

# Chapter 22

D R. CLARKE PRESSED his ear against the receiver of his stethoscope as Benji took in a series of deep breaths. Each inhalation only lasted a short moment, stalling in plateaus as if there was something blocking his airway when he attempted to fill his lungs. But Benji clenched his fist tightly and continued through the struggle, determined to follow the doctor's orders.

"That's it, Benjamin, you're doing great," Dr. Clarke assured him.

Benji remained on his back atop the sweat-infused sheets of the bed, his face pallid and nearly gray. The outline of his ribs protruded from his opened shirt as the cavity of his chest fluttered like the wings of a young bird. Henry stood across the room with his back against the wall, observing him from a distance.

Dr. Clarke moved the instrument across Benji's chest and over to his other lung, repeating his instructions. "Just one more time," he said.

Benji inhaled again; the air entered in the same short, staggered gasps. Dr. Clarke listened intently and attempted to conceal his concern from the boy, not wishing to further exacerbate his malady with additional, unneeded worriment.

"Very good," Dr. Clarke said as he removed the stethoscope from his ear and placed it on the nightstand. "Go ahead and put your shirt back on now."

Benji slowly leaned up in bed and began to feebly button his white shirt, light-headed and dizzy as if he had just spent the past hour running at a sprint.

"Rest up, son," Henry said to him as he placed his hand upon his forehead. "Abigail and Rosemary will be home from town soon."

Benji nodded and slid himself underneath the covers, promptly falling asleep. Dr. Clarke quietly put his medical devices into his satchel and motioned for Henry to join him in the other room.

"I won't lie to you," Dr. Clarke began as they stepped into the living quarters. "His condition is getting worse."

"I don't understand," Henry said, shaking his head. "We've been giving him his medicine exactly as you've instructed. It used to work right away whenever he had a problem."

Dr. Clarke paused to gather his words tactfully as not to rouse anger in his friend.

"Henry . . . has Benji been getting enough to eat?"

"Of course he has! You know I would never let my children go hungry."

"I'm not saying that you are failing to provide. I am merely asking if his meals have been entirely sufficient lately. He seems to have lost weight since the last time I saw him,

Henry. It's important that a boy his age, and especially one with his condition, get all the nutrients he needs."

Henry felt the red heat of shame come across his face as he considered the past several months and the paltriness of their diet. Henry lowered his eyes and sighed to himself.

"I just don't know what to do, doc. With everything that has been happening in town, no one is looking to purchase any winter grain supply. It's all changing so fast. The merchants are focused on gouging those new pilgrims with imported goods; the ranchers are starting to auction off their land to industrialists and whomever else will buy their property. Jacob White told me that he is selling everything but his house—the pasture, his barn, his livestock—so that he and his family can devote their time to that daily worship next to the church. You know I rely on those customers to make a living . . . without them, all we have is whatever I can manage to harvest here and what little we can afford at the market."

"Yes, the Second Coming is having an effect on us all, I'm afraid. I've had fewer than half the house calls I'd normally be getting, even with all of the newcomers in town. People just aren't bothering to treat their sicknesses in the face of an incoming rapture. I even spoke to one man who had come down with a terrible ulcer, and he told me that he'd rather be taken by it now than risk a chance of being here for the bowls of wrath. It's the fear itself that is the greater danger to us all, if you ask me."

"There's no reasoning with them! I thought we might be able to get by with what we have until the people started to wake up, but they are showing no signs of stirring."

Dr. Clarke placed his hand upon his friend's shoulder with a note of avuncular encouragement.

"I'm sure it will all be over once October passes. Until then, you just focus on keeping your boy strong and properly fed above all else. I've seen you soldier through worse times before. I know you can do it."

Henry remained in place as Dr. Clarke lifted his satchel from the floor and bid him farewell. As the door closed behind him, Henry was left with only the cyclical sounds of stridor emanating from Benji's bedroom.

Henry clenched his eyelids shut as he attempted to quell the thoughts and images of his greatest worries in his mind. Benji and his daughters were the only things in the world that had kept him from the bottom of a bottle of rye or the end of a rope the last time this happened. It was his children who spurred him to lace his boots, who impelled him to take his plough to the fields. It was his children who helped him to find a routine and restore order to his daily life, and it was his children who gave him purpose to carry on through it all. Without them, he would not have been able to stand.

The rasp of Benji's breathing began to envelop Henry's consciousness as if he were right next to his ear. He began to think about what the future would hold. He thought about Benji lying there in bed, unable to go to school, unable to help on the farm, unable to learn a trade or leave home to start a family of his own. He began to think about it happening all over again. Another illness, another piece of him dying. Another burial, another funeral service. More neighbors arriving with stale muffins and maudlin blubbering. More friends bringing over more ale, more excuses for them to imbibe until they could no longer walk. More blessings and more condolences, when all he would want was more solitude to grieve alone.

He opened his eyes. Henry had to escape these moribund thoughts at once, and briskly exited his house to the porch. He grabbed a field sickle and held it in his hand as he looked out to the rows of half-harvested wheat that would cease to mature once the air began to cool. He calculated the motions in his mind. Each swing of the blade cuts ten stalks of wheat. Each stalk averages five heads. Each head holds about twenty kernels in a dry season like this. That's one thousand kernels of wheat with every motion—one thousand kernels to feed his family with every aching, relentless swing of his sickle.

He knew it was not enough. Henry stepped down from the porch and walked along the edge of the fields as the wind dragged the dust across his boots. He continued past the outer perimeter of the plowland to the pen beside his cellar. His sickle still at his side, he paused to look at the four sheep whose wool filled his family's pillows and outfitted their clothing year after year. The largest of the four plodded toward the timber fencing and stopped at the gate, its black eyes bulging from their sockets as it stared back at Henry while chewing on a mouthful of cud.

Henry entered the pen as the white-woolen ewe remained in place, waiting for him to approach. Henry slowly knelt down next to the animal and placed his free hand on its cheek as he drew his sickle with the other. Its tongue protruding from its mouth, the sheep stopped chewing and began to twist its head and bleat desperately, as if it knew what was going to happen next.

Henry clutched its neck and tightened his grip. As the sheep kicked and writhed in his arm, Henry planted his feet into the ground and swiftly crossed the blade over its throat in a single motion, still holding its head tightly to prevent any escape; the blood pouring from its neck, the sheep collapsed into the dirt. Its legs began to jerk with less intensity the more the blood spilled out and turned its white wool red. The other animals stood at the opposite end of the pen and watched as the life slowly drained from the oldest sheep's eyes—eyes that continued to bulge open and gaze into those of Henry, until it summoned the last of its energy and took its final breath.

# Chapter 23

ABIGAIL PLACED A hearty plate of meat, gravy, and carrots in front of each member of her family as they sat at their small sawbuck dinner table. Rosemary looked down with sadness and disgust as the steam billowed off the dish.

"Is this mutton?" Benji asked excitedly.

"It is," Henry confirmed as he folded his hands in prayer. "And we ought to give thanks that we are finally eating a square meal like this again. Benji, would you like to lead us this evening?"

Benji nodded and closed his eyes, repeating the same prayer used at school, with the appropriate substitutions. "Our Father in Heaven, who has blessed this family with another day, come grant us a continuance of thy protection and blessing during the next. Come then, and be in this house and likewise grant us the help we need to be faithful and successful in our duty. Amen."

Henry and his daughters repeated the end of the benediction, and the four began to eat their dinner. Benji, eschewing a fork and knife, picked up the mutton bone with his hands and began to ravenously devour the helping of meat. Henry looked over at his son and said nothing of the impropriety, happy to see that his appetite had returned.

"It tastes great, Abigail," Benji said as the gravy dripped down his cheeks.

Rosemary appeared nauseated by the sight of it all and stared at her plate apprehensively, slowly beginning to cut into her carrots instead.

"How have you been liking your walks home from school by yourselves these past few weeks?" Abigail asked Benji, breaking off a small piece of bread.

"Good," Benji answered without looking up.

"I think Rosemary has been doing a fine job with it," said Abigail to Henry. "Perhaps this can be a more regular occurrence in the future."

Rosemary lifted her eyes to her sister, who looked away obliviously without noticing her vexed glower. Feeling some tension at the table, Henry declined to respond to Abigail's suggestion and continued dining in silence until he heard footsteps approaching their home, followed by a knock at the door.

Henry placed down his fork and pushed back his chair but was swiftly halted by Abigail.

"Please, let me answer it. You've been in the fields all day."

Abigail dabbed her lips with her napkin and stood up to walk toward the entrance. She opened the front door, and it seemed as if a ghost had appeared before her.

"Thomas?" Abigail asked with astonishment.

Thomas held his hat across his chest at the threshold as Abigail waited breathlessly.

"Miss Smith," he replied, equally taken off guard by her presence at the door.

The pair continued to stand together in an awkward daze as Henry stood up to greet his unexpected guest. A warm blush filled Abigail's cheeks; and likewise, Thomas's eyes glinted in the candlelight like two fireflies as he laid them upon her, unable to conjure up any explanation for his sudden visit.

"Pastor Aleman." Henry greeted him behind his dumbstruck daughter. "What brings you here?"

"Good evening, Henry," Thomas said, as he noticed the family was eating dinner. "I apologize, I can come back later if this is an inopportune time."

Henry waved off Thomas's concern, inviting him inside. "No, nonsense. Come in."

Thomas walked in the house and stood inches away from Abigail, who did not move from her position in the entryway. The two remained at a loss for words until Abigail suddenly blurted out a proposal.

"We're just sitting down for supper. Allow me to set up a plate for you . . . if you'd like."

"That's very kind of you," Thomas answered with a smile. "But I will really only be a moment."

"It would be our pleasure if you'd join us," Henry insisted.

"Actually, I was hoping I could speak with you privately. It's rather important."

Thomas's solemnity gave Henry pause, and he understood that something must be afoot to warrant the sudden call at this hour.

"Of course," said Henry. "We can discuss outside on the porch. Please, come."

Thomas followed Henry across the room, meeting Abigail's eyes once again as he walked toward the rear exit. Abigail staggered back to the table and exhaled deeply, her heart beating madly.

"What's gotten into you?" Rosemary asked.

"Nothing," said Abigail. "Let's just finish our dinner before it gets cold."

Henry shut the door behind him as the clatter of the silverware against the sides of his children's plates resumed inside, and he stepped out onto the porch. He lit the whale-oil lantern hanging from the nearby post, bathing the two men in its shallow glow. The fire reflected in Thomas's eyes.

"I'm sorry for the sudden intrusion, but I needed to speak to you about something urgent."

"This is certainly a time of urgency for everyone. I know you have only been away for a few months, but I imagine the town must seem like it's gone through a generation of change already. What can I do for you, pastor?"

"Truthfully, I came here because I wanted to talk to you about the advent."

"Yes, it seems like everybody wants to talk to me about it these days," Henry replied with mild exasperation.

"It's a lie, Henry."

Henry was taken aback by the audacity of the statement, not expecting this kind of talk from the normally reserved pastor.

"It's a lie," Thomas repeated. "A grift. A hoax. Call it what you may. Whether William truly believes what he is saying or not, I am still unsure. But I do know he has reached the point of no return. He cannot go back on his word."

"I've heard that the Baptist ministers who attended his sermons confirmed that what he is preaching is all accurate," said Henry. "Are you saying they are a part of this, too?"

"Craven fools—all of them! They are all simply afraid of not taking action—either out of fear that their parishioners will leave them or fear of God's wrath if William's claims do come true. Think about it, Henry. They are in a position where, on October twenty-third, they can merely say that they overreacted or were hoodwinked or any other excuse for preaching what they have, and hope that their congregants will just forget about it and move on—or even thank them for their caution. But if they do nothing until then, they will have these radical zealots accusing them of condemning their parishioners to eternal damnation by not ordering them to prepare for Judgment Day. So they are going along with this whole charade."

"I suppose William always did have a particular skill for persuading others to fall in line with his plans," Henry recalled.

"I didn't know you were so well acquainted."

"When we were kids, he had everyone our age wrapped around his finger. Nothing too serious, just childhood mischief—getting us to help him with one scheme or another or convincing us to follow whatever trend he deemed fashionable at the time. He just had a way with words, even back then."

Henry looked out into the night as if he could see the past manifesting in the moonlight.

"You know, the only one who ever actually saw through the beguilement was my wife. William took a real shine to her when we were all in school together, but brilliant as he was, a life with him just never appealed to her, and so she rejected each of his many attempts at courtship."

"A smart woman," Thomas remarked.

"Pursuing Mary was probably the only thing that made him stay here as long as he did. And that's why I think it really drove him over the edge when she chose to be with me instead. He seemed to resent the town after that, like we weren't capable of appreciating his intellect and thus were no longer worthy of engaging with him. It wasn't long after she and I began a relationship that he left for the seminary, and we never heard another word about him again until now."

"I see. Perhaps that memory has faded for the rest."

"I can't help but remember that feeling every time I hear his sermons, as if my wife is there next to me, whispering in my ear to remind me. William speaks to us as if we are all peers, part of a single collective that is united in one mission. But these are the same people that he once manipulated with ease all those years ago. Part of me knows what he really believes, though: that he is the sole authority on all matters of which he speaks, and we are merely his students being graced with his seminar."

Thomas stepped closer to Henry and lowered his voice. The lantern flame reflected in Henry's eyes as he listened to Thomas closely, the light growing ever brighter with each word from the pastor.

"That is exactly it. William and the other ministers all want you to think that you are not capable or worthy of judging the facts for yourself. That you have to rely on his expertise and his expertise alone. But you are, indeed, the *only* arbiter of truth. And I want to make sure that you and everybody else here is empowered to make that judgment for yourselves.

Good men like you have no other choice currently—

window. Unbeknownst to him, at that moment, Rosemary sat with her back pressed against the wall, slumped onto her bed, rattled after having heard the entire conversation. She sat motionless with her eyes open wide, peering into the void of darkness before her, and thought about the temptation laid before her father—the decision between heresy and righteousness, sin or salvation—as the feeling in her stomach returned once again.

# Chapter 24

ROSEMARY WAITED RESTLESSLY in her seat until the summer winds carried the music from the organ into the classroom, calling her to detention. Her pre-sermon discussions with William had been enlightening for her—not only as much-needed respite from the half-measured lessons taught by Mrs. Edwards, but for the profound, often transcendent, metanoic feeling that grew within her over the course of several weeks. In those moments reflecting upon Scripture with William directly, she at last felt that she was a part of the larger worship in spirit—a suitable recompense for her absence in physical form.

But her meeting with William the day following Thomas's visit felt different. She was filled with an unmistakable sense of guilt, as if there was a sin that she needed to confess—though part of her knew that the penance was not hers to make. While she waited in the chair in William's rectory for him to return from the camp, she was unable to concentrate on the subject of their coming lesson, instead repeating the scene from the night before over again in her mind.

"Have you begun to read the latest I gave you of St. Bonaventure?" William asked as he entered and took a seat across from her at his desk.

"Yes, Brother William," Rosemary replied, snapping out of her daze. "But I'm afraid I haven't finished it yet. I've only been able to read it on the nights when the moon is high."

"What bearing does the moon have on your studies?"

Rosemary was overcome with a sudden sense of trepidation as she considered her reply.

"I don't want my father seeing me with the book. And I know my sister, Abigail, will tell him if she finds me with it. So I've been sneaking out of my bedroom at night and reading on the porch when the moon is shining and the sky is clear."

William leaned back and nodded wistfully. "I used to take pine plugs from the woods and place them in the stove when I was reading in secret. I found that the glow was just dim enough to not disturb the others in the house, but still bright enough to not strain the eyes when reading."

"You used to have to hide your studies from your family too?"

"My father was something of a fundamentalist—one might call his religious philosophy Johannite, primitive. We only had three books that were allowed in our home: the Bible, the Psalmody, and the Book of Common Prayer. Anything else was profane in his eyes. But just about the time I was your age, I began to understand that there was still much to learn and much to uncover on the path of truth, so I would read whatever I could get my hands on by whatever light was available until I left for the seminary."

"I wasn't sure if this was a kind of sin," said Rosemary. "I feel like all of this—the concealed readings, discussing the advent with you here behind his back—goes against the fifth commandment. But is it really wrong to betray my father's wishes if they are keeping me from a better understanding of God, to save my soul when it would be otherwise lost?"

William thought to himself for a moment and slowly stood up from his chair, walking over to the bookcase next to his desk.

"The Bible can sometimes seem like it's filled with contradictions," he said, pausing to pull out and push back one book. "But remember that Scripture is infallible; any perceived inconsistency or contradiction is merely from man's misunderstanding of His word. That's why my father was mistaken all of those years ago when he forbade the readings of anything beyond the holy books. Because man is imperfect, we need scholars like St. Bonaventure and the like to meditate on these often-complex questions before us, to help us understand the nature of the Bible and bring us closer to its true perfection—closer to God."

William continued searching the bookcase as the dust from the shelves glinted in the sunlight.

"You know the fifth commandment well, it seems. It clearly and rightfully instructs us to obey the orders of our parents. But what do we do if our mother's or father's wishes go against those of God?"

William found the book he was looking for and removed it from his shelf, then turned around to Rosemary.

"That is a long-debated question for biblical scholars, who likewise noticed the ostensible variance in Scripture. But they note that, when considering this subject, it is important that we recall one of the most fundamental precepts of our spiritual world: that God is the Father of Fathers."

William opened up the book and began to turn the pages that he had marked and notated at some point in the years prior.

"This is a text by Flavius Josephus, one of the great Jewish historians and authorities on the laws of the Old Testament. Herein he explains the punishment for breaking the fifth commandment, as outlined in Scripture: 'That son who does not requite his parents for the benefits he hath received from them, but is deficient on any such occasion, shall be handed over to be stoned.'

"However, there is an important passage that follows it: 'Honor to thy parents ranks as second to honor to thy God.' Listen to the purposeful juxtaposition of these two thoughts. Josephus specifically outlines the drastic punishment that is reserved for disobeying one's father per the biblical law. But then, if this is but a secondary commandment compared with those that require honoring God, how great must the punishment be for disobeying the Father of Fathers! It is instead a punishment of the spirit, a denial of salvation. It's therefore that God's law is the only law which may countermand those of our parents—lest we face a retribution even worse than a stoning of our mortal flesh."

William shut the book dramatically and handed it to Rosemary as she looked up at him from her chair.

"If there is any doubt that remains, let me further reinforce this notion by reciting the words of Jesus himself from the Gospel of Matthew: 'He that loveth father or mother more than me is not worthy of me: and he that loveth son or daughter more than me is not worthy of me.' So, Rosemary, if you feel that your father is commanding something of you that goes against God, then it is indeed your duty to disobey him."

Rosemary lowered her eyes, feeling a renewed sense of guilt. Her palms began to sweat as William stepped toward her and leaned in closer.

"Now, is there something else you want to tell me?" he asked, casting a dark shadow over her.

Rosemary looked up as William stood before her, blocking the light from the window. She remembered the words between Thomas and her father that had continuously hung in her mind since the night before, the disavowal of the church teachings and the blasphemy that he allowed in his house. Her tongue became dry in her mouth as she debated to herself whether or not to speak them aloud.

"No," she managed to say at last, as she shook her head.

William slowly pulled himself back from her chair and returned to his seat, the sunlight now pouring in on him, as he looked at her with his blue eyes glowing.

"It's important that you come to me should you witness any actions that may jeopardize the souls of you or your family. For we will not get a second chance at redemption after the clouds break in October."

Rosemary nodded her head fearfully, taking in his words as they continued their lesson until the church bells reverberated through the wooden bones of the church.

Dozens of believers clad in white linen lined the pathway to the residential district as Rosemary accompanied Benji home from the school grounds. Looking down at the center of town, they could see that most businesses had shut their doors for the day, and the large majority of worshippers were heading to the church camp for the afternoon services, the spirit alive and electric among them. As they continued past them to the base of the hill where the first cluster of houses was located, Benji paused and raised his eyes to the sky, pointing to the top of one of the homes.

Rosemary stopped with him and looked up, shielding her eyes from the sun. Standing atop the roof was a woman garmented in a flowing ascension robe, her eyes closed and arms outstretched to the heavens. Pushing herself higher on the tips of her toes, the woman puffed out her chest and lifted her shoulders into the sunlight.

"What is she doing?" Benji asked in wonderment.

Rosemary kept her eyes focused on the woman as the light shined upon her face and she inched farther toward the sky. Rosemary marveled at her as she cast away all worldly concerns and continued basking in the sunlight, fully faithful that she would soon be taken.

"She's bringing herself closer to God," she whispered to herself.

Benji shrugged and walked ahead as Rosemary stayed in place, continuing to stare at the woman in white as she held her eyes closed and fervently waited for the Lord to accept her. Rosemary imagined herself there in her place, basking in the brilliant light of Christ, ascending to Heaven as the houses in the town became smaller and smaller the higher she rose. She thought about her family there with her, becoming smaller, too—and considered the coming months that would determine their eternity.

# Chapter 25

BY MIDSUMMER, THE *Calvary Crier* had become a sensation. Every resident in the town, native or pilgrim, had no choice but to purchase a copy twice a week if they wanted to stay abreast of William's sermons, which ran so frequently that only the most dedicated and most ascetic of the lot were able to witness them all in real time. Outside of Calvary, circulation of the paper had increased by more than a thousandfold, and Josiah's small press could no longer stay ahead of the demand.

"We're getting requests for distribution as far as Savannah," Josiah said to William as he accompanied him back to his rectory between sermons. "I don't know how we can keep pace. My press can only produce so many copies per day."

William placed his hand on Josiah's shoulder to allay his concerns.

"God is just. I am certain that He will not condemn the lot of creation out of their own ignorance to the times. We will find a way."

By the next morning, Josiah had received a half dozen offers from local artisans and business proprietors bequeathing their workspace to the *Crier*. Overwhelmed by the benevolence and magnanimity of his neighbors, Josiah accepted one offer, selecting the largest space—that of a devout blacksmith who had recently closed down his business to spend his remaining time at the camp—to build the printing press he had long dreamed of operating.

Over the weeks, Josiah transformed the smithy into a stand-alone press capable of fulfilling the incalculable amount of requests coming in from across the country. At last separating his home from his business, he likewise could finally hire a staff to assist with the enterprise—a pair of copy editors, three laborers to work the machinery, and a brigade of delivery boys who took care of the allocation and distribution duties required to package and ship the publication to the larger markets.

The *Crier* soon became the biweekly vehicle not only for William's latest sermons, but for detailing the zeitgeist of his movement as a whole. The paper quickly conquered local markets across a great expanse of the country—a feat so prodigious that some commentators began to refer to Josiah as "The Napoleon of the Press." But Josiah saw himself as more of a foot soldier than a general, and he took great pride in writing the cover stories himself, which imbued him with a sense of purpose and power as he channeled William's teachings and story into everlasting prose.

*OF ONE ACCORD: A CONSENSUS OF*

*FAITH HAS BEEN REACHED*

*AUGUST 12, 1844*

*Holy, holy, holy is the word! And the word of the Second Coming of Jesus Christ rings true for all men of God who hear. The good Br. William Miller has announced that he has received via post a signed letter from ministers near and far who have studied his interpretation of prophecy in great detail. Foremost experts in all matters spiritual across denominations—Baptist, Methodist, Presbyterian, &tc.—have reviewed his exegeses, cross-referenced the histories which support his conclusions, and validated the mathematics behind the calculations that foretell the coming advent on the eve of October the twenty-second. Thirty-eight ministers had requested the full body of proof from Br. William. And all thirty-eight ministers have now confirmed its authenticity.*

> We, the undersigned, jointly declare that the case for the Second Coming of our Lord and Savior Jesus Christ on October 22, 1844, is unassailable—its support resting solely on the divine and infallible word of God and our Holy Scripture. May He grant us mercy as we rightly begin preparing our souls for the privilege to stand with Him at the eternal throne.

*It is a unanimous agreement—a remarkable testament to the supreme rigor and precision of Br. William's teachings. And perhaps, importantly, this portends a final coming together and unity in Christendom, for as we are urged by the Apostle Paul: "I beseech you, brethren, by the name of our Lord Jesus Christ, that ye all speak the same thing, and that there be no divisions among you; but that ye be perfectly joined together in the same mind and in the same judgment" (1 Cor. 1:10).*

*Truly, our spiritual shepherds have all joined in one mind, one judgment, and one accord that the end times are upon us. Br. William's prophecies have been confirmed by the leading experts, the truth as clear as the sun shines overhead. No one can any longer deny the consensus—let ye who doubt be cast aside with scorn and derided as fools.*

After the letter of certification had been published in the *Crier*, a flood of requests entreating William to guest minister at various congregations came like the breaking of a dam. Pastor and parishioner alike eagerly wrote to the United Calvary Church requesting, often pleading, for William to speak but one sermon in their local venues—and within one week, William had more than twenty invitations to lecture at various congregations across the Hudson River Valley and throughout the Northeast.

The church leaders had been facing an inundation of congregants who were terrified by the apocalyptic pronouncements they read about in the paper, and thus without hesitation they paid for William's transport and lodging in order to help quell the budding frenzy in their towns. In smaller hamlets, tents and makeshift meetinghouses were quickly erected to contain all of the avid worshippers in the region, many of whom traveled from nearby farming communities, fishing villages, and backwoods settlements to witness this once-in-a-lifetime calling. But the more populous towns and cities were better prepared for the visits. Many opened the doors of the larger churches or theaters to accommodate the multitude of worshippers—and as the size of the sermons grew with each new stop, some of the greater destinations used their town squares to host sprawling open-air lectures. Without fail, Josiah accompanied William to every one of the guest sermons to document the great occurrence.

### BR. WILLIAM MILLER PREACHES IN PORTSMOUTH
#### AUGUST 23, 1844

*Br. William received a welcome in his latest stop in Portsmouth, N.H., that would make governors and kings alike green with envy, as hundreds of devotees flocked across the New England coastline to hear him preach. Men, women, and families waited in line for hours under the oppressive August sun, crowded together like a shoal of Atlantic herring to attain the nearest position to the central podium. Young boys sat with legs dangling from the roofs of the seaside homes just to get a glimpse of the reverend and lend an ear to his lecture. Seamen foreign and domestic perched themselves atop the rigging of their ships moored to the nearby wharves in hopes to catch the echo of the sermon and bring the word with them to both the waters and shores anew.*

*Standing amongst the crowd in the clearing by these great piers, Br. William spoke at length about the undeniable proof of Scriptural prophecy. He opened by acquainting the crowd with the vatic signs from the Old Testament that told of Christ's first coming, how they were described in Scripture and how they came to pass. He spoke of the prophet Isaiah, who foretold the arrival of the Messiah with such exactitude that there could be no denying that it was any other than our Lord Jesus whom he referenced—prophesizing a son born of a virgin (Isa. 7:14), despised and rejected by men, wounded for our transgressions, and finally brought as a lamb to slaughter (Isa. 53:3–7). Br. William then turned the conversation to the prophet Daniel, who out from a divine vision states that the time "to make an end of sins, and to make reconciliation for iniquity, and to bring in everlasting righteousness, and to seal up the vision and prophecy, and to anoint the most Holy"—that is, the time when the Messiah would rise from the dead and walk among men— would be seventy weeks, or 490 years by our Gregorian calendar, following the decree of Artaxerxes to restore the temple in 457 B.C. (Dan. 9:24). One could hear an audible gasp of epiphanic understanding amongst the skeptics as Br. William then performed a simple calculation: 490 take away 457 is 33—the year of the Messiah's death and resurrection foretold in Scripture, which came to pass precisely as stated.*

*Br. William concluded the series with a simple pos-tulation: if the first coming of Jesus Christ was prophesized with such accuracy—both in date and in description—then why would one believe that the Second Coming would be any different? For we are told with no ambiguity that "The first man is of the earth, earthy: the second man is the Lord from Heaven" (1 Cor. 15:47). And here it squares that we shall look to the heavens for the second and final coming of the Son of God!*

*By the end of the sermon, all hesitant or nonbelieving were made to be believers, and those already devoted were spurred to perform their spiritual duty and deliver to others the tidings that Br. William had brought to their town. The sermon was so powerful that several ministers were told to have repeated the very teachings of that day to those who were not fortunate enough to attend or be within earshot of the sermon. Local reports indicate that the prophecy of the Millennium was met with such passions of the Portsmouthers that many dozens of men followed behind Br. William's carriage on foot, shouting their thanks and their praises for saving them and delivering these blessings unto their unworthy spirits.*

*Think, reader, of a man who inspires these feelings in so many! And not for the payment of a single penny to his purse—but his is a payment in the joy and satisfaction of bringing salvation to others.*

William's visitations were not without his detractors. Holy men of other denominations and general skeptics often showed up at events to voice their criticism or challenge the authenticity of his interpretations, which William, with years of experience engaging in academic debates as a professor, was well-equipped to counter. Josiah quickly realized that the retellings of these clashes were often the most circulated articles of his paper and found that they, despite the intentions of the naysayers, did just as much to spread the teachings of William as the sermons of his that were met with universal praise.

### *SHOWDOWN IN SALEM AS BR. WILLIAM BEWITCHES THE NONBELIEVER*
### *AUGUST 27, 1844*

*The spirit was hot in the outdoor mall of Salem, M.A., as Br. William's sermon was intruded upon by a dastardly sect of scoundrels and impish dissenters. The leader of the rogues was a man claiming to be a descendant of the settlers at Plymouth Rock, who interrupted a most beautiful and serene homily to levy claims that the reverend was no more than a Pharisee practicing rhetorical priestcraft and spitting blasphemous venom upon the congregation.*

*But our Br. William was not shaken by such rudeness, and called the man to the center floor where he was lecturing, not one modicum of hatred or hint of ill temper in his heart. He asked the man calmly to repeat for the audience the issues to which he associated this charge of priestcraft. The oafish man, suddenly dumbstruck as soon as the eyes were upon him, clumsily laid out his imputation—stating that he believes that preparing for salvation ought not be induced by fear of hellfire or warnings of damnation, for God is merciful and a merciful God forgives and accepts the imperfection of his creations.*

*Br. William, hearing the argument before them, responded in kind with an indisputable rebuttal. "If God is universally merciful," he said to the man, "then you should have no hesitation to curse Him right now—to publicly take his name in vain to prove that you do not fear retribution." The oaf, tongue-tied and now sweating like a pig on a spit, tried every which way to deflect from the point at hand, but still would refuse to take the Lord's name in vain. "My brothers and sisters," Br. William concluded after several minutes of verbal jousting, "I give you your Pharisee." The crowd exploded into laughter and the man returned to the shadows, glowing with shame but perhaps unwittingly responsible for a dozen more souls saved through his own exemplary iniquity.*

As word of the magnificent spectacles of logic ascribed to William's sermons continued to spread, the waning weeks of summer brought upon him a cascade of circuit-tours throughout the region. Although he endeavored to honor as many requests as he could, the timing of the schedules necessitated that difficult decisions be made and certain offers refused. William began to discuss terms and conditions with the local parishes: only those that could fulfill the promise of an ample meeting location would be entertained, and the invitation would not be accepted until the church could prove that their viewing capacity was up to his standards.

Financial inducements quickly became the norm as each of these larger locales battled with one another for William's presence. Donations to United Calvary were frequently advanced, with many parishes outfitting the original camp in Calvary with provisions and supplies from the regions they served, until it became so overwhelmed with imported goods that the parishioners found themselves refusing delivery or dumping the excess food items into the river lest they rot under the sun.

But the most resourceful of the church officials knew the most efficient way to court his favor was the promise of extending the reach of his teachings, and several in the metropolitan centers offered to publish and distribute hard-bound editions of his lectures by way of the larger publishing houses in the cities. Josiah himself negotiated the stipulation that these copies be imprinted with the logo of the *Calvary Crier* and that a portion of the profits from each volume sold would be reinvested in the operations of his paper. The churches were more than willing to oblige.

The requirements of celebrity came naturally to William. At every destination, he and Josiah were provided with bountiful meals and comfortable lodgings, as many a devout innkeeper would remove current tenants without hesitation to make room for the new guests of honor. The stagecoaches provided for the initial excursions soon gave way to steamboat and locomotive when possible; thus, by early September, William was able to deliver ten sermons per week without missing a single Sabbath in his hometown. The invitations were soon coming in with such frequency that William quickly found himself only accepting the requests from the largest urban centers—Boston, Rochester, New York—for these offered him the greatest opportunity for the greatest audiences and, therefore, the opportunity to save as many souls as he could. The rest of the responsibility would have to lay amongst his brethren to continue spreading the word to those whom he could not reach directly.

By the time the heat had abated and the days became shorter, William had successfully preached throughout each of the northeast states—as far north as Portland and as far south as Philadelphia, wherein he decided the city named after the church addressed in the very Revelation of John itself would be apropos to be his final destination before returning home to Calvary for good. At the tour's conclusion, Josiah estimated that some half million Christians across the country were readying themselves for the October date, with William's sermons being preached by proxy as far away as London. The world was beginning to open its eyes to the signs of the times, which were dutifully catalogued by the *Calvary Crier* for all to see.

*A GREAT EARTHQUAKE SHAKES THE NEAR EAST*
*SEPTEMBER 2, 1844*

*Quite truly the world is in its final cosmic turns as we bear witness to the signs foretold in Revelation. News from the four corners of the globe confirm what the most devout of us already know: the sixth seal has been opened, and we are marking the death throes of our earthly existence. Seismic tremors have decimated part of Asia Minor this past week, with reports indicating that the ground has been shaken so severely that the land has split in two. Some fifty thousand souls are said to have been swallowed up in the chasm—the first but not the last victims of God's supreme wrath.*

### THE STARS OF HEAVEN FALL UPON THE RUSSIAN EMPIRE
#### SEPTEMBER 5, 1844

*An explosion in the cosmos disrupted the typically placid plains of the Russian tundra as fiery stars rained down from the heavens like a brilliant blizzard on a cold winter's night. The frozen Siberian forests are said to have thawed from the fire above, transforming the snow into ash and the pines into burning embers. It is not yet clear how many Cossacks and Siberian Eskimos perished in the destruction.*

### A MIGHTY WIND BLOWS ACROSS THE ORIENT
#### SEPTEMBER 9, 1844

*It is reported that at least seven great typhoons appeared throughout the Orient, from the Arabian Sea to the coast of Japan. The cyclones have left nothing but decimation in their wake, blowing countless ships off course, flooding rivers, uprooting crops, and razing the straw villages across the region. The winds seem to have appeared suddenly and without warning, leaving countless unprepared to fortify their land. Chaos and famine have followed in course—and many fear that some will be forced to resort to cannibalism.*

*MOUNTAINS MOVE OUT OF PLACE IN THE PACIFIC*
*SEPTEMBER 15, 1844*

*An historic volcanic eruption in Sumatra was spied from a nearby whaling ship. Reports from the twenty-two crew members aboard indicate that the cataclysm has disappeared an entire island—sinking it into the depths of the ocean, where now only the blackness of the abyss remains. A young seaman on the ship described the subsequent scene as the ash and clouds fomented in the sky in baleful yet familiar apocalyptic prose: "The sun became black as the night, the moon red as blood."*

*By all accounts, the evidence has mounted that the sixth seal has indeed been lifted. And as we humbly await the seventh and final seal, we pray for God's merciful deliverance.*

The once-resounding atmosphere of anticipatory jubilation and unity in Calvary gradually mutated into an undercurrent of fear and disquietude as the Day of Atonement approached. The residents had read the stories of the signs from abroad with unease as they wondered if their town would be spared from much of the death and destruction. The end times, and what they entailed, were only now truly dawning on the believers in town.

Many retired completely from their daily lives at the start of the final month, removing themselves entirely from the day-to-day tasks that would soon be of no concern to them, and focusing their efforts exclusively on worship and ceaseless acts of contrition. Those who did not participate in turn were often looked upon with suspicion and tacit disdain—for they were not taking the times as seriously as they should.

*WAITING FOR THE MIDNIGHT CRY*

*SEPTEMBER 23, 1844*

*The town of Calvary has become a model of spiritual purity and righteous behavior for the coming of our King. All but a small sect of nonbelievers are busy preparing for the end times, and those who choose to remain in denial know to keep to themselves and stay in the outskirts of town. Br. William's tour has ceased, as he has vowed to spend the rest of the time we have amongst the people who first accepted his teachings not six months prior. It is now every dusk that the worshippers congregate at what has come to be known as "Ascension Rock"—the lawn next to the United Calvary Church that overlooks the western horizon.*

*The sermons may be going on day and night at the camp, but the spirit of the advent lives on throughout the town as well. One cannot walk down the main street of Calvary without passing scores of men and women dressed in the garments of piety, the white ascension robes; one cannot stand in a shop without overhearing a recitation of Br. William's blessed lectures passing through the mouths of the patrons. Everywhere in town, residents are affixing crosses upon their front doors, passing out literature of the advent, painting verses from Revelation upon their silos. And the most salient reminder of all may be the countdown markers that are changed before sunset daily, noting just how long we have until our judgment come.*

*To quote Br. William, there is now a harmony seen throughout the community just as there is a harmony seen throughout the Scripture. All of the mysteries and numerologies that confounded generations of scholars are finally revealing their perfection as God's plan is unfolding; and likewise that spiritual harmony is no doubt imbued in the minds of His followers. The prophecy and signs of Christ's imminent return are becoming clear to all, and we the people of Calvary now open our arms for Heaven's embrace. God bless us all.*

Josiah read through the final proofs for the week's issue through his pince-nez glasses, punctiliously ensuring that no inaccuracies could stain the perfection of the subject matter. The time for printing additional issues was running out, but he would continue to work until the very last grain of sand fell in the hourglass. He removed his pince-nez and placed them on the counter before him, then folded the proof back as it was given to him and handed it off to one of the three press operators, motioning to his colleagues that it was ready to be printed. Bidding the men adieu, Josiah put on his hat and proceeded across the town before the day's end.

Josiah walked down the street beaming with a pride that he had been seeking to find all his life. He breathed in the crisp autumn air and felt a sense of duty fulfilled that day, just as he had with each run of his paper since it had taken on a new focus, and he now walked with his chin high, chest held out.

"Good day, Brother Josiah," a gentleman said to him as he passed by.

"Hello, Mr. Young," a young lady greeted him courteously on her way home.

"Thank you, brother," another said, stopping to shake his hand. "The latest *Crier* may have been the best one yet. You're doing the Lord's work, my friend."

Brightened by the words of the passersby, Josiah looked at the homes on the main road and imagined what was happening at that very moment in each. In one, a family prays over their final month of dinner rations. In another, the shopkeeper puts away the rest of his wares, concentrating his efforts exclusively on worship and atonement. And in another, the children count down on their calendars until that day will arrive, when all of the worldly pain, all the hunger, all the distress is lifted up from them as the Bridegroom awaits their ascent.

Josiah arrived at his own home and stopped before the sign that he had placed on the walkway to his front door. Observing the dusk falling in the sky, Josiah replaced the wooden numbers on the post with eager anticipation: 29 DAYS HE SHALL COME.

## Chapter 26

ABIGAIL KEPT HER head low as she walked through town. Although the brim of her white calash concealed her face, she could still feel the eyes of her neighbors upon her. The time of the end was approaching, and nearly everyone seemed to be on the brink of panic. Fear had evolved into paranoia—and those who were not at the daily worship were singled out with suspicious glares.

"That's the last of the shipment," Nathaniel said to her behind the counter of his general store. "I'll be closing up shop for good by day's end."

Abigail took the supply of herbs ordered by Dr. Clarke and placed them in her wicker handbasket.

"Thank you, Mr. Harriman. Please give our regards to your family," she said, turning to leave.

"Abigail," Nathaniel called out as she stood at the exit. "Tell your father that it's not too late, that there's still time for him to join us. The Lord will accept even the tardy so long as their atonement is true."

Abigail nodded uncomfortably and walked out the door. The town center had been particularly quiet for the past several weeks; stores were now closing permanently, their owners and employees retiring to spend their remaining time at the camp worship throughout the day. The shutdowns had rapidly progressed not long after the *Calvary Crier* began reporting on the terrors and calamities across the globe when the sixth seal was opened. The people read in great detail about the cosmic upheavals, the natural disasters, the conflagrations, destruction and death—millions throughout the world suffering and longing for the coming of Christ to end their tribulation—as they were waiting for the same reckoning to come to their small town. It was imminent and it was inevitable. All they could do was pray that it would be quick.

As Abigail continued on the road home, the prevailing silence was disrupted by a commotion in the distance, near the foothills up to the church. Seeing a number of residents assembled at the crossroads, she redirected herself from the pathway toward her house to observe the ruckus.

"My neighbors, strangers from afar, you must not simply obey an order because a consortium of those in power will have you believe it's true. You have been beguiled by florid prose and deceitful, alarmist rhetoric for too long! And I fear you all may lose yourselves to hysteria forever if this willful submission continues on."

Thomas stood at the base of the hill with the shadow of the United Calvary Church extending over him from behind. His once-youthful face seemed to have aged twenty years in the weeks since Abigail had last seen him. His hair was frizzled and mad, his cheeks full of stubble. His eyes appeared as if he had not had an adequate night's sleep in months, his mind perhaps too fraught with worry and disillusionment to allow for a proper rest.

Thomas spoke at the junction of the path to the camp and the town proper, intentionally positioning himself at the most traveled intersection where residents and new arrivals were forced to pass if they wanted to attend William's worship. He had gathered a hostile crowd.

"The devil's words!" one man shouted. "Close off your ears, friends, lest ye be tempted in the final hours."

"Lies and deceit!" another hissed. "Nothing but foul duplicity."

"Liar!" another called out. "Liar! Devil! Bastard!"

Thomas was unbent by the truculent clamor. Abigail could see him sweeping his determined eyes across the growing crowd, hoping that there was even one face behind the panorama of ascension robe hoods who might listen, who might begin to think for themselves and consider the possibility that their current reality was not as it seemed.

"Has not history taught this lesson to us before?" he continued. "Have we learned nothing from the countless false preachers who drew multitudes into the path of wickedness? Let us not forget what happened to the sorcerer Barjesus when he encountered the Holy Spirit inside the Apostle Paul—blinded for his iniquitous prophecies, just as he blinded his followers from the truth. And just as he was not able to see the sun for a season, so, too, have you all been clouded by the lies of the reverend throughout these past months."

The oratorical devices of the pastor only angered the crowd further. Thomas's exhortation was soon drowned out by the countervailing shouts of contempt from the gathering. The most ardent believers had had enough of the public blasphemy and attempted to silence any further opposition to their cause. Their vitriolic words were quickly replaced by an artillery of apples, quids of chewed tobacco, and whatever small objects were in their hands, hurled at Thomas before each person turned their back to him. Throughout the barrage, he never yielded.

"Do you see what madness William's words have wrought?" Thomas asked as he wiped the pulp of the fruit and the wads of spit off his overcoat. "If you find yourself repulsed by this ugliness, tired of these jackals skulking amongst the ruins of our once-great community, then join me at the new church of Calvary—where we will worship in love and commune, as God intended."

The crowd began to disperse without further disturbance when the church bells started to ring. With no one around him who would listen, Thomas finished cleaning the mess off his clothes and began to walk alone back to his home.

Abigail watched helplessly from afar. She hadn't spoken to him since the night he came to their door. It was too painful for her to consider. Things used to be simple during their budding romance; it seemed to progress naturally, burning like the steady wick of an overnight candle. The secrecy with which they saw one another was not born of indecency, but out of practicality. It was merely to keep their lives stable until they were ready—until the town was ready. But everything changed when William returned. She had sensed something different inside Thomas the moment he walked past the pulpit; there was a new fire that glimmered in his eye. She knew that flame was brighter than that of the simple wick of their relationship—it was one that grew more intense the greater William's influence became; perhaps one that could never be extinguished. And still, she missed him.

Leaves fell before her as she followed in his trail. The country road to Thomas's homestead was dying a vibrant death as autumn began to overtake summer. The once-verdant pastures that lined the dirt paths on the outskirts of town were beginning to desiccate and dry into straw. The wildflowers had begun to wilt and sink into the ground; and the bees that once splashed in the pools of pollen crawled wearily across the infecund stamens of the faded flowers in a hopeless search for any remaining sustenance. Untended rows of Indian corn and apple orchards speckled the scenery with yellow and purple as the fruit went unharvested and fell to the ground. Abigail could smell the rot in the air.

As she approached the homestead, Abigail heard a dull pounding in the distance. She felt her chest, thinking for a moment that it might be her own heartbeat, and continued toward the open barn where she had spent her idle days with Thomas some months before. She entered quietly and found him inside with a half-constructed pew turned on its front as he hammered together the wooden base. She waited for him to notice her.

"Abigail?" Thomas asked, at last lifting his eyes to the familiar silhouette at his door. "What are you doing here?"

"I waited until no one would notice me following you back," she said, stepping deeper inside the barn. "You seem to have made a lot of enemies in such a short amount of time."

Abigail looked around the small barn that had once been nothing more than a slipshod receptacle for hay bales and secondhand farming tools donated by the ranchers to the church. But Thomas appeared to have transformed it into something dignified. The floors were swept clean, the roof was re-thatched and impenetrable to any leaks, the chicken coops were replaced by several neatly arranged lamp tables. The barn now held four rows of benches gathered intimately together, facing a modest pulpit in the rear, which was situated beneath a wooden crucifix that hung from the ceiling. The sun shined through the window above the entrance and onto the altar, angled in a perfect square.

"That may be true, but for every ten who curse me, there is one who will see the light." Thomas rose from the ground.

Abigail walked down the rows of benches before her and inspected the seats. "How many people have joined your congregation?"

"Only a handful of regular worshippers so far. The sexton, his wife, and a few others who can no longer stand the pomp of the services at the camp. I expect there will be more at the end of the month. I hope that I can count you and your family among them."

"I don't know . . . My father likes to stay out of these kinds of things."

"Your father is a decent man. I've always respected him, and always will no matter what he decides to do. But this isn't the time to remain neutral. It's important that he realizes this. You can help him."

Abigail clutched the basket with her brother's medication, wrapping her fingers tightly around the handle.

"I don't know what's going to happen then. Whether

you're right, whether William is right—but I do know what is happening now. I saw the end of your speech in town before. I'm afraid you're going to get yourself into trouble."

"There is such a thing as good trouble. I can't just stand by while this nonsense is happening in front of my eyes."

"But why can't you, Thomas? If you think this will all be disproven, then why not simply wait and let them come to that realization themselves? Why risk all of this antipathy? Why not just remain silent?"

Thomas sighed and turned to face the light.

"I don't know," he conceded. "I am aware that I could simply bite my tongue and wait for this all to pass. God knows it would have made these past few months easier on me. But there is a gnawing feeling inside me that refuses to accept it. It feels like if I do not say something, if I remain idle while this madness continues—then it will all become normalized. Even if I do appear as the lone voice crying out in the wilderness, that of a raving contrarian, at least I know that I was speaking the truth."

"So you are doing this for your own personal satisfaction then. If no one listens to you, then that is the only value this has."

"I believe there is great importance in virtuous opposition, even if it ultimately changes nothing. I cannot quite explain how or why, but I know that it exists. There must be a purpose to it. Perhaps even if only God recognizes it."

Thomas turned his eyes to the crucifix above.

"So help me, I must continue. No matter how many lashes, floggings, and defamations I must endure, I will not fall to my knees unless it is the Son of God who appears before me."

Abigail felt tenderness and compassion radiate through her as she saw the exhaustion and torment on his face and the toll that the stress was taking on his soul. She wanted to wrap her arms around him, press her hands over his wounds, heal him with her warmth and give him the strength to continue. But she knew she couldn't—it was not her sacrifice to make.

"I have to be going now, Thomas," she said achingly. "My brother needs his medicine. Please stay safe, for me."

Abigail pushed away the sadness and turned to the door. Lowering his eyes from the cross, Thomas turned around to reach out and place his hand on her back, to touch her softly and let her know that the light was still there for her. But she was already gone.

# Chapter 27

ABIGAIL STOOD BESIDE the stove and methodically turned a pestle to the side of the mortar as she ground the supply of herbs for her brother. With only one day until the Day of Atonement, Harriman's general store was already long closed, and she had to make sure that they would get all they could out of what remained of Benji's medicine, turning a small quantity into a fine paste to maximize the oils needed for the vapor.

"The rhythm can sometimes be soothing, wouldn't you say?" said Henry as he entered from the back door, covered in the leftover thickets of his wheat field.

"Anything to keep my mind off of tomorrow. You can feel the anticipation in the air like it's being carried by the wind."

Henry wiped the sweat off his forehead with his sleeve and grabbed a loaf of bread that Abigail had placed in a basket near the doorway. With no other food in the house,

Henry tore off a small piece and ate it dry, making do with what little he had at his disposal for lunch.

Abigail's deliberate strokes were interrupted by the sound of the front door opening, as Benji darted inside with Rosemary entering behind him.

"What are you two doing home so early?" Henry asked as he raised his eyes from the table.

"Brother William gave the students a holiday today and tomorrow," Rosemary answered. "All of town is preparing for the millennial services."

"Is that so?"

"Everything in town is already empty," said Rosemary. "The only people we saw on the way home were those ministers and their drivers arriving in the ports."

"I suppose that'll be the last batch of visitors we'll have. There must be a thousand new faces here just in the past month," said Abigail.

"At least that. And Mrs. Edwards says there are millions more preparing on their own. The whole congregation is at the churchyard. We should be sure to leave early so we aren't stuck in the back tomorrow."

Henry placed another piece of bread in his mouth.

"We aren't going to United Calvary tomorrow," he said.

The house fell quiet as if the air was depleted from the room. Only the sound of the pestle scraping resumed as a palpable tension emerged between Rosemary and her father.

"But the entire town will be there," she argued. "All the kids at school, everyone we know!"

"Pastor Thomas asked that we join him for services in his new church. I've put it off since then out of concern for how you and your brother and sister might be perceived by the others. But it's almost over now, and I think it's only right we accept his offer tomorrow."

Rosemary snapped her eyes to Abigail. "Was this your doing?"

"I don't know what you're talking about," said Abigail. "This is father's decision, not mine."

"You just want to be with him, even if it sends us all to Hell, don't you?"

"Hold your tongue, Rosemary," Henry said, stepping forward. "I don't want to hear that kind of talk in this house."

"But Brother William says that Pastor Aleman is a false preacher. That he's trying to ruin salvation for everyone who follows him."

"The pastor has served this community well for these past few years. And I believe it will be doing right by him to join his congregation, to at least hear what someone else has to say for a change."

"First you say that you don't want us at the worship because you don't want us worrying about the rapture. But now it's here! There's no more ignoring it."

"It's my decision—and it's final," said Henry.

Rosemary began to shake with resentment as she stared at her father.

"You don't even care, do you? You don't care about me, you don't care about Benji. These are the last days that we have on earth, our last chance at salvation. And you want to tie us down with you while everyone else ascends to His altar!"

"That's enough of this," said Henry. "We are going to the pastor's church, and we shall go there together, as a family."

"We'll spend our eternity in perdition, so long as we go

as a family," Rosemary grumbled, as she stormed off into her bedroom and slammed the door behind her.

"Rosemary! Get back here!" Henry demanded, to no avail.

As the rancor settled in, Benji stood up from the table and slowly followed after his sister in an attempt to comfort her, closing the door quietly behind him.

Henry bit the side of his cheek. "The devil is starting to overtake that girl, I tell you. Ever since she turned thirteen."

Abigail pondered to herself for a moment and walked over to stand beside him.

"Father . . . may I make a request of you?"

Henry remained silent.

"I think we should go to Reverend Miller's service tomorrow."

"You, too, now?"

"What is the risk in it, truly? If nothing happens, then there is no harm done. And if it does . . ."

"Something doesn't sit right with me about those sermons. True or not, I don't like what they're doing to people in this town. Look what they're doing to my own daughter, my own blood."

"But that's just it. Shops are being boarded up, farms abandoned. Our neighbors, everyone in Calvary, they believe this is the end."

"And I don't begrudge them for that. Let them believe what they believe. This is the United States of America, after all. But I am doing what I think is best for us. It's my choice to make, not theirs."

"Are you not concerned that Reverend Miller is right about all of this? That this might really be the end?"

"Of course I'm concerned!" Henry exclaimed. "What fool would not have fear struck into his heart when hearing that crack of doom."

Henry turned his back and walked over to the window to look outside.

"I never told you this . . . but I think you're old enough now to hear it," he began. "About three years ago, when your mother first got sick, Dr. Clarke pulled me aside and informed me how little time she had remaining. He wanted to tell me in private as not to compound her suffering with news of the prognosis. I'll always appreciate him for not saying it in front of her; but God help me, not an hour later I broke down at her bedside and let it all out. I told her that I would tell you and your brother and sister—so that you all would know to cherish every last day with her before she was taken by God. But do you know what she said to me? I'll never forget it—she didn't have a tear on her cheek or a moment of hesitation in her heart. She sat up and took my hand in hers and said, 'All of our times must come one day; but when we live life preparing for death, we're not doing much living at all.'

"And so that's why I never spoke a word of it until her last moments were here. Rosemary still hates me for it, I think. But these were your mother's wishes. She didn't want to spend what little time she had left in dread, in sorrow, in despair, surrounded by the inevitability of death. She wanted those final months filled not with sadness or anxiety, but gratification and joy and fondness; not worrying about what was to come, but rather, until the very end, only thinking about the present. So I shall keep that vow to her, and I'll go across lots to make sure her children don't live their lives in fear of the end, until the moment that our maker says otherwise."

Fighting back tears, Abigail stood behind her father as the image of her mother came across her like a wave. She caught her breath, speaking at last.

"You've shielded us for all these months the best you could. But I think it's possible that those final moments just might be here now. And I know mother wouldn't want to look down and see them being spent with such animus between you and Rosemary. Come what may, at least we can face it together as a family."

Henry mulled over her proposal to himself in quiet rumination. Without a word, he turned from the window, walked to the children's bedroom, and opened the door. He found Benji sitting at the end of the bed, hands folded as he stared at his shoes dangling below him. Rosemary lay down on top of the covers with her face buried into the straw pillow.

"Let me have a moment alone with your sister," said Henry.

Benji immediately obliged and slid off the bed, leaving the room and closing the door behind him. Henry sat down beside Rosemary at the edge, displacing her position as he weighed down the side of the mattress. Rosemary shuffled her head and lifted the corner of her eye from the pillow.

"Now I know you don't want to hear it, but you have to understand that I am doing what I think is best for this family. I don't expect that you'll understand now, but when you're older and have your own children, I believe it will become perfectly clear."

"'When you're older, when you're older,'" Rosemary

repeated. "But what happens if tomorrow really is the end and that time never comes?"

"Then we'll be together to see it through."

Rosemary turned herself over and sat up in the bed. The anger upon her face dissolved, and Henry saw the true fear that remained latent inside her finally surface.

"Father," she said softly. "I'm afraid."

"There's nothing to fear," said Henry, placing his hand on hers. "You don't have to worry about dying, I promise."

Rosemary shook her head as her eyes teared up and shimmered in the light.

"I'm not afraid of dying . . . I am afraid for you."

"Afraid for me?" Henry repeated. "Of what?"

"That you'll be left behind."

Henry could finally see the truth in his daughter's eyes as they sat together in silence. He thought about Abigail's words from earlier as Rosemary turned her face back into the pillow and attempted to will herself to sleep. Perhaps there was indeed a greater thing to fear than death: separation—irreversible, eternal separation. And that he could not allow to happen, whether in this world or the next.

The following day, the Smith family put on their Sunday clothes and headed for the United Calvary Church.

# Chapter 28

CLOUDS GATHERED ATOP the steeple as the church bells tolled one final time. The gray blanket upon the lower stratosphere carried the sound waves in a steady current across the town, resounding throughout each home and each farm across the valley below. It was a calling for all to hear: the time was upon them.

As dusk approached, the last of the worshippers made their way up the hill toward United Calvary to congregate on the lawn overlooking the western horizon. Henry and his family, freshly bathed and adorned in their best church attire, followed in the end of the line as they walked up the slope to the church landing and convened with their neighbors.

Not a word was said among them. Scores of townspeople and recent transplants waited demurely with eyes lowered, mouths dry, and hearts beating rapturously inside their chests. To Henry's right, the normally outspoken George stood silently with his hands tucked into his breast pocket, forsaking the pleasantries that he'd built his life upon for quiet introspection. To his left was Marigold, dressed entirely in black, staring into the gray void before her with anxious hope that the dead would soon be rising amongst them. Dr. Clarke stood with his wife and son, peering down at his pocket watch as he counted down to the precise moment of the sunset. Jacob waited nervously with his family huddled closely at his side, his arms wrapped around them as if to ensure that if one ascended, they would all travel together.

Reverends Storrs, Marsh, and Fitch led a group consisting of several of their more intrepid parishioners who'd accompanied them from across the state to Calvary for the final services. Many desired to end where it all began, under the auspices of William's ministry, and perhaps be closer to Heaven atop the sacred hill. But the unease was present even in their eyes, as Josiah guided them to the correct spot on the lawn where they would have an equitable viewing of the sermon. Josiah made quiet small talk with the three ministers and their foreign parishioners, remarking what an honor it must be for them to be spending their final hour in the place where the secrets of the prophecy were first revealed. He, too, then took his place near the edge of the overlook, so that his position would be the closest to William when the time came.

The white hoods of the ascension robes dotted the gathering like snowcapped peaks of a mountain range. Henry could feel the hypnotic zeal emanating from within them and thus sought out a cluster of worshippers wearing traditional Sabbath clothes like his own family. Locating a clearing beside them with a view of the horizon, Henry led his children into place as they positioned themselves amongst the crowd. All was quiet as they stood and waited, until he heard a familiar voice whisper discreetly.

"Henry, you brought your family," Nathaniel observed. "I'm so glad you decided to join us after all."

"Well, it's important that we all be here together, isn't it?" he said, looking down at Rosemary, who responded with a clement smile.

William stood at the foreground of the precipice with Josiah at his flank and his back to the congregation. There was hardly a sound in the atmosphere as they waited for him to begin the services—the bells ceased tolling, the birds were no longer calling, no chatter amongst the crowd. All that could be heard was the howling of the wind.

The sun fell behind the gray curtain and began to bleed into the horizon. William raised his hands to draw the attention of the worshippers and cupped them upward to the heavens. The silvery sky outlined his figure as if he had been traced by electricity. All eyes were on him.

"The time is upon us," he announced as he turned to face the crowd. "The hour of that auspicious day of which the prophets so sweetly sung."

There was a dull whimper amongst the worshippers as the preparation of the past six months began to bear its fruit. The infant child of the young parents from Raleigh started to cry, as its mother attempted to lull its wailing with a desperate rocking in her arms. All of time seemed to be condensed in the moment William commenced the services, and discomfort and dread pulsated throughout the gathering.

"When I first realized how soon the end would befall us, I, in truth, knew not how to react. I love this world. I love its people. It moves me to bask in God's creation, to feel the warmth of the hearth in the winter, to drink the fresh water from the brooks in the spring, to hear the sounds of nature proliferating in summer, to be with my community in worship every Sunday throughout the year. And so my heart sunk in my chest and froze like a block of ice as I first learned that all of these joys would be left behind at dusk on this day, never to be experienced again."

Henry gulped as he took in William's words. He considered how he had spent his time on this earth—laboring from sun to sun, attempting to fulfill the responsibilities of fatherhood and the God-given challenge of raising his children alone. He thought about his missteps and travails and wondered if he had done right by his maker. He thought about his wife waiting for him behind those silver clouds, about her judging him for his works and forgiving him for his shortcomings, and considered in earnest, for the first time, if he was truly about to meet her again.

"But fear should turn to hope when we think of the eternal bliss that this moment will bring," William continued. "This is not an end, but a beginning—the beginning of Christ's glorious millennial reign. For as soon as the sun goes down, a sun brighter than one thousand stars shall rise in its place, the light from the Lamb filling the void where the darkness would be. And we shall be saved—O we shall be saved—from this life and brought into His everlasting kingdom! When I close my eyes and open them again, I hope to see all of you with me, robed in the spotless garments of Christ's righteousness, crowned in glory, as we stand by His side. We will meet again, my friends."

William turned around to again face west, and he watched

the sun scrape across the horizon, cutting lower with each passing second. Josiah took one step closer and whispered imperceptible words to him, dabbing the tears from his eyes.

Henry looked around him as the crowd seemed to consolidate, as if all were looking to one another to find unified solace from their fear.

"The time has come," said Reverend Marsh to his group as the sun sunk lower.

"The prophecy of Daniel shall be fulfilled!" Reverend Fitch exclaimed.

Many in the crowd began to sway nervously. Some began to sing hymns, masking their dread with a veneer of hope as they watched the sun slowly disappear. Henry could feel the tension resonate through his children as they gathered closer to him.

"It's but a few more moments until the world will be silent," Reverend Storrs assured his parishioners, who were all beginning to shake. "A few more moments, and then Christ shall come!"

The wind carried the mewling of the infant and the cries of the other worshippers across the lawn, as many began to break down in tears in the final seconds.

"I'm scared," said Benji with a sudden twinge of panic.

Abigail rubbed her brother's back consolingly as they watched the sun continue to sink. The infant cried louder and more frequently with each passing moment. The congregation was now one singular huddled mass.

The bottom edge of the sun at last crossed the horizon, and William puffed his chest into the air.

"He is appearing," he announced exuberantly. "I feel Christ near!"

The inevitability of the ascension caused many to lose their wits and begin to scream out loud. Some fell to their knees while others raised themselves closer to the heavens on the tips of their toes. Rosemary squeezed her father's hand as tightly as she could.

"Behold! It is accomplished!" said William. "The Bridegroom cometh!"

The sun fully disappeared behind the western horizon as William closed his eyes. The screaming stopped—even the cries of the infant ceased. There was not a stir in the air as the congregation collectively held their breath. Darkness fell upon the hill.

Several moments passed in what felt like an eternity. Many were afraid to look out ahead of them. William at last opened his eyes and peered out across the skyline. Nothing had occurred.

Time passed by slowly as a faint murmuring began to propagate amongst the crowd. The murmurs grew to whispers, whispers to chatter, chatter to debate. After several minutes of waiting in place, some of the more dispassionate members of the group waved their hands dismissively, and started to leave.

Henry looked around him, his heart returning to normal pace and the feeling returning to his legs. Little by little, the congregation began to dissipate. He breathed a sigh of relief as those around him continued to depart. It was all over.

"Come on, let's go home," he said to his children.

William continued to stand in place, his back to the crowd as the night began to fall. Henry gazed at him one final time with a peculiar sense of pity. He did not understand it, but his heart stirred for the man—further even, as he looked down to see Rosemary wiping tears from her cheeks, still clasping on dearly to his hand as they left the hilltop.

The crowd emptied from the lawn—the skeptical, the devoted, the ministers, and even Josiah, who waited in good faith for the full thirty minutes of silence—until William was left alone on the precipice. He continued staring ahead, unmoved, his eyes affixed to the sable void that was materializing beyond the gray sky.

# Part Two

---

"Because thou hast seen me, thou hast believed:
Blessed are they that have not seen,
and yet have believed."

# Chapter 1

THE WORLD KEPT turning. The winds continued to blow. Fire hung bright in the day, the moon
reflecting its radiance in the night. Time crept by
slowly and the days marched on. The dead remained in the
ground; the living still walked the earth. Nature continued
its course. Temperature fell with the leaves; seabirds flew
south; color faded downstream. Animals burrowed for the
winter; the ground began to harden. Hearts of men kept
beating. But they, too, were hardened. Although the world
had not ended, for them, it would never be the same.

The cold draught whistled through the narrow gap of
the entranceway as Abigail shut the door behind her. The
nights had swiftly succumbed to the autumn chill, the
remaining warmth of October given unto the coming Feast
of All Saints. Abigail shivered as she entered her home and
took off her wool coat and frosty bonnet, placing an empty
wicker basket on the floor. She paused to warm herself by
the fire.

Abigail extended her hands toward the hearth that glowed with the dull embers of a fallen oak. As the heat reached her fingertips, her mind began to thaw. She thought about the prophecy that had not come to pass, the static she felt throughout the atmosphere, and the latent discomfort that still lingered inside her. It had only been a few days since that evening, but it felt like a thousand years. She had thought she might be filled with relief—a finality to the general worriment and angst that struck the town. But yet, there was still a gnawing fear, an anticipation of what was yet to come, of which she could not let go.

The stove was not hot enough to shake the cold from her bones, and Abigail abandoned her momentary solitude. Her father was waiting for her. Removing her hands from the lukewarm heat, she turned tepidly toward the children's bedroom and stood in the doorway without a word, peering inside. Henry and Rosemary flanked Benji on the bed, who desperately curled the covers over his shivering, supine body. His face was ghostly white and saturated with febrile sweat; he was barely conscious as he moved his head side to side in a liminal delirium, his eyes shut tight. Rosemary sat on the edge of the mattress with his hand clasped in hers, while Henry positioned himself on the other side, gently stroking the hair back on his forehead.

An odd feeling of sentimentality came over Abigail as she watched her family together, united in woe. Before her was a scene of purity and love, captured like a work of Renaissance art that she had read about in school yet could never understand why it was considered divine. But she knew then: in that brief moment, they were all as one—Benji's illness like a loose thread that wove her small family together, and sometimes seemingly the only thing that kept it from coming apart.

Henry spoke to her without turning from the bed.

"Were you able to find more medicine?" he asked quietly, as not to wake his son.

Abigail shook her head soberly. Benji had become progressively sicker since the long night at the churchyard, remaining bedridden in the days since. She watched her brother's chest heave as he struggled to retain each noseful of air he was able to take in. Her feelings of pity and sorrow quickly turned to anger as she recalled her failed attempts at procuring more help from the vacant town. She was angry at the residents for continuing in their hermitage; she was angry at the believers who held on to the idea that their ascension was still to come; and most of all she was angry at William for allowing others to remain paralyzed in fear. She knew he could put an end to it all with one simple address, one plain admission that he was wrong.

"I'm afraid the stores are still empty," she said. "I'll have to go again tomorrow, first thing in the morning."

"Did you try knocking on Mr. Harriman's door? He must just be taking his time restocking his wares."

"Several times. Their lamps were on—I know they were home, but no one responded."

Henry lowered his eyes and shook his head in disbelief.

"The streets are completely deserted," she continued. "Hardly anyone has left their houses since that night, other than the outsiders packing up their camps to return home. Nary a wagon, a peddler—not a single sound a stone's throw from anywhere in town. It seems everyone is afraid to come outdoors. The only face I recognized passing through was

Marigold Chandler. Poor woman looks like she has seen the devil. Probably has nothing more to do but roam the streets with the church still closed."

Henry looked out the window at the pale shadows from the moonlight. He began to stroke the whiskers of his beard in quiet contemplation as he absorbed the news.

"We'll have to conserve as much as we can until the town reopens," he said. "There's still enough supply of the medicine here for now if we are judicious with it. We have a half bin of wheat plus two sheep and four hens. And I have the squirrel traps set out in the woods."

Benji groaned and tossed in the bed. Henry caressed his forehead again to allay his pain.

"Is there any sign of Reverend Miller?" he asked with a note of bitterness.

"No one has seen him in nearly a week," Abigail replied. "I'm beginning to think that he skipped town after that night."

Rosemary raised her eyes and looked at Abigail askance.

"Brother William wouldn't just abandon us like that," she said.

"Of course he would," said Abigail. "His prophecy has become unraveled; the con has been exposed in front of the whole world. I suppose the public shame is too much for him to bear."

"That's not true! He told us that there would be a long silence after the opening of the seventh seal. You said it yourself—the world has been quieted."

"Forget the silence—open your eyes, Rosemary! Can you not see what has happened? This was all one big lie. And you fell for it most of all."

Rosemary averted her eyes as she attempted to stave off tears of anger.

"I bet you're glad this all happened," she said under her breath. "You and that lover of yours both."

Abigail felt her heart skip a beat as her father raised his eyebrow and turned his head toward her.

"Excuse me?" she said. "You don't know what you're even saying anymore."

"I know more than you think," said Rosemary. "You've doubted everything Brother William said this whole time. You wanted him to be wrong so that Pastor Aleman could take over the church again."

"The nerve of you to say such a thing!" said Abigail, stepping toward her sister. "You haven't the slightest idea of what I've done for you in these past weeks—following along with your stubborn demands like fools ourselves just so you wouldn't break this family apart. But we can only tolerate your fable-chasing for so long. It's time to wake up and admit your error so we can all get back to our lives as normal."

"If you say that I am wrong and Brother William is wrong," Rosemary began, "then you're saying science is wrong; that history is wrong; that God is wrong. And you'll be going straight to Hell if that is the case. You'll see."

"Enough!" Henry growled. "You're going to wake your brother."

Abigail and Rosemary continued glaring at one another but withheld any further bickering as they watched Benji stir more aggressively in bed.

"It's all behind us now," said Henry. "It's time we focus on getting through this winter with the short supply of food and medicine that we have. It's not going to be easy, but once things return to normal, this will be our season to begin anew."

The antipathy faded as the hardships that stood before their family began to dawn on Abigail. Benji winced in pain as he lay beneath the wool, attempting to stay warm while his body was burning from the inside. The weather was getting bitterer by the day. The cold wind cried outside.

Henry stood up from the bed as Abigail and Rosemary put their enmity aside for the evening. Abigail opened their dresser, pulling out her night-robe, while handing Rosemary her matching set. Henry lowered the lamp in their bedroom as they prepared for sleep, where the only warmth that could be found was from the bodily unity of the three children together in the bed.

# Chapter 2

JOSIAH'S BREATH HUNG in the cold, stagnant air of the printing press. The machinery for the *Calvary Crier* rested inoperable beside him, a heap of iron and wood that had not moved its gears since printing the final edition the week before. Behind it, amongst the towers of leftover paper stock, stood Reverends Storrs, Marsh, and Fitch, who had gathered together in the dark room to discuss what must be done next.

"I've received some troubling accounts of the situation at my home parish," said Reverend Fitch, holding a letter in his hand. "Mine may be the nearest to Calvary, but I am sure that it is not the only church feeling the repercussions of that night. Our acting pastor writes to me that the skeptics have now taken it upon themselves to persecute the believers. Meetinghouses preaching the October date have been pelted with rocks and eggs, advent signs on the homes of the worshippers have been vandalized, and there has even been some talk of tarring and feathering anyone who was peddling the *Calvary Crier* from their newsstands."

"And what of the congregants?" asked Josiah. "Are they holding true to their faith?"

"Our pastor writes that the plaintive wailing of the believers can be heard throughout the city in the evening time—cries and lamentations to God for forsaking them after they had sacrificed so much to be saved. But he notes that the only sounds louder and more ubiquitous in Albany are the jeers from the naysayers during the day, directed at the members of our church as they walk the streets in shame and embarrassment. Confronted with the ridicule, even the most devout are slowly beginning to admit that they were mistaken. Some are renouncing their views outwardly, while others are joining in the taunts and sneers as if they were never believers in the first place. And a few have been seen dyeing their white robes black as a public act of contrition."

"So just like that, they have abandoned their beliefs, cast aside all of the signs and the science like rotten food? A movement of a million strong ends in a single night?"

Reverend Fitch closed his eyes and nodded. "I am told that believer and nonbeliever alike have come to know that day as 'The Great Disappointment.'"

Josiah began to pace the floor with manic perturbation as he deliberated to himself. Just over a week ago, the building had been warmed by the constant turning of the press, the floors treaded with the boots of a dozen employees— all volunteers who refused to take a single penny for their labors. Josiah had not heard a word from any of them since the Day of Atonement. Most, he assumed, had returned with the other outsiders to their hometowns with heads held low, filled with regret that they had invested their time and sweat into a seemingly empty cause. There was now no one left but him to operate the machinery, and he knew the newspaper would be doomed if he missed the next issue.

"At ease, Brother Josiah," said Reverend Storrs.

"Bringing yourself to conniption is not going to help us find the answers we need," added Reverend Fitch.

Josiah stopped pacing and took a deep breath, his mouth tasting of the acrid odor of ink and oil.

"What do you propose we do then?" he asked, his voice trembling with desperation.

"Firstly, we must locate Reverend Miller," said Reverend Marsh. "He is the face of this movement, after all."

"I agree. The people will be looking for him to issue a statement one way or another," said Reverend Fitch. "Josiah, do you have any idea of where he is?"

"I stood beside him that night in the churchyard after the last of you had already left," Josiah replied, regaining his composure. "When it was clear that the hour had passed, I begged him to return inside before he freeze to death in the evening cold—but he wouldn't stir or say a single word to me. He just kept staring into the sky, waiting. That was the last I saw of him."

"And what came of him after that?" asked Reverend Marsh. "Surely he did not become a pillar of salt."

Josiah had heard the rumors slowly circulating through the town. Some said that William absconded the next day across state lines, returning to the university where he'd formulated this very prognostication in the decades past. Others claimed that he was spotted at the port, chartering a merchant ship to England or France, taking off with the

donations given to United Calvary to live like royalty over-
seas. And the direst scenario, which chilled him most to
hear—that after the shame and humiliation of that night,
William wandered alone and eventually took his own life,
the agony of failure too much to handle.

But the thoughts were too profane for Josiah to consider
aloud. For now, all that mattered was that they were without
their spiritual shepherd, and they would have to find a way
forward without him.

"William is not the only one who propagated this
prophecy," Josiah said. "My paper, your preachings. Every
leading expert, every scholar—biblical and otherwise. You
all validated it as the truth. The ministers of all Christendom of Upstate New York agreed, for land's sakes."

Josiah leaned over his machinery as he began to work
through a plan in his mind.

"I believe it is time that we start to generate a response.
But we do so without taking away from the gravity of the
reverend's prophecy or implying in any way that the overall
mission was wrong. Rather, we search our hearts and find an
explanation for why it did not transpire in the precise way
that we once believed."

"And what might that explanation be, brother?" Reverend Marsh asked scornfully.

"Everything that Brother William foretold was aligning
perfectly with Scripture until this very last moment. The
opening of the seventh seal, the half an hour of silence, the
first trumpet—they should have come to pass exactly when
he predicted. But maybe there was some kind of error in the
calculation, some small aberration that was not accounted
for when coming to this specific end date. Everything else

in his teachings was correct—and perhaps when we revise the calculus, we see that it will only be another short while until the final moment is here."

"Go ahead and tell them that, and you will bring down the whole of the Convention with you," said Reverend Fitch. "We all signed a letter confirming the accuracy of the numerology, if you recall. How can you ask us to amend the conclusion of the prophecy without coming across as liars or buffoons?"

"Then perhaps it is a matter of interpretation. We tell them that the date of the Second Coming was correct, but the manifestation of the prophecy is not to be taken literally. There have been some who said Christ will return only in spirit—that the advent is not something to physically behold. 'The kingdom of God cometh not with observation,' says the Gospel of Luke. Brother William always stated that the eschaton is the unification of Christ and His church, and that the church is the spirit within us all. It is plausible, then, to reason that the kingdom of God shall exist for us beyond the flesh. That seems to be an elegant reconciliation, wouldn't you agree?"

"Mr. Young, you are not a priest," Reverend Storrs countered. "Scripture is unambiguous about Christ's return in bodily form. Do not forget his ascension on the fortieth day after his resurrection. Jesus did not rise to Heaven in spirit—but in body—and the Acts of the Apostles tells us that 'this same Jesus . . . shall so come in like manner as ye have seen him go.' Anyone paying attention to the services over these past several months will realize this. So do not think so lowly of our congregants to believe that they will not see through your so-called elegant excuse for this Disappointment."

Josiah paused and thought to himself, raising his eyes from the press before him.

"Then what if the ascension of the righteous actually did occur?" he posited. "What if the number of worthy were so few in this wretched world that we did not witness a single soul rising among us? Could it be that the Millennium has begun—that we were all left behind, and this suffering we feel in our hearts marks the beginning of our eternal torment?"

"What a thing to say!" said Reverend Storrs.

"Foolishness!" Reverend Fitch jutted forward.

"Gentlemen," Reverend Marsh interjected. "We did not come here today to rationalize the events that did not come to pass. We are here to talk about the future—a future where I believe life will go on just as it always has. Disappointed those in our congregations may be, they cannot live in such sorrow forever."

Reverend Marsh pressed against his cane as he leaned in to speak to the men candidly.

"I used to worry about the dangers of change—these new sects and denominations springing up all around us and capturing the ears of our parishioners. It's that very fear which brought me to this town in the first place. But I've learned something since my stay here: the hearts of men can be as capricious as the wind. These people will see their neighbors dressed in white, and they will soon weave themselves the same linens so they do not stand out as contrarians; and just as quickly as they join them, so, too, will they shed their garments when they are no longer fashionable with the masses. It is not the first time they have done this, and it will not be the last."

"And what are we to say in the meantime?" asked Reverend Storrs. "What tack can we take that will not lead to a stain on our ministry?"

"We concede that we were led astray by a single man—by the counterfeiting and contrivances of William himself," said Reverend Marsh. "And then, we simply wait for them to put it out of their minds and move on to the next trend."

Reverends Storrs and Fitch looked at one another and exchanged a confirmatory nod, satisfied with the unified line of the elder minister. Josiah stared at the men with revulsion.

"I cannot believe what you are saying. Don't you understand what will happen if you admit that all of this was wrong? We put all of our efforts into this mission and to raising awareness of the gravity and imminence of this cause. All of us were firm in the belief that this was not merely a prediction—this was an inevitability. If we back down now . . . your ministries, my newspaper—they'll never trust us again!"

Josiah's pleas failed to move them as the reverends settled into a firm concord. They would acknowledge the error of their teachings, deflect blame unto the intimidation and coercion of William's church, and allow the seasons to pass and hope that the memories would quickly fade.

"That is something you must work out on your own, Josiah," said Reverend Marsh. "We've been away for long enough, and it's time for us to resume our lives and our commitment to God."

One by one, each of the ministers walked past Josiah to gather what was left of their parishioners and sail away from Calvary, never to return. The door shut with a loud, carceral echo as Josiah watched the vestiges of his final allies exit his building for good.

Josiah felt his spirit leave his body as the draught curled across the corners of the empty room. He began to think about the future that lay before him—being forced to close his press as the circulation plummeted, driven out of Calvary in ignominy, moving west to some Indian territory where word of the Great Disappointment had not yet managed to reach. Worse than his own fate, he thought about the future of William and of Calvary itself—reputations desecrated, now laughingstocks to the world.

Josiah slumped down amongst the towers of papers as the sheets gently floated to the floor from the force of the wind. For the first time since William had returned, he was alone.

# Chapter 3

WITH THE SHUTDOWN of town operations persisting longer than anticipated, Thomas saw fit to hold daily sermons for the gradual influx of residents who came to outwardly accept the erroneous nature of William's calculations. In each day after the Disappointment, new parishioners hesitantly began to fill the converted barn, slowly shedding their reservations as they realized they were in safe company, free from judgment and criticism. The church eventually became a sanctuary for them, a refuge where they were finally able to come together and speak openly for the first time since the spring, where they could have the freedom to express their misgivings about the past six months, and could at last feel comforted by the fact that they were not alone in their skepticism or disbelief.

Of the twenty worshippers who constituted the parish by the end of the first week, only eight had attended his small services on the Day of Atonement. But in Thomas's eyes, there was no special privilege for the inaugural members, nor was there any malice to those who arrived at the truth later than the rest. To him, the thought of treating the more recent arrivals differently was not only immoral but impractical, as he hoped to continue growing the community and one day restore some comity to the town at large. And so, he welcomed all of the new congregants with open arms, ensuring that they would feel in good spirits despite their errant ways.

"'Rejoice not when thine enemy falleth, and let not thine heart be glad when he stumbleth,' says the Lord God," Thomas reminded the congregation in his Sabbath sermon. "Remember that it is a sin to relish and gloat, but a virtue to forgive those who were once led down the wrong path and now choose to travel the road of enlightenment."

Thomas looked out at the audience before him. Nearly all of the pews that he had installed were filled for the first time since building his temporary house of worship in the summer. The narrow corridor of the barn was only wide enough to fit a handful of parishioners on each bench; but despite the limited space, there was one row that he asked to always be kept empty—the seats that he hoped would one day be occupied by Abigail and her family. He pictured it clearly: the door of the church gently gliding open, light flowing in as if the face of God were shining before him; her visage there, backlit by said grace, a silhouette etched in the entryway, slowly walking in with a demure but relieved smile and taking her seat with her family in front of him. Thomas looked at the unoccupied pew in the first row and back to the door and waited longingly for that day to come—the moment when all of the chaos and bedlam of the year could be put behind him and his life could move forward once again. But for now, he waited.

"Over the coming days, I hope that we will see even more victims of the adventist chicanery come forth to join us here in this church. Perhaps these will be the formerly devout, those who once stood on their rooftops each night waiting to be taken, those who gave up their farms or their shops to spend their days worshipping at the camp. Perhaps they will be the ones who were the vilest in spirit, who out of fear and insecurity would spit at us, tell us that we are the wicked and the damned for refusing to believe in the same divinations as they. Or perhaps our new congregants will be the neutral parties, those who closed their eyes and said nothing as the others hissed and cursed at you while you walked to join us here in worship.

"But Scripture tells us how we must accept our brethren who deign to humble themselves and enter this church, ready to start anew, regardless of their past iniquities. We are told that we must greet them with a holy kiss—a kiss of peace—a phrase that is repeated no fewer than five times in the New Testament, and that is central to the entire foundation of our congregation. This is not a kiss in the literal sense, but rather it is simply a metaphorical embrace from neighbor to neighbor. It represents a wish for concord and harmony—and an end to suspicion, contempt, disagreement. It is a gesture of forgiveness and reconciliation, unity amongst brothers. And we must remember that the Bible does not say for us to *end* our services with this symbol of peace—but to *begin* them with it. And that is exactly the kind of new beginning we must endeavor to make."

The parishioners nodded along as Thomas continued, putting aside past grievances with those who sat beside them.

"As we humble ourselves in this church, we thank God for showing us what can happen when we fool ourselves into believing that we can fully understand the divine ways in which He works. What a providential lesson for us to be taught these past months—one that more and more are beginning to comprehend by the day. Just as the bird knows not how or why the wind moves under its wing, we, too, must learn to be carried by the divine forces that move this world. For we know the end is not to be known: 'of that day and that hour knoweth no man, no, not the angels which are in Heaven, neither the Son, but the Father.' My friends, we must trust in God that our judgment will be just and that our faith will be duly rewarded—no matter when that time of deliverance may be. Amen."

Thomas escorted his congregants out of the church and into the dew-dropped pasture in front of his homestead, shaking their hands as each prepared for the venture back to town or to their own farms or ranches. Despite his urgings, he felt like he was shaking hands with freed captives—prisoners held for so long that they were always looking over their shoulders, living in constant fear that they would be sent back. There was still a latency of doubt hidden deep in their eyes, and he knew his words could only do so much.

As the last of the parishioners retreated into the forested horizon, Thomas paused to reflect in the brisk autumn air. It was a cold but beautiful morning on his farm, a breeze-less day with a boundless blue overhead. But across the tips of the trees, a collection of clouds hovered over the town. Thomas looked at the hill in the distance and could make out the shadowy outline of the steeple of United Calvary amongst the silver swirl. The church the elder Reverend Miller had built with his own two hands—that now risked being torn down by the tongue of his son.

Thomas felt a sense of nostalgia as he looked at the church and recalled the wayward path that had eventually brought him to where he was that day. He'd spent his youth plucking from the proverbial pear tree, a popular and roguish boy who made a name for himself as a schoolyard jester. The daily lessons in class failed to maintain his interest, and so he turned to foolish behavior to keep himself entertained—making snide and irreverent remarks to his teachers in front of his classmates, leading a band of peers to dalliances with mischief and minor thievery, stealing bottles of rum from the sailors at the ports, letting pigs loose from their neighbors' pens to run roughshod throughout the town. But it was at that church where the course of his life began to correct itself, and where his journey toward righteousness began.

He recalled that day when, in a desire to shock and entertain his companions, he stood on the steps before the church door and dared God to strike him down in that very moment, lest He truly not be all powerful. "Tremble before me as I prove my might," he said mockingly as his friends chortled in return. And just as he uttered the profane dare, the large hand of Reverend Samuel Miller fell across his shoulder, and he spoke the words Thomas would remember forever: "The Almighty exercises more power in granting mercy than delivering wrath."

The reverend took an interest in the boy from then on, perhaps in part owing to his own son's absence, and invited Thomas to make penance for his blasphemy during services after school. The church was typically empty except for the two of them, and thus the sermons were often more akin to Socratic dialogue between him and the reverend. Thomas found himself returning daily, long after whatever penitence was needed had been reached, for the private lessons were far deeper and more interesting than anything he was learning in school. Although they centered on a single book, Thomas felt challenged and humbled for the first time as they explored the cavernous depths of Scripture, new questions arising as he thumbed through each leaf that illuminated the path before him.

It was on his seventeenth birthday that he asked to be baptized—not out of fear for what would happen if he did not, but out of the love he had for God's boundless love. With Samuel performing the ceremony in front of his family and his community in the warm waters of the Hudson, he gave himself to God and committed his life to his maker.

All of the years of ennui-induced rebellion were long behind him under Samuel's tutelage at the church. By eighteen, he had become the first new member of United Calvary's clergy since William had left for the seminary some years before. And while Samuel remained the principal minister, Thomas was happy to help with the sermon preparation, to keep up the church grounds and interior, and even assist with the duties of sexton when needed. It gave him a satisfaction, a novel feeling that he belonged and was fulfilling his duties to himself and to his creator—and he would repay Samuel in whatever way he could for this gift that he had given him.

Samuel had rarely spoken to Thomas about his son. But

in his final weeks, he confided to him that he believed William was likewise on the winding path of truth, and that the road would one day lead him home and away from the distractions of academia and the higher class of society. It was here that he belonged, he told Thomas, and his final hope was that he would realize his place in due time. And so when he asked that Thomas one day cede control of the church to William, Thomas obliged out of good faith to his mentor and kept his promise.

He reflected on the vow he'd made with a helpless feeling of remorse. There was no correct action he could have taken. If he refused to relinquish the church to William, he would have caused a rift in the town and would have broken the dying wish of the man who had helped him find his purpose in life; and in keeping his word, he set a course of strife and discord that stretched far beyond Calvary. But still, he could never have known what was going to ensue—and he had to put this chapter in his life behind him as well.

Thomas turned from the sight of the church and began to walk back to his home. He thought about Samuel's words to him, about the journey that William was undertaking just as Thomas himself had taken in his youth. He had a sense of empathy and understanding of the man as he wondered where he might be at that moment. He, too, must still be on a wayward path—but Thomas prayed that he would soon correct his course toward enlightenment.

# Chapter 4

ALONE SHADOW PASSED by the church as the waning sunlight glowed upon the face of the structure like a dying ember. It was a sorry sight to behold—the once-vibrant building, overflowing with faith and prayers and music and calls of the Lord's name, was now dormant, resting as if there was no one left on the earth except the solitary wanderer.

*Perhaps the world really did end. Perhaps I am the only one remaining who did not ascend into His arms.*

The figure walked to the back of the church, past the empty school building as his shadow extended farther upon the hill with the setting sun. Vestiges of abandoned shelters, discarded provisions, and tattered tarpaulins dotted the path before him like incongruous cobblestones leading to the larger tent in the center. The banner continued to flutter from the masthead atop it as a cruel reminder of what once was expected: THY KINGDOM COME. He paused to watch the words undulate in the wind and shook his head in despair.

*O Lord, what can console me when thou hast forsaken me? My life, my studies, my faith in thee and thy infinite wisdom all brought me to this moment; and the moment has passed without deliverance. I beseech thee to show me the way as thou once showedest me before. For where can I now walk when the light no longer shines upon me?*

The figure pushed open the canvas door and peeked inside to inspect the empty space. The anchors that once kept the tent firmly planted into the ground had been raised, leaving gaps between the grass and the canvas where the cold air could wildly wriggle itself inside. The entropy of the atmosphere and the gusts from the hillside lifted the loose corners of the tent and allowed for the pastel light to shine through and illuminate the open room. With no soul in sight, he entered.

The canvas bobbed in the wind as he set foot inside the vacant hall. The tent appeared to have been abandoned in a hurry, like the ruins of Pompeii or the salted ground of Shechem. Everything was left behind exactly where it had remained at the end of the final services—sheet music resting upon the portable organ, hymn books tucked underneath the wooden benches, and Bibles left open atop them. The wind screeched as it passed through the small gaps under the canvas and swirled across the room, the cold updraught turning the loose pages of the Bibles like the deft movements of an invisible hand.

Seeing the desolation of the once-glorious camp was too much to bear. The figure pulled back the door and hastily made his way outside.

*My Lord, if thou hast turned thy back on me, then I must turn myself to the words of thy vessels for guidance. Thou know-*

*est I find consolation in the great men before me who dared attempt to understand the mysteries of thy ways, just as I have likewise dedicated my life to those same pursuits.*

*Let them help me find solace now. "Narrow is the mansion of my soul; enlarge thou it, that thou mayest enter in. It is ruinous; repair thou it." This open church—this is the mansion of my soul, for it was from my soul that I found my mission to build it and through my soul that I preached thy word within it. And now it, too, is in ruin and disrepair, and I know not where to seek shelter. O saints, burn the smoke of thine incense to signal the way!*

He ambled slowly toward the precipice of the hill that overlooked the town. Candles were beginning to glow from within the windows of the homes below—hundreds of souls moored to the earth still. Perhaps that meant that he was not alone after all, that they, too, felt as wandering stars emitting twilight, lost and disconsolate that their God had not accepted them into His kingdom. Or perhaps it was indicative of a more sorrowful state: that they felt no such desertion, and had already begun to move their lives forward, abandoning their holy cause.

The figure hung his foot above the steep descent, daring his conscience to consider how easy it would be to end it all in that instant.

*How can I have been so wrong, O God, when I was so certain with every fiber of my being that I was right? What else must then be illusory? Where else must I be mistaken in the midst of such feelings of certainty? Is the sky not blue? Is the water not wet? Is there no danger from a fall if a body were to leap from this cliff?*

*No, that is not the same, my Lord. Others can confirm the*

*truth of those examples for me if I begin to question my facul-
ties of reason. But the realities which I begin to doubt are those
within myself: whether I am a good man, whether I am living
according to thy will. If I could have for so long gone on with
such surety that my translation of thy word was unerring and
absolute, then how can I thus go on with faith in the rightness
of myself?*

He placed his foot back on the grass and steadied his
stance. It would not be today. Others before him had been
through worse—and now their spirits were as eternal as the
words they had written.

*Is it Boethius to whom I may turn, the martyred and per-
secuted of thine early sons, when thou hast cast me away, my
Lord? He, too, finds himself abandoned by the whims of Fortune. "Thou hast found out how changeful is the face of the
blind goddess."*

*But Lord, thou art not blind—thou rewardest thy servants
justly in kind for their faith! I followed thy plan, I followed thy
path back to this town where I was born and where I discovered
thy love. And I preached as thou toldst me to preach, yet I have
now led so many of my friends to despondency. And why?*

The figure walked back to the front of the church to
descend the hill into the heart of Calvary, where the narrow
pathway turned to pavement as the terrain became more
level with the horizon. No living souls stirred in the vicinity, but the figure nonetheless tightened the white hood of
his ascension robe around his face to ensure that his visage
remain in the shadows and his identity be concealed from
any who might pass.

*Aquinas teaches us that no man can behold the truth unless
it is illumined by the light of the invisible sun, which is God. If*

*the truth is a work of art, we are merely the chisel; and therefore truth ought be credited to He who giveth the light, just as the art ought be credited to the artist and not the instrument. Lord, thou shinedst on the truth for me once—was it that I was just a faulty tool?*

*Where was it that I was led astray? I dare not question what was written by the hand of Moses and the prophets thereafter in whom the Holy Spirit resided. No, should there be any fault, it is the fault of man—the fault in our worthless works and my understanding of them hence.*

*Perhaps it was the histories that took me off course. I lie awake ruminating over details that I once thought were settled in my work long ago: was the end of the pagan rite of daily sacrifice misrecorded in the time of Clovis? Was the year copied incorrectly in the Dark Ages as the records passed from empire to empire, kingdom to kingdom? And that twelve hundred and ninety years began one or two years later—and we are thus one or two years behind the eschaton?*

*Or perhaps it is an error in my own calculation and a weakness in my understanding of the ancient languages? Was it the Rabbinic calendar to which I should have been ascribing the Day of Atonement rather than the Karaite? What meaning would that have to the interpretation of Daniel? Perhaps a difference of months until the blessed day when the Son of Man returns.*

*I may ponder these distinctions and minutiae endlessly, but it brings me no comfort. For then how do we explain the signs of the times, all that we have witnessed across this year of tribulation with our own eyes? O God, please grant me thy light!*

Making his way to the base of the hill, he stood at the crossroads of the church and the town and surveyed the landscape before him. Dusk was turning to night, and the few who were outside were beginning to return home. Those in the town at this hour seemed to be drifting without purpose, no goods in their baskets nor lanterns in their hands to guide their way. They appeared as if they were in their fortieth year in the desert, bereft of hope that the Promised Land was near and beginning to lose kinship with the others in their tribe. He observed this in two pairs of townspeople as they silently passed each other, their eyes averted, looking down only at the road ahead—as if they shared only a common shame that could not be admitted nor could be taken away.

*Was it for my pride, O Lord, that thou hast forsaken me? A pride that I did not speak, but may have felt in the deepest cockles of my heart, to believe that I have solved thy profoundest puzzles and uncovered the eternal mysteries of thy plan?*

*No, how shameful to think! What pride that would be now to propose that thou hast delayed thy Son from redeeming the whole of the world just to teach one wretch a lesson about pride. But then why? What motive am I missing, my God?*

The figure walked through the center of the town as those remaining on the street gradually disappeared inside. He looked into the houses he passed along the way as families were sitting to eat their dinner together behind the windows. There was an air of solemnity in each scene he observed, as they slowly raised the food to their mouths without speaking a word to one another—always just staring ahead in a vacuous daze.

*I recall the words of Augustine, who repeats the plea: "Say unto my soul, I am thy salvation," who begged for that nourishment just as I beg of thee now, Lord. Look at thy creation in this house of pain. Though they have food on their table, it gives them little sustenance now, my Lord, since thou hast left us wanting. But the Bible is a feast of reason. Be there something in Scripture that can satisfy the hunger for an explanation? Speak to us, O God!*

The cold air carried him through the residential district as he continued passing house after house on those empty streets, winding his way to the outskirts of the town, finding the same solemnity in the rooms of each family. But as he neared the windswept woods, a cluster of brittle autumn leaves tumbled before his feet and rolled across the road, attracting his eye to the words that were painted on the fence before him: FOR AT THE TIME APPOINTED, THE END SHALL BE.

*The words of thy angel Gabriel! At the time appointed, by thou, God. Thou art the architect and maker of all things, and if thou decidest to unmake your creation, then it is only thou who decidest when. Of course it must be that thou hast a grander plan!*

*Please forgive me, my Lord, for these terrible thoughts that have passed through my mind. Thy plan may not be clear to me yet, but I implore thee to grant my understanding in time, and I have faith that thou wilt it provide. I know that thy light, as dim as it may seem, will only appear brighter the darker these times become. And the sustenance these poor people so greatly need will be revealed to them—through me as thy merchant, or otherwise, my God—when the time is right. "The eyes of all wait upon thee; and thou givest them their meat in due season."*

The figure continued walking along the perimeter of the town as blue gave way to black and the night rested upon Calvary. Early in the evening though it was, the residents were not of the heart to remain awake for longer than needed, and the lanterns inside each home began to turn off one by one along the cobblestone rows.

*Is it thus thy mysterious plan, O Lord, to see that thy grace is thousandfold repaid after the despair in which we are left? I come back once more to Boethius:* Quam multis amaritudinibus humanae felicitatis dulcedo respersa est! *"With how many bitternesses is the sweetness of human felicity blent!"*

*I must think about what felicity can be had from waiting in sorrow without giving up hope, should the moment of deliverance finally come. What joy it must be to think a beloved is lost at sea, only to find them returning after years of continued faith that they had not perished. And for thou, the most beloved of all, to return as such would bring an indescribable joy infinitely more than our shipwrecked lover, for thou art our Lord God, thou from which all love springs and propagates.*

As he continued to ponder the nature of God's plan, the figure stopped outside a forested path and sat upon a rock with a vantage of the whole lot of Calvary. He watched as all of the light disappeared from each home, until the town fell into complete darkness. As he lowered his eyes, feeling as though he again was the only inhabitant of the world, he caught sight of one beacon in the distance—a glow from one solitary home before him that shined like a lighthouse in a tempest of self-doubt. Raising himself from the rock, he proceeded to the light as though drawn by a magnetic force and followed it like a North Star.

*O please, Lord, let this sensation in me be that of thy guidance that is rekindling in my heart. I feel it now, that same splendor I felt as I first started to truly comprehend thy works, as I began to decipher the meaning of Daniel and John. But I know now that that understanding was incomplete, that I did*

*not follow thy guidance clearly, for I am imperfect, and how
can one who is imperfect truly fathom perfection?*

*Thy words are now coming to me! "Reprove not a scorner,
lest he hate thee: rebuke a wise man, and he will love thee."
And how I strive to be as wise as a man can be. And how I love
thee, my Lord, and my love for thee shall grow stronger, for I
have faith that thou shalt correct me in my interpretation of thy
word. Please, Lord, show me now the error of my ways! Help
complete my grasp of thee!*

Finding the light amidst the darkness, he approached
the home slowly and peered inside the window. He could
feel the warmth radiating from their lantern from outside the
glass as it brightened the interior of their single room. Inside
he saw a family—a mother, father, two children—kneeling
in prayer, their hands clasped, eyes closed. He watched them
intently, and a feeling of understanding began to come over
him. Theirs was a light that was still burning bright while all
others were beginning to dim.

*Is this the light which guides me to thy blessedness and thy
glory? Is this the light to which thou hast led me? My Lord, could
this be that sensational, divine feeling that Augustine described
of when he came to know thee? "Thou calledst, and shoutedst,
and burstest my deafness. Thou flashedst, shonest, and scatteredst
my blindness. Thou breathedst odors, and I drew in breath and
panted for Thee. I tasted, and hunger and thirst. Thou touchedst
me, and I burned for Thy peace." My God, is this it?*

William pushed his hood back with his hand and felt
the brisk air upon his face. This family had answered his
prayers, and now he would answer theirs in turn. In that
moment, God's plan and the final remaining mystery of
Scripture had been revealed to him. He was renewed.

# Chapter 5

JOSIAH OPENED HIS bloodshot eyes and lay in his bed languidly. Each morning since the Disappointment had been the same for him. For a brief moment, his consciousness would remain snugly tucked away in the sanctuary of a dream, removed from the external realities of the world. But as his eyes adjusted to the light, the same dismal truth materialized day after day—and his hopes were fastly fading behind it.

This morning was another bitter realization that their cause was over, the final blow struck by the sharpened trident of the three departing ministers. Spurred by his mind's waking recognition of their abandonment, Josiah sluggishly removed himself from his bed and walked outside, past the countdown marker in front of his home, and across the empty street to his printing press. There was nothing more he could do to advance the mission, and he knew it was time to pack away the excess supplies and the movable parts of the machinery and close the operation for good.

Shoulders slouched and arms heavy, Josiah summoned what little remained of his willpower to force himself to audit and collect the materials throughout the day. Every box of paper stock and every barrel of ink were monuments to his failings; every calling card for his distributors was a harsh reminder of how much loss was swiftly bound to befall him. As he finished carrying the wooden crates across the floor, he lit a candle to inspect the intricacies of the machinery and attempted to calculate how many of the parts he might be able to sell downriver. The equipment was in good condition, only used for a few short months, and new publications were springing up in Manhattan almost every week. Perhaps it would garner enough for him to pay a fare for his journey west.

Josiah lowered his head and began to weep, not just for the end of his dream, but for the beginning of the misery that awaited him. He feared that this new life would be a return to his previous one—a life where those with less knowledge than him were in charge, where no one would listen to what he had to say, where verity was anything but a virtue. He leaned against the machine and pounded his fist against the metal frame, losing himself to his tears—until he felt a sudden rush of cold wind behind him.

Josiah turned around and found William standing at the doorway, garbed in a frayed white ascension robe and clutching a Bible in his hand. There was a mystical gleam in his eye as he stood there, as if he had seen the Morning Star and its glow had become etched in his iris.

"Brother William! You've come back!" he gasped.

"While the Bridegroom tarried, they all slumbered and slept . . ." William began, entering the room as if in a trance.

Josiah stared back at him in wonderment as William removed the hood of his robe and walked farther inside with heavy, plodding steps.

"And at midnight there was a cry made: 'Behold, the Bridegroom cometh; go ye out to meet him.' Then all those virgins arose, and trimmed their lamps. And the foolish said unto the wise, 'Give us of your oil; for our lamps are gone out.' But the wise answered, saying, 'Not so; lest there be not enough for us and you: but go ye rather to them that sell, and buy for yourselves.' And while they went to buy, the Bridegroom came; and they that were ready went in with him to the marriage: and the door was shut. Afterward came also the other virgins, saying, 'Lord, Lord, open to us.' But he answered and said, 'Verily I say unto you, I know you not . . . '"

William moved toward Josiah until they were face-to-face. William's eyes appeared to not have seen any rest in days—dried out and drooping like a cave, open only under the influence of some divine or cosmic stimulant.

"Watch therefore," he continued, slowing his speech so Josiah would comprehend clearly, "for ye know neither the day nor the hour wherein the Son of Man cometh."

The wind blew the door shut and bent the flame of Josiah's candle like a forceful gale upon a loose sail. Several moments of silence passed as Josiah attempted to gather his words.

"Forgive me, Brother William, but I don't understand," he admitted at last.

"Matthew, chapter twenty-five. It is the final piece missing from my interpretation of the timeline."

"But if you cannot know the hour," Josiah ruminated,

"then how have we for so long and with such certainty dis-
seminated the date of October the twenty-second?"

William placed his Bible on the table.

"Brother Josiah, I have walked among the people since
that night, ever treading the path of enlightenment. And
at my darkest hour, it came to me like a brilliant light sent
from Heaven: that date that Daniel and John led us to recognize as the time of the Second Coming is but the first and
earliest of which we can expect the Bridegroom to return.
That He has not called for us yet does not mean we have
been forsaken; rather, this is all a part of His divine plan to
ensure that we are prepared for our eternity together. It is
now more important than ever that our faith remain strong,
for we have entered the most critical test in all history. And
if we are to save the people of this community from damnation, I will need your help to explain to them why the
advent did not pass as we once said."

"I am here to offer you any assistance you need. But
things have changed since you've been gone that you must
be made aware of. The other ministers have already left town
with their congregants and are on their way to sully your
name as we speak."

"Let the rats abandon the ship! They have their words,
and I have *the* Word. I may have made an oversight in
my explication, but Scripture cannot be wrong. To deny
the imminence of the advent is to deny God's word. Do
you understand?"

"I do," Josiah said with a new emergence of tears in his
eyes. "Just tell me what must be done."

"Wet your pen in the ink, and heed my words," William
instructed. "Together, we will need to deliver this news in

the *Calvary Crier*, and by tomorrow morning, it shall be on the front step of every home, every tent, and every barn in town."

His heart beating like mad, Josiah dashed over to the crates of supplies and removed a pen and inkwell. Locating the closest paper he could find, he glided to his desk and brushed off the dust of inactivity that had gathered over the course of the week. William continued to stand while Josiah readied himself for dictation, pulling his pince-nez from his breast pocket and lifting his head to signal that he was prepared to fulfill his duty.

"Blessed is he that waiteth," William began as he paced across the room as if it were a pulpit. "The time of the ascension has passed without incident. But we must take care not to doubt the veracity of Scripture, which tells us that the Bridegroom is soon to come. Rather, we must instead ask ourselves why we were not ready to accept Him—why we were too busy looking upward, not inward, for salvation.

"We may find the truth in the Parable of Ten Virgins from the Book of Matthew. In this passage, we, the loyal and patient children of God, are likened to ten virgins who await the coming of their Bridegroom on the eve of their matrimony. As the Bridegroom tarried, the ten virgins took rest and waited to be summoned to their eternal union. But when that midnight cry of the Bridegroom resounded, only the wise who had readied their lamps were ready to enter His chambers, whereas those who were unprepared were forever rejected from sharing in His grace.

"This Tarrying Time in which we now find ourselves is the same test from God. It is our Lord's way of unmasking the imposters; it is His way of exposing the devils who feign faith to immanentize their salvation, the wretched pretenders who will pack up at the first challenge of spirit. And so now our faith will be tested most forcefully, as we await the midnight cry for ourselves."

Josiah's hand began to tremor as he not only transcribed the speech, but listened deeply to the elusive truth he desperately sought each waking morning. He pressed on, careful not to err or misconstrue a single word, as William continued without pause.

"How, then, can we be readied to meet the Lord when we are awoken from this sinful slumber we call life? Some may read the parable and say simply that we must find the lamp to guide our way. But, good Christians, we already have the lamp: God's word, the Scripture—for His word is a lamp unto thy feet, and a light unto thy path.

"It is therefore not the lamp that we must seek, but the oil to keep it burning; and the oil that kindles His word is in the actions and preparations we must perform to make these grounds worthy for the Holy Kingdom. Rejoice, brothers and sisters, for we have been given this Tarrying Time as both a challenge and a blessing from God—to cleanse ourselves and our land for the Bridegroom's return, and to render the oil through the tryworks of penitence and belief.

"Salvation requires that we work together, to separate the wise and ready from the foolish and unprepared. The hallowing of our grounds begins on the coming Sabbath—where all who wish to prepare shall gather inside the United Calvary Church if ye truly yearn to be saved."

Josiah raised his eyes from his desk as William completed his recitation, watching as he turned away and located a seat against the wall, then promptly sat down on the chair.

As if the last remaining energy had been exerted in his final words, William closed his eyes and immediately fell asleep. Daring not disturb him, Josiah left William to recuperate and penned the title of the article himself.

### THE TARRYING TIME BY BR. WILLIAM MILLER

Josiah worked throughout the day and into the evening on the typesetting process, unpacking the necessities with which he had come so close to parting as he loaded the press and began the initial run for the paper. William remained in the seat, sleeping soundly through the cacophony of the machinery and the malodorous ink fumes, as the candle upon Josiah's desk burned nearly to its base.

It was not a moment past midnight that there were enough copies of the *Crier* to circulate throughout Calvary. There was no ability nor need to go beyond the confines of the town; Josiah knew that their only concern was the immediate community. Riding throughout the darkest hours of the evening and into twilight, he placed a copy of the paper on the doorstep of every household in the heart of town and across the small farms around its perimeter. By sunrise, the people of Calvary would find William's sermon folded at their feet before them, with the promise of answers and a solution by the next Sabbath.

# Chapter 6

THE CONGREGATION ANSWERED the call and amassed in the United Calvary Church on the following Sunday. The spirited nature of the worship at the camp was gone, as were the bodies of the hundreds who used to regularly fill the tent throughout the day. Most of the outsiders had already left the town, either returning to their homes or attempting to find a new calling elsewhere—traveling westward to the frontier or finding work in the factories that had begun to appear in the urban centers throughout the region. Many locals continued to attend Thomas Aleman's service across town as a quiet act of rebellion against the movement, but the majority of the residents decided to give William one final chance to redeem himself before they joined their old pastor. Though their souls were dampened, there was still a fuel within them that could be rekindled.

Josiah stood in the back of the church and glowed with confidence as he looked out upon the throngs of weary parishioners. Those around him had only a single column in the *Crier* to help restore their hope, but Josiah had much more. He had seen the truth with his own eyes—he had felt the same epiphany as William, its spirit transmigrating from the reverend's soul to his—and he knew that it would all become clear to the believers in due time.

Footsteps from the upper chamber echoed through the cold silence of the church as the congregation braced for William's arrival. Despite the prevailing air of uncertainty and even resentment among some in the church, the congregants collectively leaned in toward the sound as if it were the Bridegroom himself coming to deliver them—waiting for any kind of sign or direction to help them find the path to salvation. The footsteps became louder as William reached the ground floor and stepped through the doorway to the nave. He strode toward the pulpit without dither or delay. His black gown was neatly pressed, his body washed clean, his face shaven and eyes well-rested. He was ready.

William extended his hands outward and began.

"My friends, your presence here today warms my soul and fills me with hope that mankind shall indeed find redemption after all. As the camp behind this church lies deserted, as others turn their backs and leave our town at the first sign of adversity, you remain here with your faith intact, wounded though it may be. I, too, am not unscathed by the pain that we all experienced on the Day of Atonement and the days since, and I, too, am not unharmed by those arrows of fortune. But as we reconvene here today to consider why the Bridegroom has not yet come for us, we must remember that it is the poor in spirit, the bruised and lacerated and tormented souls, who shall inherit the kingdom of Heaven. And I assure you now, just as I have all along, that the prophecies of Daniel and John are not false and our readings are not mistaken. There is simply more work to be done before that kingdom come."

The church remained still as William paused his sermon, as if to instigate a reaction from the parishioners. He would offer no further explanation until they beseeched it from him.

Stirring in her pew, Mrs. Edwards could no longer control the inner workings of her consciousness and was the first to raise herself from her seat and plead for clarity.

"But why!" she cried. "What has made us unworthy of His love? We waited for Him dutifully and in good faith and yet Christ has rejected us!"

Her interjection stimulated a concatenation of implorations, prayers, and petitions for clarity that had been festering within the congregants for days. The clamor drew out the tears in many who had previously not been able to cry out of the shame they felt; but surrounded by like-minded neighbors, they finally bared their souls and purged their emotions. Satisfied with the response that he elicited, William waited for the room to quiet and answered calmly.

"My brothers, my sisters. Scripture identifies the Bridegroom as the Son of God, our Lord Jesus Christ, so clearly that even the most illiterate of us may understand its meaning. But we seldom speak of His bride in such transparent terms. Many of us may naturally assume that we ourselves are the bride, each of us individually trimming our lamps to prepare for the midnight cry. But alas, this is not the true meaning found in the Scripture, for the union of the Bridegroom and the bride is the union of Jesus Christ and His church—that is, His union with all of us collectively.

"Now, I ask ye believers," he continued, gazing into the eyes of the congregants, "how can we say that His church is ready for Him with what we see happening across the whole of this town? Think now: why should the Bridegroom return to this land when the wicked and weak of faith still desecrate it so? Why should He desire to unite with the church for all eternity when there are still so many impure among us?"

The parishioners began to covertly glance at one another, wondering who might be standing in the way of their salvation.

"It is fair to ask why we, the righteous and believing children of Christ, have not yet been chosen to be saved. And that reason, I have assessed, is because our work to prepare has only just begun. There are still those among us who act in an effrontery to the teachings of this church and the teachings of Scripture—those who follow the diabolical words of a corrupt man who once claimed to be of the cloth.

"I speak of that temple that has sprung up across the valley," William declared with a gesture to the south. "The 'church' of our former pastor and all the apostates who dwell within it. Do not think this is unnoticed by our Lord; the more who choose to join that congregation, the more corrupt and unworthy this land becomes. I wish that God had granted me this wisdom to see it before, but it is clear to me now: this schism is a sign of the times in itself—Christendom riven into the sides of good and evil."

"This is Thomas Aleman's doing!" one of the congregants announced. "Both of my neighbors went to his services rather than join ours on the day we were to be saved."

"I knew it must be his fault," said another. "He knocked

on my door asking me to join him as well. He cursed our lessons from the Scripture and said that they were false— that God's word was false! I turned him away, but I ought to have struck him down there."

The church began to echo with tales of the temptations of their former pastor—spreading misinformation with his toxic speeches at the base of the hill, his wild pronouncements about the root motivation of their cause, his profane denouncement of William and the visiting reverends and all the ministers of the state who confirmed the date in October. Inspired by the exchange, William elevated his voice and continued as if he were in the camp once again.

"Yes!" he bellowed. "As we prayed for salvation, they prayed for continued sin; as we opened our congregation, they built a house of Satan. It is they who keep us locked out of the kingdom gates. It is they who anchor our ark to the lake of fire. Thus, it has now become our duty to prepare for the midnight cry by sanitizing these grounds onto which New Jerusalem shall descend. We must work together to make it worthy and fit for a king of kings, to transform it to a holy city that will be home to our God. Our lamps will thus be filled by our actions henceforth.

"This is the start of our new mission," William concluded, quieting the congregation. "Life needs to be hard for the unbeliever. For this tarrying will never end until we are finally cleansed and His church is made pure."

## Chapter 7

A SECOND WAVE OF faithfulness flowed into Calvary as the worshippers shrugged off the torpor of the Disappointment and began to prepare once again for the end of days. But the indeterminate amount of time until the advent meant that, in order to survive, shop owners and artisans would need to resume their work—though now with limited output, concentrating not on long-term profit but rather on securing enough of an income to take them through the coming weeks. Those who had already sold their houses or their farms were not as fortunate and instead spent their time importing what they could from the merchants who supplemented the production shortages with food and supplies from nearby villages, praying for a swift ascension before the money and resources they'd saved from the liquidation of their livelihoods would run out. The worshippers returned to church and children returned to school, where Mrs. Edwards reoriented her lessons to the Tarrying Time and explained to her students the virtue of patience and preparation. No one knew how long it would be until that day would come—but all who were faithful were instructed to act as if the midnight cry could sound at any time.

Abigail entered Harriman's general store the first week it reopened and looked over the vanishing merchandise. Nearly everything had been sold off in October, and the shelves were not yet restocked; all that was available were leftover supplies for the pilgrims to build shelters at the camp—canvas, rope, spikes, and handheld tools—which had begun to collect dust and soot as they outlived their utility the month prior.

"Mr. Harriman, has my brother's medicine arrived from the port yet?" she asked Nathaniel, who stood behind the counter and catalogued his inventory.

"It has, Miss Smith. Dr. Clarke ordered a fresh batch from Albany for you last week."

Abigail breathed a sigh of relief as Nathaniel handed her the herbs to place in her basket. Their remaining supply at home would not be enough to get Benji through another severe episode, and the cold weather saw to it that they were now happening with increased frequency.

"How long did he say this stock would last?"

"Surely until kingdom come."

As Abigail counted the last of her family's coins on the counter, she heard the chimes on the door ring behind her. Entering was the former sexton of United Calvary, who began to browse the aisles and take measure of the limited items that were available. Nathaniel raised his eyes and saw who had come inside and immediately placed down his pencil and ledger. He walked out from behind the counter with a sense of urgency and hurriedly stepped in front of the sexton so that the two tall men were shoulder to shoulder.

"What do you think you're doing in my store?"

"I've run low on sperm oil," replied the sexton. "Have you replenished your stock?"

"That's some divine irony, neighbor. But of course you have neglected the reservoir of your lamp as you spend your days worshipping in that awful cult."

"Mr. Harriman, have you oil or not?" he asked again, nonplussed by the store owner's ire.

"The only oil you need can be found at the United Calvary Church. Join us for the afternoon worship today, and I assure you that we will see to it that your lamp burns brighter than ever before."

"I'll do no such thing. I want no association with that crooked reverend of yours."

Nathaniel's face turned pink as his lips fell into a scowl.

"Then see it that you leave. We do not allow heretics to patronize this store."

"I am a paying customer. What difference does my presence make to your salvation?"

"No more than a tree ought to allow ivy to take root near its base can I risk having your apostasy anywhere near me when the Bridegroom calls. Now get out before things get out of hand."

Nathaniel seized the sexton by the collar and spun him forcefully toward the door. Readying his fists for a brawl, the sexton looked up to find Abigail watching in fright in front of the counter, and thought better of escalating the altercation. Adjusting his shirt and overcoat, he stood upright and quelled his hostility, then stoically exited the door. Nathaniel returned to his counter.

"Mr. Harriman?" Abigail began tepidly as she looked at him in shock.

"Don't you mind that, Abigail," Nathaniel assured her. "Any pious store owner would do the same. Those nonbelievers may choose to stay in that church and hide from the truth, but nothing gives them the right to infect the rest of us here, yourself included."

"That man . . . that's the old sexton. He's with Thomas's church now?"

"Has been since the beginning. Josiah Young has published a list of all the townspeople who attend so we can keep track of those who hold us back from salvation."

Abigail gripped the handle of her basket and averted her eyes, attempting to hide her apprehension. Nathaniel looked at her curiously.

"Speaking of," he began, "you and your family haven't been worshipping with them, have you? I can't recall seeing you or your father at church since the Day of Atonement."

"No, Mr. Harriman, never," said Abigail guardedly. "It's my brother. He's too sick to make the trek up the hill, and we have to care for him at home. That's why I needed to get his medicine from you today."

"Well I reckon being at the church with his neighbors could do more to heal him than any kind of herbal concoction. But that is for your father to decide. I just hope he understands that we are all in this together."

Abigail nodded silently as another customer entered, jangling the chimes once again and elevating Nathaniel's eyes to ensure it was a fellow believer. Confirming it was a friendly face, Nathaniel turned back to the counter, only to see Abigail swiftly exiting with her basket in hand.

Abigail found more townspeople walking the streets than she had seen in nearly a month. The ascension robes had again become a common sight, and she ascertained that a majority of the residents were now cloaked in white regardless of the time of day. She breathed in heavily as she hurried through the cobblestone roads, anxious to get away from the center of town as quickly as she could, fearing that she might be further accosted for her family's absence from the church. But her momentum was slowed as she passed a cross street, where she was nearly knocked over by an older man who was thrown to the ground before her with a loud thud as three others in ascension robes stood over him.

"Take your blasphemy elsewhere, devil," said one.

"It belongs right there in the gutter," another added.

The man slowly raised himself to his feet as the blood dripped from the scraped palms of his hands, not willing to take on the three assailants by himself. Abigail waited on the curb until the men in the ascension robes eventually turned to walk away, then knelt down to pick up the victim's hat from the pavement.

"Are you all right, sir?" Abigail asked as she handed the man his hat. "You're bleeding."

Abigail remained at his side as he looked up at her with empty, sullen eyes—eyes that quietly expressed his gratitude, but also a deeper, underlying weariness and pros-tration. Looking to his flanks to ensure that no one had seen the exchange, the man stood up, placed his hat upon his head, and walked away without a word. Abigail was left holding her basket in the middle of the road as she watched him limp away toward the southern end of Calvary, where she surmised he must be heading toward Thomas's church.

She recalled the conversation that they'd had the last time she and Thomas were together. *Why not just remain silent?* she had asked him desperately, a selfish attempt to convince him to choose her love over his convictions. She thought about the moment she'd lobbied her father to decline the invitation to his services on the Day of Atonement, and she wondered what life would have been like if she had instead been there with him and their previous parting had not been their last.

In that moment, she was overcome with a sudden desire to follow behind the man—to go see Thomas and at least warn him of the dangers he would face if he were to show himself in the town. But though he was suffering there alone, she knew the separation itself was his solace— that mile of wooded paths that separated her from him also separated Thomas from the center of town and the source of such violence and antipathy. What kept them apart, for now, was the only thing keeping him safe.

The church bells began to ring in the distance. School would be letting out shortly, and Abigail estimated that she could cross paths with her sister if she began to make her way up the hill now. Benji was still too frail to return to class, and she did not like the idea of Rosemary walking home alone with the town on edge, so she made haste to the schoolyard to keep her company on the way.

A horde of young children scampered past as Abigail approached the entrance to the school. She stood on her toes as she waited near the open door for the remainder of the class to file out, but she could not find her sister amongst them. Her heart began beating faster as she felt a pang of dread with each student who exited and each minute that passed by. But as the echoes of the children's laughter receded behind her, Abigail turned toward the church and saw the large wooden door open in the distance.

Out from the church stepped Rosemary, followed closely by William as he escorted her across the threshold. Abigail watched curiously as the two conversed in front of the doorway. They seemed to be engaged in a deep conversation; Rosemary was looking up to the reverend with an expression of deference and adoration that Abigail had seldom observed in her sister's eyes. There was something personal about their exchange—a familiarity between the two of them that seemed as though they had known one another for years, or perhaps in a different life before this.

Abigail waited until their conversation came to a close and William reentered the church before she approached her sister.

"Abigail, what are you doing here?" Rosemary asked as she traipsed down the path in front of the building.

"I was just picking up Benji's medicine from the store," said Abigail, careful to not let on that she had been watching them. "I figured we could walk home together."

Rosemary shrugged unsuspectingly and accompanied her sister down the hill and into the town on their way back to the trails to their farm.

The clouds rolled across the sky as they passed by each believer who was trimming their wick for the midnight cry according to their own spiritual discretion—the volunteer who would continuously distribute the local run of the *Calvary Crier* over the coming weeks; the shop owner who would post signs to announce the prohibition of the apostates in their store; the magnanimous evangelical who would proselytize to as many nonbelievers as they could, leaving daily notes upon their doorsteps in hopes that they could save one more soul in time for the advent; and the common worshipper, who, like all the rest, would close their home and storefront in the afternoon to attend the daily worship, where they waited for Christ to come at the fall of dusk.

But each sunset was a heartbreak as the days became shorter and the waiting began to take a heavier toll on the believers. Some wondered what they themselves were doing wrong; others blamed their neighbors and suspected that there must be a secret, prevailing sin that they were not seeing. They knew this would be a period of tribulation and strife that tested their fortitude and their patience, and they would have to persevere. But as the ground became harder, the trees became more barren, and the wind blew more bitterly, they were still waiting. He had not yet come.

# Chapter 8

JOSIAH TOOK A seat in the front pew next to Marigold, occupying the space that her mother had routinely taken for years. There was palpable anxiety in the room as he listened to the soft whispers that abounded between the narrow walls of the church. Several weeks had passed since they had entered the Tarrying Time, and many in the congregation were beginning to worry.

"What are we doing wrong?" lamented a nearby congregant to his companion across the aisle. "We cut off our ties with the apostates. We converted the few who were willing to be saved. So why has our Lord still not come?"

"My cousin writes to me from Philadelphia," his companion replied. "He insists that all Sabbath services there have resumed as they once were, without mention of the imminence of the Second Coming—and all jeering and mockery of those who expected the advent have likewise ceased. It begins to make one wonder how long this must go on before we follow their lead."

"Indeed, brother," said the first. "The peace and concord elsewhere only makes the torment of waiting that much harder to bear."

Josiah turned his attention away from the nearby conversation and toward the entrance of the church, where George Wainscott was arriving at the top of the aisle. Several parishioners immediately swarmed him as if they had been long awaiting his counsel. George was taken aback by the sudden solicitation as they each began to simultaneously voice their concerns to him and implored him to give them some kind of direction.

As George attempted to listen to the frantic entreaties, a young, pale-eyed woman managed to break through the crowd and grab him by the hand.

"Please help us! It's been weeks of tarrying, and yet we are still here. My husband closed his smithy in preparation for the Day of Atonement. But now my family is running out of food as we wait!"

Though visibly shaken by the earnest plea, George could do no more than console the woman with a sympathetic rub of the arm as the questions of the other parishioners became louder and more fraught the longer they waited for William to arrive. Before long, their initial diffidence faded as the majority of the church was ablaze with speculation about when the tarrying would finally cease.

Josiah calmly adjusted his position in the front pew as he waited for the services to commence. He exchanged a glance with Marigold sitting beside him, whom he could see was working through her own silent deliberation.

"They're right to ask," she said, turning to him. "Some

are not as fortunate as you and me to still have our means for survival. How much longer must this go on?"

Josiah leaned in toward her and placed his hand over hers. "Our waiting is what fortifies our faith. We just need to be patient and keep following Brother William's lead."

As the rest of the congregation took their seats, William appeared as if an apparition before the stairwell and immediately chilled the air in the church. Noticing the flurry of conjecture, he began to speak before taking to the pulpit.

"'Let us not be weary in well doing: for in due season we shall reap, if we faint not.' I've said to this congregation before—the time of tarrying is a test from God. Jesus is watching our every action to ensure that these grounds that will one day carry the walls of New Jerusalem are worthy of the site."

William walked with a calculated stride toward the altar as the congregation waited for any kind of answer as to what more needed to be done.

"I ask you now: will the oil of our lamps be filled merely by waiting? No! It does not rise from nothing—we must go out and take it ourselves. Indeed we have not done enough to decontaminate the future site of the holy throne. Across the way, in this very town, Thomas Aleman is preaching his false sermons. He is denying the words of Scripture that cannot be denied. He is literally damning each and every one of us in our community—and yet how little ye do to stop it."

A steady rumble reverberated through the church. Many nodded along, confirming what they had suspected all along—that the only ones to blame for their continued abandonment were those who were actively praying for it.

"How can we expect the Son of God to grant us eternal salvation when we cannot even prevent a select few heretics from infiltrating our small community? We have been too passive. We have to shake people at this point and say, 'Come on now.' We tried voluntary. We could not have been more kind and compassionate—everywhere you turn, another chance being given to them to join us and believe; granting incentives to them; promising a friendly, warm embrace. But the voluntary phase is over. The time has come that we protect ourselves and see to it that our suffering ends forthwith."

The congregation responded with a roar as they were filled with a sudden jolt of determination. William himself became energized by their response and continued to spur them into action.

"It is one thing for these heretics to put their own souls in danger. But it is unforgivable that they now risk the spiritual safety of everybody in this town."

"Amen!" Mr. Edwards barked as he leapt from his seat. "Thomas Aleman's services are happening right now as we speak. I say that this may be our best chance to find all of them together and excise them from these grounds!"

Many began to stand up, aroused by the zeal of the foreman. In the front of the room, George surveyed the crowd with concern. Seeing that the levee was about to break, he quickly took to the aisle and voiced his opposition.

"My neighbors," he began. "I know there are passions stirring within you, but we must remain civilized. There are processes that we have to follow."

"Let us delay no longer!" another added, ignoring

George's plea for civility. "God has told us what must be done to the heretics!"

"I know you blame Thomas for our troubles, but the town has no recourse to deprive him of his property," said George. "It is his land where he holds his services—and we cannot legally tell him what he can or cannot do with it."

George could see that his points were falling on deaf ears as calls to march across the town to Thomas's church continued. He looked at William with a sense of vain desperation.

"Are you going to put an end to this? It is getting out of control!"

William glared at George as the rest of the parishioners rose to their feet. They had never hated anyone more than they hated Thomas and those in his church at that moment. United by their animus and the desire to put an end to their anguish, the congregation massed together into a single entity and burst open the door of the United Calvary Church.

As the tail end of the mass exited, only George was left standing in the aisle, helpless to stop them. He turned around and met the eyes of William at the altar. George looked at him in silent abjection as William closed his Bible and walked back up the stairs to plan his next sermon.

Chapter 9

DOWN THE HILL and across the valley, over the slanted roofs of the broad stone homes and through the untrodden streets, a cold wind swiftly swelled and forged a trail to the outskirts of the town. It slithered and wended throughout the bridle paths, sweeping through the stock-still woods and into the open air of the nearest homestead, where Thomas Aleman held a dueling Sabbath service in the small barn beside his house.

He hoped it would be the last. The same loyal group of parishioners, save a few who were lost to coercion or had been convinced to give William one more chance at redemption, gathered together as they had every Sunday since the Tarrying Time began. But with the season beginning to turn its page, Thomas believed that it must only be a matter of time before it would all be over.

"What you witnessed on the Day of Atonement was the restoration of the natural order of Christendom," he said to the parishioners, who huddled closely together in the cold barn. "If there was one thing that was inevitable, it was that Reverend Miller's prophecy would be exposed for the fraud that it is—for deception is the bedfellow of the oracle, and it is the Lord who will always pull back the sheets."

Thomas looked out at the faces of his congregants and could see the disillusionment in their eyes. They had been cast aside as heretics by their neighbors, friends, and family. They had been blamed by the believers for their own unfilled salvation—mocked, cursed, abandoned, and shut out of the town. But they were still here, and he owed them more. He owed them the uninhibited and total repudiation of the man who caused them such harm, no matter how dangerous speaking out had become.

"I understand the appeal of the reverend's words. His vivid pronouncements and extravagant divinations. Prophecies of doom, redemption, and ultimate glory. But these are nothing more than the devil's temptations masquerading as the truth of Scripture."

He looked at the empty pew that he held for Abigail and her family. He imagined her sitting there, nodding with encouragement and giving him the motivation to continue.

"You are here today because you refused to fall victim to these traps. You are here today because, despite the whole of the world seeming to cast you as an obdurate sinner, a rotten and infectious presence, you know the truth. You have eyes—and you can plainly see it for yourself."

As Thomas paused between sentences, he heard distant rustling outside the door and across his lawn. The blustery November air carried the noise like a steady trumpet. There was never a sound beyond the call of a bird or a gust of wind at his remote farm, isolated as it was on the edge of town, but he could now feel the ground vibrating beneath him. Thomas knew what was coming, but the image of Abigail inspired him to carry on.

"Only our Lord God can ask us to be faithful beyond reason, to carry a faith that defies all logic," he continued as the rumbling persisted. "But you were not asked this by God. No, you were asked to trust in the words of a mystic—to trust invisible calculations, hearsay, and reports of events you cannot witness yourselves. All along you knew that your eyes were not deceiving you, even if the public tide was too great to say otherwise. And then these predictions never came to pass, and we learned to trust our senses again."

A crescendo of voices suddenly resounded from outside. A series of booming knocks followed, pulsating the old barn door like a beating heart. The parishioners shifted in their seats and looked back nervously, then returned their eyes to Thomas for guidance.

"It is the most holy among us who are able to separate God's truth from Satan's lies," he said defiantly, ignoring the clamor. "Even my namesake, the Apostle Thomas, did not believe in Jesus Christ's resurrection until he felt his wounds for himself. And now, my friends, we ourselves can feel the wounds that Reverend Miller has inflicted upon this town."

The knocking grew louder, and the door began to bubble at its hinges as if it contained a wild beast behind it, pawing the ground and rearing for a charge from the outside. Several of the parishioners began to cower together, whimpering and shrieking in terror now that they, too, realized what was to come.

Thomas closed his eyes to collect his thoughts, and the room was empty. A brightness engulfed the church as he found Abigail standing before him, bathed in the same light as she had been during the final time they had spoken. She repeated her question to him.

*Why not just remain silent?*

Thomas opened his eyes and looked out at his congregation, screaming and recoiling at the sight of the battering of the barn door. He finally knew then the reason why he couldn't.

"The signs of the end were not true, but these wounds are. Reach hither thy hand and touch them thyself! For these wounds to our community are wounds which we must behold in order to begin to heal, lest history repeat itself. Let their scars be a reminder for our progeny—so they do not fall for the same deceit, caught up in the same manic winds as those which swirl within our neighbors today. Let us set a lesson for the generations after this that we will not be carried away by them. Never again, I say!"

The door burst open from the outside. The congregants ran to the back of the barn and families huddled closely together to protect themselves as the mob entered. Mr. Edwards and the parishioners who'd led the calling at United Calvary entered at the vanguard and stopped at the end of the aisle. They turned around and nodded to the group, as Josiah emerged from behind several other townspeople.

Thomas took a deep breath and dutifully walked toward the entrance as his congregation remained in a defensive position behind the front pews. With each step he took, he was able to further view the extent of the group behind Josiah, which stretched back like a sinuous viper as far as he could see.

"My friends," he began calmly, "I know the anger you

feel. But do not misdirect your indignation. It is the false-
ness of the other preacher that has led you astray."

"No, Brother Thomas," Josiah said, shaking his head.
"We know the truth."

"And what truth is this you speak of?"

"That it is you who has been corrupting our community.
It is you whom God sees as unworthy. It is you—and the
rest of your disciples—who are preventing our salvation."

Thomas felt Abigail's hand upon his and he gazed into
the depths of the crowd before him. She was there for him,
assuring him to stand his ground.

"Please, why don't you join us," he offered. "You are
all welcome to attend our service and see for yourselves—"

"We don't want to join your fiendish rituals, blas-
phemer!" a man shouted before Thomas could complete
his entreaty.

Others in the crowd began to harangue the congregation with unfettered rage. Thomas gripped Abigail's hand
tighter and turned to check on his other parishioners. He
found them shaking in fear, helpless to defend themselves.
But he knew there was no longer anything he could do
for them.

Time stopped. All of his life came upon him in one
simultaneous flash. His defiance of God as a troubled youth.
Samuel Miller's hand upon his shoulder. The grandness and
mystery of Scripture revealed; the feeling of God's love filling him as he was warmed by the light of knowledge. The
happiness and worth he felt when he was told he would be
leading the church services, guiding his neighbors toward
righteousness with the hope that he could pass on the

same feeling to them that he had when he first understood God's truth.

He thought of the first time he met with Abigail, when she volunteered to help organize the previous year's Christmastime gathering. Getting to know her in those early morning hours as more than just a member of the church. The revelation of her past, her dreams, her interests, and her musings filling him with the same feeling he had when he first read through Scripture. It was another way of God revealing Himself through her, through love, in a way he had never felt before.

He wished he could tell her. He wished he could hand her the letters that he was keeping locked away inside the nightstand in his home until the day this would be over. He wished that he could articulate why he could not simply let this go. He wished he could say that if he were to do nothing, then this would continue to happen again and again—perhaps not in the near future when the memory of these mistakes was still fresh, but in generations when William Miller was long forgotten, the actions of Calvary lost to the flow of time. But the inheritance of those who stood athwart would be passed down. She was a part of that, even if she never knew. She was there, holding his hand, holding him up, as he faced down the inevitable.

"Your service is no longer welcome here, Thomas," Josiah declared. "It is time to come out of Babylon."

Thomas closed his eyes and embraced Abigail in his arms at last, as the crowd descended upon the church and enveloped him in the squall.

# Chapter 10

"WHY? WHY? WHY hasn't He yet come?" the pale-eyed woman shrieked. "We've done everything as you've told!"

An electric tension surged throughout the United Calvary Church as the congregation attempted to rationalize the Bridegroom's continued delay. Many expected to be taken after the final nail had been struck to board up Thomas's church for good; others allowed for a full day and night of prayer before they expected deliverance to be achieved. But few anticipated that more needed to be done, that they would have to wait this long before they would be called to their maker.

Mr. Edwards stood up and shouted. "It's been a full seven days now. Surely a holy number to bring the end. The apostates are gone, only the pure remain—so why have we not been delivered? We cannot bear this much longer, Brother William!"

William remained stalwart in the face of the desperate pleas.

"Sacrifice." His voice resounded throughout the church while he paced the pulpit like a Napoleonic general. "Let us remember the sacrifice made by our Lord and savior to pay the ransom for our sins and redeem all mankind. Let us remember not just his death, but the agony he faced in waiting for that day—the blood that he sweated as he prayed, the heartache he endured as his people turned against him, the weight of his cross as he marched toward his fate. Think of the wounds he suffered for our transgressions, the bruises he faced for our iniquities, and then look at thyself here! Think now, supposed child of Christ, and ask thyself: hast thou done enough?

"I see before me a community that is engaging in performative piety—one that finds it easy to join in daily prayer and repudiate those in vocal opposition to our call, but one that finds it too much a demand to devote the full spirit to salvation. I see before me those who still go about their worldly machinations, who still find pleasure in their secular idols each night as they return to their homes without having ascended to the Heavenly throne. What a wonder that the Bridegroom has not yet called when He sees how unwilling we are to give up these earthly delights!"

As the other parishioners lowered their heads in shame, Jacob White could no longer withstand the castigation. He rolled off his seat and placed his hands upon the shoulders of his wife and daughter as the congregation turned toward him.

"Brother William!" he called out. "When my family learned that the Second Coming was near, we did not delay. As soon as my last hen was plucked, we gave up our land, our ranch, and our home; and since then, we have been living as modest lives as lives can be, waiting patiently for the Lord to take us. So I dare any man to tell me that I am the reason why He has not come, and I'll have a pitchfork in his damned eye!"

"Yours is certainly a sacrifice worthy of the Bridegroom, Brother Jacob," William granted him as Jacob returned to his seat. "But can the same be said for thy neighbor?"

William looked out across the nave at the bleary eyes of his parishioners—those who had sold their homes, their land, and livelihoods. He looked at the fatigued faces lining the rear pews, then turned to the front. There he saw George Wainscott, outfitted in his navy-blue coat, thin walking stick gifted to him from a Parisian merchant at his side, as he sat calmly—comfortably—and listened to the sermon.

"On his journey from Galilee across the desert of Judea, Jesus encountered a wealthy nobleman," William began. "This young, rich ruler sought of our Lord to understand what it takes to achieve eternal life. 'What, good rabbi, must a man do in this mortal realm to receive the keys to the Heavenly gates?' he asked Jesus. And sayeth our Lord, 'Noble youth, follow the commandments of thy God and thou shalt be awarded that eternal blessing.'

"But when the young nobleman assured him that he already follows the commandments and commits no sin nor effrontery to God, Jesus shook his head, for he knew that this could not be entirely true. Sayeth the Son of Man, 'If thou wilt be perfect, go and sell that thou hast, and give to the poor, and thou shalt have treasure in Heaven: and come and follow me.' For it is he who eschews his treasures on earth who will be repaid thus. 'Every one that hath forsaken houses, or brethren, or sisters, or father, or mother, or wife, or children, or lands, for my name's sake, shall receive an hundredfold, and shall inherit everlasting life. But many that are first shall be last; and the last shall be first.'

"We have indeed rid this community of those who outwardly sin, but now it is time that we look inward and ask who among us refuses still to fully live by His word?"

William shifted the timbre of his voice as he turned his eyes unmistakably toward George in the front pew.

"I speak of the covetous idolaters, those who are still connected to their earthly wants. Those men who have plenty while others go hungry in the name of our cause."

The congregation focused their attention on the front row. George began to feel the eyes upon him.

"I speak of those who continue to labor for capital while we rightfully cast aside our land, our valuables, give all as alms," William continued. "For these chattels and gold are but the ropes and anchors that fasten us all to this earthly domain. Let us instead untether our ship and sail the clear waters to salvation!"

Josiah stood up beside George and raised his hands to the sky.

"Yes, amen!" he shouted, as others in the congregation followed his lead.

"Why should their sacrifice be any less than mine!" Jacob added.

William slowed his tempo and concluded definitively. "Remember, no man can serve two masters—that is, the service of gold and the service of God. It is only after we dedicate all our spirit to this cause that the Tarrying Time will cease, and we may find redemption."

"How much longer must we wait once that happens, brother?" Mr. Edwards asked from the aisle.

"Give thyself to God in full," William began, "and it shall be no longer than the farmer waits for his precious fruits of earth after he receiveth the early and latter rain."

# Chapter 11

ABIGAIL SHUDDERED AS the outside draught infiltrated their home through the gap of their door. Although she wore multiple layers of wool, a row of goose bumps rippled down her arms from the back of her neck as if a phantom had entered the house and whispered in her ear. She could not shake the sensation that something was wrong.

Abigail walked closer to the stove and attempted to warm herself by the fire. All was silent except for the monotonous, hollow popping of her father splitting wood outside, the logs tumbling over with each strike of his axe. Across the room, Rosemary knelt on a chair and leaned over the dining table, where the latest edition of the *Calvary Crier* was spread out before her.

"I don't know why those keep getting placed at our door," said Abigail as she lowered her hands to the heat. "No one here is paying Josiah a cent."

"The church covers the costs of production now," Rosemary replied without looking up. "It's free for everyone in town."

Abigail shook her head as she considered to herself a list of more charitable and righteous ways that money could have been spent.

"I suppose there is no news of the rapture yet," she said sarcastically.

Rosemary raised her eyes from the paper and looked at Abigail over her shoulder.

"Brother William says that the delay was due to Pastor Aleman and his church. It takes time to cleanse the town of his lies."

"Of course he says that. He'll look for anyone else to blame but himself."

"I am just grateful that I was able to convince father against taking us to those services. We'd have just been a part of the problem."

"You're so naïve sometimes, Rosemary," said Abigail, attempting to suppress her frustration. "The longer this goes on, the more people are going to realize that they are being strung along on this journey to nowhere—that all of these mandates and directives are accomplishing nothing. In fact, it just might be high time that we give Pastor Aleman's church a chance ourselves, if you were to ask me."

The light from the fire reflected in Rosemary's eyes as she stared at her sister.

"It's too late for that."

"What do you mean?" asked Abigail without turning her body from the hearth.

"It says in the paper that Thomas closed his church,

boarded it up overnight. He left the town the Sunday before last and took all his followers with him."

Abigail froze in place as the cold chill returned. The room filled with an orange glow as the back door swung open and the blustery winds brightened the embers in the fire like bellows. Henry entered with a fresh stack of wood for the evening and began to place the split logs beside the fireplace. Rosemary quickly tucked the newspaper onto her lap so that he would not see. Abigail remained motionless, her heart numb, as she thought about Thomas. Part of her hoped that the story in the paper was true—that he had had enough of the persecution in the town and willfully absconded with his loyal congregation to start a new life elsewhere. But in the deeper depths of her intuition, she knew that he wouldn't just leave her without a word. Something else had happened. She could no longer feel his warmth.

"How is Benji doing?" Henry asked. "Has his fever broken?"

A lump rose in Abigail's throat as every touch, every whispered word with him came rushing back to her at once, along with the image of the final embrace that she had denied him and now would never come. She continued to stare into the fire as she watched the flames dwindle before her.

"Abigail?" Henry asked again.

Abigail collected her senses and turned to her father.

"Not yet . . . The fire is running low. I think the heat will help him."

"What he needs is the warmth of God," said Rosemary.

"We should take him to the church while we still have a chance—before it's too late."

Henry looked over at Rosemary and noticed the corner of the *Calvary Crier* peeking out from under the table.

"That explains it," he said as he walked over and lifted the paper from under her hands. "Still with this obsession over the Second Coming. It's no wonder everyone in town won't relent when they are all reading about it in the news every week."

Rosemary lifted her eyes to Henry. "Father, please. It's important."

Ignoring her appeal, Henry walked over to the stove with the newspaper in hand and knelt down beside the hearth. In a single motion, he shoved the paper on top of the hot cinders and waited for it to catch fire. The three watched as the ink began to rain down the sides of the white pages until a flame burst forth from below. The *Calvary Crier* was soon ablaze and bathed the entire room in an incandescent, yellow glow.

Rosemary crossed her arms at the table and gritted her teeth as Benji's coughing began to echo from the bedroom. Henry finished stacking the wood beside the fireplace and then grabbed his overcoat to brave the evening chill.

"It may be late before I return," he said to them at the doorway. "Be sure that the house stays warm and that Benji is able to get his rest."

"Father, I have a bad feeling about all of this," said Abigail. "Do you have to go tonight?"

"I've received word that all able-bodied men must attend the town hall. George Wainscott doesn't call these kinds of meetings unless it's something important."

Henry opened the door, and the cold winds again rushed inside.

"Hopefully it means we're finally putting an end to this madness once and for all. Don't wait up, you hear?"

Abigail and Rosemary nodded reluctantly as Henry turned to leave the house and walk into town by lamplight.

✍

"Remain calm, everyone. Let us not descend into a mob," George said in hopes to mollify the rabble that had gathered in the town hall.

George banged the gavel onto the small desk on the dais as the hall brimmed with residents eager to voice their opinions about William's latest proclamation.

Henry entered the back of the meetinghouse and looked over the crowd to the front of the room. He had not been inside since it all started. Gone were the old portraits upon the walls, the odes to the founders and the celebrations of the region's history; instead, lining the spaces the oil paintings and framed documents once occupied were portraits of William himself—visual hagiographies donated by the other regions he'd visited in the months prior or brought by pilgrims who'd journeyed to witness his sermons in the camp. The American flag that once traditionally draped across the banisters behind the dais had also been removed—and in its place now hung an oversized replica of William's chronological chart of the end of days, swaying above the center podium from the rafters. GOD'S EVERLASTING KINGDOM was the new backdrop for the town's civic affairs.

"I've called this meeting tonight since many of you are

rightfully concerned about the challenge laid before us," George began. "This talk during the Sabbath services is not something I take lightly. We are still a rational society and thus we must deliberate rationally among ourselves before making any further hasty decisions."

"You heard the reverend—we must begin to do more lest we risk being left behind!" one of the townspeople cried, beginning a series of vociferous opinions.

"We are all to blame for His delay!" another shouted. "We are not yet worthy!"

An uproar carried across the audience. As those in the crowd continued to debate over one another incoherently, George banged his gavel again.

"Please, please. I hear what you all are saying. But what more can we do? How much purer can Calvary be? Are we to live as monks until our day of judgment?"

Parting the townspeople in the front of the hall, the slender frame of Josiah Young stepped forward and onto the dais. Josiah faced George and slid the gavel from out of his hand without resistance, as George stood hopelessly confounded by his temerity. Josiah turned toward the crowd.

"Brother George has a point, I believe," he said as the townspeople listened closely. "There is an abundance of faith, hope, and charity among us in Calvary. So it is indeed fair, then, to ask each of us how much more we can offer to pay for our share of eternal grace."

Josiah thrust forth the gavel to draw attention to Nathaniel in front of the group.

"You, sir. Tell us what you have sacrificed as you await the coming of our Lord."

"Me?" Nathaniel asked, taken aback. "Why, my family

has vowed to put all of our efforts into purifying this community for the advent. The door of my shop was the first to be closed to those black-hearted apostates so they could not spew their venom in the presence of the believers."

"But your door is still open to the rest of us, you see," said Josiah. "What matters to you if your business is operating if you truly believe the rapture is imminent? Look now at your friend Jacob White, and observe how much further he has gone to prepare."

"That's right," a voice in the crowd called out. "Some of us are going hungry because we closed our businesses last month."

"It's true," added another. "My family has sold off all our wares so that we can spend our time preparing for Jesus to come."

Judgment echoed through the hall as Nathaniel began to sweat from the heat of their growing ire. Clasping his open hand to his heart, he could bear no more of the reproachment.

"I see now," he said with tears in his eyes. "O how vain the Bridegroom must think I am! You are right to shame me. If closing my store and spending my days in worship is what it takes to bring us all closer to salvation, then I shall board my doors tonight!"

Scorn swiftly turned to praise from the crowd as some standing nearby patted Nathaniel on the back of his shoulders. Others wrapped their arms around him as they accepted his pleas for forgiveness.

Inspired by the plaudits, a newfound vitality came across the eyes of Marigold as she raised her voice next.

"And I, too, offer more than words," she announced. "If

any family has sold their farm or their home in preparation for the Second Coming, consider my door open to you. The rooms in my family's estate are far more than I could ever need myself, and no one here should have to worry about freezing to death outside before our glorious ascension."

Cries of gratitude reverberated throughout the meeting-house as the most impoverished of the believers embraced Marigold and wept at her generosity.

"Behold, there are indeed so many righteous among us!" said Josiah. "But yet there still remain those who are not doing their part commensurate to their means."

Josiah turned to George and pointed the gavel in his direction.

"George Wainscott: what sacrifices of yours can you recount for the people in this hall?"

Surprised by the sudden inquiry, George stammered through a response.

"Why . . . of course . . . you all see me in church, wor-shipping beside you each day. I have been championing this cause from the beginning—there ought be no doubt of my faith in the movement."

Josiah stepped closer and leaned his tall figure over him, covering him in his shadow.

"Yet you continue to operate your shipping ventures to and from Albany throughout the year, do you not?"

George looked out into the crowd and saw a hundred eyes upon him. His dock foreman, Mr. Edwards, stepped forward to interpose.

"What Josiah says is true. Mr. Wainscott keeps the ports open daily, compelling those like me to do his bid-ding instead of giving ourselves to the services!"

"I have," George answered, gathering his composure. "But you see, there are essential operations that must continue for the good of this town."

"What could be more essential than the collective salvation of your neighbors, Brother George?" said Josiah. "How can you say you are devoted to our mission when men are forced to work on your merchant routes instead of being at United Calvary, praying with us? How can you claim to be doing all in your power to bring about the Parousia when Jacob White lives off of crumbs, Nathaniel Harriman closes his business to atone for his sins, and Marigold Chandler opens her home to those who have none?"

Henry could feel the animosity burning hot around him as others began to murmur to themselves or exclaim aloud the examples of their own suffering. He had never witnessed this kind of hostility in the town, even in criminal proceedings, and began to grow fearful at the unpredictability of his neighbors in this state of mind.

"What about you, Josiah?" George struck back. "I think yours is perhaps the only venture that has grown in profit since the news of the Millennium."

"Blasphemy!" one of the residents shouted immediately.

"The *Crier* has saved countless thousands by spreading the word across the nation!" another screamed. "How dare you!"

"That is the Lord's work that you're denigrating. There is no more righteous a mission than delivering the tidings that could mean the difference between eternal bliss and eternal damnation."

George took a step back as the crowd began to inch

closer to the dais, continuing to berate him. Josiah was the only one standing between him and constriction by the mob.

"Mine is a humble donation," said Josiah. "I was not gifted with the hand for farming, nor the voice to uplift the masses, nor the fortune to spread my charity to others. But the Lord did grant me one thing: the power of the pen, and I chose to wield it to save as many souls as I could. And so I continue this business not for myself, not for glory or fame, but for the redemption of good Christians across the world—for all who are pious and believe!"

The audience immediately showered praise upon Josiah, who closed his eyes and breathed in their approval. George stared at them in bafflement as Josiah turned his attention back toward him.

"We are here because we are a democratic community. So I propose now that we take a vote: that all business operations to or from Calvary that are not directly related to our church shall cease as of this moment."

"This is outrageous!" said George. "We cannot just lock down all commerce in the town indefinitely."

"We all suffer for the actions of the few who continue to profiteer off of our pain," said Josiah. "It is only fair that we now bring this matter to a poll. Or are you against democracy, too, Brother George?"

Henry watched as the crowd around him lifted their eyes at George menacingly while they conferred with one another as to how they would vote. But through the debate he remained silent, lest he become a target of their fury himself.

Josiah issued a proclamation. "I ask now: all in favor of terminating all business in town as we wait for kingdom come, say 'aye.'"

The crowd loudly responded in unanimous agreement. Josiah waited for the men to quiet their voices and continued.

"And all those opposed, say 'nay.'"

George stared back at the rows of townspeople as no one dared cast a vote of opposition.

"The 'ayes' have it," Josiah concluded calmly.

George shook his head to himself as he raised his arms.

"But wait," he began. "What are we supposed to do about supplies, about food? You all have said it yourselves— some are already going hungry as we tarry."

"The solution is precisely what Brother William mentioned in his last sermon," said Josiah as he stepped closer to him. "Remember that it is easier for a camel to go through the eye of a needle than for a rich man to enter into Heaven. You are the wealthiest man in Calvary, and yet those like Brother Nathaniel and Brother Jacob seem to be giving up a greater share of their humble earnings for us all."

"What are you implying, Josiah?" George said, nearly in a whimper.

"It's simple: you need to do your part if you wish to ascend."

Henry grew more concerned for George's safety as his neighbors around him began to bare their fangs at the dais. He wondered whether he should try to stop them, if he could say something to quell their contempt—or if any opposition would only provoke them further. But he knew that George was a pragmatist above all else. He must realize that if he did not give it to them, they would take it by force.

George raised his hands in submission.

"You are right," he said to Josiah, then repeated louder for all to hear. "He is right! Those who have given up their farms, their trades, still need to eat while we await His return. No man shall have to worry about going hungry so long as I have bread to spare. The church will henceforth have my payment to provide for those who are in need!"

The crowd erupted in a cheer, as if all of their past sacrifice had finally been rewarded. The men in the front of the congregation moved forward to congratulate George for his piety, who exhaled a sigh of relief and dabbed the cold sweat off his forehead with a kerchief.

"Let this be an example for everyone!" Josiah declared. "It is not just our wealthiest who need to give up their holdings. Brother William says that covetousness is idolatry, and no idolater shall inherit the kingdom of God. All artifacts of this life will be useless in the next! To show your faith in His return, who among us shall cast aside these ephemeral indulgences of their own—anything that cannot be shared with our community—just as our brother George has done just now? Tonight! Tonight! Let us rid ourselves of that which anchors us to the lake of fire tonight!"

With each person in the room who volunteered to sacrifice more of their secular life or who pointed to a neighbor whom they knew had more to give up than they, Henry began to feel less safe from accusation himself. Believing that it was only a matter of time that he would be next, he waited until the crowd was momentarily distracted by self-congratulation or remonstrance, ducked between the rabid believers, and surreptitiously backed out of the meetinghouse to exit into the cold air of the late autumn night.

❧

The breaths of the townspeople dusted the moonlight as they descended on the town square. From all corners of Calvary, man, woman, and child exited their homes, carrying out their worldly possessions—clothes, tools, books, toys, dolls—and casting them into the raging bonfires that blazed outside their doors.

"Burn it all, brothers and sisters!" Josiah shouted from the middle of the street. "Build no more houses! Plant no more fields! Forsake your shops, your farms, and all secular pursuits! This earth shall soon be scorched far more than your goods are now."

Some fell to their knees and praised God once the last of their belongings were incinerated. Others acted as if they were possessed, silently operating by some higher force above, as they followed along in automatic compliance with an emptiness in their eyes and tossed their items into the fires. Yet a few performed the ritual while wiping tears from their cheeks, helpless to resist the tide that had beset the town, as they watched everything they'd worked for go up in flames by their own volition.

Henry stood in the shadows on the outskirts of the main square, witnessing the event unfold with abject horror. Across from his vantage point, he saw William standing on a plane slightly above the rest, surveying the scene from afar with a look of satisfaction as the flames cast a pulsating glow across his face. As Henry stared at him, William turned his eyes and caught the reflection of the fire in those of Henry. The two looked at one another from opposite ends of the town square, William irradiated by a burning light and Henry alone in the darkness.

Having seen more than he could bear for the evening,

Henry turned away to walk the wooded trail back to his home, as the smoke purled into the moonlight behind him.

෴

Henry closed the door and slowly removed his overcoat and hat, still in disbelief of what had transpired. He wondered if it all had been a dream or a hallucination. But he could taste the smoke from the fires sticking to the back of his tongue; his nostrils were still clogged by the tar and ash that once made up his neighbors' possessions and livelihoods. He knew it was real.

The fire in the hearth had turned to a dull ember, and Henry estimated that the children had long been asleep. He added a log for the evening, then entered the children's bedroom, careful not to wake them with the sounds of his boots upon the floor.

All three were resting soundly on the bed—Abigail in the middle, with Rosemary and Benji cuddled tightly into her breast as if they were seeking the warmth of their mother. Henry watched them silently as he fought against the demons of his imagination and the bleak images of the future that lay ahead.

Sensing his troubled stare, Abigail slowly opened her eyes and sat upright in the bed, attempting not to jostle her siblings.

"Go back to sleep. I didn't mean to disturb you," Henry said softly.

Abigail rubbed her eyes and ignored his instruction.

"How did the meeting go?" she asked groggily.

Henry stepped forward to kneel beside their mattress.

"I want you to promise me something, Abigail," he whispered as she waited anxiously. "Stay out of town. You, your brother, and your sister. Don't go in no matter what. Not until winter is over. Not for anything, understand?"

Abigail nodded at the gravity of the directive, as Henry kept staring ahead.

"Father," she began nervously, "what happened tonight?"

Henry took in a breath as the frenzy, the furor, and the fire repeated in his mind.

"The world came to an end."

# Chapter 12

THE MILLENNIAL FERVOR fully enveloped Calvary in the wake of the great expurgation. The town was now an island amongst a sea of sin. No carriages moved within the outer limits; no steamboats nor wooden fleets passed near the cold harbors. The ports were closed indefinitely, save for one weekly trading vessel owned by George Wainscott, which he used to import basic living essentials such as grain, sugar, and printing supplies at his own expense. The residents were likewise shut off to all outside correspondence or news that could propagandize false temptations of another way of life. There was only one source of information, and that information was the verified truth of the *Calvary Crier*, each article certified by William himself.

*Write: for these words are true and faithful.*

The town collectively began to lose weight under William's new orders. All of the stores were closed for business and all commerce was forbidden; all produce from the farms still owned by parishioners was given directly to the church, and the food supply was to be shared equally in commune. The weekly imports from George's ship typically provided an allowance of bread and butter, and the local farms a meager portion of potatoes, beets, and winter parsnips for stews. These humble refections brought them closer to salvation, according to William, who assured the believers that their hunger and their suffering was nothing other than the very oil that would fill their lamps for the coming midnight cry.

*He that overcometh shall inherit all things.*

What was once a voluntary call to worship was now a de facto daily requirement. The church was the only place where rations were distributed to each man, woman, and child evenly; and so it was there where every hungry resident would come to receive their prepared meals and listen to the morning sermon, leaving to eat their scant victuals in their homes in the afternoon and marching back before dusk, where they would watch the sun set and signal that the cycle would yet continue the next morning. Formal schooling was suspended as each of the remaining days were treated as holy as the Sabbath. But when the children became fidgety from the never-ending sermons or querulous from the hunger pangs, Mrs. Edwards resumed her role as a headmistress, often shuttling the children to their old classroom to distract them with new hymns to sing for their parents and the other worshippers while they watched the sun go down, day after day, with a painful pining for it to be their last.

*Here is the patience and the faith of the saints.*

While the residents established a city of God atop the hill of Calvary, a second dominion continued afar, across the forest and farmland plains, at the Smith residence. Here, the family kept to their own isolated way of life and maintained a level of subsistence as they bided their time for what Henry imagined would be the town's inevitable second, and final, reopening. Remembering the advice of Dr. Clarke, Henry did what was necessary to ensure that his son was well-nourished as his illness progressed, and he continued to farm what little he could to feed his family and to prepare their home for the coming winter. Benji continued to breathe, though confined to his bed for most of the day, and continued to spend his sleepless nights gazing outside the window to count the stars in the sky and keep his nascent mind from disintegrating during his convalescence. And with their lives revolving around the care for their brother, Rosemary and Abigail continued to drift apart the closer together they became.

With the school now closed, Abigail took it upon herself to begin teaching her sister the practical skills of housekeeping while their father tended to the fields. She demonstrated how to change the linens daily, a necessity as Benji lay ill in his sweat-drenched sheets; to launder them in the wash bucket outside and ensure they were dried before sunset; to brush the coals from the stove until her cheeks were powdered in soot; to scrub the wooden floors until her elbows were sore; to clean, condition, temper, and mill their small storage of wheat into flour; to make good use of what they had from their limited supply of food; to set the table, serve their dinner, and clear the plates before going to sleep; to wake up and repeat it all again the next morning.

Rosemary begrudgingly followed her instructions as she quietly longed to be elsewhere. She imagined being in town with her neighbors, singing songs with them as they bonded together in the trials of the Tarrying Time, until the righteous among them would at last be delivered. She pictured herself in William's chambers between the sermons, helping him unravel the mysteries of Scripture as they returned to their lessons of scholars past. Amidst the most arduous of her labors, her back aching and her hair caked in flour and dirt, she dreamed that a powerful storm would come and sweep her away—a gust of wind to carry her yonder to the hill, up to the entrance of the church, her arms outstretched as she joined her congregation to be nearer to God.

Tiring of the endless cycle foisted upon her by her sister, Rosemary awakened before her siblings at the break of dawn to perambulate the farm and surrounding woods. It was a peaceful morning—the air unmoving and nature still at rest—and for the first time since the school had closed, she found some temporary respite from the travails of the day. Under the lilac sky, Rosemary walked far from the house, across the patches of wild pumpkins and gourds, and to the edge of the woods, where she found a cluster of shrubs and winter berries lining the forest trail. Rosemary knelt beside the vibrant red fruits that glowed amongst the shadows of the trees and began to methodically pluck them from their stems.

The solitude of the cold morning allowed her a moment to finally think about something other than her daily chores or the escape thereof. She began to ponder the last book that William had given to her, the works of St. Bonaventure, which she had only recently completed by the dull light of the pine plugs she had placed in the fire per William's recommendation. She pictured him standing beside her as she opined about the writings.

334 | GARRY HARPER

"There is a part of the book that makes me wonder about our existence after salvation," she wished she could say to him. "St. Bonaventure reasons that if something is generated out of nothing—our lives, this world—then one must logically deduce that such things cannot be everlasting, since eternity stretches infinitely backward just as far as it moves ahead. So then how can we exist for eternity in the kingdom of Heaven? We know that our *lives* are finite, so then that must mean it is our *souls* that are infinite. And if our souls are truly eternal, does that then not also mean that they have likewise always existed?"

Rosemary paused and returned to her previous deliberations on infinity, the triune God, and the nature of time itself.

"Perhaps the soul is like God then," she continued in her imaginary discourse. "It is something that is not bound by the same laws as our universe. What if, before the world was born and before we each descended to our corporeal form, our souls existed with God outside of time as we know it; and as such, if the world must one day end, our souls are then fated for the eternal kingdom where time will no longer be, and all of the past, present, and future merge into one. Eternity, therefore, is when we become as the Trinity—in union with God, unbound by time—returning to that state of existence just as we were before Creation. It is the completion of our cycle."

Rosemary could see William beside her, smiling at her notion, complimenting her logical deduction and expounding upon her thesis with a perspective that only a lifetime of knowledge and scholarship could bring.

"And by that same reasoning, the souls of the unworthy

will likewise exist in eternal damnation," she heard William add. "This, too, is a kind of cycle—one in which the soul, separated from God forever, is destined to repeat the same cursed existence given to man since his expulsion from Eden. Only now the greatest torment is knowing that there is no longer any hope for a finite end."

Rosemary continued to ruminate on the subject, wondering which form of eternal life awaited her, as she anxiously plucked each red berry from the shrub.

"I wouldn't eat those if I were you," the voice of her father warned.

The sudden sound startled Rosemary, and the berries jumped from her palm onto the forest floor.

"Those are chokeberries," Henry explained. "They didn't name them that because of their sweet taste."

Rosemary spun around, annoyed by the interruption.

"I wasn't going to eat any. I was just counting them."

Henry looked at her askance as he folded his arms.

"The sun is barely risen. You journeyed out here this early just to count berries?"

"I was trying to be by myself."

"I understand things are difficult lately, but your sister needs you in the house—not gallivanting in the woods."

Rosemary threw down the rest of the berries as she raised herself to her feet.

"I just needed some time to think."

Placing his hands upon his hips, Henry looked up at the evergreen boughs that quietly bristled above them.

"I remember when you would come out this way when you were younger. You used to point to anything you could lay your eyes upon and ask me all sorts of questions about the world around you. What makes the days shorter in the winter; what the meaning was behind the calls of the birds; why, why, and why. You looked to me like I would have all of the answers, no matter what you wanted to know."

"I suppose I'm still looking for them," said Rosemary, turning her eyes away.

"Well I may not know everything, but perhaps I can still help with whatever is on your mind today. Your father isn't as oblivious as you might think."

Rosemary hesitated as she looked down at the trail of cracked berries on the dirt.

"I sometimes wonder if time stopped that night in October," she said at last. "The days all seem to blend together now—like we're living the same cycle over and over. And it seems like it's never going to end."

"I suppose you'd experience this sooner or later," said Henry, smiling to himself at the thought. "That feeling you have is part of getting older, being an adult. I feel it, too, out on the farm day after day, season after season. You soon begin to realize that the earth itself works in cycles and so you must as well. It's humbling, in a way, to become part of that natural order."

"Even when that labor feels like a torment? Even when we feel like we could be doing so much more with our time, something more gratifying than these endless works?"

"That repetition is how we survive, how we continue forward even when our hearts are elsewhere. Those negative thoughts will eventually become dampened by it, I promise you, Rosemary. You'll find that out soon enough."

Rosemary looked in the distance down the dark, hollow tunnel in the woods that led into town. There was some space between her and her father, and she considered how far she might get with a running start ahead of him. She stood up and planted her shoes into the dirt, pivoting her feet toward the westward wooded corridor. But as she readied herself, she heard a familiar coughing emanating from the house—the heavy wheezing that carried through the air every morning with the consistency of a cock's crow. Rosemary looked at Henry's eyes, and he motioned for her to join him back to the house. She hesitated at the edge of the forest and loosened her stance on the soil. Together with her father, she turned back, ready to begin her day of labor.

*And there shall be no more curse: but the throne of God and of the Lamb shall be in it.*

# Chapter 13

AS THE EVENING wind whistled outside his bedroom window, Henry fell into a vivid dream. There was a troubling stillness to the air as he found himself standing outside his farmhouse. The sun was overcast by a milk-white fog as if a single celestial cloud had enveloped the entirety of the globe, and he could not determine whether it was the early morning or the high point of the day. The world was lifeless. There was no sound around him—no calls of animals or insects nor breeze between the leaves—except for the light echoes of children's voices in the distance.

Henry followed the sounds of the shallow voices away from his home, toward the grassy terrain that he preserved by the side of the house. The children's voices grew louder as he slowly marched to the hill and stood before the tall sycamore tree that towered into the sky. He stopped to listen, until the sounds were suddenly muted by the flitter of a bird's wings overhead. Henry looked up to find a mourning dove descending onto the bough of the tree, perching itself on the edge of the branch and staring at him with its dark eyes. He looked back in silence as the dove tucked its head into its breast, tightened the grip of its talons over the perch, then puffed its feathers and shook its chest before letting out a plaintive call that resounded through the empty sky.

A second dove descended from the ether, flapping its wings rapidly to slow its trajectory and land on the branch beside the first. Both birds perched themselves atop the bough and continued to look at Henry, who became lost in the spellbinding blackness of their eyes. The doves leaned their beaks forward and called their doleful melody to him once again—but as soon as Henry blinked his eyes, they were gone.

The bough where the mourning doves once stood now held a nest of thickets in the corner of two divergent limbs. The voices of the children had returned, though Henry still found no one in sight. He looked up at the nest and walked closer to the sycamore tree, which hung against the bleached white sky like a fossilized remnant of a former world. With each step, he inexplicably became more nervous, filling with a sense of foreboding and dread as he neared the heavy trunk.

As he approached the tree, the soughing of wind in the branches began to overtake the sounds of the voices. Henry could feel no breeze around him, and the brittle brown leaves on the tree did not bend; but still, the wind continued to whistle louder with every movement toward it. By the time he at last stood beneath the bough, the roaring had become so forceful that he could no longer hear anything else—until it, too, ceased in an instant.

Henry stopped underneath the tree and looked down

at his feet, where he found the nest of the mourning doves, fallen from the bough and overturned on the ground. Three eggs lay broken, the white shells shattered on the cold soil, as the unborn hatchlings spilled out before him. Henry knelt down into the dirt and was filled with a profound, helpless sorrow as he clutched the nest in his hands and felt his heart slowly tear in two. The hatchlings were all dead, their beaks open but eyes not yet developed. He continued to look down at them and was filled with immeasurable, indescribable regret.

The wind resumed its howl above him—and he awoke.

The sky was heavy and white, auguring an early winter tempest in the distance. The wind whipped around the corners of the church on the hilltop, wheezing like a choked scream or a dying gasp of air. The draught spiraled around William as he stood at the precipice of the hill facing westward, gazing out into the morning sky before him. He watched as a flock of seabirds floated across the ivory expanse like a roving blemish across a blank canvas.

"We are getting closer," William said to Josiah, who stood behind him deferentially. "I can feel it in the air."

"It's been twenty-one days since the town has closed and the people have purged their material goods," said Josiah. "But there are still no signs of the advent."

"God has given us enough signs. The burden lies on us now."

"Respectfully, the people have done all that we've asked for. Excised the apostates. Sacrificed their belongings. Closed their shops. Sold their farms. They are living on stored food and Brother George's generosity. But there is only so much they will continue to do without seeing the fruits of their labor."

"I would not let that trouble you, brother."

"I'm sorry. I feel like I must have laid out the instructions incorrectly, perhaps set the wrong expectations with them."

"You did everything exactly as we planned in convincing them that night. They had to hear it from someone other than me; they had to feel like they were making the decision for themselves. And now those ashes cannot be unburnt."

"I'm not sure I understand . . ."

"They've come too far to stop now. You need not worry about the faithful reversing course. It's the others who are the concern."

"So what does that mean for us? What more must be done in town to ready ourselves?"

"It's become clear that until every one of us truly believes, we will never be granted salvation. It is not enough for only the believers to purify themselves—this whole land is sacrosanct. It's time that we tell those remaining few in town who have not joined us that our patience is wearing thin. Silence is just as profane as blasphemy; inaction just as unholy as sin. This is not about freedom or personal choice. They who do not comply put their entire community at risk."

Josiah scrawled the declarations in his notepad as William looked down onto the roofs of the houses below.

"Remember that the neutral angels are likewise fallen—they who have been neither rebellious nor faithful to God, but only for themselves, bound to perdition," William continued. "And as such, should we observe our neighbor refusing to believe, abstaining from worship, it is our duty to inform the church. For these are the final bodies who hold us back from deliverance."

"I understand, brother," said Josiah. "In short time, I'll ensure that they all will have this edict."

"And in short time, God will take notice," William promised. "We are almost there. We are almost there."

Josiah placed his pencil and notepad in his pocket and hurried to his printing press as William continued staring out into the horizon. He watched the wings of the seabirds beat on successively, gliding across the firmament as their caws echoed through the air. Banding closely together against the rising sun, they followed the Hudson south to find an escape from the winter in a warmer clime, and vanished into the clouds downstream.

# Chapter 14

THE SOUNDS OF scattered footsteps echoed across the puncheon floorboards as Henry and Abigail desperately scoured their home. Amidst the thuds and creaking of the wood, a faint, high-pitched whistle continuously whirred as Benji lay in the bed, struggling to open his airway. His face had taken on a ghostly white pallor and his lips were blue as a robin's egg. Specks of dark red blood stained his pillow beside his mouth.

The pulpy remains of the herbs rested in the bottom of the cauldron next to the bed, oversaturated to such a degree that they were no longer of any medicinal use. Henry rummaged through the bedroom, searching for any vestiges of unused medication—a basket or a satchel that might have been misplaced or left over from the previous month, a loose leaf or stem that may have fallen to the floor or into a drawer—anything to help his son persevere through one more episode.

"This was the last of the supply," said Abigail. "I'm sure of it."

"That can't be everything! Dr. Clarke told me that he ordered enough to last through the end of the year."

As Benji writhed atop the sheets and Henry and Abigail anxiously continued their search, Rosemary remained steady and calm as she knelt on the floor beside the bed. Placing her elbows on the mattress, Rosemary folded her hands, closed her eyes, and began to pray.

"Dear Father, who art in Heaven. Please accept my brother's soul, for he has not the strength to repent."

"Please listen to me, father!" Abigail cried. "That is all we have. Not a single order has come in since the shipping lanes were closed last month."

Henry slammed the last cabinet shut and covered his face with his palms.

"God damn it all!"

"God, grant him thy everlasting grace in this time of need."

Abigail took her coat from the hook on the wall. "I will go find Dr. Clarke. He'll have another solution. I'm sure of it."

"No," said Henry, shaking himself out of his despair. "The town is too dangerous right now. This is my responsibility."

"Open thy Heavenly gates and allow his soul to join in thy glorious banquet."

Henry stood upright with newfound determination as he formulated a plan of action.

"I'll be back by candlelight. It's important that you stay here with Benji and make him feel at ease. The more panicked he gets, the worse his breathing becomes."

"And one day grant us the mercy to all join him in thy kingdom."

"Rosemary—silence!" Henry snapped brusquely.

Rosemary remained unperturbed and kept her eyes closed and hands folded, lowering her voice to a whisper to continue her prayer. Henry quickly put on his coat and shut the door behind him, making haste to the town while the light still remained.

❧

The frost from Henry's breath cut through the air as he made his way through the wooded trails without delay. His farmhouse quickly disappeared into the dark void behind him as he ceaselessly pumped his legs with a stride that he had not managed to employ since his youth. The images of his son's anguish had kindled a dormant energy within him, pushing his lungs and his body to new extremes as the long dirt pathway soon gave way to the sight of the cobblestone pavement.

As his boots pressed against the road, Henry at last slowed to catch his breath and scan the vicinity for help. To his surprise, he found that the town was awash with worshippers who made their daily pilgrimage in unison toward the United Calvary Church, the bobbing ascension robes flowing like whitecaps in a stormy river. Henry approached the center of the town and waded between each faceless figure as he attempted to look for any open storefront or any home that was still occupied at that hour. The streets became fuller the deeper he went, but not a word was spoken to him as each devotee blankly ignored his brisk movements and continued to march solemnly ahead in the opposing direction.

Pushing his way against the current of believers, Henry found a clearing to continue toward the town square. He moved past the barren town hall and vacant houses, beyond Josiah's printing press and the Chandler estate, at last coming upon Harriman's general store. Henry pulled on the door and quickly found that it was locked, then turned his attention to the window beside it, frantically rapping on the glass in the hope to get his friend's attention.

"Nathaniel! Nathaniel!" he cried. "It's Henry. Please open up, it's urgent!"

Cold sweat began to drip down his temples as he heard no response nor any sign of life in the building. Spotting a resident in an ascension robe passing nearby, Henry ran over to the figure and grabbed him by the arms.

"Please," he said as he shook the man. "Where is the Harriman family? I need to find medication for my son."

Despite the desperation of Henry's actions, the person in the ascension robe replied to him sedately. "Why, it's nearly sundown. They should be on their way to the church, of course."

Henry looked at the hilltop in the distance to discover a row of worshippers forming along the ascending pathway, plodding ahead with a solemn, drone-like monotony. Releasing his grip of the man, Henry turned to the north and ran as quickly as he could toward the church.

Henry's hair was matted in sweat and nearly frozen from the cold air by the time he reached the fingerboard at the base of the hill. His lungs were burning and his tongue parched and swollen, but his legs nevertheless continued to move him toward the crowd. As he came upon the line of worshippers, Henry attempted to identify the faces behind the robes one by one along the way.

"Nathaniel? Nathaniel?" he asked each person, growing more agitated with every successive figure who silently dismissed his calls.

But as he questioned a small group of pilgrims, a robed man soon overheard his pleas and removed his hood. Henry saw his face from afar and dashed toward him.

"Nathaniel!" he exclaimed.

"Brother Henry," Nathaniel returned calmly, staring back at him in a trancelike state. "I haven't seen you at the sundown services lately. Is everything all right?"

"Listen to me, it's Benji. He's having another attack, and we've exhausted the remainder of his medicine. Do you have any more supply in your store?"

"I'm afraid I do not. We ceased our orders altogether last month."

"But . . . we need those shipments . . . my son—"

Nathaniel placed his hand on Henry's shoulder. "We're doing this for him, Henry. And for you, too. Christ's arrival is near. And soon you won't have to worry about these earthly ills anymore."

Henry looked up at him in disbelief as Nathaniel pulled over his hood and continued up the hill. Henry remained stuck in place as more worshippers passed him by on their way toward the church. He was adrift, surrounded by a sea of unrecognizable strangers.

"Please . . ." he begged hopelessly. "Anyone . . ."

The sun receded farther toward the horizon as each robed believer walked past him without slowing. But as the last of them entered the base of the hill, Henry noticed one of the figures carrying a familiar limp.

"Dr. Clarke?" he asked from across the path.

The figure stopped as Henry hurried toward him.

"Dr. Clarke!" he said again. "Thank God. It's Benji . . . we need your help."

Dr. Clarke remained stolid as the surrounding worshippers slowed their pace and cocked their ears toward their conversation.

"Brother Henry, it's nearly sundown."

"Listen to me, man. Benji's breathing—"

"I'm sorry, Henry, but it's too late now."

"Too late? Too late for what?"

"The ascension could come tonight. We've been preparing so diligently for so long."

Henry felt the contents of his stomach come to a boil. In a sudden bout of fury, he reached out his hands and seized the doctor by the collar of his robe, pulling him closer to his face.

"Damnit, Dr. Clarke!" Henry blared. "Are you not listening to me? My son is going to die if we don't do something!"

Dr. Clarke looked around as the other worshippers began to take notice, keeping his voice low as not to draw further attention.

"Henry, please stop this," he said quietly. "If I leave with you now, they'll think I don't believe."

Henry loosened his grip and stared at him with confusion.

"What are you saying?"

"These people will look for any excuse for why they haven't been saved yet," Dr. Clarke said with his voice trembling in fear. "If I'm not here with them, they'll blame me for it next. And Lord knows what will happen then."

"That's absurd. They must understand that this is a matter of life and death."

"There are more important things to them than that. Go see what Thomas Aleman and his church have become if you don't believe me."

Henry dropped his hands to his side, and Dr. Clarke readjusted his robe.

"I'm sorry, Henry . . . I have to go."

Henry looked out at the tapering tail of white robes ahead of him as Dr. Clarke resumed his hobbled march toward the church. He felt as if the entire world was parading to oblivion. But amongst the madness, Henry hoped that there might be one remaining vestige of rationality. And so, heeding Dr. Clarke's charge, he gathered what was left of his dwindling vitality and made his way toward Thomas's church.

As he hiked through the empty streets of Calvary, Henry could hear the choir of schoolchildren singing hymns from above. He thought about the young students who were compelled to carol for the coming of their own deaths and remembered Thomas telling him long ago how evil would persist when good men remained idle. But he'd never thought it would come to this. The memory filled him with regret, a guilt that he had not stood with Thomas and the light of his church before his own town descended into darkness.

However, he knew that it was no time to bewail what was already decided. His only concern was for Benji and giving him the proper care he needed no matter whom it was from. If he could reach the pastor or what was left of his new parish, they could perhaps find a solution. There was still time left, still hope that they could help get Benji a different treatment or transport him to the nearest location that had not been overrun by the hysteria.

But as the sight of Thomas's home emerged in the distance, Henry's heart sunk into the cavity of his chest. There were no sounds of worship, no signs of life, nor any people in sight. The homestead stood abandoned before him—frost covering the untrodden grass that led to the unlit home and deserted barn. It seemed as if all who had ever set foot inside had turned to dust.

Henry was out of breath. His legs could hardly support his weight, and his knees began to wobble as his energy was at last depleted. His pace became but a crawl as he neared the barn. Afraid of what he might find, he gradually forced himself toward the door—but it would not be opened. Looking up, he found a wooden plank nailed across the entrance to the church with words from Scripture painted in what looked like blood: DEPART FROM ME, YE CURSED.

Devoid of any remaining strength, Henry turned his back against the barn door and slumped to the ground. He looked out to the north across the treetops at the single beacon of light emanating from the church on the hill. With no further recourse, he knew that there was only one left to seek—the only one who might have the power to help.

❧

Henry entered the halls of the United Calvary Church, which were empty following the sundown service at Ascension Rock outside. The world had lasted another day, and the worshippers had returned home, wondering what they must have done wrong or who among them might still be preventing Christ from bringing an end to their struggle.

The only person inside late in the evening was William, who was lighting votive candles at the altar with his back to the entrance. Henry stood at the threshold as William turned around slowly.

"Brother Henry."

"Reverend Miller," Henry said in a whisper.

Henry stepped forward hesitantly.

"It's my son . . . I don't know what else to do."

"The midnight hour is drawing near. There is only so much time left for him."

"Please . . ." Henry continued. "I can't lose him."

William put down the candle, vibrating in its glow.

"God has given your son a gift. He has spared us one more day before our reckoning."

"I'll do anything. I have nowhere else to turn."

"Bring him here, brother. Let the light of the Lord cure what ails him. I promise you, Henry. This is the only way."

Weary and weakened, Henry lowered his head and acceded to the instructions. He had no other choice but to bring his son to God.

## Chapter 15

WILLIAM DREW OPEN the canvas door from the inside of the tent to find Henry holding his unconscious son across his arms.

"Come," said William. "It's ready."

Henry tucked Benji against his chest as he ducked below the canvas and crossed into the vacant structure. William had lit two lanterns at the station of the former pulpit, which illuminated the cross-shaped baptismal font beside it. The water lay calm and stagnant, most of it having already effervesced from the past month of inactivity. Henry looked at William with uncertainty as he felt the cold draught permeate the gaps under the tent, but William returned with a confident bow of his head.

"The water may be cold, but it's not yet frozen," he assured him. "It's no different than those springtime currents in which you were baptized by my father all those years ago."

Henry nodded meekly as he carried Benji over to the

wooden steps and ascended to the top platform above the pool. William followed behind and removed his heavy bear-skin overcoat, draping it over the empty bench and revealing his black frock. Moving ahead of Henry, he slowly walked down the steps and into the frigid water as he beckoned for him to do the same.

Benji moaned unintelligibly as Henry gently glided his legs into the water with them and held on to his underarms to ensure that he would not sink any further.

"Scripture teaches us that all but Christ and the Blessed Mother are born with the sins of Adam," William began as Benji shivered in the cold. "But the supreme benevolence of the Lord lies in His forgiveness of the betrayal of His creation—as long as we willingly seek our absolution and choose to be reborn in the waters of His mercy."

Henry caressed Benji's cheek as he felt his body shaking in his hands.

"Benjamin Smith, do you reject Satan and all of the forms he takes to bring temptation to man?"

Benji's teeth began to chatter as he managed to open the slit of one eye. He nodded wearily to William.

"Please hurry," Henry pleaded. "He can't be in the cold for much longer."

"Do you accept that Jesus Christ is the Son of God," William continued apace. "Do you beseech Him for forgiveness of your sins and give yourself to Him as your one Lord and savior?"

Benji nodded again as his head fell back into Henry's hand. He began to toss in the water as he struggled for air.

"And do you accept that His Second Coming is true and imminent—that the advent is near?"

Benji attempted to move his parched lips in search of a reprieve from the cold as his eyes rolled into the back of his head.

"He says yes—he does!" Henry exclaimed. "He accepts that this is all imminent! Now take his pain away. Please, I beg you!"

"In the name of the Father, the Son, and the Holy Spirit, let these waters wash away thy sins."

William nodded to Henry, who let go of his grasp from under Benji's arms as William submerged his body in the water. As he resurfaced, the shock of the cold sprung open Benji's eyes, and he took in a deep breath of air. For the first time that evening, Henry felt his hopes resuscitated as he knelt into the pool and pulled his son toward him.

"It's going to be all right, Benji," he said as he held his head against his heart. "I love you. I love you."

Henry wiped the tears from his eyes and loosened his arms around his son. The awakening of his senses, even temporarily, filled Henry with a divine sensation. Perhaps it was going to be all right in the end, he thought. Perhaps this was all he ever really needed.

Henry continued to look at Benji, who gradually began to fall back into unconsciousness.

"Let us bring him inside the church," said William. "There he will find the warmth of God."

Henry's eyes concealed a dull void as he leaned forward with his forearms pressed against his knees. He sat in the front-most pew across from Benji, who lay on his back on a makeshift cot at the church altar beneath the etching of the crucifix. His clothes had been removed, and his body was now dry and wrapped in wool, brightened by the shimmering candles that surrounded him like a miniature city of lights. He remained entirely still as he drifted in and out of sentience, drained of all vitality and oxygen, his breathing no more than a faint whimper.

There was nothing more Henry could do but sit and watch. His son was slowly drowning. In the logical hemisphere of his mind, he knew that Benji would not live past the night; but still he maintained an irrational, spiritual hope that he would find deliverance here in this house of worship. There was a certain mystical aura to the empty church at that hour, and he felt as if he were in a separate space between Heaven and earth, halfway between dream and reality—a limbo where time had stopped, and he just needed to make it through one final test before the end.

William quietly prayed over Benji at the side of the small bed. Only the distant rumbling of thunder punctuated the silence, as a winter storm began to slowly sail across the sky toward the hill. As he concluded his prayer, William opened his eyes and raised himself from his knees, then softly walked toward the pews and sat beside Henry.

"We must be patient now," he said. "The rest is up to God."

"I can hardly hear his breathing anymore," Henry said without taking his eyes off his son.

"The struggle is subsiding—his soul is finding peace. That is the power of prayer."

Lightning lit the interior of the church through the eastern window as the thunder echoed again in the distance. Henry listened to the coming storm and hoped the rains would come and wash away the chaos and the sorrow for good.

"William, can I ask you something?"

William shifted position in his seat to face him directly.

"Why are you doing this?"

"It is never too late to write another chapter in our book of life. Your son still has time before his judgment, and I am duty bound to help him find his salvation."

"I don't mean why you are here, in this moment. I am asking why you are doing this—all of this?" Henry gestured to the whole of the church around him.

"You are asking me why I came back to Calvary. I don't believe it's uncommon for a man to seek a return to his home later in life."

"You say you've found irrefutable evidence for the Second Coming, the end of days. Information that affects everyone—all life on earth. Yet the first place you think to go and bring that news is to this meager village of three hundred. Why not instead deliver your tidings in Boston or spread the gospel in New York or London? Why bother with us?"

William's eyes flashed in the light of the storm as he considered his reply.

"Remember what I said about the words my father once told me? That truth is an undeviating path?"

Henry nodded, recalling his sermon on the day he announced the coming rapture.

"By the grace of God, I have discovered something about this path that I did not expect. The path of truth, for me, was not a straight line—but a circle that brought me back to where it all began. I left here because my father could never understand that we as individual men are limited in our capacity to understand the fundamental questions found in Scripture; and as such, I believed that it would take the sum-mation of countless generations of scholarship and intellect, a rich understanding of language, history, and science to truly grasp the wonders of the Bible. My father thought I would one day return and admit that he was right, that a more basic reading was all that was needed to understand God's plan. But what I realized after discovering the truth of the end was how limiting his approach was—and why this house of worship that he built and for so long struggled to have recognized by his peers was dying before his eyes.

"When I uncovered the date of the advent, I knew it was a sign from God telling me to honor my father's wishes and return to the church that he had left for me. The people here are the salt of the earth, those who are in the greatest need of direction and instruction. They are the people who most need saving, Henry. God called me to my studies, to tread the path toward enlightenment, and to return and lead the blind by the light of my teachings. I am here because it is my duty to help my fellow neighbors before it is too late. Everything I am doing is for their own good, for the good of this town."

"But why the constant shifts of your demands?" Henry countered. "If this is God's plan, then why bring these false promises of salvation, only to then command more from your followers with each successive week we wait?"

"It's been clear since the tarrying began that more must be done if we are to truly bring an end to it all. But imagine if I told them this from the beginning—that our sacrifice must be consummate, that the only way to find ultimate salvation was through ultimate suffering—do you think anyone would have listened?"

Henry deliberated to himself and then shook his head.

"That's why this cumulative, stepwise approach was necessary. It is human nature, after all. Tell a man to jump into icy water and he will refuse. But ask him just to go in up to his ankles, and then his knees are only one more step. After that, it will make no difference to him if he wades in deeper. He is already cold and already wet, and returning to the air will only make him further still."

"But you are not asking them. Shutting them out of commerce and life in the town. Ensuring that those who do not comply are seen as pariahs amongst their own neighbors. That is no choice—that is oppression."

"That is a natural consequence of their own selfish aims. How can one be expected to be treated fairly when those around them know that they are putting everyone's soul in danger?"

"They believe that because yours is the only voice they are allowed to hear. How can you call that the will of the people when you have silenced all dissent? When you have forbidden any outside influence from entering the town?"

"This is a matter of achieving eternal life or being committed to the second death. What if those dissenters and their misinformation are convincing? One person persuades another, then that person another after him. It begins to grow and spread like a cancer. We know that there will just be a select few who will be chosen to weather the storm of sin and find salvation—and it may be that these influences see to it that we are not among them. And I say thus that you are no longer free to choose when that choice can affect all others around you."

"And so you silenced them permanently. You burned the heretics at the stake—Pastor Aleman and his congregation—a mortal sin in the name of spiritual purification."

"Oh please, Brother Henry," William said with a dismissive shake of his head. "I stated that Thomas Aleman and his followers should merely be excommunicated from this town, removed from the public sphere so they could no longer poison our well. Whatever else my parishioners may have done to see that through in the moment was their decision—not mine. And I am sure, no matter what their actions, they were decided in the name of good for us all."

"And now you've really done it," Henry said as the thunder roared once more. "You've gotten everyone to believe, to live for the sole cause of salvation, even if it destroys what we've made for ourselves. Is this what your father would have wanted when he asked you to return to us?"

"Before I came back, no one in this house of worship was awake. No one was singing. No one was atoning for their sins," William continued, rising to his feet and pointing his finger toward the sky as he fixated his eyes on Henry. "I alone awoke them from their spiritual slumber! There is no greater aim than to save a soul, brother. And no sacrifice is too great for the promise of the glory that awaits us."

"And how many more offerings will it take?" Henry asked sharply. "What more needs to be done for Christ to rise again?"

"That, Henry," William said as he leaned in closer, "that is for you to decide."

As the two men stared at one another, the remaining

gasps of air from Benji came like a silent scream, and his body began to violently convulse on the bed. Henry leapt across the altar and knelt down over his son, clasping his tiny hand in his own.

"Easy, son," he whispered to him. "Easy—I'm here."

As he rubbed his thumb softly against his palm, Benji let out one final breath, and then all was still. Benji lay with his mouth open, his chest no longer moving. Henry continued stroking his hand as tears surged from behind his eyes. The sounds of thunder began to recede in the distance. The rains never came.

"You promised me he'd be cured," Henry said without taking his eyes from his son. "If only I took him here."

William slowly walked to the altar and stood beside him.

"Brother Henry, he is cured indeed. Glory be to God, he is now free of all his ills!"

Henry lowered his head to Benji's hand as the last remaining light inside him faded away.

# Chapter 16

" '*S*UFFER LITTLE CHILDREN,
*Forbid them not to come unto me:*
*For of such is the kingdom of Heaven*
*And I shall soon return for thee.'*

*O when, o when will we be worthy*
*Of His promised eternal grace?*
*How long, how long must we toil*
*Just waiting for thine embrace?*

*Suffer little children,*
*Our voices now beggeth of Him:*
*Please open the gates of Heaven*
*And swiftly take us in.*"

Mrs. Edwards dabbed a warm teardrop from her eye as she finished conducting the chorus of her former schoolchildren in the front of the church. The robed choir wobbled restlessly before the pulpit as they waited in a starved delirium for their next instructions while the pipe organ continued to play.

Henry remained expressionless in the front pew, flanked by his daughters on each side. As he stared ahead blankly, he looked into the hollow eyes of the children who waited at the altar and felt a profound pity for them. None of them appeared to understand what was truly happening—that they were delivering a requiem for their young friend and classmate who not long ago would have been singing along-side them in church or in school. Between the hunger and the constant worship, the line between life and death had seemingly become blurred for them. The funeral services were just part of that fever dream from which they could never seem to wake.

Abigail and Rosemary began to softly sob to themselves as the final notes of the organ rang throughout the nave. But Henry remained unmoved, surrendered to a feeling of futility as he continued to gaze into the eyes of the children before him.

"Thank you, sister," said William to Mrs. Edwards, as she led the children back to their seats before the altar where Benji had taken his final breaths.

William stepped forward and replaced the choir in the front of the room, standing behind the lectern to address the full congregation.

"Today, we remember our young brother Benjamin Smith, who was sadly taken from us before he could witness the glory of our savior's return."

The parishioners in turn wiped away their budding tears as they remembered the vibrant youth who used to sit with them every Sunday since he was old enough to walk—the small boy who would run around the church grounds with the other children after services, the boy who would pass out hymn books as a kindness to their former pastor, the boy for whom they prayed when his mother passed away at such a young age and for whom they prayed when he, too, was stricken with a sickness of his own.

"But on this somber day, we must not let our grief overcome us. We can take solace in knowing that Brother Benjamin leaves this earth pure of heart and pure of soul, baptized in Christ and freed now from all corruption, all sin. And for this, there is no doubt in my mind that we shall soon find him waiting in the great banquet hall as we celebrate our eternal union with the Bridegroom in the imminent future."

William paused as he looked out across the congregation with a stern furrow of his brow.

"But let this occasion also be a reminder for us all of what is to come," he warned, shifting the cadence of his voice. "There has never been a clearer message sent by our Lord than His taking of this young life just as he began his time living for Christ. I trust that it is a sign for our community at large—a sign that we, too, can ascend only when all of us are collectively giving ourselves to Jesus. There shall be no more tolerance for those who refuse to commit to our cause and thus prevent our eternal union. I believe this is the final message we shall receive; there can be no more warnings, no more examples set for us. So thank you, Lord—and thank you, Benji—for helping us recognize what we must now do in this time of waiting. And may He have mercy on us all."

As Henry locked eyes with William, the sounds of the services faded around him and everything else in the pulpit dissolved to black. He began to see the reverend in his true form: for all of his talk of enlightenment, he saw not a man who cared about uncovering the truth—but rather one who sought, above all else, to find validation of his own theories regardless of the reality before him; every victim of his teachings a proof point, every missed date or unmaterialized prediction a mere aberration, footnotes in an endless dissertation that could never be refuted nor corrected because it continued to evolve in perpetuity.

The light came back to the room and illuminated the parishioners around him next, as they wiped the tears from their cheeks with the sleeves of their white robes. But Henry would not forget the faces behind the hoods, each person who had turned away as he begged them to help the very child for whom they wept that morning. As he looked into their eyes, he knew that it was no longer William alone who could bring an end to the wildness that had overtaken the town. William had once assumed that the people were too uneducated or too simple to realize the truth of his prophecy without his guidance. But in that moment, Henry understood something about his neighbors that William never could—that through all of the waiting and rationalization, they, too, had now become coauthors of his thesis. And Henry hated them for it.

Henry's empty expression slowly contorted into a deep scowl; his burning contempt was all that could thaw his sorrow. He stared into William's eyes throughout the sermon until the services concluded, when Mrs. Edwards stood up and indicated to the students to join her at the altar for the processional. A dirge began to play on the pipe organ, and the children began to sing:

*"How long, O Lord, our Savior,*
*Wilt thou remain away?*
*Our hearts are growing weary*
*Of thy so long delay;*
*O when shall come the moment*
*When, brighter far than morn,*
*The sunshine of thy glory*
*Shall on thy people dawn.*

*How long, O gracious Master,*
*Wilt thou thy household leave?*
*So long hast thou now tarried,*
*Few thy return believe.*
*Immersed in sloth and folly,*
*Thy servants, Lord, we see,*
*And few of us stand ready*
*With joy to welcome thee.*

*How long, O Heavenly Bridegroom,*
*How long wilt thou delay?*
*And yet how few are grieving*
*That thou dost absent stay:*
*Thy very bride her portion*
*And calling hath forgot,*
*And seeks for ease and glory*
*Where thou, her Lord, art not.*

*O wake thy slumbering virgins,*

*Send forth the solemn cry;*
*Let all thy saints repeat it:*
*The Bridegroom draweth nigh.*
*May all our lamps be burning,*
*Our loins well girded be,*
*Each longing heart preparing*
*With joy thy face to see."*

The display was beginning to make Henry sick. Unable to remain seated any longer, he stood up with his daughters and led them down the aisle toward the exit of the church.

Henry focused only on the door ahead of him as he passed Nathaniel and Jacob at each side of the exit, brushing past their bowed heads and extended hands without a word. The two raised their eyes and grumbled aloud as he walked past them, wondering why their old friend would show them such discourtesy on a day like this. Keeping his view fixed ahead, Henry opened the door to find several townspeople immediately approaching him to offer his family condolences for their loss.

"Henry. Girls," George began, reaching out his hand. "May God be with young Benji. I pray for the boy."

Henry ignored George's embrace and sidestepped him to continue out into the cold morning air as the organ echoed behind him. Abigail and Rosemary stood at the threshold, nonplussed by their father's sudden lack of propriety as he kept walking forward without them. Realizing that he was not stopping for anyone, they turned to one another and quickly ran ahead to catch up with him.

"Blessings to your son, Henry!" Marigold cried to him

from the side of the pathway. "He is surely in a better place than we."

Henry continued onward without acknowledging her, picking up his pace down the hill.

"Father, what are you doing?" Rosemary asked as she struggled to keep up with his speed. "Why are you in such a rush to go home?"

Henry ignored her questions and remained focused on the walkway in front of him as the rest of the congregation began to converge on their path. Dr. Clarke was the first to break away from the crowd and hobble toward Henry, noticing that he and his family were quickly leaving the church grounds.

"Henry, you must accept my family's condolences," Dr. Clarke said, removing his hat and placing it across his heart. "I am certain that Benji's suffering has now ended."

Henry felt a sudden tension travel from his gut and into the muscles of his hands as the doctor neared him. Resisting the urge to lunge for his throat in front of his daughters, Henry stepped toward Dr. Clarke and leaned in so that their eyes were inches apart.

"If you don't get out of my sight this instant," Henry said in a low whisper through his clenched jaw, "then I'll see to it that your suffering has just begun."

Dr. Clarke hastily backed away to allow Henry and his daughters to pass, and they at last made their way through the rest of the churchgoers and away from United Calvary.

"Can we please just stay with them for a while?" Rosemary pleaded to Henry, looking up at him as they walked down the hill. "It's been weeks since we've seen or spoken to anybody in town."

"I want nothing to do with this flock or this cursed pasture," said Henry. "This will be the last time we set foot on these grounds."

"But that's not right!" Rosemary declared. "Did you not see the tears that were shed around you? Did you not hear the songs that were sung for him? They all loved Benji, too!"

Henry stopped in his tracks and turned around to face Rosemary.

"And where were they when he was dying and in need of help? Where were they yesterday when I buried him with my own hands?"

Rosemary gulped as she continued looking up at her father.

"Do you know why I had to dig his grave alone?" Henry continued. "Because these neighbors you claim love their community so much forced the sexton out of town—or perhaps worse. They do not give one thought about anyone's survival or livelihood. All that matters to them is their own supposed salvation."

"But you heard what Brother William said. We must all work together to achieve that. We are united in that mission."

"Damnit, Rosemary, your brother is dead because of this madness! Because of that exact rot you're repeating like an entranced fanatic."

"It's not their fault Benji got sick! It's just like what happened to mother. You bury your head in the dirt and pretend like nothing is wrong until it's too late."

Before Henry could react, he heard a loud crack ring across Rosemary's face and saw Abigail standing over her, pointing at her with her index finger.

"I'll do it again until the devil inside you has gone out,"

she warned. "You think you know everything, but you're still just as ignorant as ever, Rosemary. Don't you see what your church has done to this family? It's time to walk away for good!"

Rosemary raised her watery eyes to her father and looked for him to intervene—but Henry said nothing, turning away reticently as he continued down the hill. She pressed her hand against her stinging face as she watched the shadows of her family dissipate in the distance, before reluctantly following behind in their wake.

## Chapter 17

A COLD WIND WAILED across the barren plains as the winter sun began to rise over the trees. Heavy fog slowly drifted in across the farmland; the sun struggled to warm the frost-covered earth. Henry watched the white mist creep over the infecund dirt before him, shrouding the forest path to his west that led toward the riverside. He stood quietly as the air continued to thicken, rolling ahead and glazing over the grave beside the old sycamore tree.

He read the letters of her name carved into the wooden cross: MARY SMITH. The lilies he had planted in the spring were now withered and wilted, slouched toward the hidden sun. The marcescent petals had long since begun to rot, the once-white flowers now appearing no more than a starved weed. One strong gust of wind was all that it would take to commit them to a second, final death.

A fresh grave rested beside that of his wife. The dirt mound atop it had yet to settle, the soil still warm. A matching wooden cross stood next to hers. But on it was an etching of a name he could not yet bear to read: BENJAMIN SMITH. Henry looked up to the cloudy morning sky.

"You never would have thought it to happen," he said out loud, shaking his head to himself. "One day bringing new life into this world, then as quickly as he'd come in, it's taken away just like that. Our only son, gone before he was grown, before he could leave the house where he was born, chart his own course in life, see his dreams through. I curse myself for thinking it, Mary, but if it weren't for our girls I'd soon have a mind to join you both right now. Lord help me . . .

"Sometimes it seems like this is never going to end. The longer everyone waits for it to be over, the more certain they are that they are right. And the more they believe they are right, the more forceful they are in their defense of it. I know I'm never going to be the same after this—but I fear that the world is never going to be the same again either. This absurdity will last forever.

"Everything feels upside down. Black is white; truth is fiction; sin is salvation. This world just isn't right, Mary. I don't know if it's just this town or if the whole of humanity has been gripped by the same madness. But I don't feel a part of it anymore. They say that the end is near and we must do all we can to ready ourselves to die—damn the consequences and damn the daily woe. But I think about what you told me all those years ago: there are more important things to life than death. What is it to be alive without living? We are all standing here waiting for our time to come, while we instead die from the inside out. And to what end?"

As he watched the graves glinting in the faint sunlight,

Henry heard a sound approaching in the distance—the shuffling of shoes across the hard ground, crunching the dried grass of the farm. He turned to find a lantern glowing through the swelling fog and a voice calling to him.

"Father! Father!" he heard echoing through the atmosphere.

Out of the brume, he found Abigail dashing across the farmland from the rear exit of their home, holding the dim light with a look of dread painted upon her face.

"Father, Rosemary is gone. She's missing!" she panted as she approached him.

"She's gone?" Henry repeated in disbelief. "For how long?"

"I don't know. She wasn't in the bed when I awoke. She must have left before dawn."

The remaining leaves from the sycamore tree shook in the breeze and fluttered down to the earth. As Henry looked out to their home through the fog, a bitter gust of wind swirled across his back from the woods behind them. He felt his legs sinking deep into the mire, unable to move as the winds froze him in place. It was only when Abigail reached out and grabbed him by the sleeve that he at last remembered his purpose, rose up from the bog, and walked toward the house to face the inevitable.

"Check for anything that's missing," Henry instructed when they arrived inside. "Any items that she may have taken that could indicate where she might be headed."

Abigail at once followed her father's directive, and they

each focused their attention on a different area in the small house, checking for any clues or signs of Rosemary's whereabouts. Abigail entered her bedroom and scanned her eyes across the space that she had shared with her sister every night of her life for as long as she could remember. She shut the door, and the past began to materialize before her.

Abigail saw the white crib that each of the children had once slept in against the outer wall. Moonlight was pouring in from the window, basking the interior in a pale blue hue. She walked in closer and found herself and her sister, barely old enough to walk, standing on their tiptoes to lean over the railing and observe their new brother, the peaceful baby boy who never cried or let out much of a sound at all—who marveled back at his sisters with wide eyes and an indelible smile on his face.

"Where are you, Rosemary?"

Abigail heard the whisper and turned to find herself a few years older walking about the room as she searched for any sign of her sister.

"I know she couldn't have gone far."

Abigail heard a rustling coming from inside the closet as she opened the door to discover Rosemary, no more than five years old, ensconced in a game of hide-and-seek, giggling with delight when her sister located her under a pile of linens with just her eyes peeking out between the sheets.

"I knew I would find you!"

As Abigail stepped inside the closet, the specter of their former life disappeared into the dark shadows before her. She inspected the items inside and found that her sister's winter coat was missing from the rack.

Abigail turned around and made her way toward the

bed. She could still see their indentations in the sheets as their past selves appeared again, now approaching adolescence, pushing their belongings into the space between the wooden bed frame and the floor. She knelt down where she and her sister had once stored their dolls before they became too old to play with them any longer—and where Rosemary still kept hers hidden under a dress, though Abigail always pretended not to know. Abigail reached in and pulled out the wooden doll that her father had made to look just like her sister and she brushed back the dust from its face. She leaned her back against the mattress with the doll in her hand as her heart sunk lower. It was nothing more than a figment of the past now. Everything had changed.

As Abigail sat with the doll in her lap, she noticed that something had been placed on the table beside their bed. Her visions receded back into the harbors of her memory as she stood up and moved over to their nightstand. Laid upon the table was an object of the present—their family Bible, which appeared to have been left open deliberately. Her heart began to race faster as she slowly approached the book, moving her fingers across the open page. A crease bent at a right angle pointed to a passage from the gospel:

> *Think not that I am come to send peace on earth: I came not to send peace, but a sword.*
>
> *For I am come to set a man at variance against his father, and the daughter against her mother, and the daughter in law against her mother in law.*
>
> *And a man's foes shall be they of his own household.*
>
> *He that loveth father or mother more than me is not*

*worthy of me: and he that loveth son or daughter more than me is not worthy of me.*

Abigail's eyes widened as a wave of understanding came over her. She slammed the Bible shut and called out to the other room.

"Father!" she shouted. "We need to start gathering our things."

Abigail heard her father's hurried footsteps across the floor as he ran to her room and opened the door.

"What's wrong?" he asked. "What did you find?"

"We need to leave now. We can hide in the cellar if it's too late."

Before Henry could comprehend the meaning behind her urgency, a sudden knock resounded from their front door. Abigail closed her eyes as the sounds persisted, and her father slowly made his way to the entrance. The memories of their past returned and replayed all at once—the time before the sickness, before the mania, before the doom and death predominated their daily lives; the time of childhood games with her sister, the time of wonder and amazement with her brother, the time of unity and harmony amongst the three children. But she knew she would have to leave them behind if she wanted to move forward.

Abigail opened her eyes and followed her father into the main room. The knocking turned into a forceful pounding as he neared the door. Abigail looked behind her and measured their ability to flee outside the back. Henry paused before turning the knob, looking back at her over his shoulder as she silently pleaded with him to take to the rear exit—to leave it all behind. But Henry was not ready.

Henry opened the door to find Josiah and George at the entrance with a consortium of townspeople behind them.

"Brother Henry, Sister Abigail. You must come with us quickly," said George.

Abigail peered into the group of men and women, who glared back at them forebodingly behind the hoods of their ascension robes.

"What is this? Explain yourselves," Henry demanded.

Josiah stepped inside the house as Henry moved in front of Abigail to protect her from the incoming crowd.

"We found your daughter. We need you to follow us to the riverside; she is waiting for you at the pier."

"Rosemary . . ." Abigail whispered.

Abigail saw it in her father's eyes. She knew he had to acquiesce if he had any hope of seeing her again. Henry turned to Abigail to ease her apprehension.

"It's all right," he said calmly. "We're going to find her and take her with us."

Abigail nodded diffidently and slowly followed Henry through the door. As they walked farther outside, they saw the true extent of the dark-eyed fanatics that accompanied them. The dirt path to the woods before them was lined shoulder to shoulder with the greater half of the residents of Calvary—two parallel rows of townspeople, all garmented in white ascension robes, forming a corridor for them to travel westward to the water. There was nowhere for them to turn.

With a nervous breath, Henry and Abigail made their way toward the river, as the rest of the worshippers trailed closely behind.

## Chapter 18

A SINGLE ROWBOAT SWAYED slowly in the icy water, its wooden hull drumming monotonously against the terminus of the pier. Frost was beginning to form along the unused pilings and the outer perimeter of the docks. The once-bustling shipping port was now devoid of any commercial traffic, and the small vessel was all that connected Calvary to the rest of civilization.

The sounds became louder to Henry the nearer they came to the pier. Each snap of a twig under his boots, each clatter of steps against the cobblestone, every drum of the boat against the dock was amplified by the damp air, overpowered only by the beating of his heart and the cry of the wind. Henry and Abigail advanced toward the docks to soon find the rest of the town waiting for them at the end of the path. Each new figure was likewise garmented in ascension robes, the openings of their sleeves pressed together, concealing their hands so that only the dim outlines of their faces were visible in the mist. Behind their white hoods, Henry was able to recognize certain eyes—those of his neighbors and friends, those who had worked and traded with him and sent their children to school with Rosemary and Benji—each holding a dark, minatory stare as they waited for their arrival.

George and Josiah prodded the pair farther along as each member in the gathering parted one by one, forming a V-shaped tunnel to allow them to continue toward the base of the pier. As the last of the worshippers stepped to the side, one solitary figure stood at the end of the line, draped in a cloak of fog that rolled in from the water.

"William!" Henry called out as his visage became clear through the clouds. "Where is my daughter?"

Henry stepped closer but was quickly met with the shoulders of Nathaniel and Jacob, who acted as sentries stationed at the flanks of the reverend. The two men grabbed onto him and prevented him from moving any farther as he attempted in vain to shake off their grasp.

"Henry and Abigail Smith," William announced powerfully for the crowd. "It has been brought to our attention that you both have forsaken your duties in preparing for the Millennium—and have even gone so far as to deny a believer the right to daily worship."

William paused and motioned to his left. Out from the cluster of townspeople, Rosemary stepped forward, outfitted in a new ascension robe, and stood obediently at his side.

Henry attempted to charge at William, but Nathaniel and Jacob clasped his arms and shoulders, locking him tightly in their grip. Abigail waited behind her father and stared at Rosemary with anguish in her eyes, as her sister glared back with cold remorselessness.

"Throughout this year, we the righteous have toiled, sacrificed, and suffered so that we may one day accept the call of the Bridegroom when He returns to earth from the clouds," William continued. "There have been some in this town who have attempted to suppress his call with the terrible din of blasphemy, whereas others seek to drown it out with silence. But now, thanks to the faithful, that final impediment has been uncovered, and the cause of our long tarrying at last revealed."

All eyes fell upon Henry and Abigail as they absorbed the blame for the town's collective despair.

"This is ridiculous!" Henry shouted from the grasp of his captors. "We have left you all alone while you worship as you please. I have stood by silently with my family and kept to myself despite the destruction you have wrought upon the town in which I was raised. It is our right—and no business of yours—to choose what we do amongst ourselves."

"That is where you're wrong, Brother Henry. Evidence from Scripture tells us that a single impurity can delay that glorious day—and that one sinner can undermine all of the work we've done to hallow these grounds. We have seen it time and again since October the twenty-second. It is now only your inaction that remains a threat to the salvation for us all."

Josiah forcefully shoved Abigail beside her father to ensure that charges would be levied equally between them. Henry looked to his side to find his daughter shivering from fear and from the cold, staring down at the pavement below them, mouthing a prayer to herself.

"What do you want from us?" he asked. "Is it attendance in the worship? What little food we can spare from our farm? Fine—we'll hand it all over if we must. All that matters is that you give me my daughter back."

"It is too late for atonement," said William. "What kind of false piety would we garner from such pressure? If ye shall ask for mercy, ask only God now—for the well of our clemency is long dried."

Henry looked up and could see the contempt looming in the eyes of the believers that surrounded him.

"My friends, look at what is occurring among us," he said. "Look at what you're doing to your neighbors, your kin, yourselves."

The townspeople continued to stare back at him without a word as a cold sweat began to form on his forehead.

"Open your eyes!" Henry begged, his legs starting to buckle as he remained in the hands of Nathaniel and Jacob. "Can't you see? It's not happening. It's never going to happen. Are we just to forever live in fear of a judgment that will never come?"

A moment of silence permeated the stale air as Henry waited for a response, a defense, from anyone. But only one sound echoed through the atmosphere—a call that broke through the clouds above, as the last of the seabirds flew due south for the winter across the white sky.

"They refuse!" one of the neighbors shouted.

"They will not repent!" screamed another.

The throng of fanatics began to condemn the doubters before them. Voices rang out confirming that they must indeed be the reasons for their lack of deliverance, which quickly devolved into curses and calls for retribution. The robed mass stepped forward and began to close in on them.

Surrounded on all sides, Henry and Abigail sunk to the ground in terror.

"So be it then," said William, quieting the crowd. "Henry and Abigail Smith, your punishment shall be swift and unequivocal. You are hereby banished from the town of Calvary, the future site of the New Jerusalem—your sins setting sail with you."

Henry looked at the inauspicious, fog-draped waters before them. He could not see out into the river more than ten feet beyond the pier.

"This is madness! We have nothing with us—the river is nearly iced over!"

"The Lord will grant you passage if He deems you worthy," said William.

"Rosemary, this isn't the way. Tell them you don't want this."

"Your daughter has chosen the path of righteousness," William said in her stead. "She is with us now."

Rosemary stepped in closer to William, never removing her eyes from her father and sister. Henry looked at the face of his youngest daughter standing before him in her lily-white robe. He could see it in her eyes. She held a true faith, bound to the movement—not out of appeasement or coercion from the mob, nor one based in any kind of rationality or deduction. It was a trust that was unconditional, the same trust that she used to show for him when she was younger, when she believed he had answers to every question in the world. He knew he had lost her.

"To Hell with you, William," said Henry, raising himself to his feet to stand firmly before the crowd. "And to Hell is where he will be leading all of you."

As he stood upright, Henry felt a sudden, sharp pain against his temple—and then another on the back of his head. A hot sensation burned down the side of his skull as he placed his hand on his head and felt a wetness in his hair, observing the sticky film of blood on his fingers. Dropping to one knee, Henry watched as stone after stone hurtled toward him from the hands of the congregation, each attacker stepping forward and releasing them with a rabid scream.

"Move forward," William instructed over the clamor. "Thy vessel awaits."

Unable to withstand the bludgeoning any longer, Henry and Abigail hurriedly continued forward as each of the townspeople pummeled them with stones to the face and body, cursing at them to leave.

"Sinners! Heathens!" a woman shouted as she targeted Henry's face.

"Be gone! Be gone!" a man shouted as he threw a large stone against Abigail's back.

Abigail fell to the ground as the cold rock ripped through the fabric of her clothes, her bonnet sailing from her head and her hair unfurling into the dirt. A second barrage came quickly, and Henry helped her to her feet to desperately move ahead. Within moments, Henry and Abigail were tattered, bruised, and bloodied as they stumbled toward the dock in fear for their lives. William followed alongside, standing over them with fiery zeal as he barked to the crowd.

"With each step, our town becomes more pure! With each step, we rid the vile bodies that infect our congregation! O we cleanse this land so that He may deliver us from evil! Out, out, unfit beast! And bring perdition with thee!"

Henry and Abigail slipped on the frosted boards of the docks as they moved into the impenetrable brume until they could no longer stand. As they crawled toward the boat, Rosemary overtook their path and stood before the mooring with a heavy rock in hand. Henry and Abigail looked up at her from their knees.

"Rosemary. Please . . ." Abigail moaned as she gazed at her sister.

Rosemary hesitated for a brief moment, loosening her grasp of the rock between her fingers. But with the calls for exile reverberating around her, and William waiting behind them, she raised her hand over her head and cast the final stone unto her sister's face, cracking open her lip and knocking her sharply to the ground.

Henry threw himself over Abigail to protect her from any further harm as the rest of the crowd clustered along the end of the pier. With the swarm drawing nearer, Henry helped Abigail climb into the small vessel and then crawled in closely behind. Covering his face from any remaining attacks, he untied the boat from its station and pushed them away into the river.

The crowd gathered at the pierhead to ensure that the two were not able to return against the current. Abigail lay down with her face averted, her heart too heavy to look back, as they slowly began to recede to mid-river. Henry remained upright, bleeding and swollen from the assault, as he watched Rosemary stand beside William, his hand warmly pressed upon her shoulder, surrounded by the rest of the white-robed worshippers. The group grew more distant with each rolling wave, and the two gradually disappeared down the river and into the fog.

# Chapter 19

THE WORSHIPPERS WATCHED from the pier as the last vestiges of the boat were swallowed by the mist. The battle was now over, and it was time to walk back into Calvary victorious. They proceeded one by one, as if coordinated parts of a singular entity, in the same instinctive migratory pattern to which they had become accustomed in the mornings—eastward to the church. Rosemary followed at the tail end of the crowd beside William, refusing to allow herself to turn back and look at the river behind her. All she heard was the sound of the current receding into the past.

The group slowly trod the same path that they had taken before every sunset since October, silently walking toward the United Calvary Church in the distance. Cobblestone roads bridged the docks to the former center of commerce in the town, where the barren buildings rose up around them and pierced through the layer of fog. Rosemary looked up as she passed images of her former life along the pilgrimage: the shops she had begged to patronize with her sister on the way home from school, now closed permanently and emptied of all merchandise; the Chandler estate that had captured her and her brother's imaginations with thoughts of the founding of the town and the mythical years of the Revolution, now in disrepair, functioning as a public tenement building for the most destitute of the townspeople; the arched roofs of the houses where she'd played with her neighbors and friends, which now remained lifeless and vacant throughout the day as the residents committed themselves to the worship; and, farther in the distance, the church where her journey into faith all began—its narrow, wooden steeple reaching out like the figurehead of a mighty warship, imposing itself imperiously over the homes below.

The only sounds that echoed amongst the winter winds were the footsteps of the congregants as they plodded up the base of the hill. No one was singing, no one was praising—each pair of eyes hidden behind the hoods of the white robes was facing the path before them as they continued to trek up the incline toward the grounds of the church. Not a whisper was heard among them as they at last reached Ascension Rock. There was nothing more that needed to be said or done; their preparations were over. Today was the day that Christ would come and deliver them into eternity.

Rosemary looked out over the precipice of the hill into the western horizon. She had longed for this moment—to be surrounded by her fellow believers, to feel the warmth and verity of their faith that she had been missing in her time away from the church. But as she breathed in the heavy air, something did not feel complete. The atmosphere was bereft of the same anticipation and avidity that they had felt on the Day of Atonement as they waited for the advent. Instead, the worshippers now stood somberly, feebly, as they faced the church and waited quietly for William's closing words to them.

William stepped forward from the congregation and walked to the western wall, standing with his back against the building. Looking out to the people before him, he began his sermon free from the typical incandescence of his prose, speaking with a new air of sobriety and reservation.

"My friends," he began. "When we take a view of what has beset mankind for all of history—the sickness, the affliction; oppression and persecution; poverty, famine, and heartache—we are to fairly draw one conclusion: to live is to suffer. And we are right to ask why God, in all His wisdom and grace, has made man to be His most miserable creation."

Rosemary took her attention off of William as she turned to look at the rows of townspeople that lined the western lawn, their eyes continually fixated on him. She looked at each of their faces—unwashed and gaunt, weary and wanting. But behind their eyes lay a deeper truth that they dared not speak aloud: one of confusion, fear, desperation. Their eyes cried out for an end to all the madness that has consumed them, an end to existence as they know it. Yet they stared ahead, holding on to the hope that William would be proven right—that all of the sacrifice, the brutality, the physical, moral, and spiritual suffering would not be for naught. They listened intently as he continued.

"What I say to you now is that this way of life is all part of God's ultimate plan. All of your earthly woe, all of the tribulation—the pain, the hunger, the sorrow—is here by design to give a greater zest to that which shall follow this

life. For the longer we tarry in hardship, the more glorious that moment of deliverance shall be. And so we must
await that blessed moment, the triumphant appearing of
our savior Jesus Christ, with the utmost appreciation and
gratitude. For we can know no joy without hurt, no bounty
without loss, and no salvation without suffering. Amen."

Rosemary felt the cold wind on her neck as William
waded through the crowd toward the forefront of the hill.
He placed his hand gently upon her shoulder as he joined
her in the middle of the congregation. The winter draughts
crooned amongst the silence.

"What do we do now?" Rosemary asked, raising her
eyes up toward him.

William looked down at her and nodded assuredly.

"We wait."

And so the worshippers gazed into the western horizon, waiting for the sun to set and set and set. Time ceased
to have any meaning as the present bled into the future.
Rosemary looked around her as the days and years passed
and the believers grew old before her eyes. Figures faded
with each passing moment, evanescing into the air as they
continued to wait for the day to come—the older generations first, then those in the summer of their youth falling
into the white abyss of the winter. Rosemary watched as
the worshippers slowly vanished one by one, always faithful
that they would one day be delivered, as the group became
smaller by the season.

Rosemary looked at William, now shrunken and gray,
hunched over beside her as he quivered against a cane, waiting for the moment to arrive. He leaned in closely to her
and placed his cheek against her shoulder as he, too, soon

388    |    GARRY HARPER

succumbed to the passage of time and slowly disappeared into the clouds. One after the other, the rest of the believers faded away with the wind, dissipating into the shadows of the hill, until she was the only one left. Alone on the precipice, Rosemary looked at her hands, the creases and the wrinkles of her aging palms, and she closed her eyes and waited for her eternity to come.

She imagined how it would be: all of existence consolidated into one moment—the past, present, and future now as one. She saw herself there in this fluid state of being, a divine reversion to the universe before Creation, where all souls were ruled by the same laws as the triune God, freed from the shackles of time. She would be there surrounded by the souls of all those who ever existed—her mother, her father, Abigail, Benji—everyone she ever loved beside her, those whom for so long she had yearned to see again, existing as they always had and now forever would be, without age or affliction, endowed with the boundlessness of God. This was the eternity for which she would wait an eternity to find, the promise of the infinite that would remove the suffering of finite existence once and for all.

Rosemary smiled as she at last began to fade gently into the winter air; a phantom of a forgotten past borne into eternity, ascending into the infinite, until there was nothing remaining but the sound of the wind.

"These are spots in your feasts of charity, when they feast with you, feeding themselves without fear: **clouds they are without water**, carried about of winds; trees whose fruit withereth, without fruit, twice dead, plucked up by the roots; raging waves of the sea, foaming out their own shame; wandering stars, to whom is reserved the blackness of darkness for ever."

Jude 1:12–13